# SEX, RAIN
## &
# COLD FUSION

A NOVEL

## By A. R. TAYLOR

RIDGECREST HOUSE

Published by:

Ridgecrest House

578 Washington Blvd. Suite 1094

Venice, CA 90292

ISBN 0615818447

ISBN-13: 9780615818443

Library of Congress Control Number: 2013909191

# DEEP WATER

WHEN WOMEN ASK David what he does, he tells them he's in league with a god, the one who lives at the bottom of the ocean. The deepest waves are his domain; they roll fifteen thousand feet below the surface, racing along undisturbed over the bottom of the sea floor. Higher up, at seven thousand feet, slow, ponderous water slides over rocks, across great oceanic deserts, then cascades down vast canyons, carrying turbid currents of sludge, hurricanes of debris that swirl in silence. The moment one of these long, slow waves meets another of different salinity and warmth, internal breaking surf is the result, exploding up hundreds of feet into a dark underworld that contains enough food for the whole planet, enough minerals for all civilization. This deep water glides beneath us, lives on without us, waiting perhaps for the ultimate abandonment of the planet by man.

The next time you are at the beach, consider that water you behold; it knew the abyss, knew the great drum rolls of the ocean floor, and it rose up to you from a world as distant as the stars. That wave might have traveled twenty thousand miles and ten years just to touch you. It is the intersection of yourself and fate.

David's own life had reached such a point. The murky water that appeared on the surface so inexplicably, and he thought, so undeservedly, had actually been coming to him from a long distance and from the depths.

# CHAPTER 1

L IKE MANY OF David Oster's bad decisions, his escape from California to the state of Washington would be justified with an orgy of lies. The worse the decision, the more he liked to sugarcoat it to his critics, and in this instance, he prepared himself for a virtuoso performance.

Trying to get some decent food into his mouth, he eyed the dishes stacked up in the sink of his usually tidy Spanish bungalow, then the chocolate ice cream cartons and the Dewar's bottles in the trash. The mail was piled against and atop the phone, a sort of totem against those women trying to get through to him, though it couldn't block the rapid flash of numerous messages lighting up his voice mail. His cell was off, his e-mails unread, while he attempted to barricade himself against the pitiless availability of the modern world. But he knew he couldn't keep this up much longer.

Only one man could save him from a definitive female throttling, and that man was Niels Hoekstra, director of the Larson Kinne Institute for Applied Physics. As he stood in the steamy August night air, staring out of the kitchen window at the hibiscus growing halfway up the glass, he decided he had to call Hoekstra himself. The older man had trouble hearing him for a moment, but at last blared into the phone, "Oster? Good to speak to you." There was rustling in the background and the noise of a glass hitting the table. "Shh," Hoekstra said, presumably to someone else in the room, and then in a louder voice, "I am just finishing up my work."

"Ahh, I was wondering…"

"Yes?" he growled.

"About the job."

"It's still available, if you want to know."

"I don't know if I conveyed that I am very interested."

"You did not seem completely interested, to my eyes. I assumed, young man, that Scripps or Woods Hole was your destination. However, President Thornton shall know your personal leanings." He made it sound as if David liked to screw cats.

"Wherever I can get the most money for ship time, especially if I don't have to teach, that's where I'm going."

His putative boss promised to have a decision in two days.

David sipped his Scotch and drew little equal signs with his finger on the windowpane. Incredibly, he appeared to be on the cusp of getting exactly what he wanted, a job with no exposure to undergraduates at all—it was pitiful when a physicist tried to tell eighteen-year-olds how a ball rolls off a table—and he could feel his heart racing. No more grant proposals; he could pry all the money he wanted out of the institute, and that meant underwater physics that could lead to fundamental breakthroughs, and that meant, maybe someday, the *N* word, as in Nobel. More importantly, he could leave Pasadena, California, and his postdoc at Caltech without seeming to break up with anyone. This new job as senior research fellow would impress his women, and it needed to, all three of them smart, demanding, and ambitious for him as well as for themselves.

Never in his thirty years had he collected girlfriends like this, and he could only ascribe it to some serious gonadal rush, a feeling of potency and choice that first showed itself when he landed his coveted postdoc, and had unfortunately only increased with his getting a bead on a make-or-break position at a prestigious institute. From nervous little boy to second-string rugby player at Stanford to brilliant graduate student at UCLA, along the way, David's sexual fortunes had improved, but only slightly. The last couple of years, though, he could feel himself swaggering like a brainy Casanova, and he paid way too much attention to his longish black hair, hoping that it vaguely suggested the poet. Really, his face was distinguished, he kept telling himself—and why wouldn't he, since his girlfriends told him so too? But soon they'd be saying something else, possibly with a restraining order at the end of the conversation.

Around dinnertime, after another two days of telephonic tap-dancing to avoid his women, at last the all-important call came. "Do you think you would like it up here, Oster?" Hoekstra almost shouted at him.

"Love it, absolutely love it," David said, more or less in a stupor from too much sugar and Scotch.

"Why would you love it?" Hoekstra said, apparently puffing on a cigarette because there was a breathy pause.

"It's so—picturesque," David said, although the *p* word sat plumply on his tongue.

"The position is yours if you want it, but you have to start in three weeks. Any problem getting yourself up here, you know, any encumbrances?"

"None, none whatsoever."

"So, you took the job." David's advisor, a distinguished old man who was head of the oceanography group, had carefully watched his protégé's progress in a two-year postdoc that had stretched into four. Taking a white handkerchief out of his pocket, he wiped his nose and pondered the younger man before him. "Are you sure you want to do this? The Kinne Institute has a lot of money and prestige, but the university that houses it, Western Washington State, is pretty much a dump, fifth rate from what I can see. Didn't you have offers from Florida and Scripps?"

"Not nearly as good as this one, but don't worry. I plan to lock myself in the lab and do nothing but science." David proceeded to spin a long tale about how great it would be up north, where he could commune with nature. He portrayed an earthly paradise specifically designed for his benefit, a wet dream of scenery and silence perched on the Olympic Peninsula between the Pacific Ocean and the Cascade Range. His soul would expand, as would his wallet. The thing about all these lies was that he knew what kind of hole he was digging for himself. Or he sort of knew.

When he finished his screed, the old man stared at him a moment. "But it rains so much there," he said in a low voice. Alas, David would not let anything puncture this otherwise perfect piece of mendacity, and anyway, who cared about a little rain? He had real troubles.

At home that night, as the pink twilight glowed over the canyon behind his house, David sketched randomly on a pad of paper by the phone, looping curlicues and knots together and then making up fanciful equations to express their relationship. He knew what he faced, and he faced it now with controlled foreboding. He would have to lie carefully and well, over and over again, to Valerie, to Cosmo, even to poor Helena, telling them how brokenhearted he was to leave the haven of their arms and journey all alone to the Pacific Northwest. He would have to feign sadness when he wasn't, in fact, sad. He felt manic, almost possessed, since for months now he had been experiencing himself as an actor, a very bad actor at the service of someone else's muse. When he slept with too many women, each one represented an alternate reality, and he blended into that reality depending on the woman before him. Now his personalities had begun to collide, and he had to get out before the inevitable explosion.

For what David projected as possibly their last meeting, Valerie Jordan insisted he come to her apartment, a bad venue because she knew he loved it and had used it to seduce him over and over again. On the appointed Friday night, an evening he had chosen carefully because everyone was so exhausted and stressed out by then that they couldn't register much, he gazed up at those seductive bookshelves of hers. The leather-bound classical volumes called to mind their first meeting, at a café near campus. The books on her table—one Latin, another Greek—had marked her as a classicist, a profession that fascinated him. Anyone who could devote herself to Sophocles or Lucretius in these fetid times had him by the balls. It was a triumph of the ideal, because what could she ever do with these things beyond spreading their hermetic beauties to a few brainy groupies? Her long red hair and ample body were equally intriguing; she had sipped her espresso most sensuously and dipped her biscotti into the foam as if it were the milk of the gods. Shortly thereafter, he found that sex with her was warm, sensual, and undemanding.

Now, instead of the subtle speech he had prepared for this tricky evening, he could do nothing but picture her warm breasts rising on his tongue. The room swam before him, undoubtedly due to the vats of wine he had consumed, as Valerie gazed dreamily at him across the table.

At last she muttered, "I believe I'm falling in love." For one instant, without considering, he smiled with the boldness of a lover who is loved back. Then the panic set in. Thank God, before he could speak, she said, "His name is Sid. Sidney Gershon, professor of Mayan languages and culture. I met him at a dig in Tikal last summer." Those Latins and Greeks of hers must have been conspiring in his good fortune, and David nearly giggled at the image of an absent lover named Sid dusting old bones with a toothbrush.

"Very violent," he finally coughed out.

"Sid?"

"Mayans."

"They weren't so bad, if we drop our ethnocentrism."

He nodded solemnly, got up, made his way to the kitchen, and clapped his hands under the faucet, wiping water over his face and neck. It was heartening, actually, that she talked such crap. Valerie was one of those "everything is all right if it exists" people. Because someone somewhere does something, no matter what it is, it has value, hence morality, even if it involves a culture that flung its children into bottomless pits and played football with their heads. It made him feel better about leaving her. Besides, it now appeared that she was breaking up with him.

He returned and sat down beside her, while she studied him carefully, trying to gauge the effect of her announcement. She had obviously expected him to be angry, or sad, or both. In truth David felt downright jaunty, but he attempted to appear solemn.

"Don't worry, I'm happy for you. I'm actually going somewhere myself for a while, to the Pacific Northwest. You know Larson Kinne, the guy who adapted osmium, one of the world's densest metals, for engineering uses?"

She shook her head no and ran a finger around the edge of her wineglass.

"He's developed a fascination with applied physics, or rather the conviction that physicists don't apply physics anymore because they've descended down into the world of subatomic particles or up into the Big Bang. We're too busy counting quarks, something like that."

At the word "quark," Valerie stiffened a bit but didn't interrupt him.

"My work on wave patterns around the Juan de Fuca Ridge off the coast of Washington has caught the great Mr. Kinne's eye, and his institute is prepared to give me everything I need for whatever I want to do, as long as I can do it under the ocean and at the ridge."

No nonscientist, no matter how bright, actually wants to talk physics, nor can they. They want to know it exists but not how it works, and Valerie was clearly one of these. He hoped his speech would shut her up, or better yet, lull her into a state where she would fail to notice that he had made his plans before learning of her new relationship. Her response was a surprise.

"But you're here now, tonight," she said in a low voice, pulling him to her with alarming intensity.

"What about Sid?" David struggled to breathe.

"I don't fuck him the way I fuck you."

He had no idea what she was talking about, yet what could he do?

He was just short of the point of no return when she jerked her body away and stared at him, eyes narrowing as if an awful truth had suddenly occurred to her. And surely, it finally had.

"How long have you been planning this?" Without waiting for an answer, she began to button her blouse. "You know, you're a good-looking guy, David, but you're a tremendous pain in the ass."

He cleared his throat, wondering how quickly he could get out of the house, but she took the lead once again, dismissing him with a shake of her head. He walked out to his car in a state of dislocation. In point of fact, her news was more stunning than his: she had professed her love for someone else. At the same time, she seemed distraught about losing him. What could that mean? As he fired up his twenty-year-old BMW, he realized that he had never actually broken up with anyone before. His former romances seemed to have just trickled away like a failing battery. He pulled out from the curb, feeling lighter somehow, but only for a moment, because the prospect of two more such confounding scenarios, face-to-face, with two other women who might have entirely other agendas, soon had him shaking at the wheel. He had to swerve to avoid a squirrel scooting across the roadway.

"I need to see you," David yelled into his mobile phone. He was trying to set a time to meet up with his second girlfriend, Cosmo, she of the incredible legs and the short blonde hair, the flight attendant on Alaska Airlines the day he had flown to the state of Washington for his first interview at the Kinne Institute. "Where are you exactly?" he yelled again over the noise of jet engines on the tarmac.

"Let's see, I'm headed to Boise, then Salt Lake, then back here to Los Angeles, I think. I could meet you at Skeeter's, but it'll be late in the evening, around eleven."

"Fine," David said, thrilled at her ridiculous optimism. She talked as if she might live to see another day. He hated flying, really despised it, and attributed this fear to his father, an alcoholic auto executive nicknamed Dave the Bomber, who liked to test-drive cars while drunk. He used to force David and his mother to fly with him on his friends' vintage airplanes through weather that few commercial airline passengers ever experienced. Hammered, he would reach his head into the cockpit, scream at the pilot—"How's it going, Chick? Think we're going to make it?"—laugh like a crazy person, then pound on his son's shoulder. "Don't worry, kid, I'm insured. You can collect if you're not smashed into the side of a mountain."

So, he admired Cosmo for her aerial derring-do, and maybe that's why he had asked her for a drink at the Seattle airport when first she had come up behind him, dragging her little black flight bag. What happened next, though, he could hardly have anticipated. This sprightly flight attendant had pulled him past the baggage carousels, across four lanes of airport traffic, through a Chevron station parking lot to a crumbly, fake Spanish-looking Ramada Inn. Inside the green-and-brown room, by dim lamplight, she undressed down to her black hose and pale pink brassiere. The excitement of the thing, the time pressure, the job fears, the alcohol, with planes zooming overhead—it was incredible. She came just as a 747 dropped its wheels over the motel. That had been his cue to race back to the airport, where a car and driver awaited. By now, of course, he was dirty, covered in sex and confusion, and completely unprepared to wow a roomful of scientists with the highly theoretical talk he was about to give, but he sure was relaxed. Wow them he did, with his air of sangfroid as much as his knowledge of underwater physics.

He owed his new job to her, in the goofball logic that had come to dominate his thinking of late, and couldn't just skip town without notice, even though it was hard as hell for them to see each other more than once every two weeks or so. How to break the news to her? Would he even really be leaving her, since she might only regard this as a schedule change or a call for re-routing? Basically she could board any airliner in the world just to retrieve him, and for free. Such freedom across many fronts might also have led to other boyfriends on her part, something he had often wondered about. Perhaps he was in for further revelations?

Skeeter's was her favorite sports bar at another motel right near the airport, and it was noisy. He hated to have to yell his desertion into her face at high volume, but she had insisted. While a football game blared over the bar and laughing pilots and mechanics enjoyed the free hors d'oeuvres, David worked random Newtonian equations in a small notebook he always carried. $F = dp/dt$, momentum divided by time, and there was his own initial. Next $p = E/c$, energy divided by the speed of light, and there was little Cosmo. Then $p = hv/c$, Helena, Valerie, and Cosmo all in one expression of the momentum of light. To move things along, $hv/c = E/c$. At last, and this could be derived from all of the above, $E = hv$, the energy of light, courtesy of Einstein. All of these overheated particles floating around in his life, no wonder things had gotten so out of hand.

When Cosmo finally vaulted her way over the chair, David had to admit that he might miss her jouncy goodwill, but before he could say much, she spilled five or six cuttings from in-flight magazines onto the table, single words like "cool," "handsome," "bold," all meant to refer to him, apparently, and despite everything, he was charmed. He stuck his own little mathematical notebook notations into his pocket.

They ordered chicken wings, and while Cosmo kept smearing her face with hot sauce, then wiping it off again, David tried to explain why he had decided to move away.

"I can't stand Los Angeles anymore. I mean, what's with the guy on the corner who wears a Ralphs bag on his head and threatens me with a broom even though I give him money all the time? And I detest these endless academic conversations where talking seems like a substitute for living, always on some subject I know nothing about. Then, whenever I manage to track down the so-called 'normal' locals and socialize with them, they only talk about movies and money. I just want to work. In Washington it'll be all physicists under one roof doing science."

"Sounds creepy," she said with a grimace and then let her hand glance off his leg.

"But it means I'll have to, you know, be there, to do the kind of work I need to." Some football team made a touchdown at this moment, and the place erupted, but he yelled over the mayhem, "I won't be able to party as much up there."

"You'll probably want to party more."

"I'll need to concentrate."

"I don't really care where you live, David," she said as she dipped into the French fries.

Outside in the parking lot, when normally she would have lured him to her motel room, instead she kissed him on the cheek. "You make everything so complicated, you know that?"

"How do *you* know that?" he muttered lamely, but by then, all he could see was her retreating uniform.

What did they really feel about his leaving them? As he walked along Oak Grove Drive two days later, glancing down at a homeless guy feeding his dog underneath a eucalyptus tree, he wondered. David folded up two dollars and handed them to the man. It was hot and windy, and he found it hard to breathe. He had spent weeks anticipating the drama of these breakups, prepared for tears and emotional collapse, but not for this muted expression of pain, almost like background music.

Where was the foreground, and why was it hidden from him? He found himself thinking of one of Dave the Bomber's more memorable stunts, when he'd decided he had to get rid of a tree stump in the backyard and had wired it up with two full sticks of dynamite. The explosion threw nine-year-old David and his father across the yard and shattered all the windows on the side of the house; still, it was nothing to the blowup they expected when his mother returned home. Instead, she simply surveyed the damage, cigarette in hand, occasionally kicking some dirt off her golf shoes, saying not a word. That terrifying silence continued through dinner, while the glaziers worked upstairs.

Then, as now, he had felt relieved but almost letdown; disappointed was it? Surely not, he told himself, as he paid for a latte at the corner coffee shop. For him, at least, his proliferating romantic involvements had all been momentous, a spur to anxiety, plots, and finally flight. He believed firmly in some future knockdown from these women, and he knew he deserved it.

David's final farewell to Helena turned out to be similarly perplexing. Granted, he had gone out with her only three times since their meeting at some deplorable dinner party filled with her UCLA colleagues in the specialty of Finno-Ugric linguistics. Tall, thin, with a weary Modigliani kind of face, she had stared at him across the baked Brie. "I aam Helena from Hunga-ry," she had said, sounding an awful lot like Dracula. Who knew what sort of incalculable laments might lie ahead for him once he mentioned his pending exit?

In preparation, he had begun drinking vodka as soon as he arrived at her neo-Gothic apartment. This worked, so much so that he couldn't adequately frame the parting words he had crafted. Helena only seemed to register his pain, without absorbing the fact that he actually planned to flee the state, and responded by launching into her own tormented personal history. He lay sprawled on her couch while her story floated over him like Liszt—in fact, he thought he heard her mention Liszt, although he was not a close relative. When he awoke, it was light, and she was passed out beside him. She opened her eyes as he leapt up.

"I've got to go to work, darling," he said, leaning over to kiss her.

"Good-bye," she said, snuggling into the couch cushions, smiling, so apparently she was less than heartbroken, if she understood what was going on at all.

Back at home, David found himself wanting to phone each of his women with some sort of heartfelt pleading. He still felt a nagging need to justify himself. Days passed, and still no lovers called him, not even his perhaps uncomprehending Hungarian Helena. He occupied himself with packing and worrying over what he should do, never having imagined a situation such as this. Finally, in terse, straightforward e-mails, he lied once again to Valerie, to Cosmo, even to Helena, telling them how crucial the Larson Kinne Institute of Applied Physics was to his scientific future, when in fact he knew little about it beyond its fame and its well-heeled backer. In the service of these lies, he became eloquent, hyper-rational, as if he could fix his life by talking about it. Worse yet he lied to himself, thinking he could live a solitary outdoor life, perhaps hunting, maybe fishing. He would wear hiking boots and down vests while chopping logs for the wood stove. And soon enough, he would go to sea. Even if he met a gorgeous woman who offered to play mandolin by the fire, then fuck his brains out every night right after they'd eaten her home-baked blackberry pie, he vowed to say no.

# CHAPTER 2

O N THE FIRST day of his first real job, David savored a novel form of transport—he walked to work. The size of Pyke City, Washington, population nineteen thousand not including students, was such that almost every major building, including the university, could be reached on foot from the house he had rented, and he intended to take full advantage of that fact. As he set out on a crisp, clear day in mid-September, David felt buoyed by the dense trees that lined his route, but more than that by magnificent Mount Rainier looming off in the distance. Many of his consolations here would obviously involve scenery, and he welcomed their ministry, resolving to treat himself like someone recovering from a nasty operation. The silence from his three lovers unnerved him, but he vowed to discard paranoid fantasies of their detailing his sex life on the Web.

The Larson Kinne Institute occupied a remote corner of the campus. Surrounded by Douglas fir trees, with a trout stream running along the back side of the property, it appeared to David, standing before it now, as half sportsman's dream, half high-tech extravaganza. Obviously, no expense of any kind had been spared in building it. A separate wing housed the institute's famous supercomputer, Big Flora, with a processing speed of ninety-two teraflops, a single teraflop being one trillion floating-point operations per second. Only a couple of Venusians could get to thinking that fast. Two high-energy field colliders with a diameter of eighty feet each occupied another vast wing of the building, and in a cylindrical structure outside resided one of the world's largest satellite telescopes, its length limited only by the capabilities of the space shuttle's cargo bay. It was capable of observing light that had traveled through the universe for an incredible ten billion years, a fact he learned when he read a brochure about it in the lobby.

During these early days, David occupied himself with setting up his own piece of scientific heaven, his new lab. The stream was visible from his window, so he shoved his desk to a spot where he could look out at it, then took to fussing over the gleaming machinery that would advance his knowledge of underwater waves. In the corner nestled three computers and a seismograph set up to monitor the deep-sea mountain ranges, called ridges, that circle the earth like seams on a baseball, one of which was Juan de Fuca. Probably because he was having more fun than he'd had in a long time, he made no effort to meet any of the twenty or so other scientists in residence, and talked to no one except a few graduate assistants, until one morning he got a summons from his new boss.

The very tall Niels Hoekstra glowered down at him from behind his huge desk, raising and lowering his eyelids dramatically, as if he were acting out a play in his head. Unsettled, David responded by saying hello twice, each time to silence. Shifting his weight nervously, he sank ever farther down into the overstuffed green chair he occupied while glancing around at the mahogany finished walls of the older man's office.

Finally Hoekstra spoke. "Look, Oster, I know your work, although Christ himself only knows why another great mind from Caltech would decide to come here, land of sulfites and the sports bra."

"I'm sorry, sir. What?"

"The Chemistry Department discovered sulfites and their preservative properties for the modern American salad bar, and last month, some genius in engineering published a new theory on the optimum fit of the sports bra, how to keep bobbling breasts stationary or some such nonsense. The secret, apparently, is titanium underwire."

"Amazing." David had never given much thought to the actual college that housed the Kinne Institute, since he had no intention of having anything to do with it.

"The last guy we got from Caltech ran off with a female faith healer. Too much dope smoking, if you ask me. Normal Americans have abandoned science. They've all gone into advertising. We only have the nuts and the fruitcakes now. But Pelliau was very high on you, said your research in the deep ocean could lead to advancements in fundamental physics." At that moment the phone rang, and Hoekstra picked it up, waving his hands at David to stay and wait.

Trying not to listen in on the mumblings behind him, David surveyed the older man's bookshelves, where, somewhat creepily, every book and reprint was arranged in alphabetical order. He traced his finger to *P* and pulled out several papers by the man Hoekstra had just mentioned. Viktor Pelliau, pronounced "Pelliow" with a big "ow" at the end, was a highly esteemed practitioner of fluid mechanics, rumored to be close to the Nobel Prize. He was seriously famous. And he had wanted David here? Now, *that* was exciting.

Hoekstra barked behind him, and David turned back his way. "Yes, Mr. Hot Bubble Man, as everybody calls him. That old sonoluminescence work of his, creating tiny bubbles in a cylinder that he bombards with sound waves. Has anyone ever duplicated it? One or two, maybe."

"According to him, the bubbles collapsed and produced high heat, also a burst of light. He said he'd detected neutrons streaming out of the flask, which would confirm that fusion had indeed taken place. Cold fusion in a test tube, in a lab, would be a discovery on the scale of, I don't know, Enrico Fermi's nuclear chain reaction."

"The Department of Energy called it garbage."

"Not Pelliau's work." David shook his head.

"No, the experiments of those two nutballs in Utah in 1989. Here we are in the twenty-first century, and he's working away at it, even was brave enough to publish a few papers."

"I've read them. I don't know a whole lot about the subject, but I don't believe it's a complete crock either."

"More will be revealed." Hoekstra coughed ominously.

"I'm flattered that Pelliau knows my work." And David meant his five measly first-author papers.

"Don't be. It's just because it happens in water." Hoekstra pronounced the word "water" as if he'd never heard it before. Whatever Danish accent he'd once possessed had faded; he now sounded almost southern and exuded a mythic mountain-man quality, like Odin from Alabama. But he fiddled all the while he talked, either with the phone, then with a paper clip twisted into the shape of a question mark, then with the gold scissors that were part of an expensive desk set.

"The Juan de Fuca Ridge is definitely underwater, sir, a lot of water. At its deepest point, in fact, under thirty-two hundred feet of water."

"A technicality," Hoekstra said and stared at the younger man from dark gray eyes.

"And I'd like to go to sea as soon as possible," David announced stiffly.

His boss muttered some words he couldn't hear, and then declared, "Larson Kinne is a friend of mine, but he wouldn't know an oceanographer from an ophthalmologist. Look at me, a biologist, my specialty hyperthermophiles, you know, critters in geysers, but because of my government connections, he thought I could ride herd on a bunch of physics people. Head in the clouds, not here with us on planet Earth, but convinced that he knows what physicists should be doing." While making this bizarre speech, Hoekstra stood up, giving David the full force of his height and his splendid attire: gray sport coat, matching gray trousers and vest, and a gray-and-white striped shirt with a wide collar, all of which matched his shoulder-length hair. Even in these early days, David registered this latter-day Viking getup as an aberration in the state of Washington, where the down jacket was king.

"I'm glad Professor Pelliau wanted me to come here. He must be an extraordinary man," he said, trying to find a safe subject.

Hoekstra turned and yanked the pull switch for the blinds, which came down catawampus to the sill. Leaning toward David, he twisted a pencil around in his hand. "He's mad. He's completely insane." Then he paused. "Not clinically insane. He has the madness of years in a protected environment. Now he just does whatever he wants. His eccentricities—and believe me, they were never minor—have flowered like kudzu. It grows like hell, and you can't fucking cut it down. He's Latvian, for Christ's sake. Have you ever been to Latvia?" Before David could assert his lack of familiarity with the Baltic states, Hoekstra sat down again and spoke to him in a low, portentous voice. "I have an assignment for you, David. I know it's going to sound somewhat odd, or perhaps unrelated to the physics of ocean waves, your chosen area, but it is of great moment to the university."

"Sure." By now, David just hoped to get out of this office with his job intact.

"I want you to keep an eye on Shelby Burns."

"Excuse me, who?"

"Good God, the man who lives across the street from your new residence."

"I just rented the place last week. Should I know him? Is he in science?"

"He is not in a field of endeavor recognized by any institution of higher learning, that's certain. Just watch him. Do I have to spell it out for you?"

"I'm afraid so."

"Eyeball his movements. Think of it as birdwatching. Wait a minute." He went to one of the bookshelves and pulled out a pair of binoculars, an expensive military-looking set of Fujis. He paused a moment to watch someone outside his window, then swung back toward David and shoved them into his hands. "Once you've been here awhile, David, you will understand why I'm asking you to do this. At the moment it sounds unrelated to anything you would normally think of as gainful employment, but it is of the highest importance."

"You mean try to spot the guy out of my window? I don't have that much free time. I'm preparing several experiments."

There was a knock, and Hoekstra loped to the door, embraced whoever was behind it, then turned back to David. "Meet Frances."

This, apparently, was Mrs. Hoekstra, clad in a pink blouse and black pants. She had a round face, long honey-blonde hair

tied back in a ponytail, and a warm smile, but unfortunately
also the largest behind he had ever been privileged to see. He
knew this because a moment after she said hello, she turned
away and walked back down the hall. The weird thing was
that she was fairly slim from the head to the neck on down
to the waist, and then something had happened, something
immensely large.

Awestruck, David barely heard Hoekstra while he continued to natter on in a low, intense voice about Shelby Burns,
repeating several times, "Don't forget what I just told you."
Finally, he rose from his ancient swivel chair and slapped his
hands down flat on the desk in front of him. "Need I say more?"

David knew it was time to get out of the office.

Lurching toward the lobby as fast as he could, David started to
wheeze. What the hell was wrong with the guy? Why had he
hired him at all if he hated Pelliau so much? He stepped out of
the institute's front door onto a marvelous green lawn bordered
with pink rhododendron, but at this moment, the landscape
failed to cheer; instead, a sort of pastoral horror came over him.
He was actually in the state of Washington, like, forever. How
could he have forgotten what Karl Marx called "the idiocy of
rural life"? Maybe this Hoekstra fellow had succumbed, along
with the guy he seemed to hate so much, Viktor Pelliau.

As he bent down to pick up a hazelnut, he tried to buck
himself up with his scientific purpose. At least he knew what
he wanted to study. He knew where it was, right here, and he
knew more or less what it would cost. Two years earlier he had
spent several weeks on a National Oceanographic and Atmo-
spheric Administration vessel over the Cobb Segment of Juan
de Fuca. By dropping radioactive tracer material, he had confirmed his theory about the return of deep water to the surface.

Deep water seemed, at least in this one very small experiment, to rise only near the largest segments of the ridge. In itself that would be an important discovery, but it also edged him closer and closer to his personal obsession, one that he kept secret, thinking of it as a sidebar to his "real" science. The pattern of deep ocean circulation might offer a clue to the existence of a fifth force, the discovery of which would turn the world of theoretical physics on its head.

Besides the four known forces in nature—gravity, electromagnetism, the weak nuclear force (responsible for radioactive decay), and the strong nuclear force (that holds atomic nuclei together)—many physicists have wondered if a fifth force exists. It seemed clear to David that the circulation of deep ocean waves couldn't be explained by gravity alone. It required the existence of a medium-range, substance-dependent force, otherwise, how to explain the obvious violations of Newtonian gravity that his tracer data clearly showed? In his view, the scale of an oceanographic experiment was very appropriate for the discovery of a new force. General relativity well describes the actions of a galaxy, quantum mechanics the movements of a neutrino, but what about the world in between? This fifth force might account for anomalies in the physics of the middle world, our world. But to do the right experiment would cost a fortune, just the kind of fortune offered to him by the Larson Kinne Institute.

Consoling himself with these thoughts, David prepared to imbibe a steaming hot cup of coffee at the student union. Right at the entrance, however, he started backward, having spotted an eight-foot-high wooden sculpture of a steelhead trout upended on its tail, conveying fearsome aggression. Before he could read the inscription below it, a loud voice called out, "David, David Oster, that trout is not going to bite you." Then he met the man who was going to change his life.

A strange-looking fellow with a wide, flat face and spiky gray hair grinned and waved him toward his table. He turned uncertainly.

"Viktor Pelliau," the older man said, "I've been waiting to meet you for days and days. I am looking for a physical ocean-ographer to help me test out some of my theories."

David felt suddenly much better about his decision to come here.

"Your talk was good, good, good," he added, making it sound like "got," then ran his hand through the hair standing up on his head. Thick eyebrows met across the bridge of his nose, which he must have broken several times. Probably in his late fifties, he looked like an aging but intellectual boxer and wore a pair of very round glasses. "How did the old man get you to come here?"

"He promised me ship time, huge amounts of money, and total immunity from ever meeting an undergraduate." David startled even himself with his own frankness, especially in front of this esteemed physicist who had, supposedly, wanted him here. Pelliau didn't seem to mind.

"So you can do your work undisturbed by the youth of Washington. Have you seen the mighty Dane since you've been here?"

"Definitely. The guy scares me."

"Do not, under any circumstances, tell him anything."

"You make him sound like an ax murderer."

"I'm from Latvia. I understand things the ordinary Ameri-can is stranger to. Do you know any Latvians?"

"You're my first."

"That's enough." He pulled out his pipe and started stuffing it with tobacco. "Come to my house for a glass of wine this eve-ning. You have the haggard look of a man without a country.

Believe me, I know. I have had no country for decades." Then he gave David his address, which happened to be right across from the house he had just rented. "My God, I knew some poor person had moved into that monstrosity, but you! What a wonderful coincidence."

In the coming months, David would ponder how wonderful it really was.

The monstrosity Viktor referred to was the "villa" (advertised as such) David had rented from a biologist friend of Hoekstra's. Outside, it was a gray wooden two-story house in the faux Nantucket mode, but inside, a more exotic reality prevailed. Its owner had had numerous adventures in the Middle East and had acquired an imposing gold dome that hung over a mother-of-pearl table in the living room. Despite his recent vow, David must have been fantasizing about nights of sexual excess under the dome's vicious curlicues, since nothing else accounted for his commitment to this ridiculous structure. Everything in the house was out of scale, especially for a man his size, measuring exactly six feet. The dome was huge, the table beneath it tiny. The minute study had a rolltop desk fit for Louis the Fifteenth if he'd been three feet tall. There were Moroccan-style articles scattered about, giving off exotic odors, but the color scheme was an alarming yellow. All in all, it was the home of a very short man with disastrous taste. But on this particular evening, heartened that at least he had somewhere to go, David gazed up at the dome and tried to get comfortable on a silk pagoda chair underneath it. Then rain began to fall softly, one ping at a time. He looked out the window at Viktor's cozy-looking Craftsman-style house across the street and prepared himself to converse with one of the most famous physicists he had ever met.

Emerging into the wet night, he spotted Pelliau on his covered front porch holding a plate of cheese and waving him over. "You don't need that, David," he said as he grabbed the umbrella out of his hand. "No one ever uses those here." He then pulled up one of several wicker chairs for him. The evening light had darkened, and thickened, unaccountably, with the smell of smoke. "It's the burn. Farmers spread fire through their fields to make way for new plantings next year. Environmentalists fight it, but the Skokomish Indians did it the same way two thousand years ago."

"How can they burn it when it's raining?"

"This little shower is only over us, I think. I wonder what Shelby is doing?"

"Shelby?" A small explosion went off in David's gut. This was the very man Hoekstra wanted him to watch.

"The man next door. A most interesting fellow." The house he pointed to was brown and beige, also in the Nantucket style, but shabbier and smaller than his own.

Before he could ask anything more about the said Mr. Burns, from down the street a voice cried out to them, "Hello. Are you drinking without me?" An extraordinary African American woman, with hair knotted around her head in cornrows, strode toward them, and David could just make out a taut, slender body beneath the jeans and black T-shirt.

"My woman," Pelliau muttered as they watched her advance, "Lucy Fosse."

David could see her face now, nobly formed, in her early thirties perhaps.

"Can I have a glass?" she said smiling at him, probably because he was staring in appreciation. She sat down and curled her legs around to one side, stretching herself like a contortionist, then pulled a pack of cigarettes out of her pocket and leaned toward Viktor for a light.

"Lucy, you must meet this fine young man, David Oster. He comes from Caltech, only for a few days now."

She patted David on the leg. "Whatever we do, let's not talk about who grew the largest zucchini this year."

"No, vegetables are definitely out," Viktor said. "The natives often use large plantings as a show of virility or romantic intention, David, no matter how personally unattractive you may find this custom."

"I used to think rain was romantic," Lucy said as she twisted several large silver-and-amber rings around on her fingers.

"Rain is always romantic," David muttered.

Viktor interrupted, "No rain talk now, or anything about unfortunate weather patterns. You'd only be anticipating the future, and it would not be beneficial." Then he gave his weird little laugh. "Lucy is the most beautiful woman in town. Don't you agree, David?"

Lucy jabbed at Viktor's arm and gave him a look.

"She certainly is, though I don't actually know any others, and I don't plan to for a long time."

"That's ridiculous. You need to have someone to pursue," Viktor said authoritatively.

This sudden foray into a possible personal life startled him, as truly he could only think of the women he was escaping. "No more women. One woman is too many, but a thousand are not enough, if you know what I mean," David said, not wanting to encourage the smallest romantic longings in himself or others.

Lucy observed him closely. "You're an addict?"

He had never thought about it that way, but, realistically, his life in LA had gotten pretty demented. "I was addicted to personal complication. Now I'm going for simplicity. Having attained at least the geography of a simpler life, I now have to work on the mind-set."

"You've come to the wrong place." Lucy Fosse blew smoke rings into the air, while the night sky darkened, and with it came a wind that smelled of burning oats. "You have fantasies of a simple life out in the country, baking bread, padding around the house in slippers. That doesn't mean you're being simple inside yourself, quite the contrary. Your thoughts run riot. Everything you are or imagined you could be rises to the surface, and you are left to deal with it somehow. The 'It' inside you can no longer be hidden by the hassles of big-city life. You're just here, with yourself. It causes all kinds of elemental anguish and bad behavior."

"'*Et in Arcadia ego*,'" Viktor said, nibbling on a piece of cheese.

"Yes, death is in the garden too." David had seen the phrase inscribed on a tombstone.

"Darling, I'm impressed," Lucy said. "The snake in the shrubbery."

"Now, now, young woman, don't frighten him off so soon. Lucy's a musician and dancer. It affects her point of view. I will give a party soon, so you can meet all the beautiful women in town, all two of them at last count." Viktor pulled a couple of cigars out of his pocket, offering one to David, who shook his head no, and then to Lucy, who took one and sniffed at it, running it along the end of her nose.

"Will this party include Shelby Burns?" David said.

"Of course." Viktor laughed as if he knew a great deal more than he was saying.

# CHAPTER 3

AS PART OF his employment contract, Hoekstra had agreed to give David a wave tank fifty yards long. It was located in a Quonset hut adjacent to the institute, and he was standing in front of this marvel now, three weeks after his arrival, watching graduate students test the strength of new rubber tubing used to anchor instruments undersea. The water in it bubbled and churned away like a high-tech version of a child's wave-making toy.

David was chatting with his second real acquaintance at the place, a string theory man, planning a visit to the Buccaneer Bar in a dreary town called Wren a few miles down the road. They did not discuss their work, and a good thing, too. No one had ever offered up a single model of physics from string theory; they just liked to talk about it at dinner parties, and David considered it a parlor game that had mysteriously conquered, at least temporarily, the world of physics. Today the string theory man was obsessing about something else entirely, the university basketball team, the Steelheads, rattling on about their prospects. Not good was the gist.

Across the top of his wonderful tank, he spotted Niels Hoekstra, motioning him to go outside. He began to sweat right away, trying to figure out what to say about this Shelby Burns caper. He didn't know anything about the guy, and he didn't want to know anything—that was his mantra. But before he could speak, his very tall boss announced a new area of complication in his life, informing David that he must serve on a university committee.

"What are you talking about? As in the whole university?"

"Of course. You won't have to do anything."

"This isn't part of my contract, Niels." David stumbled over the man's first name.

"Just go this once and then decide if you want to participate. It will give you something to occupy your free time."

He didn't plan to have any free time; in fact, he intended to keep so busy that he couldn't possibly get into trouble, romantic or otherwise. He started to frame the words to say this, but he simply couldn't open his mouth, as if a heavy lock clamped his lips shut. It must have been Hoekstra's resemblance to David's father that put him in such a funk whenever the two met up. Before he could mount a decent protest, the man sped away.

Days later, David found himself seated high atop the administration building in a glassed-in conference room with President Royce Thornton, a tall, gangly, gray-haired man clad in a mustard-colored suit. Trying to ignore an interminable discussion of university sports, he instead concentrated his attention on the first serious downpour since his arrival. At Caltech, David had perfected the art of fixing someone with a stare while at the same moment making calculations. Counting was the trick. Watching from the front of his head, he counted at the back, and his consciousness would remain on point even though he wasn't listening. This was a minor skill, but the rain offered a promising medium. How fat were the drops, and how long did it take each one to fall from the branches of a tree? These raindrops seemed lean and needlelike, and he had just formulated their location on his new scientific creation, the Oster Wet Scale, when Thornton turned to him, shuffling through a sheaf of papers.

"Oster, Oster, is it?"

"David Oster," he replied, eyeballing the other gloomy men at the table, which predictably included Niels Hoekstra.

"We must get you to work, Oster. No point in you just catching things under the ocean, or whatever you people do."

As David opened his mouth to define the nature of physical oceanography, Thornton gave a tremendous snort indicative of a nasal problem so deep, so unreachable, he might well pull up his stomach to get rid of it. He looked around, but nobody else reacted, not even Hoekstra.

The president pressed his face into a white handkerchief while he continued speaking. "We would like to put on a show for our basketball team, the Steelheads. Something amazing, diverting. Specifically horses."

"I'm sorry, what did you say, sir?"

"Don't toy with me, young man. Horses on the basketball court! Haven't you been listening to anything the others have said?"

"I have, I have. It's just that sports, per se, is not really my area." David had been a decent rugby player in college, and his father had been ferocious at tennis, but in general, the American obsession with sports left him cold.

"Consider it your area now. In addition to the Larson Kinne Institute, as of this year, we have a new sports center courtesy of the same donor, named in honor of his wife's family, Crestole.

Naturally, it has a state-of-the-art basketball floor. The question is, can the floor of this basketball court withstand five or ten horses on it performing a show for, say, fifteen minutes, something like that? That's a physics question, I think."

"It's an engineering question, I believe."

The vision of a new, young person who was presumably a faculty member telling President Thornton of Western Washington State University what he was supposed to know already made the room seize up like a car engine low on oil. The assembled males stared in open pity. Hoekstra, however, looked sly, almost gleeful.

"I am an agriculturalist, sir," Thornton fairly shouted. "Do not play the dummy with me." He slammed his papers down and dismissed the meeting.

David's first thought was how soon he could quit, and when he spotted Hoekstra walking toward him, he grabbed his arm. "What's with that bastard?"

"Calm down, calm down. He was probably just trying to screw with you," Hoekstra said, in turn grasping the hand of a short, round man following along behind him. "David, meet Philo Smallett, engineer!"

The man stuck out a hand and shook his.

"If things get really bad, he'll tell you what to do, won't you, Smallett?" Hoekstra intoned, and the little man gave him a smarmy grin.

"Yes indeedy." He barely looked back as he rushed down the hallway.

"Why didn't he say something at the meeting?"

"He was letting you have a chance to show off your talents." The man leered in all his Nordic awfulness. "It gets bad this time of year. Wet holidays loom, and people dream up things to do."

"Fine, I just don't want to be one of those people. We had an agreement, remember?"

"Of course," he boomed. "Don't worry, I can always neutralize Thornton if I decide to."

"Please decide to," David said, anxious to get away from the man.

In his later years, having grown deaf, his father would shout every word at him two or three times, repeating the same declarative statement again and again, regardless of what David said in return. It was a communication style not unlike Hoekstra's. This almost mystical insistence was extremely wearing, since David would, without fail, have to give up and agree with Old Dave to get it all to stop. He certainly felt that way now.

David had grown up in a suburb of Detroit, Michigan, the son of the man who originated the five-part moving car seat: head, neck, shoulders, knees, back. Whenever he searched for the lumbar control button and felt that tingling at the base of his spine, he thanked his father, if only for a moment. His mother was a bony, dramatic blonde who had been subdued by her husband's outsized personality and relentless drinking, ground down until her focus narrowed to smoking and cards. Old Dad's adventures in drunken driving never killed him, but they did leave him with terrible scars, and in his worst accident, he smashed a 1963 Shelby Cobra into a tree and had to have a metal plate implanted into his forehead. Forever after, he fairly vibrated at that spot. His wide, handsome face looked as if a frying pan had worked its way into the top of his head, and his forehead grew redder and redder the more plastered he got.

His drinking, to which David was his little accomplice, was secretive and chronic. He had probably never seen his father sober. Like a small bird dog, as a youngster he revealed amazing facility at sniffing out where his mother and the housekeeper had hidden the gin, and this helpful service endeared him to Old Dave. Much given to dirty limericks, he often regaled his son with these late into the night. In retaliation, presumably, his mother had developed an odd habit of speaking for long stretches with her eyes closed, often at the dinner table. "Mae, have you made contact yet with the spirit world?" his father would bark at her, or, "Avoiding your own filthy smoke again, sweetheart?"

His mother's shock at having a baby could undoubtedly be chalked up to age, forty-seven when she produced her one and only child. David was looked upon as an anomaly of nature, sprung from the last egg. "For Christ's sake, she thought she was having the menopause," is how his father loudly related the story, usually at holidays, with other relatives present.

One wintry night his father got so drunk he fell out of the upstairs bedroom window, sat on the front lawn in a pair of green pajamas for six or seven hours, and was only discovered the next morning by the housekeeper. Apparently he was taken to the hospital and more or less thawed out. When David asked his mother at the dinner table, "Where's Papa?" she replied, "Out. Aren't you late for *Rocky and Bullwinkle*?" Alas, even as a youth, David could see that his father's "Dave the Bomber" appellation represented multiple levels of carnage. Four years ago his mother had died, and nine months later so did his father, but they remained ever present in his psyche, hating each other with a nervy sort of zeal.

Living with the Osters had left David with a set of rules of behavior, all quite dysfunctional, and if there was ever a time to toss them, that time was now. For one, he would stop with the secrets, stop being on the psychic lam, running from knowledge that he feared could hurt him, and just talk to people, ask them questions. Thus he determined to tell Viktor about the Shelby assignment and consult him on what it meant. He hunted him up in his office late in the afternoon, but Viktor was on his way out to a dance concert.

"Come with me, dear boy. You can talk to me there." Lucy was to perform, but at what? He was mysterious about the whole business, promising only "the delights of music."

The Arts Council Hall, a gray wooden structure not far from the town square, looked remarkably like a barn. Off to one side of the stage sat Lucy. Lit by a hazy green light, in black leotard and skirt, she had her legs wrapped around a cello the way Cosmo used to wind herself around David, he remembered with a start.

Blue and purple lights flashed across the stage as she produced a deep, melancholy sound while Viktor muttered into his ear, "Sartori bow, Vuillaume cello, priceless, dear boy."

Then a voice boomed out over the loudspeaker above her beautiful playing: "The lazy dog jumped over the short, fat fence. The short dog jumped over the lazy, fat fence. The fat dog jumped over the short, lazy fence," over and over again in endless combinations and recombinations.

The dancers entered, lit by these strange lights, moving to the cello, which had now dropped to a deeper register, sounding a tragic note. It was hypnotic, eerie, and in that moment, David couldn't think where he was or why he was there. He felt dizzy and only regained his wits when, the performance finally over, they met Lucy outside the auditorium. Hauling her priceless cello in a brown canvas case, clad in the same black outfit she had worn onstage, she graced them with a small smile, then turned toward a wonderful redheaded woman David had noticed bounding around in the dance as well. Off they went, leaving the men behind. Taken together, they had the two best bodies he had seen in a long time.

Forlorn and dejected, as this was supposed to have been a romantic meeting with his inamorata, Viktor insisted they visit the only serious restaurant in town, the Old Sawmill, where he ordered up two cognacs. The decor was what David called Nouveau Lumber Baron, destined to become his particular favorite in the Pacific Northwest. It involved rough-hewn walls, red leather furniture, and deer antlers perched above the fireplace. Before he could ask him about Hoekstra and his weird Shelby Burns assignment, Viktor launched into the subject of his apparently unsuccessful courtship.

"I've known her for three years, and I have yet to penetrate the veil," he said. "I don't mean the physical one. That is not so difficult. It's the soul. She is unavailable to me in her soul."

"Perhaps she's emotionally cut off from everyone." She certainly existed behind a wall of cigarette smoke, and David, as a member of the Oster clan, understood that ploy.

Downing another cognac, Viktor murmured, "How much ecstasy can a man give? To a woman, I mean?"

"Just as much as his body can stand," David wanted to say, but the man's funk was pretty deep, and he didn't quite know what to do with this sudden intimacy. He kept muttering on about his party—"give us bonds," "bring us all together," "salmon, cooked by me."

"Do you think a fish will do it?" David asked.

"It is the food of love, and you will meet beautiful women, at least I hope."

"I want to discuss something with you, Viktor. Hoekstra asked me to watch Shelby Burns, as in spy on him. Who is he really? Is he involved in something sinister?"

"Aaahh." He made a sound that doesn't exist in English, then said, "Of course, of course he is." Viktor teheed loudly. "Oh, this is wonderful. How could I have known it would all fit so well together?" He waggled his finger at David in a knowing manner. "Have you told him anything?"

"I don't know anything. I've never even met this Burns person."

"*Tiesi to es vienmer gribeju.* This is what I've always wanted, and you inspired me," he said, suddenly almost jolly. On the spot he formulated a plan for the two of them to watch Shelby together. "First, my party. It must be right away so we can understand what Hoekstra is up to. I will invite both participants, and we can observe them." His second idea, an expensive, time-consuming scheme that involved housing. "I will beg Shelby to build me a new home. He has built things before, I think. We need something real to do. If we're not chasing women, we might as well just shoot ourselves," he said and started rubbing his hands.

"You already have a house." David was startled at Viktor's speedy and extreme plan for Shelby surveillance.

"We will rent that out," Viktor declared. "Some nice family can come and destroy everything. Then I'll ask for money from the government." Crazy as they might be, the internal logic in Viktor's plans was airtight.

After their strange and gloomy dinner, David decided to survey the environs, perhaps even try to find the location of Viktor's new property, though he didn't honestly know his way around. Tonight the air blew clear and crisp, still smelling of oats, as he drove toward the hills. He passed by several large houses and then drove deeper into the woods, where there appeared only small farms and horse ranches. It was very dark, with no streetlights, and few lights on inside the houses, but at one wide driveway, he spotted an old woman getting the mail out of a mailbox that read "Scherbatskoy." That back of hers was sufficiently interesting that he slowed down the car, wanting to see more, especially more of the long, snowy white hair. She had a tall, slender body, shapely and, seemingly, young. How strange, old and young together in the oddest combination. Suddenly she turned and, eyeballing his car suspiciously, jumped into her truck. David sped off, but he'd had time to glimpse her face. She was young indeed. She had that white hair, but couldn't have been more than thirty or so. Unnerved, panicked almost, David blew his car up to eighty miles an hour, swinging it around the roads wildly. He didn't want to find any beautiful women; he certainly didn't want to react to one as he just had. He was a monk for science, such was his vow. Nevertheless, his body told him otherwise.

At home, unable to sleep, worrying over his romantic impulses, David lay in bed and forced himself to picture the current meters he had laid down two years before on his first voyage to Juan de Fuca. How many of them remained anchored where he had put them? Between the lava and the frigid water, the forces acting against them were titanic in their fury, without even positing a fifth force. Complex biological life might interfere with them too. Around Juan de Fuca's volcanic fires, strange animals had evolved that needed hydrogen and sulfur, even iron, not sunlight, to exist, blind shrimp, giant tubeworms, species that may have been the very first on the planet. A plethora of creatures and a gold mine, literally. Along the volcanic spreading, at twenty-three parts per million, the concentrations of gold were many times greater than anything ever mined on land, and it could become a real treasure trove for him if he had the nerve and the stamina to persist.

But when could he next go to sea? Climbing out of bed, he picked up Hoekstra's fancy binocs to peer at Mount Rainier, then swung them over toward Shelby's house across the street. On this particular night, he noticed a university car parked in front, the same kind of nondescript beige Ford with a state seal on the side that had picked him up at the airport. Upstairs, the lights were on, and David could see a man with a well-formed torso moving in front of the window. Unaccountably, the car moved. It moved because a dark-haired young man slammed the door and drove it away. The man upstairs must have heard the sound too, disappeared from the window, and shortly thereafter ran screaming out the front door. Was this the object of Hoekstra's interest? David grabbed a bathrobe and sprinted downstairs, to do what, he didn't know. He got outside in time to see his neighbor racing down the road, buck naked, his round rear end gleaming in the night. The car had a head start, but not by much.

The Ford and the putative Shelby disappeared around the corner. David sat down on the curb because he couldn't think of anything better to do, and though he felt safer in this hamlet than, say, in South Los Angeles, still, it was deep night. He didn't have to sit there long, maybe six or seven minutes, before tires squealed through the darkness. The same car whirled around the corner and slammed to a stop right in front of the Burns house. The dark-haired young man had vanished; the man who had given chase now sat in the driver's seat, bent forward over the steering wheel, then finally stepped out of the car, now mysteriously wearing a pair of boxer shorts. David tried to look nonchalant when he wandered over, as if he was just looking for some neighborhood gossip at one o'clock in the morning.

Before David could say anything, the other man announced, "Thanks, buddy," then hitched up the boxers.

"Thanks for what?"

"For being there." David assumed he meant this in the existential sense. "Shelby Burns," he said and stuck out his hand.

"I'm David Oster. Want a beer?"

"Sure." A stocky guy with a heavy upper body and muscular arms, Shelby carried himself like a rugby player, "set and staunch," as his old coach used to say. He had deep blue eyes, a boyish face, though he had to be around forty, and a lot of thick, sandy hair. David led him into the domed palace, and there he sat at the kitchen table in the mysterious shorts. David found the man a sweatshirt in the laundry room. "Thanks. Jesus, I thought he was going to get my car."

"It's a university car, isn't it?"

"Sure, but I use it all the time on business. Anyway, I see this asshole taking my car, so I run after the guy. Finally I jump onto the door, the driver's side because, shit, I'm ready to die for that car. Then I says, 'You gotta give me back my car, man. I mean, they'll kill me if you don't.'"

"What'd the guy say?"

"He didn't speak, just looked over at me, but sweating because I'm hanging onto his fucking door. My pubic hairs are in the door handle. Wow, I was begging. But he had to slow down 'cause I was pulling my feet along the road, like in a movie."

"You could have been killed."

"No kidding. So finally he slows way down, and I could kind of stand and slide with the car. It was tough. Then I opened the door, but I lost my balance and almost fell, so he stopped. I started talking again, just asking for the car back, and then he slams on the brakes. I think I got a hernia. He gets out of the car, holding a gym bag, and hands me the keys. It was great."

"So how'd you get the shorts?"

"I said, 'Hey man, you got any clothes with you?' and he pulled these out of the gym bag."

"Are you shitting me?"

"Hey, I don't have any time for bullshit, David." He yanked up the sweatshirt and poked at his abdomen. "Jesus, no hernia." Then he slugged down the beer very fast.

"You'd better call the police and make a report."

"Fuck no, no authorities for me. That's why I had to get the car back. Anyway, maybe I'll see the guy around and rough him up."

As he headed for the door, David resisted the urge to slap him on the back. "That was brilliant. Anybody who gets the shorts off a man who's stealing his car is a certified genius."

# CHAPTER 4

DAVID CAUGHT UP with Viktor later the next evening as he walked home, hot to tell him about Shelby's feat. "The man is priceless," Viktor said. "Soon I will tell you his entire history, but first we must engage his services."

After a brief phone call, never mind the rain and the cold, Shelby appeared at the front door in shorts and flip-flops.

"We have this project," Viktor announced, "building my new house. It will be large with green appliances, so lovely. All that my mother ever wanted."

Shelby plopped down on one of the chairs occupying Viktor's front porch. "Why would you want to do that? You already have a house."

"Land, land is all there is, don't you know."

"I suppose you feel that way because of the Russians, because of what they did to your people," he said, surprising David with his sensitivity.

"Yes, sadly. Please build it, Shelby. You of all people can do it."

During Viktor's attempt to enlist his aid, David sat silent, watching the rain, waiting to see how Shelby would respond.

He heard the man admit to never having built anything whole in his life. Though he had repaired his front porch and put up a little drywall, beyond that he seemed to exist on odd jobs, primarily replacing shingles on people's roofs. Still, he took the bait. "Where's your lot?"

Shelby reacted immediately to the address Viktor mentioned and insisted that all three of them drive out to the so-called building site, but not in his own car, which was new but mysteriously unavailable. Viktor wouldn't drive either because, in his fractured telling, his auto was "sick, very sick." Instead they piled into David's silver 1972 BMW 3.0 CSI, a gift from Dave the Bomber, who'd bought one model each year the car was made—1972 through 1974—parting with one only reluctantly on his son's twenty-first birthday.

They drove about a mile and a half out of town, in a direction opposite to David's recent late-night drive, to a beautiful hillside piece of land with a panoramic view of Puget Sound. Now this was what his scenery fantasy had been all about, the green world spread out before him, fertile, unspoiled. Viktor laid his curious architectural plans on the top of his car, hovering over them to keep off the rain. Impossible to tell what sort of style he had in mind, but apparently he'd been thinking about this project for a long time.

"This will provide us with months of activity, contemplation even," Viktor said, while Shelby appeared to be pacing off the site.

"What about physics?"

"That will take up two, maybe three hours a day. Without women, the rest is dead air." Viktor pointed his index finger to his head for emphasis. Looking back down at the plans, he added quietly, "A music room, for Lucy," as he drew a circle around a spot on the upper floor. Shelby walked back toward them but seemed to be staring at a neighboring house with some purpose in mind. He pulled down his shirt and straightened himself in his shorts. David looked in the direction of his gaze and saw a young woman crossing the patch of dirt that separated Viktor's lot from what was apparently her own.

"Hi, guys. I'm Leah Burnett. I live next door." She had luxuriant black hair, a slim torso, and large round breasts. "I teach English literature at the university."

Viktor grasped Leah's hand and kissed it, while David kept his attention focused on her breasts, about which he thought for quite a time afterward. They were big, just-right big, perfectly rounded, and apparently real. She was wearing a clingy white T-shirt under a black leather jacket, and it framed those perfect breasts like stage curtains.

"I will be your neighbor," Viktor said.

"Yeah, I'm building his new house." Shelby spoke as if he already knew the woman.

"What style will it be?" she asked, obviously ignorant of the monstrosity about to rise out of the ground like a deformed phoenix. Her own home was a soaring wooden structure, appealing by local standards and probably valueless once Viktor and Shelby executed their plan.

"It will have a Mediterranean feel, like what I used to dream of as a child in Latvia."

"Oh," the poor innocent said and looked down at her watch. "My husband Larry is out, and something's wrong with my car. I have to get to a lecture, 'Psychosexual Motifs in *Moby-Dick*.'"

"Wow." David sounded about twelve. Those eyes, those tits—he had to shake himself out of love.

As he stood staring, tongue-tied, Shelby intervened. "I'll go with you. I can probably fix the car, babe," he said. "And Moby has always interested me." The two walked away from them, hand in hand.

"What the hell just happened?" David said to Viktor, feeling blindsided by the village Lothario. Had he wanted to come up here just to see this woman, the whole architecture thing being a ruse?

Viktor grabbed his arm, whispering, "He's wonderful. This fits in with our plans. The party must be next weekend."

David was preparing to ask what plans Viktor was talking about when, just before he disappeared into her house, Shelby Burns ran his hand softly over Leah Burnett's ass.

The next day, determined to avoid all intrigue and those causing it, David locked his office and put up a big "Do Not Disturb" sign on the door. But he soon found himself casually looking up "Scherbatskoy" in the telephone book. There couldn't be too many of them, none, as it turned out. On an impulse, he tried the business listings and found "Scherbatskoy Farms," with a cross-reference to the Yellow Pages. There he saw a half-page display ad for the establishment, specializing in riding lessons and the boarding of horses. David slammed the book shut, determined to ban the subject from his mind, and gathered up seismographic maps of a section of Juan de Fuca, where he hoped to place new current meters and radioactive tracers, if and when he ever got to sea. This particular segment of the ridge, called Endeavour, was rife with frequent earthquake swarms, and just looking at these sharp spikes made him feel almost a part of its distant rumblings. In a moment, though, rumblings much closer to him sounded, as, despite his door sign, someone pounded on it vigorously. Leaning into it, he could hear Viktor giggling outside.

"David, David, what are you doing in there? This is too much work."

"It's my job, Viktor." But reluctantly, David opened the door.

"Nobody cares about that except me, and you're with me already," Viktor sniffed, then grabbed David's coffee cup off the desk and took a few gulps. "Anyway, we're wasting time. This Shelby business makes my party even more important, don't you think? I got a state truck from the motor pool, so we can go and invite women."

"Why don't we just e-mail them?"

"They must see us in the flesh, no?" Viktor insisted on his method, though he kept fretting about which women seemed suitable. "There's a schoolteacher in Wren, hmm, I wonder, and maybe a nurse at the hospital." Finally he threw his hands up. "Lucy's the only one."

"I do have another idea," David said, but then wasn't sure he wanted to go on.

"Yes? You've met someone, haven't you?"

What could he say, only that he'd seen her from behind? "Not exactly." Still, it occurred to him that the horses provided an angle of approach. "President Thornton could possibly help us out on this." He summarized their president's lunatic project to celebrate the possible victory of the Steelheads with a glorious extravaganza, cum horses, and added that he had seen a woman who owned a farm.

"A horse show on the basketball court?" Even Viktor couldn't get his mind around this one, especially while he was virtually pushing David down the institute hallway. Outside, he jumped into the front seat of the truck, adjusting mirrors and patting the plastic upholstery. "Obviously Hoekstra has singled you out as someone who needs to be neutralized, David.

This could be serious. On the other hand, it's an opportunity. We really do need the horsewoman to train the beasts. Since we have the truck for many hours, this is the perfect moment to descend upon her. Though you know, she might actually be old, and then she can't come to the party. She could serve, though."

David had to agree that this might offer a way to get Thornton off his back and, at the same time get a real look at the woman.

While Viktor piloted their official vehicle out into the green hills beyond town, he trolled through various country-western music stations on the radio, finally warbling, "Ruby, don't take your love to town," over the singer, in his worst Latvian accent, until David could stand it no longer and begged him to turn it off.

Next Viktor pulled out his pipe and tried to stuff it with tobacco at the same moment that he shifted the truck's grinding gears. "I swear I'm going to drive in a minute if you don't stop that," David said.

"I am so nervous."

"She's just a woman. Besides, we do have a genuine mission, not only the party." "But will that be enough?" Viktor sucked in on the pipe.

"It'll have to be, won't it? God, maybe she's married." He vowed to control himself with this woman no matter what, no attempts to charm or win her, none of his trickster arts, such as they were.

In the wet afternoon, they drove through the countryside until they spotted her small metal mailbox with "Scherbatskoy" printed on it. Viktor slammed on the brakes, and they slid about five feet. "Go read that sign," he said.

"I can see it from here. Scherbatskoy."

"She's Russian. The woman is a Russian!"

"I guess a long time ago someone back there may have been of the Russian persuasion."

"You are consorting with the Russians. There is no loyalty, no loyalty at all. I am the last of the loyal men, and when I die, it will be like the dodo bird." Viktor's voice was rising.

"I haven't met her yet, you maniac. Besides, you're the one who made me come here."

"You are right. I made a mistake. This isn't the home of a horse rider at all. Like all Russian women, Mrs. Scherbatskoy drives a truck. We have a curse in Latvia, 'May you go to hell, where a woman truck driver from Irkutsk is waiting to embrace you in her hairy arms.'" But he grudgingly shifted their own truck into first gear and turned into the drive.

They crawled slowly up the steep driveway, past a largish log cabin, behind which were visible a barn and paddock. "At least there actually are horses here," David muttered as they stopped beside the barn.

"Russian horses."

The two men made their way through the stalls, seeing no one, but as they moved toward the corral, a deep voice sounded behind them. David turned to see what must have been the horsewoman looking at them fiercely. She wore tall black boots and held a riding crop in her hand, like something out of a wet Washington dominatrix fantasy.

"May I help you, gentlemen?"

Despite his recent rant, Viktor paused only a moment before engulfing her with friendliness. "I'm so sorry to intrude on you and your beautiful animals. We do indeed have a purpose, a high one, which my young friend here, Professor David Oster, will explain." He gestured to him like a ringmaster at the circus.

David couldn't breathe. This was the most beautiful woman in town, in any town he had occupied. She had high cheekbones, translucent pale skin, widely spaced hazel eyes, and thick, silky white hair tied at the back of her neck with a ribbon. David decided she must be somewhere in her thirties. Delicate and strong, she held herself tall. Her face glowed with intelligence and energy, yet she was restrained, waiting for them to reveal themselves as morons, was his gloomy thought.

"I, uh, we do have a purpose," he repeated haltingly. He realized he was now standing where rain plopped directly onto his head and rolled toward his nose.

"Please, come into the tack room."

They followed her toward a cubicle at one end of the barn, and David got a chance to glimpse her trim body beneath the jacket and blue jeans. Maybe five foot eight, she walked the way that athletes do, springing on tight calves. Inside the creaky structure, English-style saddles and bridles hung on the wall, and the strong smell of leather mixed with the even stronger smell of coffee. She poured the hot liquid into mugs and then motioned them toward two old leather chairs, while she sat behind what passed for a desk. Viktor looked at David expectantly.

"We work for the university. This is Professor Pelliau," he said, and Viktor bowed. "The president has put me on a committee to explore the"—he looked over at Viktor, who stared at him as if he were Einstein reporting on relativity—"the feasibility of putting horses on the basketball floor." Here he paused, then plunged ahead. "And having them do some kind of act, for which we need a trainer." The rain fell with a thud against the shed. Viktor drank his coffee, while the horsewoman stared at David. Then she started laughing, a deep laugh from inside her chest.

Viktor laughed right along with her. "What can you say about our university? The wish of young people from the Washington farms to know anything about anything is low. But to be entertained—that is something they like very much."

"I see your problem." She turned and gave David a bright smile, in what was the daylight of her beauty.

He suddenly felt the need to separate himself from the absurd errand that had brought him here, to enfold her in his intelligence. "It's ridiculous. President Thornton is a ridiculous man." She kept looking at him while she sipped her coffee, and he felt himself blush like an undergraduate. "I'm a physicist, a physical oceanographer, and I have no idea why he asked me to do this. He's confused, he thinks I'm an engineer, but we thought of you because. . . I saw you once."

"I guess I should be flattered."

"You need flattery of no kind, my dear. You are the most beautiful woman I've ever seen. And I have seen the multitudes." Viktor was trying to be charming.

She smiled quizzically again. "What a kind thing to say. I don't know much about basketball. Is the floor slippery?"

"Very," David said.

"Well, even if the floor could withstand such a thing, it's too dangerous for the horses."

"You could put sticky stuff on their hooves," Viktor offered.

"Yes, but then they would be stuck to the floor," she said, quite sensibly.

"I'm embarrassed to be here. The whole thing is nuts. It's insane. I used to work at Caltech." He was beginning to whine.

"Yes, David, we know your provenance," Viktor said impatiently.

"I once saw a performance of the opera *Girl of the Golden West* in San Francisco. They had horses on the stage, though they never moved really." For some reason she was taking their problem seriously. "Let's see, in *Aida* there's a horse in the triumphal procession and several more later. I wonder how they protected them?"

"The spectators weren't clapping their hands, jumping up and down and screaming at the horses. People were crooning beautifully around them. This is a whole different situation." Nightmare images formed in David's head.

"It's my personal view that the affair of the floor requires further investigation, which you two may do at your leisure, with a professional floor person," Viktor declared. "After all, if they can do these things in Las Vegas, so can we; they have water, they have leopards right in the casinos. In the meantime, I'm having a party at my house next weekend, and I want to invite you, and your husband too. We'll have a belly dancer."

David looked at Viktor in alarm.

"There is no husband," she said quietly. Up until this moment, the woman before them had been quite reserved, receptive but gently ironic. Now however, she burst out, "Yes, we must have parties here. What else can we do? It rains and rains, and it rains again. People drink, go bowling, start making love to the wrong person, and then it rains some more."

Viktor stood up, throwing his arms out. "But my dear, that's why we need entertainments. We want only to make life a little more bearable until someone liberates us from the drip."

She stood now too, and David snuck another look at her shapely body. "I'm sorry. I've lived here for years. There's no reason to complain about the life I chose. Just let me know when you've found the floor expert, and we can get together, although it sounds pretty doubtful. By the way, my name is Alexis Scherbatskoy, if you're interested," she added, thrusting her hand toward David.

"I am interested." He felt like a grown-up for the first time since coming here, especially when her warm fingers curled around his for a moment.

As they drove away in the truck, she stood looking after them, not waving, just watching impassively. David was at the wheel this time, while Viktor pulled out his pipe again and fussed with it, looking worried.

"Scherbatskoy. That's a name well-known among the aristocracy, but she could still be a communist."

"She's a little young for Bolshevik connections," David said, but his friend continued musing on her origins, finally announcing that she was probably named after "the poor dead son of the czar," suggesting they investigate her more deeply on the Internet. "Get a grip, Viktor. We're already on one spy mission. We can't investigate everybody in town."

Viktor was pensive, but as they swung onto the main road, he announced, "No matter where she comes from, you must pursue her. I don't want to see your gonads rot off, David, even if it takes a Stalinist."

"They deserve to rot."

"Are you mad?" They pushed on through the pounding rain, which was getting fatter by the minute. "She reminds me of my mother. Have I told you about her?"

"Only that your family fled from the Russians."

"She was an actress, famous in Latvia. You should have seen her Portia, a marvel. *'Nav zelsirdibai robezu nekadu; ta list no debesim ka lietus maigs par vietu so.* The quality of mercy is not strained; it droppeth as the gentle rain from heaven, upon the place beneath.' In 1956 we were in Budapest, where she was performing. The uprising started, and we got stuck there when the Soviet tanks rolled in. For her it was, as you say, the last straw. We had lived in Latvia under the Soviets for so long, in an occupied country, and then to see this in Budapest! She decided we must try to get away from it all.

"It was late at night. My father had accompanied us this time, but he was bored and had been drinking Melnais Balzams with bar girls. I was only six. My name was Vilnis then, before I became American. Mother dragged me out of bed and got me dressed in three or four layers of clothing. I was so hot, my feet hurt me.

"We ran, without my father, through the streets, then got a ride in a truck to the Austrian border. There was a Russian there, young. He saw my mother and me and stuck his bayonet right in front of our faces. 'No pass,' he said in Russian, which my mother understood. She took off her cap, and her blonde hair fell all around her shoulders. He knew her, old man. You should have seen his face. 'Madame Pelliau, your Portia was superb. I carried the memory with me since four nights ago.' All the time other soldiers were looking at us. You have to imagine the panic, that half the people in Hungary were trying to go to the West. Everybody seemed to be right there, pushing behind us, like a human wall."

The rain beat even harder against the tinny front hood of the truck. What he said made David think how different his own family had been, how privileged and, of course, how decadent. They'd created their troubles, then disconnected themselves from the results. He remembered his mother's reaction to one of Dave's more outrageous stunts—the day he had had cases and cases of gin, Scotch, whisky, and various mixers delivered in a pickup truck from the liquor store, an act guaranteeing that all the neighbors could personally experience the depth and breadth of his drinking problem. Instead of flying into a rage, she had turned to her twelve-year-old little boy and said, "Someday your father is going to turn into a rose," then gave him a sad smile. Her words were a riddle that the boy had tried to solve. Did she mean that his father would be dead, that he would be pushing up flowers soon, or was it something more spiritual? David never asked but had always wondered.

By now, Viktor had become very emotional. "The soldiers were shouting in Russian, looking at documents and tearing them up. People were screaming and crying. The young man shoved us both forward, across the border, after, you know, pretending to confirm our papers, worthless, completely worthless. He waved, as we looked back at the other poor people, and shouted, 'Thank you for Portia.'"

The man began to weep. David didn't know what to say but felt more powerfully than ever a certain blank in his personality, as if there were a tablet in his brain upon which nothing was written. His family had had no words for sorrow, that was it. Beyond sadness, they burned with a fiery rage that blackened them from the inside. He put one hand on the older man's shoulder while trying to steer with the other. How could he know what Viktor really felt? For Americans, an invading army has only the rough, fraudulent outlines of the Indian war party invented by Hollywood or the video-game feel of silvery jets blowing through skyscraper windows. Surreal, strange, not of this world.

They rode on through the rain, saying nothing, until they slogged into the driveway of the university motor pool. "I owe my life to a Russian," Viktor said as he waved to a mechanic over the lineup of wet hoods.

# CHAPTER 5

"WERE YOU MAKING all that stuff up about a belly dancer to impress Ms. Scherbatskoy? There can't really be one in this town, can there?" It was very late in the afternoon two days after their little horse-woman junket, and David was trying, once again, to get Viktor out of his office. The man was fixated on his quest for the perfect party.

"You must understand that people here perfect an eccentric subset of skills. It's the first line of defense against insanity."

"Why don't you try science? Here, look at this Rossby wave that the Neptune/Naiad satellite is tracking over the Pacific Ocean. It's probably been traveling for ten years. We're watching history, think of that."

Viktor peered down at the undulating image on the computer, which depicted what was happening in real time at the latitude of San Diego. He seemed only mildly interested and kept on trying to convince David of the tremendous seriousness of the upcoming gig. "Ahh, it will be great. Like something out of a famous novel, like that one, 'old sport,' you know, on Long Island," he gushed.

"I certainly hope you're not referring to *The Great Gatsby*. They ran over a woman with their car."

Viktor put his arm around David's shoulder as he tried to hunch farther forward over his computer monitor. "I fear that the magic of the Pacific Northwest has somewhat eluded you. Think about the horsewoman. She knows you now."

"We just met her, Viktor. Besides, whatever I do about women up here, I want to do it slowly."

"Why?"

"I have other things on my mind, mainly Hoekstra. That son of a bitch is up to something. When am I going to sea? So far the old man has done nothing and won't talk to me about it."

"You're right. We must think of what to do with him. Perhaps we should go bowling. I get my best ideas there." He drew those dramatic eyebrows together over his curious nose.

David was growing uneasy about his new friend and cohort, who seemed to have drawn him into a moronic web of all things not science. Clearly it wasn't going to be easy to get Viktor to focus on how to deal with his very pressing problem. Still, he didn't want to have to adopt Hoekstra's view of him as a delusional egomaniac, at least not yet, or he would be completely alone.

Later that night, David was at home and just settling down to sample a local Cabernet when he was interrupted by Viktor yelling through his front window about a "breakthrough," a "definite breakthrough!" David hoped this was news on those famous hot bubbles of his, but Viktor kept him in suspense, racing into his house, grabbing a glass from the cupboard and filling it with wine. Despite the rain, he insisted they sit out on the porch, smaller than Viktor's own but equipped with a chaise and a swing chair, where he could properly relay the news.

"So what's this big breakthrough?" David asked him.

"I found some beaded curtains to hang, and it makes my house look like Casablanca."

"That's what you raced over to tell me about, beads?" Where was science? Where was his mind? "Viktor, what makes you think the world revolves around your parties?"

"Fiestas, carnivals, they're the center of the world. We understand that in Eastern Europe."

"Weather, the world revolves around weather." As a result of his relatively brief residence in the state of Washington, David had formulated an important new theory. Since the beginning of time, philosophers had searched for the one great engine that propelled humankind forward, more or less inexorably. First that vital force was God; then Darwin made it evolution; with Karl Marx it became the class struggle, and finally Freud called it sex. One thing they all shared was a claim to have human motives down pat. According to David's theory, though, there was a secret history of the world that had to do with drink, with sore feet, and most of all with weather, and there was nothing the least bit romantic about it. In his current location, rain was all there was, hence the Pyke City reliance on alcohol, philandering, indoor sports, and, God help them, crafts.

Viktor listened reflectively to his rant. "What we need is the sun, the warm, the yellow, the great yellow." He slapped his forehead, rather hard. "That's it. That is the answer. I have the dancing woman from the Mediterranean. Now we must have some version of the sun. How can that be? What about a light that goes round and round, bright?"

"What you could get is a mirrored ball, the kind they used at discos in the nineteen seventies. We could get a strobe light too. Ultimately they drive people crazy, but maybe we could select our victims."

"Brilliant. Where do we find such a thing?"

David stared out at the very green grass. A mist seemed to fall from the sky, the tiniest wet that could still qualify as rain. In the darkness, it was eerie. "There probably isn't anyplace around here to buy one big enough. If I find it for you, will you promise to come up with a plan to neutralize Hoekstra, meanwhile getting me on a ship?"

Viktor grinned. "Yes, I promise. The plan will be foolproof."

David eyeballed him uneasily, anxious about his growing emotional and professional dependence on the man.

The next morning, driving through the mean rain over to Wren, Washington, he could smell the sticky richness of wood chips and wood pulp, the trees rising around him in magnificent heights. His destination was the Buccaneer Bar at the center of the little town, where he'd been for drinks a couple of times with the string theory man and several other scientists at the institute. It sported a wooden pirate on the roof who shot off a cannon at noon and at 6:00 p.m. He was looking at his watch to see if he was near such a display—alas, he was an hour ahead of time—when the fat, bearded proprietor opened the door.

"Yeah?"

"Hello. I figured you'd be open a little early on a Friday."

"Yeah?"

"I was wondering if you ever rent out any equipment that you have?"

"I'll rent anything, unless it's attached to my body."

"Well, your body is not actually our object. We'd like to rent one of your mirrored balls, with a strobe light, for a private party tomorrow."

"You'll have to get your own strobe and rig something up, but you can rent the ball up there. It's hell's own shit, though, to get down from the ceiling. You'd need two men."

"You and I could do it."

"At a price, anything can get done."

David handed him twenty bucks, and he became a friendly guy. He claimed he had another, newer one with colored glass, and he didn't need the thing back until the following week. They stood on a spindly ladder, David beneath, basically waiting to catch the man's enormous ass in his hands. The ball itself weighed a ton, and between the two of them, they could barely get it into his car.

Viktor was ecstatic when David brought it to his house later that night. "We have to hire someone to hook it up." At the very same moment they both pronounced, "Shelby."

"But where is he?" David asked.

"Don't worry. If we sit out on my porch for more than five minutes, he will appear. He's always escaping someone."

"What do you mean?"

"You'll see."

They went outside, and over too many glasses of Chardonnay, sitting there with Viktor, David consoled himself with the thought that by hanging out with Shelby, or even just sitting at the house next door, he was satisfying his boss's peculiar wishes without being an odious little spy.

In happy concert with this fantasy, the object of Hoekstra's suspicions sauntered over and said to David without any preamble at all, "Have you seen my wife?"

"No, at least I don't think so. I don't know her, of course." David didn't even know he had a wife! Hadn't he just seen him with Leah, the beautiful English teacher? He glanced over at Viktor, who had screwed his face into some impossible position—pain or hysteria, who knew? "We need more wine. Care for some?"

"White wine? Shit no. You can always tell about white wine drinkers."

"Tell what?"

"Tell that nothing's going to happen."

"You mean like forever? I've been here thirty-three and a half days, not that I'm counting, but something had better happen soon." David could feel himself forming the words, like the little o's people made when they smoked cigarettes. Drunk, that was it, and sorry for himself. "I fear I'm drunk."

Shelby smiled affably, then looked over at Viktor. "My wife's probably playing in the park with Chuckers."

"Your dog?" David asked.

"My son." Shelby looked at him and laughed, slapping him on the back. "You are drunk. That's good."

"I'm glad you think it's good."

At some point in this unsatisfactory conversation, Viktor intervened. "Will you help us with my party, Shelby? We have this round ball that shines. . ." And he launched off into an unintelligible description of the object that still rested in David's car. Shelby agreed to install it and try to find a strobe.

"Viktor thinks his party is the most important event in the world," David said.

Surveying the front yard and then gazing up toward the trees, Shelby replied mysteriously, "Maybe it is." He sighed. "You know, something will happen. It's just not going to be what we think. Want a ride in my new car?"

David and Viktor were in no condition to refuse the invite, and this led them to Shelby's messy garage, where an immense black Cadillac Escalade dwarfed an old Saab sedan and various parts to some other car strewn around. Fat, high off the road, the Escalade carried them in beefy splendor through the countryside to a town called Cedarford, typical of many on the Olympic Peninsula. It had one gas station, one restaurant called Pie in the Sky, and several rickety-looking A-frame houses scattered here and there amidst the apple orchards. Shelby's avowed aim: a pecan and a blackberry pie, "for the girls," he said mysteriously.

After he jumped out of the car in search of same, David looked over at Viktor and whispered, "How the hell can he afford this thing? He's a handyman, for God's sake."

Viktor raised his eyebrows in wonder. "Absolutely no idea. Never seen it before, in fact. Usually he just borrows state cars."

"After what happened with his last one, maybe he got scared," David said, though the man didn't seem to scare too easily.

On their way back to Pyke City, Shelby drove like a Formula One racer, the huge vehicle swaying from side to side on the country road, while in the backseat, Viktor maintained a strange monologue that bubbled up out of the night in bits and pieces: "Those lying, dope-smoking weenies," then, "Motherfucker, just a schmuck with a hard-on." David could make no sense of it at all, especially when the older man leaned into Shelby's shoulder and announced, "The Cedarford swamp drains out to the sea."

Even Shelby, who presumably knew zero about science, felt moved to question him. "Aren't you in physics? There's definitely no sea here."

Viktor didn't address this remark, instead announcing, "I'm waiting for signs, from the trees. It's an experiment. Actually, it's secret research."

Their driver let loose the steering wheel to wave through the window at the landscape, in assent presumably. David looked back at Viktor in wonder, since clearly he was plastered.

"Trees are nocturnal," Viktor said, sounding an authoritative note.

"I see. Science knows no time." Shelby seemed pleased with his conclusion.

David just wanted to get out of the Escalade as fast as possible, but when they thundered into Viktor's driveway, the older man insisted they all take a look at his own car, apparently in some sort of competitive mood. It was a decrepit-looking vehicle that seemed to have been blue but had turned a dirty all-over rust color. The Buick Roadmaster, with fins and four signature vent holes on each side of the hood, circa 1954, looked like a fish dredged up from the Paleolithic era.

"You don't actually drive this thing?" David asked.

"Of course. It's a Buick."

"It doesn't look too good," Shelby said doubtfully.

"Don't talk about that. It makes me anxious."

Shelby looked at his watch, announcing, "Well, sorry, fellas, the little woman will be waiting up for me," and fled. David wondered which little woman that would be.

The next evening, over a plate of pâté on the porch, an entirely sober Viktor said, "You see the rewards this Shelby project has already brought us?"

"Which project would that be, the surveillance or the house? Because if you're talking about the latter, you're losing money. I went past your construction site the other day, and not much is happening."

"Mr. Shelby Burns appears to be an honorable man—about my money anyway. He charges me for the hours, five hours last week, one hundred dollars."

"So how'd he get that monstrous vehicle? It must have cost sixty thousand dollars. And he's not honorable about his wife. Where the hell is she anyway? Maybe he's killed her?"

"You've been in the state of Washington such a short time, David, and look at your ridiculous thoughts. Besides, the only person around here who could kill someone is Hoekstra. Then, of course, there's Leah's husband, Lawyer Larry. He came in second at the Steel Challenge. He can shoot five metal plates with a forty-five automatic in four seconds and hit the center on every one. That's from a stand-and-draw position."

"Jesus."

"My house will be built—do not fear—when it stops raining and the charming Leah is forced back to the miserable arms of her husband."

David looked down the darkening street, lined with the imposing evergreens that were everywhere in this part of the country. "'Trees are nocturnal.' We were in a five thousand-pound car going eighty miles an hour when you said that."

"I know. It was perfect."

# CHAPTER 6

THE EVENING OF Viktor's party, a windy and wet October night, David sat on his front porch contemplating the trees outside, along with concurrent rain measurements. It took one drop 0.61 seconds to fall to the ground from the lowest leaf. That moment, that gap between each drop had him transfixed, offering up a measurement of a force he couldn't see by a result that he could. Recently, astronomers using the Hubble Space Telescope had imaged the debris of fourteen supernovae. One of these super stars, in a galaxy relatively near to us, the Large Magellanic Cloud, had actually expired 160,000 years ago, but it had taken that long for evidence of the explosion to reach us. Unobserved for sixteen hundred centuries! David loved the idea of a universe of hitherto concealed powers only waiting for someone to discover them, the fifth force, for instance, which over short distances couldn't be detected but over great distances might even have enough strength to overcome gravity. This was a mixed sort of fixation, and David suspected that it explained the presence of so much ambiguity in his personal and professional life. For good or ill, though?

Counting the number of cars parked in front of Viktor's house, on impulse he picked up the phone and dialed Valerie Jordan's number. That this was a bad idea hit him the minute he heard ringing on the other end of the line, but he couldn't hang up because she would know he had tried to call her.

Before he could say anything beyond hello, she started yelling, "You disloyal bastard, why are you calling me?"

Did she know about the other women? Otherwise why would she say something like this? "I've been wanting to talk to you. See how you are."

"Really? Or are you just stirring things up and jerking me around? I didn't think you cared that much in fact, but it bothered you that I wasn't heartbroken, right?"

"No, absolutely untrue," David said, not entirely clear about what he was denying.

"You're turning into a passive shit, or maybe you always have been one. You're just living off the fat of the land, doing any old thing you want, asking as many people as possible to love you. And they most kindly do, but then you can't deal with their feelings at all."

"That's not fair."

"Who's ever fair? Listen, you love being the center of all this craziness, the apple of every eye. You're a damsel in distress, vamping the men and women around you with your wounded act, your poignant lost act. You're like a starlet!"

Caught so off guard by this tirade, David couldn't think of anything to say that would stop it, but he didn't want to let it go either. "I may have some problems that you don't understand, Valerie," was all he could muster.

"Bullshit! Think about it," she yelled. "Fix yourself."

"I'm not hopeless, no matter what you say," he muttered lamely, but by then he spoke into empty air. She had hung up.

Obnoxious woman, she wasn't exactly a paragon of good sense herself, off digging for artifacts with old Dr. Mayan Expert. Still, he knew he deserved a part of her attack, and, in fact, it was a relief because it laid out pretty clearly the dimensions of his previous romantic failures. No understanding between him and his women, no honesty, only sex and schmooze, two activities at which he was very good, and charm, altogether too much charm on his part, by way of blocking out knowing who the other person was. He never relaxed enough to let himself be known at all, either. In his own little universe, he was the unseen force.

Demoralized after this emotional exchange, David contemplated not going to Viktor's party at all, since many of his troubles in LA had started at disreputable fiestas. It was a strategy he ruled out, though, because he knew Viktor would come over and drag him there anyway. Instead, he vowed to behave with more discretion around Alexis, to approach her less like a so-called "vamp." He should use this social event to advance his scientific aspirations, not his romantic ones, and corner Hoekstra to demand a commitment for ship time.

Before he could step out into the street, though, Lucy Fosse appeared from around the corner and marched his way, holding a drink and waving at him. "I like to get a leg up on things," she said, grasping his arm and pushing him back toward his front stoop. "Want some?" she crooned and tipped her glass at him.

He shook his head, unprepared for what came next, a colorful account of her sexual history. There were details about a young man in Florida who never could get a real hard-on but was still a great lover, then two years with her errant ex-husband, a pro golfer. Flamboyantly unfaithful, as he got into bed one night, Lucy said, she had grabbed his hand and smelled it, announcing, "That's not my cunt on your hand." When men and women talked sexual adventures, at least in David's experience, it was a signal to repeat the same activities with them. He panicked. Even if she wasn't Viktor's girlfriend, she certainly couldn't be his. Jesus, not five minutes after considering the wreckage of his former romantic entanglements, he was the target of a wildly inappropriate seduction that threatened to ruin the only real friendship in his current life.

Could he refuse to cross the street with her? Hardly, since she took his arm. Right away, thank goodness, she abandoned him at the threshold of Viktor's house when her redheaded dance troupe buddy spirited her off through the crowd. David began to breathe again and prepared to relax and enjoy himself. Stage-two party sounds emanated from every room; people had had at least three drinks, felt good, and had started to sweat. Loud rock' n' roll blared from tall speakers, and the mirrored ball turned slowly, glancing light off the partygoers, but there was no strobe to be seen, only the glow from underneath several fringed lampshades. Viktor's great breakthrough, endless rows of gaudy multicolored beads, hung down from one arched doorway to another. Intriguing, eclectic, it was above all homey, and David realized with a start that he had never even been inside the man's house before. So far they had socialized only on their front porches.

He looked around for Alexis and finally spotted her in the kitchen, surrounded by people he didn't know. She managed a wave, and he was heading toward her when Viktor came up from behind and snuck a hand under his arm, guiding him out onto his back patio.

"Feast your eyes, David. Have you ever seen anything like it?" There in the pungent darkness, the town lights looked like watery torches, wavering strangely in the rain. "Aren't you glad you came here? Didn't I tell you it would be wonderful? I am always right. I could shoot myself for being right." Viktor turned to him excitedly, brushing a slop of wine off his Hawaiian shirt. "Your horsewoman love, David, how could I forget? She is here, no?"

"Please don't refer to her as that. She was in the kitchen a minute ago. And don't introduce me to any other women."

"Alas, some local beauties did not respond to my party idea. Go after her."

He shoved David forward, but when he looked for Alexis again, she was standing next to Shelby, talking to him over the eggplant caviar. Goddamn, he'd better not be putting the moves on her. Right then Lucy wandered near, her arm draped over the shoulder of a handsome young man, and she smiled at him wickedly as he caught her eye.

"Is your love still unrequited?" David turned back to his host amidst the swirl of people.

"Possibly." They stared at the very animated Lucy.

"We might be denying reality, Viktor."

"What is reality? It's nothing you see or touch. It's all inside, here." He pointed to somewhere at the top of his head.

"No. There is something real out there, and it's not you or me. I want to ask Hoekstra to go to sea with me, get him to commit for a specific date. How's that for something solid?"

Viktor got out a large handkerchief and wiped his face all over. "Yes, OK, but afterwards I must do something about Lucy." Then he yanked David toward their boss, who loomed over a gaggle of long-legged young women. In a florid speech, Viktor proceeded to glorify Hoekstra's scientific genius to such a degree that even the old man rolled his eyes. He then announced an exciting idea: a sea voyage that would include

Hoekstra himself, who could use a submersible to eyeball first-hand the vents at Juan de Fuca, little geysers under the ocean with lots of hyperthermophiles floating around. Viktor had improvised this last bit, but it was brilliant. Hoekstra, of course, agreed, genuinely thrilled by the idea. And if Hoekstra went, David went. He might have to lock his boss in the bilge to immobilize him, but at least—at last—there was a plan.

As David started off toward the kitchen for a drink and to hunt up Alexis, Viktor grabbed his shoulder. "She will begin."

David thought he'd been joking about the belly dancer, but there she was, snaking her way into the room. Wide of hip, she wore a red chiffon veil that hung from her waist over a purple G-string and big gold earrings that jangled as she moved. Her brassiere, molded onto fine, firm breasts, was red and gold, and she had braided her thick black hair with gold ribbon. A strange, throbbing melody with bells and distant drums rose up around them. The dancer planted her feet, moving through her knees, her thighs, her hips as if to the primal rhythm of sex. David could picture every part of her body beneath him, and right now, though he tried to stop himself. He was startled out of these thoughts when there, through the haze of smoke, liquor, and hot bodies, he saw Alexis and Hoekstra standing together, as if in a *tableau vivant*. Jesus, did they know each other? Maybe everyone in this town knew each other. David surveyed the landscape for Hoekstra's wife and spotted her on the other side of the room near the improvised bar. Her enormous ass, encased in white slacks, was pointed in his direction.

The music grew louder; the sinuous drumbeat of strange harmonies began to swell in that rhythm so foreign to the daily life of people in denim and Gore-Tex. As the music throbbed, the belly dancer's hips widened their circle, and these movements had an electric effect on the room. There was rustling, unease, and some women wandered away, though David spotted Leah watching closely. Why wasn't she with her husband or with Shelby, or had the phantom wife accompanied him?

At this intense moment, Alexis chose to circle her arm through his. "Hello," she breathed softly.

David started at the sudden, intimate tone, then looked into her eyes. She smiled and moved against his hip with the music, and he could feel the slight touch of her breast against his arm.

"I've been wanting to see you," he said. Dressed in a tight black sweater and slim black skirt, she looked elegant, sexy, and he pressed against her for a moment. The feeling of her body, coming on top of his wicked thoughts about the belly dancer, made him break into a sweat.

Suddenly a voice whispered in his ear, "Quite a strain on the floor, don't you think?" It was Philo Smallett, his supposed coconspirator in the basketball entertainments.

He vanished before David could respond, and the music rose even higher. Shelby now stood with Leah, moving next to her as if hypnotized, and on the other side of him loomed Hoekstra, looking disapproving, worried even. David wondered where Lawyer Larry was. Beyond the dancer's swaying body, Madame Hoekstra suddenly appeared, placing herself between Shelby and her husband. She hoisted a martini glass to her mouth and drank it down almost in one gulp, just as her husband reached out to her. While the music rose to an orgasmic scream, David heard a cry gush from her lips, then another. He couldn't imagine Frances Hoekstra seduced by the charms of the dancer. Then the heavy-bottomed woman fell facedown on the floor.

Had she fainted? He raced over, but Hoekstra yanked him aside and started shaking his wife by her left arm. The music rose ever more relentlessly into the sexual stratosphere, yet no one could seem to turn it off.

"Darling, darling," Hoekstra cried as he shook and shook her.

"Stop it." David leaned down to see if she was breathing. Her face was contorted, her eyes fixed, and her mouth wide open. By now one of Viktor's guests, a doctor presumably, had elbowed his way through the crowd. He felt her neck, he felt behind her head, and then he knelt beside her and began pumping her heart with his hands, punctuated by bouts of mouth-to-mouth resuscitation. It didn't take a genius to see that she was dead.

But she was not dead, at least not at that moment, only unconscious, according to the paramedics. After she was taken out on a stretcher, with Hoekstra trailing behind, the paralyzed partygoers—some too drunk, some not drunk enough—were at a loss. Several whispered to each other or just stared vacantly. Viktor fussed and fumbled for a bit, then loudly insisted that everybody stay and keep on drinking. A number of people complied, swilling Scotch, vodka, whatever they could get their hands on; but instead of getting hilarious, they simply froze into more and more wooden poses.

"Would you like me to take you home?" David said to Alexis, not having any idea what else to do.

"No, no, I've got the truck. Let's talk tomorrow, when we can think."

"There might be a murderer about." Her eyes were teary, and at this, she shook her head. He wanted to stroke her silky hair, be comforting, but he didn't see how he could; instead he just took her hand and pressed it. She leaned into him for a moment, but pulled away, and he let her go.

Viktor had been eyeing him all through the paramedics' ministrations and then again through his small colloquy with the most beautiful woman in town, apparently intent upon communicating something on the order of "I told you so." Finally Viktor came up beside him and whispered, "They have done this."

"Who's 'they'?"

"The conspirators. I should have known."

"What conspirators?"

"Those who would ruin my party!"

David stared at him. "Viktor, nobody cares about your party. Her death, if she dies, has nothing to do with you."

"Nobody cares, nobody cares, how could you say that? I care, and you should care too."

David drew him outside so that no one would hear his terrible words. "Just relax a minute and imbibe the night air." It smelled fresh and green, of course wet too. "Breathe in and out," he said, as if he were talking a diver up from the bottom.

"You're right, David. What do I think? I am God? People get sick, they die, and it has nothing to do with Viktor Pelliau."

"You see, there you are. Don't you feel better?"

"You sound like my mother. Are the guests leaving? Oh no." And he started back inside.

With Alexis and Hoekstra gone, Lucy nowhere to be seen, David's only other real acquaintance was Shelby, and he was locked in feverish conversation with Leah. David decided just to go back home—a peculiar move in retrospect, but he had no idea what else to do.

Alone on his front porch, swinging randomly in his hanging chair, David sipped a glass of ice water, trying to parse out the evening's events. Had the woman simply keeled over, the result of some illness? No doubt that was the case. But if foul play were involved, Viktor's new housing project would shortly become urgent, as the police would appear and forbid him entrance to his old one. He waited in a kind of daze. Oddly enough, it was Shelby and Leah who sauntered over. They squished across his lawn and sat down next to him, silent.

Finally Shelby put his hand on David's knee. "Goddamn, that was terrible."

"I can't believe it," Leah said.

"I wonder if she's going to be all right." Shelby wiped his forehead with his hand.

"Did you know her?" David asked Leah, but even at that somber moment, he couldn't stop looking at those awesome breasts floating in black satin.

"No, but didn't you do some work for her, Shelby?"

"I painted their garage and did cleanup in the attic. Hoekstra's a pack rat, and the place was full of junk. Have you seen his porno collection?" he asked David.

"Of course not." Jesus, what next?

"I actually contributed to it, gave him some magazines I brought from Walla Walla. He seemed to think they were rare or valuable, paid me good money. They were just junk I found in my father's house after he died. Whips and chains, that kind of thing. I thought they were stupid, I mean, old-fashioned and goofy looking. Couldn't place my father anywhere near them." Shelby seemed seriously upset, shaken even, and unusually talkative.

His boss's sexual proclivities were the last thing David wanted to think about. "I really do need a drink," he announced, stepping inside and producing a brand new bottle of fifteen-year-old Balvenie, honey-flavored single malt whisky that they drank neat, after which he put on a CD of bagpipe music the way his father used to when in his cups. He couldn't restrain himself from asking about the esteemed Larry. "I didn't even see him at the party."

"He came right before the belly dancer started. Then he went to the hospital with her. He's Hoekstra's lawyer." Leah gulped at her drink. "Not that I know what he does for him. I try to ask him about his clients, but he always cuts me off. 'I don't come home to talk about work,' he says. 'You don't come home to talk about anything,' I tell him. It's been like that."

David felt sorry for her, and about as sorry for himself, since the bagpipers were playing the very funereal "Amazing Grace." Just as they were about to start in on three more glasses of the "water of life," Viktor came lurching across the lawn toward them.

"You guys, you people, you. . . " Sometimes when he got excited, Viktor said the same thing over and over, as if stuck in a language groove.

"She hasn't died yet, has she?" David asked.

"No, no, not yet, or ever," Viktor said, glowering mysteriously. Suddenly he threw his arms up to the sky. "But did they like my party?" Then he chastised himself. "No, I must be serious. Perhaps we will be blamed by the Hoekstra."

"What do you mean 'we,' white man?" Shelby said.

"I remember that I was staring straight into her face, I saw her take a drink, she clutched her throat, let out a strange sound, maybe more than once, and keeled over," David offered. How easily he could replay the moment in his head.

Viktor made a web with his hands and twirled his fingers. "Shiva, the creator and the destroyer, at work again."

Shelby pulled out a cigar and bit off the end.

As the rain fell harder, Leah pronounced them unnecessarily suspicious. "Probably she had a chronic condition. She's an older woman. A stroke, that's the most likely thing."

Shelby pulled a party napkin from his pocket and wiped his face all over, twice. A relentlessly buoyant person, he had reacted strongly to her near death, or whatever it was.

"We should pool what we know about Hoekstra." The assembled drinkers gave David perplexed looks. "What? The husband is always the first suspect."

"He's not happy, that's for sure. Self-obsessed, angry, over-sexed." Shelby clearly returned Hoekstra's dislike.

"Could be describing any one of us," Leah said, frowning.

"Speak for yourself, babe." Shelby stood, running a hand through his hair. "I think we should hold our verdicts until tomorrow when we can find out more about her condition. Shall we, sweetie?"

She got up to follow him. "Oh, I forgot in all this commotion. I just received a letter from him."

"From Hoekstra?" Shelby said. "What the hell is that all about?"

"I don't know. I haven't read it yet," she muttered, but her suddenly unhappy lover was already drawing her across the lawn, through the misty night to yet another state car. Apparently the Escalade came out only for special occasions.

"It might be a clue of some kind." David prepared himself to delve into the mystery.

"Or nothing." Viktor seemed resigned, defeated even, an unusual stance. The two men sat together in a silence that was scary, weighted. Not one living soul was about, only dead leaves and a quantity of soggy hazelnuts. Shelby's house was dark, but there were lights on at Viktor's. "Lucy wanted to stay on and look around," he said, "to see if she could find out anything." He closed his eyes, and David thought he'd finally passed out, but he opened them in an instant. "What happened to the horsewoman in all this?"

"She went home in her truck, alone."

Viktor clapped his hands, then pulled David up from his chair. "That's not good. This calls for a cognac, your cognac. We must cheer you up."

Suddenly they heard a noise. "Shh," David said, and pulled his arm so he wouldn't move. "It's probably a rat."

"Or a bird."

"In the bushes?"

"It might be the killer." Viktor began tiptoeing toward the noise. Just as he did, a head peered out from the bush right next to David's front door. It was a small, not terribly attractive rodent, some sort of cross between a raccoon and a prairie dog.

"It's a ferret," David said.

"Come here, kitty kitty," Viktor started whispering.

The ferret responded, inching its way out of the bushes and heading straight for them. Close upon its heels was none other than the redheaded modern dancer. She scooped the squealing creature up into her arms.

"What are you boys doing still up?" she said in an imperious tone.

Viktor straightened himself like a Prussian general. "Apparently we are helping you find this small resident of the animal kingdom. Is he one of your acquaintances?"

"He's a pet, but he got loose when Lucy and I went into my house. I'm Marina, by the way. I introduced myself at the party, but I'm not sure you heard, what with all the horrible goings-on." She tried to stick out a hand, but the ferret nibbled at her. The men stood silent, both trying to puzzle out the latent meaning in what she had said about her house. Lucy's house was right down the street, so why would she be going to Marina's? "Are you both drunk?"

"I may be drunk, I may not be," Viktor said, "but I know where Lucy lives."

"She didn't want to stay alone tonight, since she's so upset," the woman barked, turning with the ferret in her arms and motioning toward the street. "I live two blocks down, the yellow house on the corner." The animal's little nose wiggled at them, and David made the mistake of trying to pat it on the head. It lunged at him with sharp teeth.

"Yikes." David jumped back.

"He's tame, but he's not that tame. As you probably know, a ferret is a polecat, not totally friendly. I call him Viktor."

Without warning, the man beside David went nuts. "What exactly are you doing with my woman anyway?" he yelled into Marina's face.

"Stop it, Viktor." David tried to pull him away.

"I'm taking care of her, and you're obviously not," she yelled back. Marina stood her ground, fixing the human Viktor with a powerful stare. With the animal squirming under one arm now, she raised a fist as if to attack.

David grabbed her by the arm, while Viktor gurgled in a strange voice, "You crazy bitch!"

"Get your hands off me," she shrieked at David and ground the heel of her cowboy boot into his foot.

"Stop that, " David yelled. "We're all overwrought tonight. We shouldn't be airing our personal grievances here, at three thirty a.m., on the fucking sidewalk." He pulled Viktor away and shoved him through his front door, but the older man kept looking back, muttering strange words in Latvian, as Marina stalked away. "She was probably drunk," David said by way of consolation.

"Drunk as a ferret." Viktor shoved his hands deep into his pockets. "What do women want, the great question of our age, as Freud put it?"

"They obviously want to beat us up."

"They want ecstasy. And they can have it, too, but not with us." He sank down on one of the yellow pagoda chairs.

"They don't seem to need us much anymore, it's true."

"Yes, men are being supplanted, erased, disappeared." Viktor seemed to be concentrating in order to speak. "Because we deserve it."

"I can't agree with you there, old man. What about reproduction?"

"Haven't you heard? Babies come from a turkey baster now."

# CHAPTER 7

CROSSING THROUGH THE institute's rather antiseptic lobby on the morning after the deadly party, David stopped to stare at the bronze bust of Larson Kinne. A craggy man he appeared to be, with deep, frowning eyes, friendly though, at least in this incarnation, and all of a sudden, David felt somewhat better. He unlocked his laboratory door, hoping to find some absorbing work. He wanted to banish from his mind the memory of Frances Hoekstra collapsing to the floor, and any image of her now, lying in the hospital, or was it the morgue? David didn't deal well with illness, having had the unhappy chore of putting his father in the lockup when he became unmanageable after his mother's long, drawn-out death. Sick from diabetes, overweight, suffocating with emphysema, he'd taken to wandering the house with a loaded shotgun and had twice cornered his son with it, shouting, "What do you want now, you perverse son of a bitch?" After he held a neighbor at gunpoint in her rose garden, the police forced David to take action. Two weeks later, his father died. He died in a locked ward, and his son had put him there.

Through the familial nightmare, because of it, David had acquired a steadfast reliance on the material world, the measurable world in all its possibilities. It comforted him, and he clung to it, especially in times of stress and sadness. Working to understand it created in him a bracing trust in the world's mechanics. To console himself on this day, he picked up a reprint of a 1986 research report from the Brookhaven National Laboratory. Physicists had charted the movements of a hollow copper sphere suspended from the top of the Palisades, 150 meters above the Hudson River near the New York-New Jersey border, and observed that over time it was drawn toward the edge of the cliff. This indicated a possible fifth force with a strength equal to about 1 percent of gravity. Through the mid-nineties, a number of people had tried to duplicate these results, with scant success, but it was at least clear that any such measurement was dependent on the composition of the rock. For such an experiment, water seemed to David a much more promising medium.

His plan so far: He would drop a series of current meters and shear probes—the latter to produce measurements of oceanic turbulence at the centimeter scale—that would give him a macro and micro picture of wave action around the Endeavour Segment at Juan de Fuca. In addition, several meters above the bottom of the ridge, he proposed to drop inert gas in a band around it and then trace its circulation. If it produced a pattern that defied conventional notions of gravity, he might have yet another indication, no proof, of course, but still a hint of a fifth force.

He was hard at work on a list of instruments for this project when he spied Lucy Fosse outside his laboratory window waving at him. She was done up in a colorful tunic of African Kente cloth and kept motioning to her left. He shook his head, and finally she moved closer and mouthed, "Let me in the front door. It's locked."

As he swung the heavy lobby doors open to her, without preamble she announced, "Listen, I want to do some sleuthing. Our investigation should start right now, don't you think? I saw letters last night that made me think your friend Alexis and Leah might be connected to Hoekstra."

"Leah mentioned a letter, but Alexis? How can that be?" Was Hoekstra after the most beautiful woman in town too? Or did this have something to do with David himself, as in the start of a more pointed strategic attack?

"I think they should be the ones to explain everything. But you, you're keeping secrets from me."

"I keep secrets from everyone."

"Well, stop doing it. Let's see if Hoekstra is in his office."

"Sounds like a tremendously bad idea." In addition to his more metaphysical aches and pains, David was seriously hung over. Still, he found himself following Lucy, whether from curiosity or a simple lack of energy required to resist, he wasn't sure. "I hope he's at home grieving or preparing to grieve."

Lucy frowned. "No fucking way. She's not even dead. I heard a rumor she was going to be OK, unconscious but OK."

"Unconscious is, by definition, not OK where I come from, unless it's alcoholically induced. In my family, illness of any kind was unmentionable. Whenever anyone got sick, they acted as if it was extremely gross and embarrassing. 'If you're sick,' my father used to say, 'there's obviously something wrong with you.'"

"Makes sense to me."

The closer they got to the old man's office, the more reluctant David became, finally grabbing Lucy to slow her down. "Let's not do whatever it is you have in mind."

"You have to help me, David. I can't involve Viktor or anyone else in this."

"In what?"

At Hoekstra's door, she fiddled with the knob for a moment but had no trouble opening it. She shoved David inside the palatial office before he could protest, then immediately moved to Hoekstra's desk and slid open the top drawer. Snorting triumphantly, she held up a brightly colored condom package.

"Orange Lick. Wouldn't you know it, that swine."

"We should get out of here."

She didn't even look up.

"This is the director of the institute. He just promised me ship time. . ." At that very instant, David seriously comprehended where he was and that his presence there could sink any and all ships likely to come his way.

"Wait a minute. I think I found them." She drew out of the desk a thick pile of envelopes and put them in her pocket. David turned to leave without her, but at that moment, they heard footsteps. He froze, but Lucy kept sorting through Hoekstra's things, pocketing several more objects.

The door opened, and there stood Hoekstra, head down, carrying a bunch of files. When he looked up and saw them, some weird hell rose through his eyes. "What are you two doing in here?" he growled.

Lucy straightened to attention and let loose a dazzling, insane smile, while David clasped his hands behind him and tried to think of what to say.

"Hello there," David sputtered.

Lucy interrupted. "I was just looking for something."

"In my desk?"

"Something your wife promised to give me, but didn't get the chance, and I hated to bother you, what with all the time you'll have to spend at the hospital." She remained tough and cool.

Hoekstra glared at her. "I find it hard to believe that my wife would give you anything."

"There is much that you don't know."

"I seriously doubt that, you little bitch." He made a grab for her. "Get out of my office before I hurt you."

"Niels, you'll have to watch yourself from now on, but surely you know that," she snarled and pulled away.

He clamped onto her shoulder with a large hand. "You evil cunt, don't you think I know what you're up to?"

Stunned by how quickly things had flared out of control, David roused himself. "There's no reason to get abusive. Let go of her."

"Get off me, you disgusting old man. How many women are you torturing with your peculiar brand of sex?" Hoekstra lurched toward her, and before David could stop him, the director of the Kinne Institute slapped her on the face. Her hand flew up to her cheek, and at that moment, David slugged him in the jaw, and down he went. Apparently unhurt herself, Lucy bent over him, pulled up one of his fat eyelids, and pronounced him "alive."

"Jesus Christ, Lucy, I'm looking at assault and battery here, of my boss." David couldn't believe that, for the first time in his life, he had actually hit someone.

"You were defending me. He has more to lose from the arrival of the police than you do."

"Are you all right?" David rubbed his own aching hand, still in shock.

"It stings a bit, but nothing major."

Hoekstra made gurgling sounds, and fool that he was, David helped the big lug to stand, no easy task. Upright,

Hoekstra looked him full in the face but said nothing, nothing at all. He brushed himself off and pointed at the door, like Mussolini gesturing from the balcony over the town square.

"Listen, Hoekstra, I'm very—"

The older man motioned at them ferociously, and they got out fast, but not fast enough to avoid Viktor coming down the hall straight toward them. He seemed about to speak when Lucy shook her head violently. He wheeled around and followed them out of the building.

On the sidewalk, where they negotiated rotten crab apples and a black mush that oozed under their feet, the three of them marched along together like prisoners in a chain gang. Suddenly Viktor asked, "Whom are we fleeing? Is that right, 'whom'? I am trying to perfect my English."

"'Whom' is right, Viktor. It's Hoekstra. We were investigating his office." Lucy walked very fast, still rubbing her cheek.

"He found us, and he went after Lucy. I had to punch him," David said. Then suddenly he went nuts, screaming into the air, howling really. "My career, my whole fucking career hosed, toasted. Gone forever, good-bye. I had such hopes, such dreams." Several students paused to watch him.

"Get hold of yourself, David. You sound like Bette Davis in *Dark Victory*. Don't worry, he'll respect you more now that he sees you can fight." Viktor put his arm through his friend's and turned to Lucy. "Are you injured, my love?"

"That thug slapped me, but I'm OK."

"Oh my God," he yelped and started stroking her as if to heal her injuries by magic.

"No, no, I'm fine. I wanted to get something that might be related to Frances Hoekstra's condition."

"Why not just try to find out from a doctor at the hospital?" David asked.

Viktor clasped his hands together. "I do know a doctor, but I would not want to implore further on his professional confidence. He is not within the sphere of my influence."

Lucy rolled her eyes. "They wouldn't tell us anything anyway. We're not her family."

Despite his panic at the turn of events, David couldn't help feeling more than a little curious about what was going on. "It has something to do with Hoekstra and Shelby," he declared. "I don't know exactly how, though."

"Yes, and screwing, somebody screwing," Viktor announced.

Lucy looked at David with those dark round eyes. "'Men have died from time to time, and worms have eaten them, but not for love.'"

"What the hell does that mean?"

"It's from *As You Like It*," she said.

"Shakespeare, old boy." Viktor adopted a patronizing tone.

"I've read Shakespeare, old boy, for your information."

Viktor pursed his lips, thinking, and then suddenly got excited. "But that's it, you know. Shelby and Hoekstra. You are so brilliant. I wonder, I wonder. This whole business was dreamed up to ruin me. That is the sum of what I think."

"Why would Shelby want to ruin you, or to kill Frances Hoekstra, for that matter?" David shook his head. "Oh crap, I should be spending my time trying to get a new job."

"No, no. We're having so much fun," Viktor said.

"Lucy, you're the one who got us into our current situation. What about those letters you got out of his desk?"

"I don't know if I should show them to you."

"He sent you letters also, little one? Didn't he send one to Leah? How amazing. That man is bothering everybody we know." Viktor seemed weirdly pleased.

"Lucy claims he sent one to Alexis. If she tells me she's involved with him too, I'll leave this town right now," David said.

"You can't leave town now. Where will I live? I have to sleep at David's house"—he looked at Lucy now—"so I can watch you, if you understand me."

When they returned from campus, Viktor insisted they check out the scene of the crime before it became impossible. In the misty afternoon, his house looked stained and streaked. The front hallway had bits and pieces of colored paper embedded in the carpet, all that was left of the Middle Eastern theme. The rest of the house was a mess. Beads had fallen all over the hardwood floors, and the mirrored ball seemed to list a bit. Glasses and plastic cups were everywhere, mashed cake rested on plates, and here and there a fly buzzed noisily. But the police still hadn't been out to cordon off the site. They were free to roam about.

"You know what, guys? We should be careful what we touch," David said.

"Righto." Viktor scurried off to find a package of latex gloves he kept in the garage. With these on their hands, they began their quest—for what, they weren't sure.

The kitchen seemed the natural place to start, so they peered down into each cup, some holding dead cigarettes, others the dregs of red punch. The wine and martini glasses remained full of forlorn liquids, and those drinking hard liquor seemed to have fled just as their drinks had been refreshed.

"If it was a crime of any kind, it was probably something in her drink, but we'll never find her actual glass. Let's see, it was a martini. Forensically I guess the police could locate it, though, who knows, she might have drunk out of several glasses during the course of the night." David tried to appear as if he knew what he was talking about.

"Martinis, gin or vodka and vermouth, a clear drink," Viktor said.

"Yes, clear," Lucy said.

The makeshift bar remained as if the party were still going, and among the open bottles were indeed vodka and vermouth. Lucy and Viktor smelled and swished the liquor, while David went around opening cupboards, finally crouching down to peer into the cabinet underneath the sink. There in front of him was a bottle that looked medicinal in type, denatured alcohol, 140 proof, used in scientific labs and also as fuel in camping stoves and as a solvent in construction. Next to it stood a bottle of Bombay Sapphire gin, and next to that a variety of cleaning products.

"What's the gin doing in here with this lethal stuff?"

Viktor came over beside him to look. "Anyone could have put it there, a gin drinker, hiding it perhaps."

"Maybe the killer poisoned her drink and, being in a hurry, accidentally put the gin back next to it, instead of on the table," Lucy said.

"Did you know about the denatured alcohol under here?" David asked Viktor.

He shook his head vigorously. "Why would I ever want that stuff at home?"

Before they could grill him further, they heard a car pull up outside, and David could see a police black-and-white through the window. A paunchy, gray-haired cop emerged and disappeared toward the side of the house, followed by a young blond guy, who pulled a roll of yellow tape out of his pocket, then started up the front walkway.

The three of them huddled together at the kitchen window. Viktor whispered, "Follow me out the back so we can elude the authorities."

"Shut up," David hissed. "We've already made enough of a mess of things without going to jail. Just tell them clearly and honestly why we're here."

"Why are we here?" Viktor said.

"We're getting your personal effects," David suggested.

"I really do think we should get out of here," Lucy said, and as if one body, they pulled off their gloves, stuffed them into their pockets, and headed toward the back door.

Just as they opened it, the older cop, who must have circled around from the other side of the house, tapped Viktor on the shoulder. "Care to explain yourself, sir?"

# CHAPTER 8

VIKTOR GRABBED A plate and a glass off the counter and held them up like a waiter, announcing to the policeman that he was just "getting some things." "My house has been cursed by this strange event," he added, shoving a fingertip of the rubber glove down into his pocket.

The younger cop appeared, and now two officers stared at three guilty-looking people, then insisted they drive to the police station and give statements. During the course of this little trip, jammed together in the backseat of a squad car, Viktor smoked his pipe and gazed out the car window. Several times he grasped David by the arm and squeezed it affectionately, while Lucy just stared straight ahead.

Exiting the car, David considered throwing his coat over his head the way suspects always seemed to do on TV, since he certainly didn't want anyone to see him. He thought better of it because, after all, what had he done? Besides, nobody knew him here. Instead he strolled up to the station, which was behind the courthouse, trying to look respectable, daring the world to think him otherwise. There was very little action inside the place: a few drunks, several scruffy guys, perhaps loggers. As he sat on the bench awaiting his turn, who should go by but Hoekstra himself, with a police officer on either side? He glowered at David, and the younger man smiled faintly, a gesture toward reviving his dead career. On the other hand, he thought Hoekstra's career wasn't going too well either.

A moment later, Viktor appeared at the other end of the hallway, shaking himself as if he had fleas and pulling his jacket around him. "Any news?" he whispered as he joined David on the bench.

"El Hoekstra hath been taken."

"He's just giving them a statement." Viktor stood as Lucy emerged from the room in front of them.

A policeman motioned to David to follow him across the hall. There was no bright light, no bleak room with a good cop and a bad cop, only a stolid young man who wrote everything down in a ring binder notebook. In fact, David had to pause a moment each time he said something, because the guy wrote so slowly.

"How well did you know the said Mrs. Hoekstra?"

"Not at all really."

"What about her husband?"

"He's my boss."

"Do you know anyone who would have a motive to kill her?"

"Uh, well—"

He looked at David. "Her husband maybe?"

"I don't know."

"What about some letters he wrote to other women?" While David had a moment to envision the torments of the ratfink if he even hinted that he knew of their existence, the policeman said, "We know about the letters already. We have his hard drive in our possession. Do you have any reason to think he might want to kill her?"

"I only know why she'd want to kill him," David laughed.

"Don't joke with the police."

David pulled himself together and decided to mention what they had seen in the kitchen cabinet, telling him about the poisonous properties of denatured alcohol and suggesting the possibility that someone had mixed a little into the gin, then in haste stuck the two bottles under the sink.

"Could be a theory. I'll pass it on to the hospital, make sure they check for it in the toxicology tests."

"What about fingerprints on the bottle?"

The cop looked at him as if he were an imbecile and muttered, "Maybe," then dismissed him.

David found himself sauntering out of the station, once again trying to look innocent. His smile said to the world, "I didn't do anything, and if I had, I could hide it." Lucy and Viktor waited for him on a park bench. "I assume that we all told the same story."

"Indeed, David, and why would we not? There is only one story." Viktor puffed on his pipe.

Lucy wandered off behind them, picking flowers and doing a kind of dance around the rosebushes. "But I didn't give them the letters I took out of his desk drawer," she sang.

"You nasty, nasty girl," Viktor said.

"Christ, Lucy, isn't that suppression of evidence? They asked me about them too."

"They probably have nothing to do with the case. I wonder if she's still alive? Nobody is talking about her. It's weird."

She was right; David certainly didn't want to talk about her. Even though he barely knew the woman, he didn't want her to die, or worse. "I hate to think of people wired up to machines that breathe for them, halfway between life and death." After her second bout with breast cancer, David's mother had occupied that brutal limbo for weeks, her bones so brittle they could break with any movement. Whenever he pictured Mrs. Hoekstra, an image of his own mother painfully shone through it.

"Who knows where their spirit floats, out over the sea, beyond the clouds—" Viktor got carried away.

"Stop it," Lucy said.

"Maybe we should wait here to see what happens to Hoekstra," David suggested.

"Don't be ridiculous. It could be ten years," Viktor said.

As if on cue, they watched the big wooden doors of the building open to reveal the very man. Loping down the steps, he eyeballed them for a moment, not in a friendly manner, and then moved off toward the parking lot.

"My God, they've let him go." Viktor was stunned.

"Why shouldn't they? We have no idea what's going on here, probably nothing." David squinted into the only sun he had seen in ages, though it kept passing between fat black clouds.

The afternoon *Pyke City Sentinel* was full of the party and the sad event that took place there. Viktor was furious because the publicity detracted from his reputation as a great host, and became even angrier when he learned that he couldn't move back into his house until the criminal investigation was complete. That left him living under David's dome for the foreseeable future, engaged in harassing Shelby about construction or the lack thereof.

Their first night as roommates they sat at the dinner table eating garlic bread and salmon drizzled in olive oil, listening to what had become a downpour. "I wonder when my landlords will need a new roof."

"Don't think of worldly things, David. We should be contemplating the awful burden of life and death."

"We need to contemplate the awful burden of getting Hoekstra to give me some ship time without going with us."

"Why must he get off?"

"I don't want to sail away with a murderer."

"He's not a murderer, David. You give him too much credit. It could be several others. I'm just now trying to contact one or another of them, psychically, so we can start our investigations."

"Wait, I thought you hated the Russians for being psychic."

"We Latvians have our ways too," he said, undeterred. "You know the original Lielvardes belt, discovered ten years ago wrapped around a mummy? It says the Latvians were such a holy people our ancestors could talk with the angels."

"I've read about that. It has woven into it the whole history of the world, the mystical world, supposedly."

"*Prozit!*" He beamed and clinked his wineglass to David's. "*Uz veselibu*, to your health. You know everything, David. Most Americans are boobs."

"That's exactly what my father used to say."

Viktor fell into sighing, as usually happened when they talked about his homeland, filling the room with melancholy and regret. To make matters worse, the rain pounded its way off the Oster Wet Scale altogether, every drop a thud. That momentary glimpse of the sun had been a tease.

"You and I have got to get out of here, Viktor," David said. "If we don't get on a ship, they'll start asking me to teach."

Viktor poured him another glass of Chilean wine, one of his latest discoveries. "You shouldn't worry so much about teaching, David. It's good for you, helps you feed off pure science and make discoveries, trying to explain things. You should do it. Otherwise you'll make yourself unhappy."

"Easy for you to say, Viktor. You're not the one who'd have to teach it."

From hard experience, David knew that theoretical, even experimental, physics was teachable only to the most gifted eighteen-year-olds. Beginning physics, such as he had taught to undergraduates at Caltech, was a source of annoyance and hysteria to most otherwise rational young people. They pounded on his door at night, they sobbed, they whined, all because they were being introduced to something in which they had no interest and for which they could see no earthly use. David really needed the lab and the deep ocean. He didn't want to encounter a lot of young people with messy emotions and even messier lives. Besides, in his view, trickle-down was the only possible way physics could seep into a young mind, through other beginning scientific specialties

They were working on the chocolate sorbet Viktor had whipped up when Lucy appeared at the door. Without asking them, she grabbed a plate and scooped out some of the delicious stuff, then licked it very delicately off the spoon.

Viktor handed her a glass of wine and whispered to him, "I'll get her drunk, and she will tell me everything."

She rubbed her hand along her silky brown leg, pulling her shorts down a fraction. The two men stared as she found a green lighter in her purse, lit a cigarette, then pulled out the packet of letters she had gotten out of Hoekstra's desk and shoved them at Viktor.

"Aha, we must toast to this," he said.

David realized that this so-called "case" had been occupying more and more of his mental space, and because he had so little to do, he was submitting to the supposed mystery in order to amuse himself.

"You know, there's absolutely nothing suspicious going on. It was an accident, or she's got a disease," he said, as much to himself as to his companions.

The letters Lucy produced, however, were incredibly strange, stranger still because they reminded him of words floating around in his head somehow, long, prosy screeds with a Conrad-esque feel, if Joseph Conrad had been trying to stick a hose into a geyser rather than going off to sea. David thought he recognized phrases stolen from two of his favorites, *Lord Jim* and *Victory*, with some small adjustments.

"I gave myself up to the vigorous enjoyment of my first scientific command; the romantic associations I so anxiously sought by standing before Old Faithful all fell away into the black night." Hoekstra went on and on, narrating the difficulty of getting tons of thermophiles into a bucket as if he were Lord Jim on the water, with himself as the romantic hero. The oddest thing about them, though, was that they weren't addressed to anyone. There was no salutation, just a blank space where the name should have been, like a template for junk mail, then pages and pages of this befuddled, mostly plagiarized description of the old man and his scientific work. No appeals to love him, only to depressing, damp sympathy for his plight.

One thing, at least, was clear, David thought with relief. The letters gave him immunity against being fired for punching his boss. Hoekstra wouldn't want the story to come out if it meant he might be exposed as the author of the *Lord Niels* saga. Now David just had to worry about the man ruining his career in other ways.

"Why were you trying to get these, Lucy?" David seriously couldn't fathom any connection between this music person and the head of the Larson Kinne Institute.

"They're the wrong ones." She looked over at him archly.

"I don't understand," Viktor said.

"These are exactly the same as the letters Leah showed me, but I was looking for different letters altogether."

"We don't believe you," Viktor said.

"Why not?"

"You're in love with him." Viktor fumed.

"Are you crazy?" She got up to leave and refused to say anything more. It was late, and David offered to walk her home, but she insisted on going by herself.

Consternation had fallen upon the university, as the director of its most prestigious institute, its sole claim to anything but mediocrity, was revealed to be possibly a killer and definitely a pervert. Mrs. Hoekstra was, in fact, in a coma, and police leaks and press coverage had revealed that someone must have tried to murder the poor woman, her husband now being the prime suspect. His exit from the police station was expected to be brief; everyone presumed he would be indicted.

Hoekstra did indeed have an extensive pornography collection, and it became the centerpiece of the story, in gossip and in the local press. The most outrageous items in the collection, at least in the public mind, turned out to be eighteenth- and nineteenth-century automatons that acted out various sexual postures like a Punch and Judy show. When they started moving in front of the police chief, he apparently covered his eyes and cried out, "Jesus, Mary, and Joseph." People speculated that Hoekstra's wife had discovered his degenerate habits, or perhaps had refused to comply with his sick sexual proclivities. Intrepid reporters exposed signs of marital unhappiness, including his having seldom resided at home, instead spending his time traveling the world publicizing the institute. There was much whispering about an "other woman," although her name, or their names, hadn't surfaced. As the story went, he had waited to make his move until the party, where they would have been surrounded by numerous other suspects.

David wondered whether the strange letters pointed toward a motive. Was Hoekstra in love? Apparently letters similar to the ones Lucy had shown him had been sent to Leah and maybe to Alexis as well, so it was unclear with whom. He vowed to track down these missives and find out exactly what they said. David wanted like crazy to talk to Alexis Scherbatskoy anyway, in fact had called her twice, but she hadn't called him back. He was confused and disturbed, a victim, he realized, of his proliferating sex romps in Los Angeles. Despite all the trouble he had gotten himself into there, he still expected the women he desired just to hop to.

Incessant journalistic snooping put the neighborhood people on their best behavior, for several weeks anyway. Shelby had actually been seen outside playing with his son, Lucy hunkered down at Marina's house, and Viktor was with his new roommate. Convinced that somehow he needed to help Mrs. Hoekstra, David worked himself into the view that he alone could discover the culprit. He made endless lists of suspects, mostly of people who lived within a four-block radius of his house, a comforting task a bit like macramé. Still, Frances didn't look like a woman with enemies, and he said so to Viktor.

"There's much we don't know, David, much." Viktor stuck his finger by his misshapen nose. It was just after twilight, and the cold rain had stopped.

"Had Hoekstra ever been in your house before?"

"Hmm, I can't remember, really. I've had so many parties. I think so, though. Yes, of course."

"Where is Shelby's wife, Viktor? I've never even seen her. That's odd."

"She's around here somewhere, takes classes up in Clatskanie, " Viktor said. "He did have some sort of thing with Mrs. H, I think."

"My God, you've got to be joking."

"Alas, no."

"Well, he would know how to use denatured alcohol in construction," David said, struck by the oddity of it all, and just then the errant Shelby wandered across the street to David's house. As if psychically attuned to their suspicions, he announced that his wife and Chuckers had retreated to Bellingham to get out of the "sick" atmosphere of the town and sat himself down in one of the wooden chairs on David's front porch.

"Shelby, normally I would boot around the bush."

"'Beat,' I think you mean, Viktor," David offered.

"That's what I said. But we've been sifting through the suspects, and your name keeps coming up."

Shelby leaned toward a little wooden table and scooped some of the ragout Viktor had just whipped up onto a piece of French bread. "Aha, you remember the paint job I did for them."

"I seem to recall that your job description expanded," Viktor said.

"You guys got any beer?"

Viktor, who now had taken over David's house completely, ran inside and brought back a Heineken, which Shelby proceeded to slug in between bites of ragout.

"Do you think they'll find out about me?" Shelby asked, looking concerned.

"They'll find out about everything," David offered.

"It was brief."

"How brief?" Viktor said.

"An afternoon, less than that really."

"How much less?" David chewed on a piece of bread and observed the man.

"About an hour really, by the time we finished the schnapps."

Watching the rain, which had started up again, David tried, and then tried not to picture Shelby with the very large Mrs. Hoekstra. "You didn't attempt to kill her, did you?" he blurted out.

"Christ, why would I kill her? I liked her. I was the only one who'd given her a bang in, I don't know, a fucking decade. Her hubby didn't like her, that's what she told me."

"He most certainly did not," Viktor said.

"How do you know that?" David asked.

"I know things," Viktor said mysteriously.

"No, guys, murder I do not do. I pick up ladybugs and blow them into the wind. Death is, well, let's just say I want to be a total stranger to death all my life."

As he left later that night, Shelby noticed the binoculars on the hall table and picked them up. "Damn, just like the Navy SEALs."

David had a horrible guilt-ridden moment, especially when he asked to borrow them. "What do you want them for?"

"Work, or possibly reconnaissance. Maybe I can aid the investigation."

That notion didn't totally appeal, but David had to give him the binoculars because he couldn't think of an excuse not to. So far, the only one to use them had been Viktor, spying on Lucy and Marina.

President Thornton took it upon himself to address the university in the chapel on the following Sunday. David resisted going, but Viktor refused to stop hounding him about it, arguing for "the potential drama of the thing." At his insistence, they sat close to the pulpit. The place was packed. David looked around at the oddly cheery interior, nineteenth-century

Italian meets Twentieth Century Fox. A number of large urns, strategically placed in front of the stubby pillars, had tributes to alums etched upon them; or maybe there were real ashes in there.

Clad in his usual mustard suit, Thornton glared out at the crowd, then intoned, "Man who is of woman born"—Viktor guffawed—"is as a frail flower upon the wavering sea of life."

At this Viktor jabbed David in the side. "Someone else has written this speech."

"No kidding."

"A great man has come under suspicion, unwarranted, unfounded, and I want us all now to join in prayer, a prayer so powerful that it will lift the cloud of guilt off his head."

David saw the point quickly—damage control. That's why they had all been guided to this little ceremony, the director of the institute a prime suspect in a murder and a national cause célèbre, and here was their fearless leader standing up for him. David sank down in the pew, and Viktor began to let loose with loud sighs. The speech went on. The tidy, antique-looking Mrs. Thornton was knitting in the row immediately in front of her husband, and he glanced her way several times for approval. Finally, but not soon enough, it was over. David had the immediately liberating thought that perhaps Hoekstra would be put on temporary leave if he were indicted.

"We may be on a rudderless ship," he announced to Viktor as they left the chapel.

"Not quite, old fellow," he said, gleaming in that way of his. "In fact there is a rudder, and I am at the helm."

"What are you talking about?"

Resembling Gene Kelly in *Anchors Aweigh*, Viktor now saluted him. "As captain, I will do my utmost to guide this ship through stormy waters."

"You? That's fantastic! Already? He hasn't even been charged," David gasped. It had never occurred to him that anyone with half a brain would give Viktor a position of authority, but then half a brain was quite a bit more than Thornton had. And since they had occupied their respective porches, more recently the same house, Viktor's renown had receded into familiarity, if not contempt. David had forgotten how famous he was.

"Why didn't you tell me?"

"I wanted it to be a surprise. Yes, President Thornton has found it in his heart to place me in a position of trust, as interim director. He felt Hoekstra might be too distraught over his wife's 'ill health' to lead our happy band forward." Viktor grinned at him. "I intend to honor that position by giving you a tremendous amount of money for those little experiments of yours, and many hours of ship time."

"Brilliant idea!" Perhaps Hoekstra would be in jail for the duration, therefore not with them on deck, rolling about in twenty-foot seas. "We have to be sure to keep you in place no matter what."

"Don't worry. I intend to cling to the wheel," Viktor announced with an uncharacteristic hint of ambition in his eye. "I've been working for this a long time."

# CHAPTER 9

D ELIGHTED AT THE providential exit of Hoekstra as director of the institute, David hoped that another miracle would take place, and he would be relieved of his obligation to give a talk in the coastal town of Shoop during a weekend junket for the institute's physicists. Unfortunately, the office secretary informed him that his presence was still required. At least this diversion got him out of town, and even though he felt obligated to offer Viktor a ride, happily his roommate refused the lift.

"Of course I wouldn't miss your debut, but I must drive myself. I'm testing the Buick over long distances, and I don't want to risk your possible death."

On a dreary Saturday morning just outside of Pyke City, followed closely by logging trucks rocking their loads of Douglas fir, David tried to reach Alexis on his cell phone. Being articulate over a digitized network at high speeds on mountain roads was seriously impossible, but he managed to yell into her answering machine, "Please, I'd like to see you," before being cut off. Moments later he was plunged into a world of fantastic natural beauty and very few people. Small towns cropped up every ten miles or so, containing a gas station, maybe a convenience store. Farther into the woods there were some larger ranch houses, an occasional cabin, then nothing for miles and miles.

When he rounded the last high pass, he saw before him a small fishing village and a roadside plaque announcing that J. P. Morgan had bought the town to fish in privacy, naming it after his favorite schoolteacher, Randall Shoop. As he wound up the driveway of a tree-lined resort, he observed a spectacular wall of gray wooden shingles and a series of totem poles, their stern animal glares pointed toward the sea as if angry spirits lingered still in the carvings. His hotel room had a floor-to-ceiling window, and he sat there gazing through it, savoring the jagged cliffs below. He must have fallen asleep, only to be jolted awake by the alarm clock.

David's scientific talk, which he had adapted from his second paper, involved the mysterious fact that physical oceanographers know how cold, dense water enters the deep ocean when it sinks near the poles, but not how it comes back up again, and he was waxing eloquent on the subject while trying not to look at the smirking Hoekstra. Does water return to the surface in small quantities over large expanses of ocean or in stronger localized vertical currents? He had observed the latter at the Cobb Segment of Juan de Fuca and next wanted to study Endeavour, presumably fortified with all that beautiful institute money and equipment. Somewhat naively, David had thought the assembled guests would be as interested as he was, but it soon became apparent that most of his colleagues were way too theoretical to care, purists who regarded the ocean as a messy medium more appropriate for sailboats than for scientists.

Before he could finish gathering up his papers, he heard Viktor's familiar cackle behind him and watched as his friend shoved a plastic Busy Bee honey bear squeeze bottle his direction. "Want a drink? It's Tennessee sour mash whiskey."

David pulled him aside. "Are you or are you not director of the institute? Nothing seems to have changed."

"Don't worry, dear boy. It's all in progress."

Though several people had already left, Viktor took it upon himself to introduce David to those who remained, running down bios under his breath. "He's working on fluctuations in the cosmic microwave background. There's the string theory man, but you know him, I think."

Several other people David had spoken with occasionally— a young woman involved with astrophysics, the other a kid from MIT, who announced that he "made things flat" and who congratulated him but seemed unable to ask a single question. Surprisingly, the one person who actually seemed impressed with his talk was Hoekstra; David could read it in his curling lip.

Viktor guided him toward the bar, whispering in his ear, "Listen, the big man wants us to see his porno collection. It would aid our investigations. We have to go so we can figure out his obsession with Shelby. What do you think?"

"I think it's sick. Why would he be inviting us anywhere? He doesn't appear to like me much, and I think he hates you. Why is he even here? He should be at his wife's bedside, or he should at least acknowledge that you've temporarily replaced him."

"Yes, but why force him?"

David had no answer to this, and instead contemplated the mighty Pacific below as they wandered outside on the lawn of the hotel. A chill mist rose up around them, and sheets of salt droplets moistened their clothes as they lost sight of the magnificent coastline.

"I should just move out here and work," David said.

"This American craze with working all the time is pathetic. I go in at ten, leave at three, and am more famous than any person at the institute. I've already figured out a magnificent experiment at Juan de Fuca, which you're going to help me do. For that, I could sit back and watch my toes."

"Our specialties have no relationship that I can see, Viktor."

"Possibly you cannot see it, but you will. Did you think you were invited to the institute by chance?" He folded his arms in front of him like a Buddha, but before David could probe the notion, Viktor pulled him by the collar and leaned in for an important revelation. "There is something else of great importance, and I have wanted to tell you before but did not want to disturb your dreams."

"What now?"

"Frances Hoekstra is the heiress to a department store fortune. Huge, bigger almost than anything in the whole United States, not the whole, OK, but tremendously enormous."

"My God. He tried to murder her for her money. It's so simple."

"She's not dead, though."

"Close enough. If she's in a coma, he gets to control her money."

Just then a fantastic wall of water rose up around the two men, a storm cloud, as the sea bore down upon their protected perch. David had read somewhere that Sir Francis Drake, probably the first European to see this brutal coast, had had to sail southward because of these "vile, thicke and stinking fogges," and he could see why. Eerily, the surf pounded somewhere far below, like primal thunder, but then as suddenly as it had appeared, the dense spray receded.

"Poof," Viktor said, clapping his hands in delight. "Good-bye!"

Taking his shoulder, David wheeled him around toward the marvelous scene visible once more before them. "Look out there. That's the sea, the origin of life, from whence we crawled. We should forget about these dramas and get a larger perspective."

"But why? I'm not an experimental scientist. The sea is nothing to me, and I don't like the water. I prefer the lab. Here, really, have a drink." David relented and squeezed himself a giant shot as Viktor stared out over the ocean, suddenly thoughtful. "It's God's experiment, not mine," he announced.

The following day, David spent six hours in his room going over three-dimensional echo sounder maps of the ocean floor around Endeavour, done up by researchers on the NOAA vessel *Cadiz*. He had long been tracking the earthquakes that took place there daily, but seeing the juts and cracks on his laptop screen made the violent activity of the place even more dramatic than did his seismograph in the office. Rather smugly, he felt in possession of occult knowledge about the incessant brutality of nature.

At around four o'clock in the afternoon, he emerged from his room into a gray miasma and decided to explore the impressive stands of Douglas fir and western hemlock on the resort's property. Trails led off into the forest, and finally he picked one that had the largest green arrow. Crunching over twigs and fallen tree branches, he managed to walk straight into a spider web, and after wiping the stinging filament off his face, saw a gazebo several feet ahead of him. Beneath the curlicued structure, steam rose out of a hot tub. He didn't see anyone nearby and thought maybe he'd stick his feet in, when a long arm rose out of the pool, much like that of Frankenstein's monster when he emerged from Lake Geneva. David tried to back away fast, but his feet crunched on a bed of dried leaves, and every step sounded loudly through the forest.

Suddenly two heads rose up out of the mist, one the unmistakable pate of Niels Hoekstra. He stood there paralyzed, until his erstwhile boss called out to him, "You there, David, come in and join us." It took only an instant to see that the female head bobbing around beside him belonged to none other than Leah Burnett.

"No bathing suit," David said.

"Oh, we're naked as jaybirds in here, aren't we?"

Leah peered out through the moist curtain of air and seemed to frown at him. David began walking toward them—why, he had no idea, unless to get a look at her unclothed body. Hoekstra flung his arm up in a wave, and he stopped short.

Walking backward, still facing them, like someone in a cartoon, David waved back, shouting, "I don't want to disturb you." He turned away, conscious how joyfully they must be watching his retreating ass.

Hotfooting it out of that forest, through the lodge and into his room, he kept muttering, "Jesus Christ, Jesus Christ, what are you doing, Oster? What the fuck are you doing?" And what were they doing? With his wife hovering somewhere between life and death, he was balling Shelby's girlfriend in a hot tub. If that wasn't evidence of attempted murder, then David was no scientist.

He prayed that any discussion of this incident would vanish into the wet air and the trees, but Hoekstra caught up with him at the party later that night to mark the end of the retreat. He sauntered over, cigarette in hand, and put his arm around his shoulder. "I want to explain something to you, David."

"No need, sir, no need at all." He sounded to himself like a minor subaltern in the British Raj, subservient and desperate.

Hoekstra plunged ahead. "There are certain acts that are not really sex, if you know what I mean." The specter of his dead career leapt in front of him. Whatever happened, he didn't want his boss confiding the oddities of his sex life to him, even if he might be a murderer.

"I couldn't agree more, sir."

"Refrain from calling me 'sir.' There is the sex act, and then there are extensions to that."

David stood silent, looking desperately over Hoekstra's shoulder for someone to rescue him from this conversation.

"Good God, man, what would you call a blow job?" he said, louder than David would have liked, then more quietly, "I wouldn't ever want my wife to know about it."

There were moments in life when a certain haughty indifference was the only possible recourse, at least for a member of the Oster family, which had been extricating itself from sordid situations for decades. The car wreck came to mind. When David was ten, his father took him for a ride in a classic Jaguar E-Type roadster. As they wound around the rolling hills of Birmingham, Michigan, he got it up to 106 miles an hour, and David knew it because he watched the tachometer hit five thousand at which point he yelled that maybe they should slow down. Shortly thereafter they rolled over into an open field, not once, but twice. He was thrown under the dashboard, wedged into the dark underside of the smelly leather, only to see his father emerge unhurt from the driver's side and laugh, then light up a cigarette. The car was totaled. Of all Dave's adventures, this was one of the few times he had risked his son's life, because he was even more drunk than usual.

Even though David's knee bled through his pants, and he had a sprained elbow, old Dad had more important concerns on his mind. "Don't tell your mother what happened, David.

She doesn't want to know things like this." He used a roadside phone to call for an ambulance, got his son out of the emergency room in under an hour, rented a car, and drove them home in time for dinner, all while still drunk. His mother never said a word about the limp or the bandage on his elbow or the missing car, and never asked him a single question concerning that afternoon. So, clearly, Hoekstra had planted his confession in a well-prepared pot.

"Your sex life is your own business, Niels." David pointedly used his first name. "I refuse to have anything to do with it." He turned his back on the man, moving as fast as he could to where Viktor had been peering at them through his thick glasses.

"Speak to me, David. You have offended our fearless leader." Viktor seemed thrilled.

"He has offended me. Christ, what some people do for sex."

Viktor's eyes grew wider and wider. "Go on, go on," he muttered, but the party was too loud and stifling.

"I'm going to make you wait until we see the porno collection before I tell you." This relationship with Viktor was getting entirely out of hand, and David vowed, despite the man's residence in his house, to back off from it and all its complications.

Just as he was about to check out early Monday morning, David spotted Hoekstra striding toward him purposefully. Anxious to make a fast getaway, he hunched himself forward over the front desk to hide his face. This move did nothing to thwart the older man, who tapped him on the shoulder.

"The bus will meet you to get out to the beach. It will only take an extra couple of hours."

"What the hell are you talking about? What bus?"

"The bus for the field trip. I've arranged with the Geology Department to have you experience one of their classes. To see how worthwhile it would be to meet the young people of Washington State."

"Right now? I have to get back to the lab."

"Since it has to do with the Washington coast, I thought, why not David? Then Viktor volunteered to teach the class for them. But I want you to go along. It's perfect, since you're already here."

David was staring at the son of a bitch while he said all this, considering either another right uppercut to the jaw or possibly blunt force trauma, if only he could find a club.

"I know your schedule is flexible." The wrinkles on Hoekstra's face drew back and up into a grin.

"Viktor doesn't know anything about the geology of the coast."

"Oh, I wouldn't say that. He's a man of vast information, as are you. Spread it around! Let them know the mysteries of the sea. You could teach a class in next year's fall semester. Why not?"

"You know exactly why not."

"Even Leah Burnett could be part of it. I think President Thornton's already excited."

David paused, aware that he should convey just the exactly correct level of threat. "Believe me, you'll pay for this, Hoekstra, as in specific dates for ship time, major equipment, more equipment. . ."

"Anything you want. This is really worth something to me, David, much more than you know. Besides, the weather's too bad to go to sea for the next few months. I promise you two solid weeks in the middle of April, OK?"

"I want that in writing," he said, conscious that the man before him occupied some limbo land between director of the institute and jail, so he might not be able to make any promises at all.

He waved his hand dramatically. "Done."

Which explains how one bright Monday morning in November, David Oster encountered fifty-five undergraduates rigged out in down jackets and rubber boots, loaded with clipboards, wearing ugly caps, on a bus, with himself improbably in command. Where Viktor was he had no idea. David sat as far back in the bus as he could, praying that they weren't going to start singing about bottles of beer on the wall, but no. As soon as they pulled out of the hotel parking lot, these kids put on their iPods and lit up cigarettes. The bus driver started yelling, unable to drive and beat them up at the same time, and no other authority figure appeared to be present, except a couple of frightened graduate students who kept looking around nervously and murmuring in disgust at the wave of smoke.

Within twelve minutes, David had gone from physicist and fellow of the Larson Kinne Institute of Applied Physics, winner of prizes, imbued with boundless ambition, to camp counselor. It was too gruesome for words, and for a number of minutes, he simply sat there. Then a rising tide of smoke and carbon monoxide began to saturate his brain, and he stood up in the lurching bus to yell, "Stop the goddamned smoking, or I'll call the police."

Stunned, they ripped off their headphones and stubbed out the offending cigarettes, covering the floor in ashes and butts, and suffice to say, the rest of the trip went along peacefully. He had become a hero of sorts, and several co-eds now eyed him with interest. David just stared out of the window in shock.

As he debarked near a rest area perched on a cliff above the coast, he could see at least another hundred undergraduates already there, milling around, and Viktor right at the center, dressed in a khaki safari outfit, complete with pith helmet and walking stick, a whistle dangling from his neck. His friend waved at him frantically.

"Dr. Livingstone, I presume," David said and pulled on the whistle. "I won't forget this, Viktor."

"This whole thing is my fault, I know, so when Hoekstra suggested you for the assignment, I said, 'I must go where David goes. I'm going to give the lecture.'"

"I thought you didn't want to get anywhere near the real ocean."

"I don't, but we won't be on it, will we?"

"Not unless the buses float away."

"I'm just going to keep pointing towards Juan de Fuca and talk about my bubbles. Everybody's met a bubble, after all. I'll stand on that rock there and begin lecturing. You start herding."

Herding was the operative word, as in crowding the students toward the pounding surf without having them drown. Clipboards in hand, hats pulled way down to avoid moisture, clumps of eighteen-year-olds craned their necks toward Viktor, who had balanced himself on a crag. Only a confirmed screamer could compete with the pounding sea, but Viktor held his own while the students scribbled notes on wet paper.

To hear Viktor explain how the Juan de Fuca Ridge constantly reshaped itself because the earth's core was expanding below it and erupting through cracks along the sides of its mountains, while over 150 young people dodged the surf line and sank ever deeper into the sand, was a memorable experience. David plotted his revenge as he wandered off out of earshot. There had been a series of storms lately, though they blended in his mind as one interminable downpour, but still, these had affected the beach. Rather than being shaped into a crest, uniformly, several sandbars had piled up in opposing directions underwater, and these had created a series of waves crashing into each other, like a backward surf. Just as one wave receded, it crested across another as it rushed to shore. He could have gone surfing, but toward Japan. David was wondering about the physics of such wave action, how it played out even deeper beneath the surface, when Viktor lurched up behind him, fingering his whistle.

"It's come to this, has it, Viktor? And I thought you wanted the Nobel Prize."

"Shh. Don't say that out loud, bad luck." He glanced back at the herd. They were perched here and there on benches in the rest area, writing on their clipboards. "I told them to do a geological history of the Washington coast from what they learned today," Viktor said. "Totally impossible, of course, as I never actually mentioned geology, but you see, you set them to work, and they get down to it so fast, I am amazed. They are the worker bees of the world. They can do anything, not with their minds, such as they are, but with their hands, their feet, their necks."

Suddenly David panicked. "They can't be serious about my teaching a class, can they?"

"Who knows why anything happens around here? But if it comes to that, I will help you all the way. We will get other people to talk. I already have a title for one of the lecture— 'The Mysterious Sex Life of the Salmon.'"

# CHAPTER 10

W AS VIKTOR, TOO, plotting with Hoekstra and
Thornton to stop him from working? And were
Hoekstra and Leah really lovers? Could she be in
on a scheme to knock off his wife and live happily ever after
on her money? Or were she and Shelby involved in a deeper
conspiracy of their own, using Hoekstra to get their hands
on the dough so they could run off with it themselves? As he
headed through the dreary mist back to Pyke City late that
afternoon, David suspected everyone. Somehow he ought to
apply scientific method to these mysteries, organize the clues
into a formula. Then he'd know whether there was something
truly sinister going on or whether he was just paranoid, reading
too much into what was just a tragic accident—and into a lot
of people screwing each other to cope with bad weather and
boredom.

At once he had a happier thought; Alexis's farm was on
the way home. Why not just drop in on the most beautiful
woman in town? In spite of all his resolutions to avoid romantic
entanglements, David couldn't deny this attraction and didn't
want to. In one way or another, he was going to pursue her,

but he just had to try not to make a mess of it. In any case, he needed to know about her letters from Hoekstra. The old man obviously had not been neutralized, despite his supposed removal from the institute's directorship, and David wanted as much dirt on the guy as he could possibly find. Furthermore, the idea of Hoekstra's having anything to do with Alexis made him worry for her safety, and made his skin crawl too.

One thing his depredations in L.A. had taught him: it was never a good idea just to show up at his intended's house unannounced. First off, she might not like it, and second, he might inadvertently discover something he could tolerate only when more deeply in love. In this instance, however, the situation was dire. As he marched up her driveway, he contemplated his mission and savored the landscape, the huge trees crowding out a glimmer of sky. The snorts and whinnies of the horses guided him toward the barn, where he found her in the second stall, brushing the tail of a big Appaloosa. She didn't look surprised to see him.

"Hello," she said in that lovely voice of hers. "Are you here for basketball horses?"

"God, that stuff again. No, I was involved in something more challenging, I hope, presenting underwater physics to a group of specialists in stuff like particle physics, nanotechnology, guys who could care less, out in Shoop. I'm on my way home."

"Wonderful." She flipped the brush into a bin of hairy implements and took his arm, steering him outside, where it was cold and wet. "Tell me about your work."

"I will." But suddenly he felt that he didn't know where to begin; he was too disconnected from it. Instead of trying to rattle off something to impress her, he found himself confessing the truth. "A mathematician needs just a pencil and a pad of paper, but a physical oceanographer needs an array of helpers and equipment, like a movie director. I have none of these, only lonely computers in my office spitting out news of the research of other people, so I don't know what to do. I've been waiting around to go to sea. And now it looks as if I'll be trapped here teaching undergraduates. I'll never get to go."

"Would you like some coffee or a drink?"

"Anything you're having is fine." He followed her into her spacious log cabin. On the inside it was cozily wooden and beamy, with overstuffed chairs and several Kwakiutl masks on the wall; David liked it right away. A German shepherd sniffed toward him as he came in, then sank his nose back into the carpet, while she motioned him toward the couch and disappeared. He wandered about, pausing to look at the photographs over the fireplace. There were several of a child, a boy, one as a baby, one holding a baseball bat, then one when the kid looked about sixteen, his arms folded across an athletic chest.

"They'll probably all fall in love with you," she said from the kitchen.

"Who?"

"The students."

"Naah, I had a girlfriend once who told me, 'David, you look a lot more interesting than you are.'"

Alexis laughed as she reappeared, handing him a glass of wine. "But you didn't believe her, did you?"

"Of course not."

She picked up the photo of the tall boy. "My son, Henry."

Shocked, he burbled, "You have a son? You don't look old enough."

"He's in the East with his father, getting a better education than he could get here. I knew when his teacher said she wished she had his brain, it was all over. I'm forty-two, by the way."

"You are? Jeez, you don't look it." All his seductive ploys evaporated.

"How old are you?"

"About to turn thirty."

"A mere stripling."

David paused a moment to listen to the rain pounding on the roof, a pounding that echoed somewhere in his lower body, as he tried to digest this information and focus himself on the goal he had set for this impromptu visit, getting a look at her letters. Alexis let the silence go on, gathering up several magazines and pieces of paper on the table. He glanced at her slender hands, imagining what it would be like to have them touch him, when he suddenly choked, almost spitting his wine onto the table. He had caught a glimpse of what she picked up and something about the typeface made him think that here were the very letters he was after. But of course he couldn't be sure. He shifted in his chair, feeling about twelve.

"What?" she said.

He wanted to wrest the things out of her hands, but instead he made a feeble attempt at a more subtle approach. "You know, I should warn you about Hoekstra. He may be quite dangerous. He's been writing letters to several women. . ."

Alexis interrupted him with a plaintive gesture and handed him the sheaf of pages. "So you know what these are. I just want to get him to leave me alone. He's a married man, a married man who might even have tried to kill his wife."

David groaned. "That fact doesn't seem to have sunk in particularly, to him anyway."

"I met him at some university do, a picnic, I think. He sort of swooped down and started asking a lot of questions. He had very much the air of the eminent scientist, so it didn't make me too nervous."

"This guy is seriously strange. He's supposedly director of the institute, but his status keeps changing, and he's trying to screw me six ways to Sunday. He's also trying to screw a lot of other people as well."

Alexis shivered, got up and disappeared into a back room, then returned with a whole packet full of the missives bound in a black shoelace. She held on to them a moment, then laughed. "It definitely got a little heavy on the 'Here I am at a geyser, thinking of you.'" She handed him the bundle, and he could see immediately that they were identical to the letters Lucy had taken from Hoekstra's office, very likely the same as those he had reportedly sent to Leah.

Reading the first three to himself, he was appalled by a vision of this horny old man penning these screeds and churning them out on his laser printer, never bothering to change the words, offering the vision of himself, lonely in command, braving wave after wave of blasting water across his so-called rig. What was the scope of this thing? For some unknown reason, he appeared to be trolling for women the way other men did for big game fish.

"It can get pretty strange up here in the Pacific Northwest, as you probably know." Alexis glanced at the clock on top of the fridge. "I'd like to talk about this more, but I'm taking a yoga class in town in about twenty minutes. You know, cultivating my inner Zen."

David felt himself being dismissed and jumped up. "Right, I've got to go. I don't know exactly what's going on with Hoekstra, but you should stay away from him."

"They gave me something to think about, sort of like a bad novel. You see, I was in love with someone else, but it wasn't working out." There, she was in love, and obviously not with him. With this woman there could be no mistake. "He was a lot younger than I was, and I felt it would be unfair to him, you know, not to have children, to miss the things that youth could give him."

"Children are highly overrated, that's what my father used to say, especially to me, his only known offspring."

"That was nasty."

"He had his problems." David stared at the rain he was about to plunge back into.

"Which he foisted on you?"

"Which I share, though to a lesser extent, God willing."

She touched him lightly for a moment on the shoulder and went on about her old boyfriend. "Anyway, I was first of all his friend, and that meant telling him the truth about how I saw my own future."

"Sounds like a difficult subject."

"It was a difficult subject, once."

"I wouldn't miss anything if I were your lover," he wanted to say—more eloquently, of course—but instead he helped her on with her jacket. "You probably should turn those letters over to the police. They may soon become important to the case."

"Oh my God."

Through the next several weeks, the sun rarely shone, only periodically casting a golden glimmer in the morning that was instantly crushed by fat black clouds. All work and life wilted. Thanksgiving came and went, and it rained and rained, but at least David had chanced upon the perfect formula for his note-book entries on the village mystery. One late afternoon, bored in his office, he had been thumbing through the little book, where in addition to all sorts of equations and formulations, David had jotted down thought-provoking remarks by various physicists, to comfort himself or induce shame, depending on his mood. He came upon a notation he had made of something Richard Feynman had said in one of his taped lectures: "Where knowledge is weak and the situation complicated, we must get help from the second law of thermodynamics." Ah, good old entropy, one of his favorite concepts.

He turned to a new page and wrote in small, precise black letters "David's Murder Notebook," and underneath it a subtitle, "Entropy at Work Again." According to the second law of thermodynamics, entropy—think of it as disorder—is always increasing, and every real-world process helps it increase. The fact that so many of us are always trying to produce order is a good thing—it's human nature, but it's doomed. Water cools, iron rusts, mountains turn to rubble. So, the old saying "Everything that can go wrong, will go wrong" might be amended to read, "Without continual infusions of energy, everything will stop going altogether." David wrote down Ludwig Boltzmann's classic equation: $\langle E \rangle = 1/2\ kT$. Energy equals one-half the constant ($k$) times temperature. Hot means more energy, cold means less. He figured he should start out by identifying the constant in his own little isolated system that was the Hoekstra mystery. That had to be the poisoning victim.

First off, he pictured the healthy Frances close to the ultimate loss of energy—death—and tried to draw her lying down in her bed, but he couldn't. Instead he sketched her about to sip that martini. She was $k$.

He backtracked from there in terms of who had the most "heat" in relationship to the woman. To him it looked like a random collection of real cold molecules, himself, Alexis, Lucy, Shelby, who else? Leah was way warmer, as in a hot tub, but the only really hot one was Niels Hoekstra. Now he drew a stick figure of a man in a three-piece suit jabbing his finger forward, insofar as he could draw a jab, or a suit, and inserted him into the equation. Thus ⟨E⟩=1/2 $k$T or ⟨E⟩=1/2.

Staring at his doodles, he sighed. Science never failed to comfort him, even as a gag.

About Alexis, he was at a total loss. Unsure how to pursue her, freaked out about her age and concerned in an inchoate way about her son, he was even more alarmed about his frankness whenever he was around her. This was a new development in his romantic life, and he couldn't foresee its consequences. Only work and forgetting about everybody seemed like good ideas, that and drinking. Much as he knew the folly of that method of escape, he was also well schooled in denial. Dave the Bomber had had an elaborate theory about the difference between hard drinking and alcoholism, which he expounded to his son once while he unpacked his uncle's collection of stuffed eagles up in the attic. "People who drink heavily never really get drunk, they just hold their liquor well, son. It's an art, a manly art, one that runs in our family. Alcoholics stumble around and drink on the job."

Here David felt they were on shaky ground, but with that special gift of his for posing the difficult question, he asked, "What if you're just drunk all the time? What are you then?"

His father peered down at him, his eyebrows coming together in a deep *V* over his nose. As he got older, his hair turned white and flopped over his forehead, somewhat masking the indentation at the plate. "If no one can tell, then you're a heavy drinker. If everyone can tell, you're a drunk. One's actual liquor consumption is irrelevant." Though he never consumed the vats of alcohol so dear to his father, Viktor's and his recycle bin had begun to look suspiciously like the back of a bar.

In order to curtail time with his roommate, David extended his working day to twelve hours, even eating at the student union to get away from dinnertime gossip and libations. Nevertheless, on a Tuesday evening he found a note from Viktor on the fridge marked "URGENT" with the words "HOEKSTRA'S COLLECTION" written in red. At last something to cheer him up, and also creep him out, a serious opportunity to snoop. If the police were so interested in Hoekstra's collection, he should be too. As he prepared himself for the long-planned porn showing, he stared into the mirror, noticing a downhill drift in his appearance, specifically a couple of extra pounds of fat and a pasty look to his skin. Valerie used to call him the rock star of science, but he certainly didn't look any too appealing now.

The grungy Buick ground along loudly, like a rusted-out eggbeater, excusing David from any attempt at conversation with Viktor. They wound their way behind the town toward a black hill shrouded in the rain, then arrived at a sprawling stucco Spanish-style home on a bluff. Once in the driveway, neither man made a move to exit the car, daunted by the prospect of what lay ahead.

Just as David finally opened his door, a thick-chested Rottweiler sprang out at them, followed closely by Hoekstra, who shouted, "Back, Heinrich, back." He slipped a choke chain over the dog's head and pulled him to heel, while Viktor cowered away from the snarling beast, truly frightened, as if the Russians were still chasing him. The two men advanced, Hoekstra reassuring them all the while. "Don't worry, Heinrich senses intention with the greatest accuracy." Now they were in deep trouble.

American Southwest both inside and out, the Hoekstra hacienda, of which their host gave them a tour, came complete with crucifix in a front alcove, a plethora of Mexican clay pots, and thick candles in hurricane lanterns on wooden tables. The look was distinctly feminine, clearly the work of Frances Hoekstra. When they came to the bedroom, her touch was even more in evidence. The bed was an enormous metal structure covered with white pillows and lacy white coverlets, and, considering her hubby, an odd marital landscape to say the least.

"Come have some brandy," Hoekstra said, dragging the Rottweiler behind him.

They had paused briefly in his study, and David had unsuccessfully attempted to catch Viktor's eye. On the wall of exposed brick behind them, at least a dozen guns hung from metal hooks, including a Derringer, a shotgun, and a modern deer rifle. Presumably the old man knew how to shoot, and to poison too? Back in the living room, they stood before immense windows giving a panoramic view of the swimming pool while Hoekstra poured a mahogany-colored liquid out of a bottle labeled Cardinal Mendoza, saying, "The best, the finest brandy in the world." David followed closely every single movement of those bony hands before he even thought of imbibing. After their host drank heartily of whatever was in the bottle, only then did Viktor take a swig, and finally David followed suit.

Hoekstra offered them cigars from a humidor. "Cuban, I get them from an old friend on the Farm."

"The farm?" David asked.

"The CIA training center at Camp Peary, joined up there just prior to the Vietnam War. I am Danish by birth, but came here to be in the US army. Of course, they latched on to my language skills, and I spent the war in intelligence. The military, a fine way to live. I'm one of the few men who wished that that war would go on forever."

My God, he had been a spy, a goddamned spy. Heinrich stared up at David, pink tongue lolling out of his mouth, panting. Just as he glared back at him, he recalled that one was not supposed to make eye contact with ferocious canines. Suddenly Hoekstra downed the rest of his brandy and motioned toward the hallway. They followed like dogs themselves.

What happened next David always looked back upon as a watershed in his sexual life, an epiphany about the pitfalls of getting old—old and male—a warning about the kind of person he never wanted to become. The men stopped at the threshold of a dark room, and as Niels Hoekstra switched on a light, they could see heavy black cabinets against the walls. He had a remote control device in his hand, and when he pressed it, the curtains across the first cabinet slowly parted before two puppets dressed in colorful German folk costumes. They twirled about, dancing, and David walked over to get a better look at these antique automatons that had so shocked the chief of police. They bowed, they smiled even, and then the girl dancer dropped her skirt while the male dropped his trousers, though they got stuck momentarily on his penis. What happened next was a pantomime of hearty sex in Bavaria, with the strains of beer hall music in the background. Hoekstra pushed another button, and the curtains across a second cabinet opened to reveal a glass window. Inside was a Hawaiian scene, with natives doing the hula, then dropping their grass skirts and loincloths right and left as the drums pounded on.

"This is delightful." Viktor uttered his first words in a long time.

"They're from the nineteenth century, motorized dioramas." Hoekstra led them into a smaller room filled with statues of African men with enormous erections.

"Those African women must have been very happy." David was trying to lighten the heavy air. Pornography was, by definition, a solitary art with its own secret codes. It felt peculiar to look at it in a group, especially this group.

"Of course the books are my greatest treasures." Hoekstra opened folding screens that hid rows and rows of oversized volumes bound in leather. "*La Puttana Errante*, 1531, an original copy. This is priceless. And here's *L'Ecole des Filles*, published in 1655. An older woman instructs a younger one on giving pleasure to men. *Therèse Philosophe*, a bestseller right before the French Revolution."

David leafed through something called *His Master's Secrets*, which contained tiny, delicate paintings depicting a man and woman in the most extraordinary poses. Only a confirmed yogi would have had a chance.

Was this where old men ended up, in a room looking at puppets copulating? Already he knew that the man before them performed some version of the sex act in hot tubs—though not with his wife, the well-padded owner of department stores— and liked to brag about it. But what kind of pervert had rooms and rooms full of expensive antique pornography? And what man proudly displayed it to others while his wife lay in a coma? She must have known all about it too, unless she lived out back of the house in a shed. Still, he wasn't sure what bearing it had on the central question of whether his boss had tried to do in his wife.

Back in the living room, Hoekstra insisted on pouring them more brandy, which was making David feel not drunk, but drugged. He wanted to range farther afield in the house to troll for clues, but couldn't figure out how to slip away since the old man was watching his two guests with almost gruesome intensity.

"So, tell us, please, what does it mean that you buy these things?" Viktor stood grinning.

"It is a history of erotica as it is in the known world today, and then it's an endless source of delight, in the fullest sense of the word."

Viktor started to laugh like a drunken frat boy. He'd had vastly more Cardinal Mendoza than David. "See here, old man, nothing substitutes for real sex."

Hoekstra pressed his hand heavily upon the much shorter man's shoulders. "Pelliau, I don't expect you to understand the erotic arts, only to observe them and learn."

Viktor reared back. "I did see some techniques I might be able to put into action."

The decrepit factor was getting to David, as in "I can still get it up, thanks," but he couldn't leave until he'd at least tried to get answers to some of his questions. Did Hoekstra know about Leah and Shelby? He must. Was he screwing her to get back at Shelby for something—was that why he'd asked David to watch the guy? Or was he just lonely and miserable because of his wife's illness, acting out an old man's lust?

David agreed to one more drink, biding his time, and just as Hoekstra and Viktor fell into a brief, drunken shoving match, he said, "By the way, why did you want me to spy on Shelby Burns?"

The Dane wheeled himself toward him. "Our Lady of the Hot Tub, naturally." Before David could pursue this further, their host practically pushed them out the front door.

David felt it his duty to pilot the giant Buick, which wouldn't start. It made small pinging noises, began to roll, finally catching fire with a sound like a lawn mower, and at last they slid and ground their way down the driveway, Viktor giggling to himself all the while. Driving into the wet night in a barely functional auto, David realized something complicated and peculiar was going on in this little town, something to which he had now become a party, but which he did not understand. These men were older than he by many years, and older-world too, schooled perhaps in altogether foreign categories of malfeasance. Beside them, Dave the Bomber's perversities seemed kind of ordinary.

Once again, escape into work presented itself as the solution, and that's what David did the next morning, slipping out of his own home like a felon. Later, carrying a sheaf of seismographic data down the hallway of the institute, he tried to back away when Viktor collared him and grabbed the papers out of his hand.

"Aha, a man and his charts. You've got to come with me." He insisted on coffee at the Bean.

Pasty and sober, Viktor remembered every damn thing that had happened that bizarre evening. He was especially intent on knowing about "Our Lady of the Hot Tub."

"Who is she?"

"I don't want to get involved in all this, Viktor. It's too creepy and strange."

"I repeat, who is she?" Viktor said between gulps of French roast. "I warn you, David, I will find her, and then I will not let her communicate with you."

"I don't want her to talk to me, you idiot." Jesus, three months earlier, the name "Viktor Pelliau" had meant a world-famous physicist floating in the atmospherics of genius—now David was calling him an idiot. "I'm sorry. I shouldn't. . ."

"Oh, be quiet. I'm trying to think." He stared at him from out of his round eyeglasses. "If I concentrate like this long enough, her face will come to me, as in a dream."

David couldn't stand it. "Leah Burnett. I found her in a hot tub with Hoekstra, in Shoop, and I don't think they were collecting hot-water organisms. As a matter of fact, he told me something sexual had transpired."

Expecting a torrent of Latvian hysterics, David waited, but shortly thereafter, the man across from him turned reflective, staring at the noisy espresso machine behind the counter.

"I appreciate your capacity to surprise," Viktor said finally. "Something big is going on here, don't you see? Why did he invite us to his home? What was he after? He's interested in you."

"He's interested in Alexis too, sent her the same letters."

"The very same ones? How odd."

"I think I should go find the second most beautiful woman in town and talk to her about *her* letters," David said. "It might be a question of life or death."

# CHAPTER 11

D AVID WOULDN'T NORMALLY have mentioned Leah in such a portentous vein, but he wanted to shut Viktor up and preclude his nutty speculations. Yet, just as soon as he got back to his office, he felt energized enough to go back to his murder notebook and see if he could make any progress. He drew another tiny stick figure—Leah holding *Moby-Dick*—and then wondered where he might place her in the equation.

How did she fit into anything?

Later that evening, while Viktor cooked a steak, David mentioned again that he wanted to get a look at Leah's letters and was trying to figure out some acceptable way to get to her. The older man was delighted to help.

"You could call her, ask her out on a date."

"I wouldn't feel comfortable doing that."

"Why not?"

"For one thing, she's married." Also, David didn't want to draw Viktor into his budding relationship with Alexis, so he decided to pile it on. "Anyway, I don't want to antagonize Hoekstra if he has an interest in her."

"Really?" Viktor stared at him while holding a platter and a very sharp-looking Santoku knife. "I don't believe you. I could seek her out, but then Lucy would find out and hit me. Oh well, I will think of something." Before David could stop him, Viktor set down the knife and platter, punched some numbers into the phone, and muttered in his silkiest voice, "Hello, dear. We must see your letters from our boss. David will explain," and shoved the phone into his roommate's hand.

"What the hell?" David tried to think of what to say when he heard her pleasant-enough greeting, but impatiently Viktor knocked his arm with a wineglass, and he decided on the truth. "We've taken it upon ourselves to solve this local mystery, and we thought you could help. Maybe you and I could have coffee or something?" David said this at a full rush, too embarrassed to slow down, but she understood and, surprisingly, agreed to meet him at the student union the following day. When he hung up, a crazed Latvian was doing a jig in front of him. Unfortunately, this was reminiscent of many other such displays in his life.

Into one of his landlord's alarming yellow chairs David plunked himself down. He stared into the fire, contemplating the agglomeration of crazies in his life. For some reason people always felt they had permission to say or do any goddamned thing they wanted around him. His personal mantra was, it seemed, "If you're psychotic, sit down next to me." This regrettable talent must have come from living with Dave the Bomber and years of putting up with his bizarre obsessions. David's ear had gone soft, as if he'd been inside a drum that got banged twenty times a day, and ultimately, he couldn't hear a thing. He just sat there with the sappy expression of the tone deaf and a face that cried out to the world, "Hit me! Hit me again!" He had cultivated an indifference to outrage.

Noontime the next day, not too far from the Steelhead trout sculpture, David sat at a table with two cups of coffee in front of him, watching the extraordinary Leah Burnett approach, fervently hoping that she would not prove as disturbed as the rest of his cohort. Clad in black slacks and white shirt, resembling a woodsy huntress, she sat down and pulled the sheaf of letters out of her jacket. He glanced down at the typeface and the words: "I gave myself up to the vigorous enjoyment of my pipe. Just then the gathering storm struck us full force across our rig." Indeed, the same howling winds, the same thrill of command. There he was, standing by Old Faithful, gathering microbes, the sometime director of the Larson Kinne Institute for Applied Physics, laying these missives onto yet another poor female. David noted that the pile of letters was about the same height as Alexis's.

"He's pursuing me, following me. He's at parties, he's at the grocery store, he's at the motor pool—" She glanced around the student union even now, suspiciously.

"All while his wife is sick?"

"Yes, absolutely. He wears bowling shirts and weird caps. He thinks he's in disguise."

"Has he made any threats?" David asked, somewhat embarrassed at the surfeit of personal information he was accumulating about his boss.

"It wasn't a threat really, but he said something about a surprise. He'd surprise me." She nodded at the letters. "They're awfully melodramatic, aren't they?"

"Don't you recognize the material? He stole it from Joseph Conrad."

David proceeded to point out certain passages belonging to that famous author, and she started laughing. "You're right.

How could I have missed that, and who knew you were so literary?"

"Boring trips to sea, hours in my bunk with J. Conrad to remind me about the romance of it all."

She smiled and took the proffered cup of coffee. "We, um, you know, in the tub."

Here it comes, he thought. Did she really need to tell him, when he'd already seen her *in flagrante*?

"He couldn't, you know, really do it, you know, sex." This articulate woman had suddenly become tongue-tied and red-faced. She looked away from him, and at that moment, he fully appreciated her beauty.

But did he do "blow job?" The words sounded fantastically obscene, and he refused to utter them. She must mean that he was impotent, at that moment anyway, but this, too, seemed impossible to discuss.

Finally he blurted out, "How in hell did you get in that tub in the first place?"

"It was about the class. You know, the interdisciplinary one that involves the institute? They're calling it 'Mysteries of the Sea.'"

David felt an aneurysm forming in his brain. "I've heard some mention of it," he muttered.

"Thornton told my department head that he wants that class and needs me to do it. I called Hoekstra, and he said he truly wanted me too, but he would be in Shoop, and I had to come out to talk to him about it. When I got there, it turned out he wanted to have our conversation in the hot tub." She blushed again. "I guess I should have figured out that he didn't just want to take a Jacuzzi. Of course he tried to get something going, but I wouldn't, and he couldn't. It was already horribly embarrassing, the whole business, and then you came by, and he made up that thing about our being naked." She put her head in her hands.

Goddamn, that class again. He had forgotten all about it. The old pervert was attacking him from so many angles that he'd lost track. Women, basketball, and poetry— there was a kind of lunatic beauty to it, a perfection of inanity. He tried to sort it all out in his mind. Obviously any man on the planet would find Leah attractive, but he had sent letters to Alexis and Lucy as well. Why was he spreading his affections around so freely? His original theory, that Hoekstra was using Leah to get back at Shelby, now appeared inadequate.

In any case, while his wife lay in a coma, Hoekstra was trying to sleep with someone who had slept with Shelby as well, a man he had asked David to watch. He was clearly a bad man, but was he capable of attempting murder? Growing up in the Oster clan, David had developed a list of appellations for the bad man. A jerk, for instance, is the guy who, because of a genetic flaw, just never gets it right. He constantly shows up late, he makes obnoxious remarks, he under-tips, all of it through an accident of birth. Call it the "jerk gene." The asshole has a different problem altogether. He delights in squandering any goodwill a woman might have for him. Late phone calls, broken dates, lying about his location or what he's doing with whomever, the asshole has genuine hostility for women and shows it. As for his father, he was a prick. The prick has key personality defects that run deep. A drunk, a liar, a potential wife beater, depending on his social circumstances, the prick is capable of anything in a fit of rage. In his benign state, he buys expensive cars that he drives badly, electronic objects that he never knows how to use, costly watches that he doesn't wear, but on the upper end of the scale, he escalates into homicidal maniac. During his farewell talk with Cosmo, David recalled, she had called him a "pain in the ass," and this put him rather low down on the bad-guy scale, fortunately. Right now he was trying to locate Hoekstra's proper rung, and it wasn't proving easy.

David didn't get a chance to see his antagonist again until the first week in December, when President Thornton convened a meeting on the subject of basketball. The idea not only hadn't died, but seemed to have acquired exuberant life. At least Hoekstra's presence or absence would shed some light on his professional status, and alas, there he loomed at the end of the table as the president of the university droned on. He must have still been director of the institute, despite Viktor's claims.

"It has come to my attention from Coach Mayding that the basketball team may have a real shot at the NCAA finals this year." Thornton glared down at the committee members. This puzzling remark dropped like a bomb on the conference table, since the team had won four games in seven years. The *Pyke City Sentinel* was quite clear on that fact, and as the population of the state of Washington was 88 percent white, it wasn't hard to figure out why.

Receiving no response to his exciting news, Thornton simply continued. "We need more half-time activities, to keep the donors happy. After all, we have a brand-new stadium. It's one of the most fantastic in the country." He glared at them. "Have you all forgotten the horses?" They certainly looked as if they had tried to forget. President Thornton grinned at David, who broke into a giggle, but just for a moment.

"What will they do out there?" asked Philo Smallett, the engineer on whom David had hoped to dump the whole project.

"Sheet and faart," this from a heavyset man who was Polish, an expert on the carbide teeth of large dimension saws. He had cornered David at the last meeting and conveyed to him the immense importance of his chosen subject matter.

"Horses aren't good for anything else. In the Fourth of July parade, it takes hours just to clean up after them," Smallett added. "You certainly can't have them out there at halftime."

"They can come in at the end," Thornton said and turned to David. "I want you to go out to Quinault and talk to Ludwig Tonnis, the basketball coach there. Check out his floor."

David must have looked at him with massive, total incomprehension.

"Ludwig, Ludwig Tonnis?" Thornton bellowed, as if he had forgotten the name of Santa Claus. "They've got the best basketball team this side of the Cascades. Do not reveal anything of our plans."

"Plans?" What plans? He certainly did have plans, but not these. He glanced over at Hoekstra now, who smiled back at him enigmatically

"My only worry—and something for a physicist to determine, someone like you—is tonnage." He glowed at him in the oddest way.

"I'm more an underwater man, if you catch my drift," David said, and several of the old guys at the table laughed.

"Don't be silly. What's underwater is on the earth as well, more particularly on the basketball floor. Just go get a state car and drive out there. Today."

David waited outside the conference room until Hoekstra loped his direction. Before the older man could launch whatever missile was in his arsenal today, he took the offensive. "OK, here's the deal. I'll do this basketball stuff if you promise me double the ship time you offered before, and schedule it for late April." He was conscious of a beautiful thing called leverage in the form of Leah's boobs. Those spectacular orbs struck him as potential blackmail material, more powerful for never being used, and the meaning of such info was certainly not lost on a member of the Oster clan.

"I'll schedule you for three consecutive weeks on the NOAA vessel *Elysium*, in May. How's that?" Hoekstra glared at him.

"Do you have the ability to make such a commitment?"

"Of course. I'm going with you."

"Well, things might—" He didn't know exactly how to approach the older man's possible incarceration. "And then there's Viktor," David added, really confused about what he was trying to say.

"He'll go. We probably can't keep him off the ship, but I'll figure out a way to get rid of him."

# CHAPTER 12

As soon as he could, David hunted up Viktor in his office to relay to him the alarming import of Hoekstra's remarks. "'Get rid of' you, what does that mean?"

Engrossed in one of the four computer monitors in his office, the older man barely looked at him. "I refuse to worry. Let's go out to my construction site, see how Shelby builds."

"No can do. I'm on assignment, and I want to get it over with as fast as possible. I can't spend the whole day driving around."

"Why not?"

"I'm headed out to Quinault on basketball business, if you must know. They tell me I can have a state truck, but only for a few hours."

"Very good. I will help," Viktor said.

At this point, David knew the hopelessness of resisting any of Viktor's plans, and as they headed for the motor pool, Viktor reminded him that it was still "Shelby's favorite venue," despite his new car. Soon they were rattling along over the hills with Viktor at the wheel. Every few minutes he reached his hand outside the window and banged on the Washington state seal, declaring, "I feel like an official in the Latvian Bureau of Mines."

Quinault, Washington, turned out to be a small town on a lake, bordering a stretch of the Olympic National Forest. Bigger than Wren, it sported at least two major thoroughfares and several gaudy taverns. Washington Teachers College was set high on a sloping lawn, and its imposing exterior harked back to another era—one that had never existed in the United States but had made an appearance in Venice, possibly when the doges were in power.

"I'll be back in twenty minutes." David climbed out of the truck.

Viktor looked at him in disgust and shook his head. "We're running out of time for our investigations. The woman could be dead before we figure everything out. You work too much."

"Wait here, Viktor. We'll discuss that later."

The college secretary obligingly hunted up Coach Ludwig Tonnis, who turned out to be a tall Washingtonian in a checked shirt. Jolly and self-confident, he stood with David on the immense basketball court, explaining its construction. "First the concrete, then sleepers of two-by-two inches are laid on edge, and then the wood finish. Maple tongue and groove, but you know that." The man seemed genuinely enthusiastic about the magic of it all, and David made a show of taking notes, then raised the question of the actual load-bearing strength of the floor. "Let's see, ten men who weigh anywhere from two twenty-five to two sixty, plus clothes, plus shoes. Can you add that now, in your head? I'll bet you can. You sci-fi types really know the times tables cold."

Sci-fi, that was about it. "Actually, this will be a pretty complex computation," he replied, lurching across the court toward the exit.

The coach trotted along after him. "What's that fruitcake Thornton up to now? So what if he has that sports center and that new floor, increased ball bounce, and shock absorption, ha! His team never wins, no matter what kind of floor you give them. They would need a trampoline, believe me."

David interrupted him. "This involves something more like entertainment."

"If you don't win, you can't entertain." These wise words floated past David as he shoved his way out the door.

Viktor stood beside the truck smoking his pipe, looking edgy, jiggling in his shoes. Once again, he insisted on piloting their official vehicle himself, trolling all the while through country-western music stations on the radio, until David could stand it no longer and shut it off. They drove on through the sodden countryside in the twilight, while gray clouds, heavy with rain, hovered over the peninsula.

"So, what questions must we ask Shelby?" Unlike his passenger, Viktor seemed energized and wanted to hunt up the man immediately.

David sighed, regretting once again that he was wasting so many hours thinking about who had tried to off Mrs. Hoekstra. Did he give a rat's ass if her husband was a murderer? Yes, certainly, of course. He cared in the purely moral sense. He also cared because the man was harassing the woman David wanted. And while he wasn't just a grubby little careerist, he cared because what happened to Hoekstra affected his professional fate. He seemed to have no way to answer the most pertinent questions—who the hell was the head of the institute, and when could he go to sea?—except through essentially witless investigations. He could wallow in outrage at this reality, or he could just plain give in to the fact that this must be politics as it was practiced in the Pacific Northwest. Better still, he could go back as soon as he could to his little notebook and use all this to increase his own understanding of the second law of thermodynamics and maybe even find the poisoner, too.

David turned to Viktor. "OK, why would Shelby want Mrs. H out of the way? There seems to be no reason at all. Was it a failed murder attempt against Hoekstra, but still, what motive would he have? The big guy's after him, that's for sure. Was it jealousy over Leah? Shelby knew he'd put the moves on his girlfriend, and he wanted him out of the way? Not likely. Did Shelby put the denatured alcohol under the sink? Maybe that's the place to start."

"How should I know? None of this makes any sense. Let us feel our way towards the truth."

"Peachy."

As they rounded the hill and came into view of the construction site, David could see that Shelby and his crew had framed the house. There was a floor, and the three of them were putting up drywall. Neat drainage ditches surrounded the foundation. There were a few lopsided two-by-fours, but other than that, the house rose like a sodden phoenix, not out of fire and ash, but out of a swamp.

Shelby waved as they walked over. "The ocean men. Hey bros, how's it going?" He put his arm around David as if they were buddies and guided him toward the shell of the house.

"It doesn't look half bad." David was amazed really. The two other guys hardly glanced at them, occupied with loud staple guns.

"It looks magnificent, but you need to go faster," Viktor announced. As they crossed the threshold, David was conscious of stepping on a new floor, and it dawned on him that even if he was a murderer, Shelby might be able to help with

his basketball problem. He started across the creaking floorboards, jouncing a bit as he went. Viktor moved away from
them toward the back of the house.

"Testing something?" Shelby asked, bending down to pick
up a hammer out of his toolbox.

"I'm on a mission." David bounced up and down several
times, registering the spring in the wood. "Wood is an amazing substance," he opined while the construction guys watched
him curiously.

"Fiberglass is cooler," Shelby said. "You know, that fucking
stuff will withstand anything. I swear a goddamned atomic
bomb can go off, and everything will be reduced to powder
except the fiberglass."

"The beauty of wood is that it absorbs so well, water, oil. It
changes; it shifts in an earthquake, it sways." David defended
the substance he was trying to learn more about, despite the
stupidity of his assignment.

"Yeah, wood is cool too." Shelby laid down the hammer
without doing anything with it, focusing his attention instead
on Leah's house. He stretched himself, reaching his arms to the
ceiling, then hitched up his jeans. "See you later, gents. I'm off
to a woman."

"You're leaving? You can't leave," David said, startled, as
Shelby sauntered down the makeshift front steps and waved
back at him. "Wait, Viktor wants to ask you some questions."

"Later," he yelled, and David couldn't think of any way to
stop him since Viktor was still stomping around in the inner
reaches of the house.

One of the crew guys stood next to David and lit up a cigarette, then looked toward the retreating Shelby. "I don't know
how the fuck he does it. A new lady every six months, his wife
doesn't care, and he never seems to get shot."

"Shot?"

"There's always a husband, and husbands don't like people like Shelby," the man said. "I'm Terry."

"David," he said and stuck out his hand. "Have they heard of divorce at all here?"

"They've heard of it," Terry said. "They just don't believe in it. Why should you pay a lawyer when you can take care of the problem yourself?"

"The husband's a lawyer in this case. A lawyer with a gun." David listened for Viktor's footsteps, wanting him to hear this discussion.

"Shelby likes to up the ante," Terry said. "That last one, shit, the wife of someone really big, some major who-ha. They used to meet in the Bel Air Hotel, you know, up on Route Five. They would start out in the bar and end up in the bridal suite. He said it was because hotels reminded her of New York, and she liked to pretend they were screwing in New York. New fucking York!"

At that moment, Viktor emerged from his walk-through and pronounced himself completely satisfied. "Keep going, men. I want to have another party very soon."

"Didn't someone die at your last one?" Terry said.

"She didn't die," Viktor yelled. "Someone's out to get me, that's what!"

Later that evening, as he piled up logs in his ornate fireplace, David pondered the identity of the Bel Air Hotel woman. It couldn't be Leah or his so-called wife. So there must be a third female player on Shelby's personal stage, aside from his brief encounter with Mrs. Hoekstra, whom David immediately ruled out. It was too much; he needed a chart, and by now he was prepared. Viktor had gone to some gruesome klezmer concert with a friend, and David was alone while the fire blazed up and rain fell on the roof. He took out his notebook, deciding to complete his stick figure cast with Shelby, Viktor, and Lucy so that later he'd be ready to insert them all where they belonged in his equation.

He smiled at his little people so obligingly dancing to his tune. If only he could control all these forces in real life, but alas, he had given up on that a long time ago. Right now he was out of his element, with too little to do, giving way to goofs. Where he really belonged was at sea, lowering instruments into the depths of the ocean, mechanical current meters to measure the speed and direction of the underwater waves, shear probes to log current speed directions at two points less than one millimeter apart. That was how he planned to map the circulation patterns around the Endeavour Segment of the Juan de Fuca Ridge. Right now, though, he amused himself with his so-not-scientific drawings.

The next morning he went to hunt up Philo Smallett. If the last few days had convinced David of anything, it was that he needed to generate his own personal life, no matter how tentative, rather than endlessly meditate on the lives of others. He wanted this life to include Alexis, and for that, the basketball project had its own peculiar uses. Down a bleak hallway covered in curling yellow linoleum, he found the engineer's office. He recited his findings so far, such as they were, to the strange little man.

"So my question is, really, is it possible for the horses to be there, and"—he paused because so far there had been absolutely no response to what he was saying—"would it matter at all what they are doing?"

The good professor just looked at him. Then he stood and began pacing back and forth in front of incredibly messy bookshelves piled high with books, papers, and what appeared to be an exerciser for the upper arms. "I've been at this university for thirty years. When I came here, students were out on the lawn playing field hockey. Basketball was a form of recreation, just a bunch of guys out jumping around. We played Washington Normal College and Washington Tech in Yakima. They had blue outfits, blue and orange." He turned, staring him down. "It was sport, the 'sound mind, sound body' idea. Now what is it?"

"To be honest I don't—" David was about to convey his cavalier attitude toward sports.

Smallett bent toward him menacingly. "Commerce, traffic in young bodies. Money, TV, money, TV. So some apple farmer from Wenatchee can sit and watch and yell and write out checks. You know whose fault it is?"

"Umm. Society's?" He was feeling like an idiot, on an idiot's errand. It had been David's experience that if somebody thought he was stupid, he started acting stupid. It was as if he immediately plunged into the other person's reality or crossed through a mirror and became someone else. All in all a terrible spectacle, and it was definitely playing itself out now.

"It's the president's fault."

"Of the United States?"

"Of this university! Thornton has never read a book, he's never seen a play, he wouldn't know a sonnet from a sing-along!" Philo was cranked up, no doubt about it. The phone rang, and he yelled into it, "What? Yes, yes, sir." He quieted down immediately. "He is, in fact, sitting right here. I am being nice to him, very nice, as you ordered. And how is Mrs. Thornton? We are, we are indeed debating the question of the floor. I believe the whole matter needs further study. Yes, I certainly hope so too." He dropped the phone into its cradle and glared at David. "Guess who? Father Christmas himself, nattering on about the team."

"How did he know I was here?"

"He ran into Pelliau, who couldn't resist telling him. Pelliau blabs all the time."

"Jeez, I hope not." He confided in Viktor about almost everything. Knowing they both worked on discredited theories was a secret bond, a shared strong stance against prevailing scientific winds, and David had decided to think better of his friend because of it. Still, the outside world wasn't as charitable, and quite a few people thought he was a nut. No way around it, his best buddy worked on cold fusion and at the moment had about as much credibility as an alchemist.

"Oster, was it?"

David nodded.

"You and I have forgotten one very critical thing. The team has to win. I don't see horses parading around if we lose, and believe me, for this basketball team, losing is an art form. We have a short, all-white team. They're doomed."

"My view exactly."

"OK, here's the plan. It's about the middle of the basketball season. We do nothing for a few weeks. He'll call us again, and we can make something up. By then they will have lost so many games, it won't matter. Of course, as you may know, horses can never be allowed on that floor."

"Obviously. I'm a physical oceanographer, so I really have no idea what all this is about. I tried to explain my work to Thornton, but it seemed to confuse him."

"The man has cheese for a brain."

"I've already talked to an expert in horses."

"If you mean those nitwits out by the barn, forget it."

"No, no, a woman who owns a farm. She wasn't optimistic."

He snorted. "That's a good ploy. If it becomes necessary, we can lay the whole thing off on her. Call me in two weeks, and we will formulate further inaction."

This plan didn't seem to offer much of an opening with Alexis. Nevertheless, David called her and asked her to come meet him for coffee. When he saw her again walking slowly toward him at the Bean, he almost couldn't speak. Her wonderful silvery white hair hung loose and thick over her shoulders. She took off her jacket, dropped it over the chair, seating herself across from him.

"Hello again. Strange goings-on in this town."

"I know. All I do is work and get more depressed."

She shook her head. "Me too."

He got up to fetch her coffee and tried to collect himself. Sitting back down, he turned to practical matters. "Just for laughs, have you solved our floor problem at all? The president feels it would cheer everybody up."

"Actually, yes," she said and handed him *Horses and Indoor Theatricals: The Art of Animal Entertainment*, a homespun-looking publication, more like a pamphlet than a book.

"My God, this could be it."

"All you can do is use it to tell them no."

"Good thinking."

She stirred a spoonful of sugar into her coffee and took a long, slow sip. "My son plays basketball," she sighed. "I miss him."

"When will he come home again?" David was nervous asking too much about the boy, but knew that he had to.

"This summer." Alexis brightened and said, "Perhaps we should go to a game? I think there's one this weekend."

"I'd like to do that." At last the sun came out. She had asked him on a date. Yes, that was exactly what she had done.

# CHAPTER 13

L ATER THAT EVENING while sitting on his porch, David watched his Latvian roommate balance a tray of cheese and fruit with one hand like a waiter, while Lucy swayed silently in the swing, apparently lost in thought.

"You look good." Viktor patted him on the head.

"I feel better, slightly." David was trying to figure out when to fill Viktor in about this upcoming research-sports-romantic outing with Alexis but couldn't seem to find the right moment. Instead he decided to grill Lucy about the letters she had been trying to find at his boss's office and, by way of an opening said, "You were right. Leah has letters exactly like the ones you got out of Hoekstra's desk."

"At least he's not doing it via e-mails." Viktor didn't seem terribly interested.

"Alexis has them too."

"Aa, the most beautiful woman in town, didn't you say, Viktor?" Lucy inhaled on her cigarette. "Have you made any progress with her?"

Rather than share news of his basketball date, David expounded on his romantic situation. "When I came up here,

I decided to change my life. In Los Angeles I was sleeping with friends, lovers, sometimes total strangers, and it was a waste. Now I'm avoiding involvement, I think." Lucy looked at him quizzically, but David forged ahead. "So what do we make of all these letters? What do we make of the fact that those weren't even the letters you were trying to find? You've never said what you were looking for."

"I was looking for other, different letters. I don't want to say which ones."

"Not from him?" Viktor seemed edgy, anxious about what further revelations might do to his courtship.

Waving her cigarette about, Lucy said, "Wouldn't it be fun to show those Joseph Conrad things to Frances Hoekstra?"

"We can't show anything to a woman in a coma."

"Maybe we should break into his house?"

David gestured at her with his wineglass. "We've already been there. It's filled with guns and pornography."

"We have to do something. I wonder what the police have found out?" Lucy picked at her fingers now.

David thought of the intrigue they were creating around the plight of a helpless person they barely knew and felt a rush of guilt. "How is the poor woman anyway? Is she on life support or what? We should go visit her."

"A brilliant plan. I shall distract the nurses with charm while you look at the charts to determine the source of her poison. But I wonder if we need Hoekstra's permission?" Viktor had drunk a lot of wine and looked slightly queasy.

"All Hoekstra seems to care about is that goddamned class they want me to teach. I think they're actually going to make me do it. Leah mentioned it too." Before this, he hadn't really wanted to acknowledge its existence, but it was becoming impossible to avoid.

"Oh, don't worry about it. Just lie to everyone." Viktor laughed.

"If you really were head of the institute, you could kill it, but are you? Who the hell would know?"

Instead of answering, Viktor gave a discreet burp.

Confounded, David went inside to the kitchen to pile more Brie and crackers onto a plate. As soon as he did, the phone rang, and the great man himself, Hoekstra, barked into his ear, "I'd like to meet with you tomorrow at two. We must discuss matters important to the institute."

Were these Shelby matters or scientific matters? Or was it that dreaded class?

"Sure," David said. Whatever he needed from whoever was in charge of the institute, he had better get it fast.

The next afternoon, in Hoekstra's cavernous office, the old man stared David down through magnifying half glasses and fiddled with a pencil, stabbing it into his index finger every now and again. He handed him a pile of papers marked "Mysteries of the Sea: A Course for Undergraduates Sponsored by the Larson Kinne Institute."

"This is unusual stuff for a physicist like yourself, and I know you'll be working at sea too, but this would be a major contribution to our goals. 'Our' goals. I speak in the imperial 'we.'" He laughed like a camel—not that David had heard one laugh lately.

"I don't know what you're talking about, Hoekstra. You owe me ship time, and I owe you research. It's all spelled out in my contract."

He squinted with his wrinkly eyes, ran a hand through that gray hair, and burst into laughter again. "Don't be an asshole, David. You haven't the foggiest idea what this is about or what I want you to do."

"Why don't you explain?"

"Larson Kinne has a dream to explore any and all practical applications of modern-day physics, for which reason he has gathered, or I have, as his emissary, you and all these eminent scientists." He smiled and kept working that pencil as if to sharpen it with his fingernail. "There is nothing more practical than teaching students, wouldn't you agree?" He glared at him triumphantly.

"My contract is clear: no teaching."

"We could sweeten that deal significantly if you set this thing up. You certainly don't have to teach it yourself. Just get other professors and some famous people to come in and give lectures."

"On what? The work I do is way too complicated for the average undergraduate."

"Look at the sheet."

David glanced down at a list of titles: "Sturgeon, Who Are They, and What Do They Do?," "Tide Pools and You," "The Poetry of the Sea."

"Think it over. If Larson Kinne is happy, Thornton is happy. If they're happy, I'm happy."

"Yes, but I'm not happy. Besides, I've just made a significant breakthrough in my work regarding Juan de Fuca, and I need to prepare for the *Elysium* trip that's already arranged." This little lie came to him spontaneously while he mentally fingered the leverageable items in his possession: letters, porn, Leah in a hot tub.

Hoekstra stood up. "Yes, you're on the schedule for June, but you can do this in your spare time. It's worth millions to me and to the department and would make you irreplaceable."

"June? I thought it was May."

"Had to juggle you."

David hadn't hung around with Philo Smallett for nothing; a deceptive show of action was his mantra. "Maybe I could put together a list of people who know about this stuff, and we can see how it would work." Nobody would want a course with the outlandish hodgepodge he determined to dream up, so he could strangle the idea right there. If word ever got out that David Oster was teaching about fish, he could hammer his career into a pinhole.

Suddenly, David remembered another bargaining chip he might throw on the pile—if he could manage to bluff a bit. "There's another matter, Niels. Shelby Burns, watching him."

"Do you have something to report?"

"Well, I might. Then again, I might not."

"Don't play with me, Oster," Hoekstra said, turning the full force of his Viking rage toward David. "The assignment is one of seriousness and purpose, which you obviously do not as yet grasp. Good Christ, man, I loaned you my binoculars!"

"I might remember something if I weren't so busy worrying about this class and my ship time. Otherwise I might forget it." David clambered out of his chair and turned away from his sometime boss. Headed for the door, he shouted over his shoulder, "I've seen your letters. I know who you are."

Outside, it was raining again, cold, mean rain that felt like needles under the collar. David felt mean himself, and why the hell not? At last he had begun to grasp some part of the older man's strategy. He saw why Hoekstra was stymieing him at every turn. It made sense. Though neither ever mentioned it, David had actually knocked this guy down in his own office. What Hoekstra wanted now was a ritual acknowledgment of his greater power, like a fat king sitting on his throne in some South Sea island. David's job was to waggle his tongue and move his knees in and out as a sign of submission, which would have been easy, figuratively speaking. He could have gotten anything he wanted out of the old degenerate if only he had known what form that submission should take.

But he didn't want to submit. His long years with the Oster clan had taught him one thing: submit and you die. Then and there he planned to enlist Viktor in his own plot to bring the monster down, if the police didn't do it for him first.

When he got back to his office, a basketball ticket rested on his desk, along with a message from Alexis telling him what time she'd pick him up—she had offered to drive since he lived so near the university—and another phone message from Philo. As he watched to make sure nobody was in the hall, he affixed a yellow radiation warning sign to his door, marked "DANGER, *PELIGRO*," and then in a fit of fancy scribbled "Biohazard" underneath. Was he going nuts, as in balls-out fucking certifiable, or was it just his usual craziness? He saw plots everywhere.

He called Alexis right away to confirm, and even hearing her voice calmed him down. Unfortunately when he got home, Viktor occupied his front porch again and eyed him very suspiciously as he ran upstairs to put on some decent clothes.

"What are you doing, avoiding me? I made some eggplant caviar just for you."

"I'm going to a game," he yelled down the steps.

"What game?" Viktor said, and as David came back downstairs, he handed him a cracker with some black stuff on it, scowling over at him accusingly. "Basketball, no doubt," he hissed into his ear. "I must go too."

"No."

Shortly thereafter Alexis's truck pulled up in front, and Viktor sprinted off the stoop, leaned through the window, then ran back over to him. "The most beautiful woman in town has graciously invited me to join you. I want to take some booze. You wait for me or else."

As David piled in beside her, he apologized. "I couldn't keep him away."

"And I couldn't help but invite him. It's fine."

"I think it's the rain. I haven't been doing much thinking these days. I've run out of random access memory."

He watched her lovely smile as she turned slightly away from him. She wore a dark sweater and slacks and managed to look elegant and homey at the same time, as if she would be equally at ease with pig farmers or kings.

They stared at the rain splatting onto the pebbles in the driveway, and inexplicably, he forgot every seductive ploy in his romantic arsenal. "Lived here long?" he finally managed.

"Forever. Since the troglodytes roamed the earth. Did they roam?"

"They were cavemen. Roaming far from the cave was out. Only in Japanese movies do they roam. Like the buffalo," he added, apropos of nothing. His mind had gone.

She touched the steering wheel, and he noticed that her hands were long and graceful, soft and smooth despite all the horse work she did. "I came here to get away from the city, the East in particular. Mountain men, adventurers, I wanted them all."

"And got them?" He said this before he realized how it sounded. To be close to her, in the front seat, was hot.

"Some." She smiled.

Before David could examine this stimulating thought, Viktor, muffled up in a down jacket and scarf, carrying a red Styrofoam cooler, leapt in beside them.

"I am ready." He patted the container. "Martinis, to get us in the mood."

Having never before crossed the threshold of the magnificent new Crestole Pavilion, David hadn't realized that they
would have some of the best seats in the house. They were
down front, a location that made their doings highly visible.
The game was already in progress, and David's own vantage
point was peculiar right from the start because all he could
think of was the floor. How strong was it? The noise was deafening, a pounding the likes of which he assumed no normal
surface could withstand, and every time someone jumped,
he could almost feel the panels bounce. He listened carefully,
not to the shouting, not to the cheers of the crowd, but to the
relentless hammering on that floor.

Suddenly he spied a pair of black legs, very long. According to Smallett, weren't all the players short and white? But
there he was, the genuine article, so tall he made the six-footers
look like very short guys; when he hit them from way out, the
crowd went nuts. Though his mind was generally a basketball-
free zone, even David could spot a serious player. Damn, he
had better get a plan B fast because these blasted Steelheads
were about to win.

He obsessed over this until Viktor grabbed his arm and
gestured grandly toward the other side of the gym. There was
Hoekstra, elbowing his way past several apple farmers to take
an honored place right in the center, next to the president of
the university.

"Your hero," Viktor said, loudly.

At this, the man sitting in front of David, in the local costume of down jacket and Gor-Tex boots, said, "My hero too."

"Really? How do you know him?" David bent down to tie
his shoelace and assess whether he could crawl under the seats.

"He's at every game."

How does he get the time, he wondered?

Viktor took another snootful out of the flask from the cooler and jabbed him in the shoulder. "What are you doing, dear boy, on the floor? The game is above ground."

David glanced over at the slim black boots on Alexis's feet.

"He's made this university what it is today," the fellow said, shouting up at him. "His wife makes all his suits herself."

The cloud lifted as David realized President Thornton was the man in question, and now he could account for his mustard yellow getups. He reached over and grabbed Viktor's ankle. Without looking down, Viktor handed him the flask, and he choked on the gin.

Viktor yelled, "The Steelheads made another basket."

"We're going to win," Alexis announced.

The man in front of David screeched, "Only one more team to beat, and then it's on to the Final Four!"

David's head ached from all the blood rushing to it, and he had to sit up. The game went on and on. Only Alexis's occasional warm smiles made it all worthwhile. David wasn't sure how much he drank out of the flask, but it was a lot. He had obviously forgotten his father's maxim—you can drink anything you want, but never drink gin unless you plan to get mean. The pounding on the floor grew worse, and in his mind, a nightmare vision arose: horses with red tutus slung around their middles clomped up and down to the sound of a disastrous marching band. then the farting would start, the horse droppings would plop down amidst the cheerleaders, who would dance on, smiling maniacally, covering themselves in brown crud.

"I'm going outside." David slid past the cheering hops farmers.

It was cold. The rain had thinned out into a mist. This was the kind of night on which he would have lit up a cigarette and smoked reflectively—if he had smoked at all—while staring out at the hills beyond, where a life even duller than his was being lived. The roars from the crowd were muffled now, but he could still hear them. The sound only served to scare him even more about what would happen during the wet time tunnel toward March. It was so dark, and had been dark that morning, and promised to be dark the next day. Darkness, wetness, that was all.

# CHAPTER 14

HYSTERICAL CHEERS FOLLOWED David all the way back to the basketball court. Yes, the grisly truth was upon him—victory, screams of triumph as the basketball team of Western Washington State University did indeed win the game. The uproar that followed convinced David that nothing would be more disastrous than those horses clattering around on such a surface. As he rode home with his companions, he said almost nothing. Calamity loomed at every turn. Despite Alexis's reassurances, basketball was entirely different from opera or theater, since at a game there were a host of unknown players in the drama, each one with a wholly unpredictable agenda.

Slow to anger, too slow, David was finally good and pissed about his situation. Then and there in the jiggling truck, he decided to go macro on Hoekstra, nuke him with something big enough to make him stop messing with his work, not to mention his personal life. First part of the plan: kill Thornton's basketball follies with a masterful report. Never mind that he had only dim ideas on how to evaluate the strength of the floor, but why corrupt his world with truth? He would phony up the whole thing. Just pretend it was the ocean they were talking about, calculating the shock absorption of the floor based on comparatively similar ratios he could scope out somewhere. The whole project would go down in flames anyway, so why not go straight for fiction? He felt light as a wet feather in this terrible rain, and when Alexis dropped them off that night, David walked into his house like a man with a purpose.

He labored on this fraudulent analysis for the better part of a week, and it read like a dream, spitting itself out of the computer like the perfect fabrication that it was. The title page looked particularly fetching, "Basketball Floor Load-Bearing Capacity: Applications and Analysis." At twelve pages, it had just about the right heft. The conclusion—horses would strain the basketball floor in forty-eight places, and his analysis was harrowingly specific as to where, in relation to the basket, all these dents and cracks in the floor would appear. He even added particular tasks the horses should be restricted from performing and their relationship to stress fractures. Hypothetically, they could stand, they could do a four-legged prone sit-down—although they would never get up again—or they could even perch on each other's hindquarters the way elephants do. Amusing himself with all this, David thought of ten ways to say "horse's ass" without ever using the words; however, he was careful to emphasize potential damage to both the floor and hooves. He dropped this missive into the committee members' mailboxes early one morning just before the winter break, because there was no way was he going to stand there, pages in hand, explaining the thing.

He felt so good that he decided to put into action the second prong of his "Get Hoekstra" strategy, and that was to convince Leah to drop the whole class business, no matter how closely it was tied to her hopes for advancement, even tenure.

In service of this, he drove over to Viktor's new house to see Shelby, planning to enlist his aid. As he wound up into the driveway, he saw, to his amazement, that serious progress had been achieved and that the guys were painting the outside of something that actually resembled a viable residence.

Before he could collar Shelby about his mission, though, the man yelled over to him, "You're not above painting, are you?"

David really didn't have the time, but he needed Shelby to work his will and figured that complying would give proof of his good-guy status. With a smile, he grabbed a fat brush and dipped it into what looked like peach soup. It dripped all over, until Shelby finally yanked the brush out of his hand.

"Watch us first," he commanded.

Living with Dave the Bomber, David had learned a fairly eccentric set of skills, among them definitely not how to paint the outside of a house. Shelby painted professionally, and the smoothness of the act, the rippling around the corners was hypnotic. He handed the brush back to him, and off he went to work nearby, though David kept waiting for the small, inevitable tinkle of rain. By the time they stopped for lunch, he had covered a largish swath of an outside wall and felt proud of his accomplishment, but when he backed away from what he'd done, it looked astonishingly pink, as in flamingos.

"Could this be the right color?"

"Absolutely," Shelby said, then added, "Actually, it's not the color he chose. We mixed in some red, because we thought it looked too dull."

Dull it was not. Mediterranean it was not. It had a fast-food look, which, while somewhat bracing in the dead of winter, might appear alarming come spring. All it needed was a drive-through window.

"Has Viktor seen this?" David really couldn't imagine that he had.

"Not yet, but I know he'll love it. He's got a great sense of color. He lived with communist gray for so long, this will cheer him up."

Or kill him, David thought.

"It's quick drying," Shelby offered.

"Hmm." David looked at a large cloud overhead.

"Have some lunch with us, and we'll see what it looks like when it's dry."

"Lunch" was what he heard, but as he sat down and chomped into a ham-and-cheese sandwich, he realized what his life had come to. He was in the state of Washington watching paint dry. They stared at the pink building until, sure enough, small droplets of rain hit the top of his head and rolled down his nose. Shelby raced over, tapped slightly with his finger on all the portions they had painted, and pronounced them "set," so they continued to watch the rain splashing off the flat pink surface. When David stood up, he was dizzy, probably due to paint fumes, and had forgotten entirely why he was even there. Shelby pulled on his arm, and instantly he remembered the horrible class and the necessity to convince Leah to kill the whole thing.

"Let's go find your girlfriend."

Shelby stared at him a moment, then said, "Fuckin' A," not even asking why. They slogged through the mud of the construction site and passed over onto Leah's beautiful green lawn, circling around toward the back of the house. Pressing his nose against some French doors, Shelby announced, "The bedroom," smirking all the while.

"Do you see her anywhere? I want to get her to drop this whole fish-and-poetry class thing."

"She'll do whatever I want," Shelby said as he went to another window. "Unfortunately, I don't see her at all, whole place looks empty. Crap, I'm obsessed with her. I should be obsessed with getting the house done. Then I could get paid." As he spoke, he pulled a pipe out of his pocket. "I'm off cigarettes too. My theory is, if I have something in my mouth at all times, I'll be fine, so now it's this."

"Why don't you take one of her courses? Then you could see her and listen to her talk for an hour at a stretch."

"They would never let me into this school. I dropped out of a community college, flunked out really. I hate sitting there while some goofy guy tells you what's right. It makes me fucking nuts. Course, I could watch her boobs."

"At most universities, only a handful of professors really keep current in their own specialties. The question is, are they capable of telling you what they know? If they are, you learn. If they can't, you sit in a chair and rot."

Wreathed in a halo of smelly smoke, Shelby squinted at him, apparently mystified.

"Listen, if you do see her, could you tell her we need to kill that class idea dead? Maybe she can think of a way to do it. It's extremely important."

Shelby nodded, but David had no confidence in him.

David bided his time, but two weeks after the holiday break had ended, still not one single person had mentioned the load-bearing capacity of the basketball floor. This had a depressing effect. He had tried to kill something, but who knew when it might reappear, like the corpse that refused to die in a horror film? Neither did Leah get in touch with him about the class and its hoped-for demise, despite his having left several messages for her. In the midst of working on a new current meter design, one in which a paddle wheel rotated back and forth with the waves so that its measurements were unrelated to extraneous water motion, he managed to put off calling Alexis. He thought about her all the time but couldn't bring himself to call. What was it—ambivalence, inertia? It felt like a wall in front of him.

In truth, David didn't feel worthy of someone so beautiful, apparently both inside and out. And his last encounter with her, at the basketball game, had been somewhat feeble, to put it mildly. He'd been so obsessed with Hoekstra, and eventually, so drunk that he'd barely spoken to her. Thus, despite his recent forays into action, he floated in a daze of wet and damp, and even the local mystery languished in his notebook. Walking on his front lawn meant sinking half a foot into the mud. His one serious hobby was drinking, the perennial favorite of residents of the state of Washington in winter, and with Viktor hanging around, it was easy to pursue. David came home about seven, settled down to a Scotch and water, then another, and finally a shooter. By this time, Viktor could have served planked wallboard, and he would have eaten it, along with plenty of wine, of course. Their Christmas celebration, such as it was, consisted mainly of liquids.

In L.A. David and his friends drank so that later they could go out and do something else, dance, watch the sunset, make love. Here they drank just to drink, and because Viktor seemed to have an infinite capacity, there was nothing to slow them down. Of course, all of this reminded him of Dave the Bomber. He had an image of himself thirty years hence, looking an awful lot like his father, then forced it out of his mind as he and Viktor sat on the porch waiting for the nonexistent twilight. It was a gray, grayer, black scenario up here in the Pacific Northwest, no soft California light that shed glow and grace, just a darkness that began in the morning and grew deeper as it pulled itself into night. Occasionally he drove out to look at Viktor's new residence, which was about as much activity as he could muster.

David sipped his wine. "Your house has been painted," he said to Viktor, randomly, with a blank mind.

"What?" He jumped up and grabbed his arm. "We must go see."

"Now?"

"Of course now."

They rode out to the construction site in the belching Buick. When they pulled up over the top of the hill and spotted Viktor's abode in the distance, it was all curved surfaces and arched walls, and unmistakably, absolutely pink. David didn't dare say a word. "Beyond monstrosity" entered his mind, but it was Viktor's project after all. He stole a glance over at the older man, who stared intently through his owl-eye glasses. Dismayed, shocked, David couldn't tell. They drove in silence up the circular driveway and stopped. Viktor just sat there staring straight at it.

"Are you all right?"

The older man nodded but didn't move.

"Is something wrong?"

Viktor shook his head, but then put his hand flat against his forehead as if in pain. Finally David patted him on the back, not knowing what else to do, other than the Heimlich maneuver.

Viktor inhaled deeply. "It is magnificent, is it not?"

"Amazing, incredible." David grew more emphatic on the second word. Viktor opened the car door, and he did too, as soon as he could reattach the handle. Viktor walked slowly to the front door, pushed on it, and they walked onto the naked floorboards, finding themselves amidst arches, wet walls, and a kitchen with a giant window that looked out on the town below.

"My dream." Viktor grabbed David in a bear hug, but before they could discuss the dimensions of his dream, they heard a noise coming from what he had dubbed in his plans the family room—hoarse panting, then huskier cries. David moved toward the sound, but the floor beneath him groaned like ten timbers in pain. Viktor stopped him, putting his finger to his lips, and tiptoed forward to peer around the corner. His eyes opened wide, and David snuck up next to him. Coiled around each other were four legs, all naked, two hairy, two not. Judging by the tension in those legs, David deemed them midway through their lovemaking. He and Viktor just stared at each other, and then the moaning stopped. Had they been discovered?

But no, nothing. The floor creaked as David turned away toward the door, and then the moaning began again, this time longer and more ragged. He was paralyzed.

"We have to get out of here," he whispered.

Viktor shook his head. "We must not distract them. Leah and Shelby must have their love moment."

So with the two rooted to the spot, the lovemaking went on for several of their respective lifetimes. When it finally reached its loud climax, David yanked Viktor by the arm, and they raced out the front door, making horses on the basketball court sound like fairies on an eyelash. Before they could shut it behind them, they ran smack into a tall, beefy man in a red shirt, sweating and carrying his golf clubs. Just to ratchet up the hideousness of the last ten minutes, David thought, this would have to be Leah's husband, the gun-toting lawyer.

Sure enough. "Larry, old dear," Viktor bellowed at the man, "what are you up to, hockey, croquet?"

"I guess they don't have golf in Latvia," Larry Burnett growled. Viktor shoved him back from the front door, though Leah's lawyer husband was not easily shovable. "What the hell do you call this monstrosity, Pelliau? I've been meaning to talk to you before the damn thing got too far along, but you seem to have made faster progress than I thought."

David was wondering about the happy couple and glanced over his shoulder to see Leah's black head of hair darting toward the side door, apparently headed for another exit. She was being pushed or pulled, he couldn't tell which.

"It's wonderful, is it not?" Viktor said, a little too loudly. "I've waited my whole life for a house like this, and next door to you, Larry, what an honor, me, a humble man from such a small country."

"Shut the fuck up and tell me what you're going to do about this. It looks like fucking Disneyland. I could sue, you know, Pelliau, and since I get free legal work, I can just sue you for fucking ever."

"What can I do, Larry? It is my dream."

"It reminds him of the Kremlin," David said. Viktor guffawed.

Larry's face swelled to match his shirt; he put the golf bag down and extracted a club, a four wood from the looks of it, then made as if to whack it against the pink side of the house. Viktor grabbed the head and tried to wrestle it out of his hands.

"Come, come," David said. "There's no need for physical violence."

Leah chose this moment to appear around a corner. "Larry, stop that. What do you think you're doing?"

"I'm getting a jump on tearing down the place." He kept on struggling with Viktor over the club. "What were you doing here, anyway?" he yelled at her as he finally yanked it away from Viktor and landed a few shots on the wall.

"I'm introducing myself to the neighbors." She moved toward him. Sweat beaded up on his forehead, and a vein swelled. He lowered the club, put one hand on his hip, and they all stared at her tousled, slightly damp black hair, her pink cheeks, and eyes that swam with sex. Those lovely nipples pushed against her shirt. She was saved by the fact that married men don't look too closely at their wives, at least this one didn't, because Larry mainly continued to scowl at Viktor. To help the situation, Shelby now appeared, apparently having smeared half a bucket of paint on himself to confirm his worker status.

"Here we all are," Viktor giggled.

"You!" Larry shouted at Shelby, and for an instant, David thought he knew what was going on, but then, "You're the one who constructed this eyesore. Do you know how this reduces the value of my property?"

"Now, now, sweetheart, a man's home is his castle after all. He can paint it any color he likes," Leah said sweetly as she tried to pull him away.

Larry refused to move, instead yelling at Viktor, "That's what you fucking think, you Latvian idiot." He banged away again at the wall, this time with real effect.

Viktor seemed too delighted with the whole interchange to care about insults to himself and stuck his hand under his jacket like Napoleon, saying, "Latvia, home of my heart."

Then something miraculous happened. Larry dropped the club and addressed David. "You can forget whatever project you had with my wife, science and great books of the sea or whatever the hell it was." Leah tried to propel him toward their own house, but as they walked away, he swiveled back toward David, shouting, "Watch yourself, buddy boy!"

The assembled party stood huddled and happy, relieved that his rage was a shot over the wrong bow, and David was ecstatic, since without his having done anything at all, the dreaded class appeared to be D.O.A.

He and Viktor started for his car. The old Buick belched like a sick grandmother, refusing to budge, and David was holding his head in his hands, laughing, sobbing, he hardly knew which. Viktor seemed immobilized.

"Get us the hell out of here before Larry comes back with a gun," David said. "He's bound to figure all this out."

Instead of speaking, Viktor took David's arm. "Wave," he said, as there, on the front stoop, stood Shelby Burns, gesturing their way.

"What the fuck?"

Viktor waved his arm like an idiot. "Oh, it's so romantic," he intoned.

"If you don't get this car going, I cannot be responsible for my actions." By way of emphasis, David placed his foot over Viktor's on the gas pedal, and, after a moment's hesitation, they shot forward into the mud. Viktor kicked his foot away and then floored it himself, and they sailed out of the driveway in their ruined ship. The moron in front of the house was still waving.

"It's wonderful, David! What a way to open my new home to the flow of good feeling. The lovemaking will flood the house."

"That couple," David began as the impossible Buick lurched along, "have disaster tattooed all over their skulls."

Viktor was rubbing his chin. "They are creating a small world in which danger swims like a shark."

As they pulled up in front of his own house, David went on and on about the fortuitousness of Larry's arrival, since at least one outrage, in the form of students, papers, poems, and sturgeon, had been laid to rest. Over a cup of espresso, he put it to Viktor that now was the time to take firm action against Hoekstra before he thought up anything else to consume his time. He insisted that the first step toward neutralization of the man would be to verify him as poisoner of his own wife. Viktor giddily agreed.

"I wonder how we can do that? No doubt we must fall back on entropy, dear boy."

"What? Why do you say that?" Had that bastard been reading his notebook? Was he a spy of some kind? "Why are you talking about entropy?"

"It's one of the great mysteries, like our own little home-town one. I've never really understood it—nobody does really, but they know it exists."

"And?"

"Whatever plan we devise will change into something else, something we can't foresee, and that will dissolve our problem."

David didn't want to accuse the man or apprise him of any of his dark thoughts, but dissolving problems was something he could get behind, and this seemed like the moment to do so.

"We should drink to that," he said, reaching for the Scotch.

# CHAPTER 15

AS OF FRIDAY that week, David continued to be grim about his prospects. The rain had taken on a vicious power, seeping into every corner of his house. The rugs smelled moldy, and leaks had started to spring, but when he tried to inform his landlord, he learned that the man was soaking up the sun in Antigua. David knew it was definitely time to call Alexis, but his self-confidence had reached a new low. And deep in the dark heart of January, he was suddenly oppressed by the fact that none of his old lovers had made any effort to contact him, even the flying Cosmo. Not that he felt he needed to see any of them, but their disappearance, which he had so awkwardly engineered, now struck him as a mark of his lack of value in the world.

Worse yet, his murder notebook seemed to have drizzled off into doodles rather than any clean formulation. He might need a different equation altogether. How about $\Delta S = \Delta Q/T$? Entropy change equals the energy dispersed divided by the temperature. Could he fit his little stick figures into that? Hmm, not very promising. He was dispirited too about Viktor, who seemed to be avoiding him—because of the notebook, was it?

Had he truly read it and not admitted it? He didn't seem to do much except go visit his new house every day. Only occasionally did he appear at the institute, so when David found a file folder on top of his computer labeled "Hot Bubbles at Juan de Fuca," he was somewhat heartened. Now he would learn the reason Viktor had wanted him in this gruesome state in the first place.

For the last several years, Viktor had been working on creating acoustic standing waves in cylindrical containers in the lab, and he claimed to have proven that fusion took place in the imploding bubbles. Now he proposed that same experiment, carried out by none other than David Oster, inside one of the volcanic outcroppings, called "chimneys," near an active part of Juan de Fuca. Did an acoustic standing wave exist therein created by oscillating high-frequency water waves, and if so, was a kind of fusion taking place within these bubbles too? The ingredients were there—hydrogen, heat, a cylindrical structure. Nevertheless, the experiment was expensive, outrageously complicated, and mad. As he had suspected, Viktor needed him primarily for instrumentation, but placing any delicate equipment inside these smoking towers under the ocean would require a technical expertise that he wasn't sure he had. His own work with wave circulation required attaching current meters to mooring cables with a tensile strength rating to eight thousand kilograms, but this location might require even stronger ones. David also planned to drag injection sleds along the ocean floor to leave a band of $SF_6$, an inert gas, which he could later measure, but that would be much easier to do than what was proposed here.

Viktor's proposal read like science fiction and might, given what David knew about him, actually involve some sort of joke. Was Hoekstra right that he was a fruitcake sponging on the

people of Washington? After all, how many years had he been in
this place? He'd gone bonkers, and so would David if he stayed
here much longer. Standing up to kick the office wastebasket, he
glimpsed his reflection in the window. Black hair long and strag-
gly, collar crooked, jeans rumpled and dirty—how much lower
could he sink? He was no longer Helena's beautiful man; he was
nobody's man, a heavy drinker, and a spy to boot. Straightening
up, he slicked back his hair and made a decision, forgetting that
all-important rule: if you're going to decide something, never
do it at 3:00 p.m. on a Friday afternoon, when you're exhausted,
depressed, and out of your mind. He decided, nevertheless, to
quit. Old Dave had left him some money—not all that much,
since he'd lost a bundle on his Chilean trawler fleet scheme. Still,
David could always go make bombs for the Office of Naval
Research. With that happy thought, he marched toward Hoekstra's office, neglecting to call first or even to knock, forgetting
even that he might or might not be director of the institute. He
just strode in like a Hollywood producer.

Smoking a cigarette, at work on a huge pile of papers,
Hoekstra glared up at him, then broke into a grin. "I've got
some bad news for you," he said, still smiling that fearsome
smile.

"I've got some worse news for you. I'm—"

Hoekstra interrupted. "It won't work. You know that, don't
you?"

Suddenly he had David's attention. "Why do you think
that?"

"I know what you've been doing, but it won't work. You
said so yourself."

An evil tide rose up in David's ears. This was it. Hoekstra
knew about his plot and was going to bring him down first.
How far would he go?

"Yes, your conclusions are sound, but his little henchmen will make it happen anyway."

Henchmen? David had visions of contract killers and concrete boots.

"I know the president. When he gets a bee in his bonnet, that's where it stays until some brave fellow plucks it out with tongs."

Breath flooded David's body as he began to understand.

"So, as wonderful as your report is—how did you learn all about load-bearing capacity? Never mind. Your last line should read more like, 'The proposal of the president seems acceptable by the commonly applied standards of structural engineering,' you know, hogwash of that species."

"Horses will wreck the floor, Hoekstra. Once they're out there getting yelled at, exposed to outraged fans, you can't control what happens. You know that, and I know that. I mean, if you have any conscience at all." At which point he stopped.

Hoekstra stared at him from out of that imposing Nordic face. "They won't wreck it. They'll just stress it. What can happen? It has nowhere to fall. There are joists underneath it, or joints, or something strong. At the very least there's ground. It will make the old guy happy to think of Trigger and Silver jumping up and down on a floor that cost eight hundred thousand dollars. It's what those apple farmers donate money for every year. So, at the next meeting, which will be tomorrow, I expect you to carry the ball, as Americans always say, and by now you certainly know where. Another thing, I overheard the president talking about your class for undergraduates. He's already dubbed it 'Wet and Wild.'"

"Sorry. It's dead." Weirdly, though, David thought the nickname was perfect. Karma, kismet, whatever it was, it was all bad.

"No, no, Thornton's very excited, said you would have three hundred kids sign up at least. Are you ready to give me a syllabus?"

"Absolutely not. I thought you were joking. Look, we have a contract, Niels, and you've already promised me ship time. We set a date."

"True, but Thornton told someone you were doing it with Leah Burnett, she of the mighty breasts."

"Doing it?" Wait a minute, David had already seen him "doing it" with her at Shoop. He couldn't breathe.

"Doing the class," Hoekstra almost shouted.

"I believe as of last week, the whole class thing is off." David relayed to him various threats uttered by Larry in his capacity as homeowner.

"True, he's definitely a menace. Even I'm aware of that. He's one of the toughest guys in town, came in second at the Steel Challenge."

"Yes, I heard that."

"Guess who won first prize?"

David waited for the inevitable.

"I did," Hoekstra crowed. "So I'm prepared. I'm sure we can convince Larry that it's for the good of the university. After all, he's my lawyer. I do have some influence with him. Did you want to say something?"

For a moment David was impressed. Hoekstra was screwing—or at least attempting to screw—the wife of his lawyer, an ace shooter. But he remembered his mission. "I want to quit."

"Everybody quits in January. I quit to you. You quit to me. Now we're done."

"Seriously, I'm quitting." Damn straight he was. Much as he cared about the general good of universities everywhere, at this point, he was indifferent to the fate of Western Washington State University.

"Don't be an ass. You just got here. By the way, whatever happens, I wouldn't want you to tell my wife about me and Leah."

"How could I tell her anything? She's in a coma." He would never do such a thing, in any case, but under the circumstances, the request seemed especially bizarre, even for Hoekstra.

"Later, I mean."

Instead of continuing this strange, harsh conversation, David opted to retreat from Hoekstra's presence, not a bold move, but a political one. He popped his head into Viktor's lab, where his roommate hovered over a computer piled high with copies of "Hot Bubbles at Juan de Fuca," consuming a gigantic mozzarella-and-avocado sandwich, much of which fell onto a computer keyboard.

"I hate to tell you this, Viktor, but surely you know that your experiment is completely undoable, not to say outlandish."

He waved him off as if he were a fly. "It's nothing, just a little summary. Perhaps you don't understand it. I'll explain it to you later."

"I understood it fine. It would cost millions and probably kill us both. Of course, I won't even have time to do anything because Mysteries of the Sea remains alive, and actually, I quit my job."

"You did?" he said.

"I tried to. It didn't seem to take."

"You can't quit. It's like the Gulag. Sadly, I know all about the class already. I know things, David. I'm not an idiot."

David was in mental dispute about that one but didn't say so.

Later, as they walked down the leaf-strewn sidewalk, David still morose, Viktor muttered, "I always like it when the facts allow my lies to become true."

"How about making something factual happen to Hoekstra? And why the hell is he still head of the institute? I thought you were."

"My status is unknown at the moment. I am a man without a country, ha, as usual," he giggled.

"We need a serious plan. Otherwise I'll go crazy with this rain."

"Yes, wet, the eternal wet. I look to God and ask him, why so wet? But, if you do this class, you get money and things out of them. Make them do things for you. They will, you know."

A small light flickered in David's mind, and for a moment, he considered this a good idea, but then he remembered that Viktor hadn't taught anyone but a handful of graduate students in years. "You have no idea how demanding eighteen-year-olds can be. I observed them as a teaching assistant at Caltech, and believe me, they don't want a single physics concept to penetrate their universe."

"David, you give me no credit. I've been thinking about your problem, and I do agree with your previously stated little idea. Let's go see the sick woman at the hospital, find out if she breathes."

"I don't know, I don't know."

"What's wrong with you now?"

"I don't like hospitals." Even the thought of visiting such a place could work David into a sweat. Hours and hours he had spent at his mother's bedside, waiting for news, for help, for medications, for someone even to talk to him about her condition. He loathed the state of mind that deemed secrecy a better path to health than full disclosure, since for him medical doctors were the very embodiment of half-truths, guesses, and false hope, the ultimate experimental scientists trying out substances on their helpless patients. A hospital was a place where you couldn't refuse their bungled machinations.

Viktor seemed a bit disgusted with his confusion but said nothing more. As the two of them sauntered past the Washington state flag at the entrance to the campus, a gloomy, out-of-breath Royce Thornton came jogging up behind them. Without preamble he announced that Viktor was now interim director of the Larson Kinne Institute—whether for the first or second time, David didn't know. Strangely enough, Viktor didn't seem at all surprised.

"What about Hoekstra?" David asked.

"I have been informed that the police have incarcerated him, wrongfully, of course. He will be out soon if I have anything to do with it."

"How can that be? I talked to him just two hours ago in his office," David said.

"Things seem to be moving quickly." Thornton steered them back around the direction they'd just come from. "I've called an emergency meeting. We need someone official in charge. Otherwise work cannot go on, though I know you guys don't do anything over at that institute there."

So they had finally nailed the old bastard. David felt like dancing. When they reached the president's office, Thornton hurried them through the door to his conference room, where the usual suspects awaited. He practically shoved the two men into their seats, announcing loudly, "The horses, that's why I convened the meeting. We need entertainment."

Without missing a beat, David tried for the deathblow. "But is this, sir, the thing we should do at this time of sorrow and uncertainty?" His platitudes brought no reaction.

The others at the table hung their heads over doodles or were dozing, even Philo, but after a strained silence, finally the Polish saw expert blew his nose into a large handkerchief. "Tremendous number of trout over in Hoh Head last weekend."

"Quiet!" Thornton said sharply. "I seem to notice a certain foot dragging in this whole business, and I don't like it. I'm not accustomed to it."

"I will explain." Finally Viktor had spoken up. Operating in his capacity as substitute for Hoekstra, he was supposed to sandbag this nightmarish project; at least that's what David expected.

"Silence, Pelliau. I haven't believed a word you've said in the eight years I've known you."

Viktor just kept puffing little smoke rings at him from his pipe. "Why did you make me head of the institute then?" A wave of anxiety swept over the table.

Thornton snorted a moment. "You're famous, people know you, and they'll do what you say, which is more than I can say for myself."

Visibly expanding his chest, Viktor said, "Since I do head the institute now, for as long as Hoekstra is subject to the inquiries of officials and possible indictment—"

"Get on with it," Thornton blasted through the room.

"I say we do the horses. They will be fun. Bread and circuses for all!"

The yes-men around the table nodded their heads in unison, and Thornton, having gotten what he wanted, clapped his hands in approval and quickly adjourned the meeting.

"How could you have said that?" David shouted as he followed Viktor back to his office. It was now six o'clock on the evening of a very bad day.

"I lost my head completely. It was power, the mad power of knowing that I, yes I, could work my will on the basketball floor. I say the sooner the better, David, because who knows when this murderer will get out of jail?" He placed his finger to his chin and started scratching. "I did it for you too, though. Here's your chance with that Russian horsewoman."

"I'm not pursuing any more women. Look where it leads."

Viktor shoved him into his enormous, very messy lab. It was more like a compound, with three or four cubicles surrounding a central worktable, upon which rows of clear cylinders were clamped to small turntables, some of them vibrating up and down furiously. Viktor waved away several graduate students as they approached him with clipboards.

"David, just because of several little accidents in your past, you cannot make this your motto. We'll stop having all our fun. You don't wish to antagonize the director of the institute, do you?"

"I don't know who I should antagonize next. I've done such an extensive job so far."

"Whom."

"Are you correcting my English?"

"Yes. Now, one more thing, David. Remember Mysteries of the Sea?"

"I'm vigorously trying to forget it."

"If you could just give a little consideration to teaching it." He unfolded a photocopied piece of paper that read "Addendum to the Fall Catalogue: Mysteries of the Sea with David Oster" in bold type, then a list of course topics. "Waves Deep Deep Down," "A Whale of a Mammal," "The Mysterious Sex Life of the Salmon," "Hot Bubbles at Juan de Fuca," "Sturgeon, Who Are They, and What Do They Do?," "Tide Pools and You," and "The Poetry of the Sea."

David stared at him in horror. "You bastard, you must have been plotting against me in secret. Did you dream this up with the demented Hoekstra? I see his lunatic titles here too."

"Of course not. Don't be crazy. You wound me with these suspicions. They forced me into this if I wanted to be head of the institute."

"Now I get it. You sold me out to get the job."

"Dear David, you will enjoy our students. They will flock to you like geese, all those beautiful little girls from the Washington farms and Indian reservations. Wet and Wild it will be, I can promise you. See, I know what it's called already."

"Are you pimping for me among the youth of the state?"

"Of course I am not. There you see my subject, the bubbles. Other people will teach everything; you are just the overseer. Besides, you can work with the beautiful Leah. She can teach poems with waves." Viktor giggled.

"Her husband won't let her."

"Oh, I think he will." Viktor seemed quite certain of this. He continued whining about how much he needed David, how central he was to all his plans, his work. Finally, just to shut him up, David gave in, but he demanded that Viktor get him all the institute money Hoekstra had promised in his contract. Otherwise, he would do neither the class nor the basketball horses. "Yes, yes, that's my first agenda," Viktor announced and scooted off, leaving him alone in the hallway.

Oh well, David consoled himself, what with silly lists and stupid meetings, the whole state could be blown up by the Hanford reactor before he really had to do anything.

Philo Smallett proved his responsiveness to an emergency phone call from Thornton by showing up in the institute lobby moments later, cornering David as he was on his way out. The strange man looked haggard, if not actually failing.

"I have received a letter from Miss Alexis Scherbatskoy. It appears you know her." He peered at David over his glasses. "She informs me in her report that a short gala, cum horses, might be possible, depending on their correct feeding and the timing of, how shall I put it, their digestatory functions."

"I catch your drift." Report? He couldn't remember reading one.

"Don't confuse me with those California expressions. I propose that we hie ourselves to Crestole Pavilion and block out the suggested choreography."

David really couldn't concentrate on any of his research this disastrous Friday—reportedly the same day of the week Eve temped Adam—so he agreed.

In the vast, empty gym, sweaty dampness seeped out of the walls, from the seats, from the scoreboards, even though everything was plastic and new. Philo marched across the floor like a drum major, turning on a dime, spinning to indicate horse activity.

"Their movements will be limited, of course," he said, waving what must have been Alexis's diagram in front of his face, and then he bobbed his head up and down several times, actually imitating a horse.

David sat down on the floor, looking up at the immense iron girders vaulting the ceiling. The rain sounded like bullets attacking a military structure.

"David," Philo said, then "David," a little louder. He marched over and pulled him up to act out several more horse moves.

"What will they be wearing?" David asked.

"The horses or the girls?"

"What girls?"

Philo became irate when he found David hadn't even read Alexis's proposal, which presumably lurked in his pile of interoffice mail, and he regretted it himself because it would have given him a concrete reason to call her. From Philo's copy, he could see that the girls had a hell of a lot more to do than the horses, mainly dancing around them, waving batons and pom-poms that reproduced jumping trout and other northern fauna. The young women would be practically naked—to deflect attention from the lack of horse action, no doubt.

"Where do the basketball players fit in all of this?"

"They'll make a parade right behind the horses, then come the girls. Stunning!" Then he glared at David. "Did I say that? I said that! Hit me, hit me right here." He made frantic gestures toward his forehead.

"Philo, get hold of yourself."

"It's madness. You see how you get sucked in, David. Be vigilant. Bad ideas, bad ideas everywhere, what did I tell you?" Now he started slapping his head with his hands, but before David could help him, he slammed his hands into his pockets as if to stop their mad motion.

"Well, I think that's about it," David offered, feeling that they had better get out of there before Philo killed himself.

"We've forgotten something."

"What have we forgotten?"

"We only have to do it if they win, and they can't win!" Philo smiled triumphantly. "Still, we've got to keep tracking their play, because, you never know. Those miserable sons of bitches could keep on winning as they are now."

"I'm sure they're trying to win."

"Bastards."

David called Alexis early Saturday morning, feeling uncomfortable about the fact that he hadn't called her sooner. But she offered to meet him that night at the Old Sawmill, where, if he was not mistaken, they'd added another pair of deer antlers to the decor. Admittedly, knowing she had a son, knowing her age had given him pause. None of this lessened her attractions, but she seemed more substantial, more significant, no longer a player in some outdoor summer theater the way all his L.A. lovers had been. Somewhere in his mind still resided the conviction that he had to stop encouraging people to love him before he understood the nature of his own feelings.

As Alexis paused at the podium near the hostess, she looked sleek and sophisticated in a black sweater and skirt, infinitely better than the other patrons. The moment she sat down, he tried to launch into the horse business, but she stopped him. She wanted to discuss the Hoekstra case.

"I gave the police my letters, but they didn't seem to care much."

"I've been playing with one of the formulas for entropy"— and here he waited for a guffaw, but she continued to look at him expectantly—"just out of desperation."

"The inevitable increase of disorder, as in a coma, I suppose you mean."

"That is what I mean!" He was stunned that he'd once again told her the truth and, even more promising, that she had a real notion of what he was talking about. "I'm trying to figure out the roles of all the players by calculating their relative 'temperature' regarding the poor victim. It's weirdly fun, but I'm still stumped." He gulped some water, afraid that he might sound too nutty, and rushed into whatever other news he possessed. "Viktor's been made interim head of the institute, and the guy's in jail, so they must have enough to charge him. Police tape still blocks off Viktor's house, something about how they're waiting for the state crime lab to produce their findings. Months after the event!" Alas, so was the mirrored ball a poor prisoner of the investigation, to the outrage of the owner of the Buccaneer Bar.

Alexis shook her head and brushed that gorgeous white hair back from her face. "Well, I suppose my letters really don't mean much. These infatuations, you know, they just go on and on without anyone ever doing anything about them. When the sun comes out, people get rid of their bad sex partners and straighten up."

"Please tell me you weren't infatuated with Hoekstra?"

"No, no, of course not. But I have to admit that I've gotten a bit obsessed with this case—just as everyone else has, it seems."

Suddenly David had a strong sense of events and people bearing down on him right here in this very restaurant, not a good place to converse with any seriousness, but he had the moment and for that moment, the words. "Listen, I want to talk. I just want you to understand that I don't necessarily like my own defects."

She gazed back at him, receptive, he thought, and seemed ready to speak when suddenly the place stirred with excitement, as none other than Hoekstra himself appeared at the doorway with Larry Burnett. There was a dead silence followed by a hum of curiosity; some heads turned, while others bent over plates, feigning disinterest. Interrupted mid-confession, David nonetheless couldn't help joining Alexis in feeling, as she apparently did, a hint of ghoulish pleasure.

"They've let him out of jail," she said.

"My God, that was fast. He just got picked up yesterday."

Their waiter arrived and scribbled their order, but kept peering over in Hoekstra's direction, asking them to repeat their requests. Finally he whispered, "Isn't that the murderer?"

"She's not dead yet," David hissed. At least he didn't think so. He would have heard about it.

"Now that will be the Dover sole and the filet, right?" The waiter still glanced over his shoulder, and David as well eyed the lawyer and his client, who hunched toward each other in intense discussion.

"I had another letter a couple of days ago. I'm sorry I didn't tell you before," Alexis whispered. "It was almost the same as the last few, but then he wrote something about the violence of my affections, how he was afraid of them."

"Were your affections for him violent at all?"

"Don't be crazy. The man is capable of building a fantasy out of nothing. I was merely pleasant to him when we ran into each other. He's intelligent and not uninteresting, and it's so boring here. Or it was." She smiled at him slightly.

"Oh my God, what next?" To David's horror, Hoekstra rose out of his seat and started toward them. Alexis only had time to swallow and then greeted him—too effusively and too loudly.

"How are you? Good to see you," she said.

Hoekstra nodded, then turned toward David. "No matter where I am, no matter what happens, I am forever your boss." With that, the formidable Dane walked back to his table, scowling all the while. Predictably, this entire scene electrified the room, and every eye fixed upon their table.

"So much unhappiness that man creates. He's like a misery machine," was all David could think to say.

Alexis laughed. "Forever, as in forever? He seems to have a thing about you."

"Maybe he knows that Viktor and I have been investigating this poisoning matter ourselves."

"Tell me more about your defects?" she said, turning more intent.

That night they had their first real conversation. Over coffee and a cognac, he spoke of his family, and although he had a horror of whining about childhood miseries, especially since his own had occurred in a privileged environment, he managed to detail the dimensions of his nightmare. Venturing into an even more taboo subject, he admitted to "vamping," as Valerie had called it, trying to charm people, all to create a circle of admirers longing for him to be around, even though he would subsequently desert them. When such talk didn't scare her off, he started in on physics. He told her that in their own lifetime, new science would emerge that accounted for the anomalies physicists had papered over for years, through overbroad estimates, assumptions that allowed vast fluctuations, theorems that had huge uncertainty factors. He even described a possible fifth force in the universe, a subject he had never even thought of discussing with his other lovers.

"I like the idea of a fifth force, something extra to account for the unknown."

"You're the first person to say that," he said truthfully. "Most specialists in the area have proved remarkably hostile to the idea, those who've even bothered to look at the experimental work."

"You do your physics underwater. You feel comfortable there?"

"At peace," he said, before he realized how that might sound. "Or maybe I like to go deep down where very few other people have gone or would want to go. If I decide to, I can ignore everyone but a few stray primordial fish. Besides, I'm pretty sure that if the fifth force is going to show itself anywhere, it will be in the ocean." He almost lurched into Viktor's idea for a hot bubble experiment but instantly thought better of it. He didn't want her to think they were both cuckoo.

"I'm impressed." Down on the street, pounded by rain, she took his arm as they walked toward her truck. In the wet darkness, he moved closer to her for warmth, and she clasped his hand. When they kissed, it was light and soft, satisfying and enough, for that time anyway.

# CHAPTER 16

ACCORDING TO THE *Pyke City Sentinel*, Hoekstra had been in jail only a couple of hours, after which he was released on bail because the charge was not attempted murder but assault in the second degree. David was on his way to his office on Monday morning when the big man himself suddenly loomed behind him.

"I want to talk to you."

David kept walking, his mind full of mayhem.

"Stop, David. We need to talk."

About what? Blood, death, lawyers, depositions?

"How's your wife?" Despite his hospital phobia, David was now determined to go see her.

"Her vital signs are fine, but she's in a coma, though, thank God it hasn't deepened. I don't know, apparently there are different levels of unconsciousness. I hate to see her like that. They say it could take several more months for her to wake up."

"It must be horrible."

"I'm not guilty, but you know that. It was just some terrible mistake."

Best to play along and find out what Hoekstra had to say, David thought. "Of course, of course." He shook his head fervently as they walked on together. "What happened, do you suppose? Maybe she had a stroke."

"They've ruled out anything like that. What about that Lucy person? She could have something to do with it. She took some things from my desk, important personal items. Did she show them to you?"

"No," David said, too forcefully, embarrassed at what had last happened in Hoekstra's office.

The old reprobate had other things on his mind. "She has tendencies, if you know what I mean, bad tendencies, subversive. I've seen her around with Pelliau. She's mad, of course. Women go mad here, especially her sort. Watch yourself, David. I see you with him. You'll be infected by that Eastern European crap he spouts."

"I think your views might be colored by your. . . situation." You would have thought David had hit him again.

"Here we are, at the crux of the matter. In jail or out of jail, I'm the one who can make possible those extraordinary experiments of yours. Everyone thinks Viktor's the genius, but I see only you. I'll give you the money and ship time. In fact, I'm going out there with you. Just tell me what you know about Frances and that Lucy Fosse."

David asserted ignorance so completely that Hoekstra seemed to believe him, and at the same time found himself irrationally pleased that his scientific stock with the man appeared to have risen. On impulse, he said, "Maybe I should go to the hospital to see how she's doing?"

"Who?"

That one remark hung in the air for a moment. How could he not know to whom he was referring? His almost-dead wife, that's who, lying all injected with tubes and wires, machines bleeping, weird noxious fluids flowing in and flowing out, her mind perhaps turned into mush.

Realizing his mistake, Hoekstra seemed to recoup. "She'll be fine, I'm certain."

"I hope so. I'd like to go as a sign of support."

"She won't know you're there, but if it makes you feel that you've done your duty."

"When are visiting hours?" David said, amazed at his coldness. Hoekstra told him to call the hospital.

The institute lunchroom was crowded, as usual, with clumps of physicists huddled, conversing intensely. Viktor, on the other hand, was alone, studying a pile of research papers, when David caught up with him and told him of the exchange he had just had with their sometime boss. He barely looked up from his plate of steak and potatoes.

"Why did you tell him of our plans?"

"To check out his reaction. I don't think he cares at all."

"I'm too busy right now getting money, David, especially for you. Who knows how much time we have? Ask the Russian horsewoman to go with you. She will relate well to death."

Although he wasn't sure he believed him, David seriously wanted Viktor to get that money. And his idea about Alexis held promise, since she had admitted to being fascinated with the Hoekstra case. When he did call her, she seemed enthusiastic about the project, and they arranged to meet up at his house the next day, then go visit the sick woman. That evening he spent drinking with Shelby and his coworker Terry at a dingy bar a few miles outside of town. Shelby was strangely horrified by the subject of Frances Hoekstra's condition, and squeamish as well; he didn't want to hear anything about David's plans to visit the hospital. On the positive side, he reported that he was able to see more and more of the divine Leah now that Larry was off representing Hoekstra. Yet he still seemed bleak and unusually cynical.

"Murder is not that extreme here, David, I hate to break it to you," he almost yelled over the noise of the jukebox and the pounding of feet on the dance floor. "Especially murdering your wife."

With his long hair and moustache, knife strapped to his belt, Terry reminded David of pictures of Jesse James, especially when he announced, "Washington is like Texas. You got an all-time OK excuse if you say the old lady bummed the shit out of you, and you just blew her away. Remember that guy, that scientist, or was he an engineer?"

"They're always scientists," Shelby announced. "They're natural-born killers, like Frankenstein."

"Dr. Frankenstein was the man who created the monster," David said. "He wasn't the killer."

"Whoever. Anyway, you're just proving my point. It's the quest for the magic spark. After a while you think you've seen it, and then when you do, you know you can kill it. There was that professor—what was his name? He murdered his wife, didn't he, two years ago? He was married to an Arab of some kind, gorgeous, big, dark, and nasty, if you know what I mean, and she was sleeping with somebody else, some local artiste guy."

Terry thought a moment. "Wasn't it one of her husband's students? Like twenty years old. I think he tried to kill him too."

Shelby poured himself another mug of beer from the pitcher. "She was in the bathtub one night, singing away, when I guess the old bastard came in, said, 'Hi, honey,' and heaved a hair dryer into the suds. *Blam*, she was gone. They arrested him, but he told the jury it was his wife's fault because he wasn't even in the house at the time of her death, and his alibi held up. She was drunk, he kept saying on the stand, the curse of his life, so bombed she must have knocked the hair dryer into her own bath."

"Where is he now?" David was a bit surprised at Shelby's extensive knowledge of the case.

"Here. He was acquitted."

"You mean he kept his job? There is such a thing as moral turpitude. They can fire you for that, if for nothing else."

"You'd have to fuck a dog on the front lawn of Crestole Pavilion during a basketball game, a dog of the same sex as yourself, to get fired around that joint," Shelby said. "His alibi was some babe, said he was making love to her all evening. He was an expert on saws, as in cutting down trees. Polish."

David sucked in a breath but couldn't get one out, and both his companions started slapping him on the back. "Did you say saws?"

"Yeah, you know him?" Shelby asked.

"Definitely."

In service of their concern, they got him two shots of Jack Daniel's and insisted he down them. "I've been in this place for four months, and already I know two murderers," he choked.

"You're doin' good." Terry shoved another pitcher of beer toward him.

"*Cherchez l'homme*," Shelby pronounced cryptically.

"Weren't you one of the *hommes* in the Hoekstra case?" David couldn't forget Shelby's brief encounter with Frances.

"I tried to be."

Terry punched his arm. "So you nailed this coma chick, Shelby? How was it?"

Shelby claimed that he would never kiss and tell, but then proceeded to do just that. "Frances was good actually. I don't think a human hand had touched her in a couple of years. The gratitude was appealing. Of course I couldn't see the ass from where I was. She didn't say much about her husband, nothing in fact, except she turned his picture away from the bed—or was it the couch?—while we were doing it."

"You were just there, and she threw you into bed?" David had trouble picturing this.

"No, no, she offered me some herbal tea, out by their patio. It was romantic because rain was dripping into the pool, like a fountain. Then she let her skirt slide up, and I realized that, uh, other forms of compensation were in my future." He sighed. "I feel tied down now."

"By your wife?" David realized once again that he'd never actually seen Shelby's wife.

"Shit no. She and I understand each other. By Leah. It's cut my activities short."

"Do you think Larry knows about you and Leah?" David said.

"No. He's too stupid to realize he doesn't deserve a beautiful, smart woman like her. He thinks because he's rich, she'll never leave him."

"You don't want her to leave him, do you?"

"Definitely not." Shelby puffed on his pipe. "Some women are best had when they're anxious and frustrated, overheated, about to seize up. But in the ordinary course of things, she'd be a tremendous pain in the ass."

"A flight attendant I once dated told me I was a pain in the ass."

Terry and Shelby laughed, and the latter pounded on the table. "Dave, Dave, don't listen to women. It's their job to complain and ours not to hear. Anyway, about Mrs. H, we did it once in the bed, then once on the couch. I fell off." Shelby stared down at the drink napkin and twisted it around his right hand. "It's all coming back to me now, sort of."

"He fucks so much he doesn't remember what he did," Terry said.

"Yeah, it was this scratchy couch covered with a Navajo blanket. We got some wine on it, I remember. Then I really let her have it, and she went nuts. I'm worried about her."

"Who wouldn't be? A coma, that's bad." Especially one induced by denatured alcohol, David thought. But it actually sounded as if Shelby liked the woman, and, anyway, he would have had no reason to kill her.

The next morning, waiting for Alexis to arrive for their hospital expedition, David went over his notebook formulations so far about Hoekstra. He had lined up the most crucial stick figures in order of decreasing heat intensity in relation to the suspect. He put Niels at the head, then Shelby, whom he seemed to hate. But why? Did Hoekstra know about Shelby and his wife's little encounter? David placed Leah next in line, assuming that Hoekstra wanted her for himself. How did that figure in with Lucy? Hoekstra certainly had a head of steam up about her. Thus far his drawing looked demented:

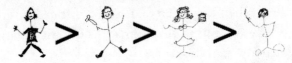

He was ruminating on all this when Alexis Scherbatskoy rang the doorbell and greeted him with a kiss on the cheek. She followed him into the house and looked around, apparently expecting to see Viktor leap to attention.

"He's out, went to work early, thank God. Want some coffee?"

"What a good plan." Her skin glistened from the moisture outside, and her beautiful hair was wound up on top of her head in a bun.

"Just in case Viktor shows up, and he could at any moment despite what he told me this morning, I should warn you that he's suspicious of your Russian background. In fact, he said he'd been researching your genealogy on the web."

She came over and touched him lightly on the cheek. "But you're not suspicious, are you?"

Before he could answer, her hand slid down to his shoulder. When she moved forward for a kiss, he found himself trembling toward her. In the moment, there was none of his usual ambivalence; he felt as if this was exactly what should and could happen right now. It did happen, several times, and it was like manna from heaven, too, as she opened that splendid body to him. Sleeping with Alexis was extravagantly wonderful, and he felt grateful to her for her warm, passionate acceptance of him into herself with no holding back.

It was near noon before they began to get dressed, and David felt his anxiety returning. He had a deep uneasiness about moving from passivity to action, becoming a participant rather than an observer in the village drama, since he'd done so poorly in his last village. Truly, he did not want to make egregious personal mistakes again, especially with a woman like this, and was often baffled as to where to venture next.

"How Russian are you?" he finally said as they put their shoes on.

"I'm very Russian. My grandfather was from Tobolsk, my mother from Saint Petersburg." She launched into a bit of Pushkin, in the original she claimed, though she could have been speaking Swahili for all David knew.

"Stop. If Viktor hears anything about this, he'll turn against you. For him, the Russians do only one thing, advance with tanks." He ran his hand over her shapely thigh. She had a strong, flat torso and elegant pointed breasts. "Listen, where did you get that wonderful hair? It's a scientific curiosity, but beautiful, gorgeous." David fell over himself trying to justify his remark.

"The doctor said it's genetic. My grandmother had a streak of white across her black hair;  then my mother had almost all white, now me."

Shortly thereafter, the enfeebled Buick rumbled noisily out of the wet mist and straight up the driveway.

"I think this would be a good moment for us to leave, don't you?" she said, grabbing her jacket.

Although it was hardly the thing to follow this wonderful uptick in their romance, David felt he had to reiterate the necessity of going to visit the poisoning victim, and Alexis agreed, but right after they got one more cup of coffee.

At the Bean, which was full of the sounds of spritzing and aerating milk, David carried two heavy mugs to their table. Alexis regarded him with those deep hazel eyes, smiling slightly. Something about those eyes made him want to tell the truth. "I was involved with a lot of women in Los Angeles…" He stopped short, horrified at how this sounded.

"You court complexity?" she said, reaching out to clasp his hand.

"Not anymore," David said decisively.

Alexis didn't seem put off, but also didn't seem especially interested in talking about his former life. The Hoekstra case was another matter. She had theories.

"I think he's setting someone up, a supposed girlfriend who was at the party and might have wanted to kill his wife."

"Two other women were getting the letters, one an English professor, Leah Burnett, and the other, Lucy Fosse, a friend of Viktor's."

"That's bizarre."

"You'll have to be careful, you know. I haven't figured it out yet, but there's something seriously wrong with the guy."

Outside in the damp morning, with Mount Rainier glowing in the mist, they climbed into his car and made for the hospital. It was a low, ranch-style structure connected to the local medical center sprawled across a hill above town, and as they drove toward it in the Beemer, he had a strange feeling that he had somehow seen it before.

"This is very seventies TV, like the Brady Bunch." It was green on the outside and green on the inside, that terrible school-wall green.

"It certainly is."

"I avoid hospitals. I hate them, ever since I had to sit and hold my mother's hand while she lay dying. My father wouldn't let her go. He hovered over her bed, making them prolong everything with exotic drugs. It seemed endless."

"How awful." She squeezed his arm.

At the front desk of the intensive care unit, David glimpsed a man being wheeled by with an immense distended abdomen, and another figure draped in white, out of whom tubes flowed in every direction. Alexis forged ahead, pulling him along. She found a cheery nurse who didn't ask questions about their relationship to Frances Hoekstra and informed them that she had been moved.

"She isn't dead, is she?" Alexis asked.

"Gosh, no. She's downstairs. We monitor her vital signs and feed her, then wait for her to wake up, if she ever does."

They slunk down to the next floor, where all was silence but
for the sound of padded white shoes on linoleum. Despite the
green paint, attempts had been made to brighten up the inside
of the hospital, with children's drawings on the walls, but still
it had that recognizable smell. Suddenly David felt weird about
going to see a woman who was on another plane, so to speak,
since he had barely known her on this one.

"Wouldn't it be an invasion of her privacy for us to stand
over her?"

"Why?"

"We don't know her that well, at least I don't. Do you?"

"No, but she needs someone to help her."

"True," he whispered, just in time to face a beady-eyed,
puffy nurse. "Mrs. Hoekstra, please. We're here to see her."

"Are you family members?"

Alexis leaned in to speak to her. "Close friends. Her husband asked us to come visit."

"To show our support, to let her know we care." David
sounded like a self-help guru.

"I doubt that that will do much. She's between an eight and
a nine on the Glasgow Coma Scale, not good."

"You never know what people can respond to," Alexis said
indignantly. "I've seen people talk other people into consciousness, just through the force of their words."

"On television. When you've been a nurse as long as I have,
believe me, you know better." However, she then pointed her
finger toward a door.

Entering the room, David saw a body buried in a cocoon
of white: white sheets, white bed, gleaming white machines
surrounding a prone human form. He looked down a moment,
frightened of what more he might see. Hooked up to tubes, to
bags, to noisy gizmos that beeped along, Frances lay there with

her eyes closed, looking like a saint in a coffin, her face pale
and gaunt. Alexis reached out her hand to touch her, but David
grabbed it.

"What are you doing?"

"I have to feel her skin. In Russia, they say if the skin jumps
back at you when you poke it, she will live."

"You might hurt her."

"How can she be hurt more than she is?"

He couldn't disagree.

She lifted up the layers of sheet to reveal a pale arm taped
with an IV drip. David hovered at the foot of the bed. As Viktor had suggested, he glanced at Frances's chart, but there was
nothing that would tell him whether she'd been poisoned, or
with what. Alexis rubbed her two index fingers together as if
warming them and placed these same fingers on the woman's
right forearm, about three inches apart, pressing down hard.

"Watch the IV," he whispered, but Alexis stared straight at
the wall, as if in a trance, while flattening Frances's arm against
the bed.

David was getting anxious, waiting for the nurse to enter
the door and throw their silly asses out. Through the window,
he could see dark clouds hovering, and there was a sheen of
moisture on the panes of glass. He could hear a cart being
wheeled down the hall as the monitors ticked rhythmically in
the antiseptic air. Four years ago, almost five now, just before
"Mae Oster passed," as their housekeeper put it, his mother had
reached out her hand to him from her hospital bed and said,
"Please forgive me, David. I hope you can forgive me."

These were the tenderest words she'd spoken to him in
a long time, and he remembered kissing that hand and laying his face along her pitiful arm. "For what? You never did
anything wrong. You should forgive me." Yes, forgive him for

always being Dave the Bomber's little buddy, for helping him plot where to hide his booze, how to get a wrecked car towed into the driveway without making any noise, how to plug the hole he blew in the side of his study when he accidentally shot off his Colt Police Positive .38.

As he sat here now beside Alexis, a woman he had just slept with, someone he was falling in love with, he felt intense pain about his own mother. Right after she died, he had dreamt about her constantly, dreams of longing and abandonment. It was as if his psyche were bolted to her soul, trying to escape her power nevertheless. Thinking about her rationally made no difference, but when David was asleep, his heart went to work to free him. Had it freed him? He wasn't sure and felt more deeply now, looking at the body of another sick woman, the challenge of love.

He turned to see Alexis still standing next to the bed, her eyes closed, now definitely in a trance. Mrs. Hoekstra's head had moved to the left, and her mouth hung open as if she were about to speak, while Alexis's eyes fluttered. Some strange Russian thing appeared to be happening, so David sat down in the chair, pulled out his notebook, and nervously drew as best he could a stick figure of Alexis because she had clearly upped her intensity relationship to the two Hoekstras in a pretty dramatic way.

He threw down his book in annoyance at his inadequate horse and looked over at the comatose woman. He looked straight into an eye that was open.

"Oh my God." He jumped out of his chair. "She's awake."

Alexis turned as if just waking up herself, then bent down by the bed. The eye was open; there was no mistaking that.

"Wait, maybe she's dead." But all the machines, which would have gone into overdrive had she expired, continued to buzz along, indifferent.

Alexis put her head to the woman's chest, listening. "She's alive," was the pronouncement.

The one eye seemed to strain and stare, not blinking at all. To his amazement, Alexis touched the woman's face with the flat of her palm, then lifted up the eyelid on the closed eye. Now both eyes were open. The jaws worked, the mouth moved.

"What?" a scratchy voice whispered, and she coughed.

David gasped something incoherent and flattened himself into the corner, afraid to breathe. He heard footsteps, the woman's eyes glared at him, and then the unfriendly nurse threw open the door.

# CHAPTER 17

INCREDIBLY, ASTOUNDINGLY, THEY had brought her back to life—Alexis had, that is. If David had helped at all, it was by upping the emotional ante, his terror transmitted through her fingers to the supine lady. Nobody thanked them, however. Instead, the nurse hustled them out into the waiting room, and instantly, the place was filled with doctors and technicians. David felt in his coat pocket for his notebook and couldn't find it.

"Wait, I think I forgot something. I've got to go back." He must have left it on the table by the chair.

"No, they won't let you in."

"It's my notebook, you know, a hundred ways to label Hoekstra the poisoner, worked out scientifically! He's the only one who would understand it, but believe me, he will understand if he gets his hands on it."

"I'll get it back for you, but we can't do it now."

"Shit, shit, shit."

"He'll be happy right at the moment, because he won't be charged with anything criminal, I don't think. Except if his wife saw him do something, which I doubt. But we can't stay here."

David wanted to wail, but by now Alexis was dragging him toward the lobby, as anxious as he was, but only to get out of the place. Once outside in the parking lot, David tried to breathe.

"You're right. He'll owe us his freedom. I'll be the hero of the Larson Kinne Institute, and he will finally give me all the money and ship time he promised. Unless he's somehow or other retrieved that book! It's small, though. Maybe he won't even notice it."

Alexis put her warm arms around him. It was warming up outside, too, and he felt a rush of joy at being with this suddenly almost-miraculous woman. But he couldn't adjust to the sudden change in the Hoekstra family circumstances, or perhaps his own. He was torn between wanting to beat the hell out of there or attempting a fast run right back to Mrs. Hoekstra's room. Despite his contrary impulses, Alexis still clung to him, guiding him firmly toward his car. They timed their exit perfectly because the great man's Mercedes came plowing up over the hill toward the hospital as they drove down.

"Do you think they'll tell him who was in the room? Did we give our names?"

"Of course we did. He'll be relieved, don't you think?"

"Or pissed if he really did try to kill her."

Over the next several days, tension lifted from the town. The rain stopped falling, the sun shone, the trees began to bloom, and the *Pyke City Sentinel* was full of the wondrous recovery of the injured woman. Their intrepid reporters mentioned two "visitors" in the room, as well as a nurse, but cited only Alexis by name. Throughout the entire time, Viktor occupied himself with Russian jokes at David's expense.

"They always say they're psychic. They have projects, gypsy women staring up into the sky trying to disarm our nuclear warheads. It was probably you stepping on an electrical wire that pushed her."

"Pushed her?"

"Into life."

"I don't think so, Viktor. I saw Alexis in a trance, using her fingers."

"Good with her hands, is she?" he giggled. Sex was never far from whatever mind Viktor had left.

David was seriously uninterested in banter about the so-called "healing," but instead obsessed about getting his notebook back. He couldn't figure out what to do except bug Alexis, who claimed she was "on it," cold comfort to him at the time. One day later he found himself sharing a beer with Shelby, a man who seemed enthusiastic about the whole business.

"You can parlay this into cash, Dave, I'm sure of it," he said.

"How so?" David rocked on his porch swing, plotting his next move. Viktor was inside cooking coq au vin.

"Why don't you tell your true story to TV? They like first-hand accounts." He seemed happy tonight, more upbeat than usual.

"Goddamn, the last thing I want is for this story to go national. Some station in Seattle actually does want to interview Alexis and me, but I refuse to do it. Besides, I was a bystander, totally, just doodling." Right at this moment, David felt sick about those little equations of his.

The next afternoon he arranged to meet Alexis at the Old Sawmill happy hour, conscious that the two of them hadn't truly talked about what had happened, but he wanted also to pressure her to somehow to get back to that hospital. As she sipped her red wine, she seemed proud of what she had done, but David was skeptical, almost resentful of being dragged into such a procedure.

"Are you a faith healer or something?" He couldn't resist asking the question because, after all, what did he really know about her beyond horses and sex?

"No, no, anybody can do that stuff."

"I'm pretty sure not me."

"Certain qualities can be developed. Everyone has them, but you have to be willing to tune yourself into them. It's a bit like being a radio and being ready to receive."

"I'd just hear static, though, but fortunately, that's noise from the original Big Bang, which I find comforting. Science, knowledge, certainty, that's what I'm looking for."

She pulled back and seemed annoyed for a moment. "You have to have faith in things you can't understand."

For David, "faith" had been the justification of all sorts of atrocities down through the ages, especially against scientists, but still he wanted to love her and not doubt her or think her some New Age aficionado. "I'll try. I believe in you anyway, hey, especially about getting my notebook back. What's happening?"

"Nothing—yet."

"You've got to do something, or maybe I should."

"Please, David, you can trust me. I'm working on it."

David hadn't trusted a living soul since about age six, but he wanted to do so now. He had to, really, since poking around in the hospital, asking questions, finding the same nurse all seemed like a ticket to exposure of his mad doings. More problematic, though, was the fact that Alexis thought it a good idea to at least agree to be interviewed on the local TV news program that emanated from the university.

"It could keep us safe from the murderer. Even if he does have hold of your notebook, the more out there we are, the more he'll get hurt if he tries to do something to us."

David definitively disagreed and said so. He knew he was right, he was certain he was right, though as they parted, he remembered Dave the Bomber's consistent counsel about the general uselessness of such a position: "Being right is the booby prize."

At dinner two days later, David and Viktor watched Alexis on television together. "Tell us how you knew she could be saved, Ms. Scherbatskoy," the earnest student reporter asked.

"I didn't know. I only hoped." Alexis seemed sincere and modest.

"You did the right thing, dear boy. This would ruin you." Even Viktor got that much. They were on David's couch, eating chopped liver on toast as they watched.

In a friendly effort to bolster David's spirits, for the next several days Viktor kept reassuring him on his decision about not going on TV, though he also continued to welcome him back to the "plane of the living," as he put it, as if he were a space alien.

"What a brilliant idea I had for you to visit her. I'm so proud of myself for not going, and my admiration for you rises like the phoenix. What will be your future now, David? You have intervened so strangely into his life. You took the faith healer with you, don't you see? He'll take note of that."

"And kill me next."

"But why?"

"I left a notebook behind in the hospital room, and he may have actually read it. It contained all my speculations, though in garbled form. But he'll understand. You may have noticed it or read it yourself?"

"Of course I have not. What an idea."

By now, David had no confidence as to whether he could trust even Viktor. "I should skip town."

"You can't. Behind your back, little elves are at work on your career." Viktor jumped up, running into what had become, perhaps permanently, his room and returned waving a piece of paper like a flag. "I am giving you everything you wanted in your contract."

Viktor had indeed supplied university money for lab equipment and ship time, days and days of ship time, for both David's experiment and his own—$4 million, to be exact. It was great, just great, but then suddenly it seemed impossible.

"Jesus, won't somebody say we're friends and that you were never really head of the institute? Has anyone signed off on this?"

"All you have to do for it is teach Mysteries of the Sea."

"No, no, what are you saying?"

"You definitely must teach that class. I had to do something for Thornton to get him to agree to all that money."

"Wait, you told me you had said something to Hoekstra, now Thornton too? I assumed it was dead because I didn't hear anything about it."

"It pretended to be dead."

"So in order to get what was promised to me in the first place, I must teach the course?"

"I fear so. Pain and pleasure, together again." He twiddled his fingers around, as he always did when he invoked the Hindu gods. "Don't worry, you just preside like a judge, and it's way off, next fall. Of course I'll help."

"Why doesn't that make me feel better? Besides, maybe now that the little woman is recovered, Hoekstra will be director of the institute again."

Instantly Viktor flared up. "You need that money, and I need you to get that money. How else can I test whether fusion is going on in the bubbles coming out of those vents?"

He took one more look at the piece of paper and shoved it into his pocket. "First thing in the morning, I take it to Thornton and tell him no matter what Hoekstra says, you must have this money, or both of us will depart for a real school."

"OK, but how can we get Hoekstra off the ship? He actually thinks he's going with us."

"It will come to me." He grimaced.

"Maybe we can look to entropy to save us," David said dryly, watching Viktor to see if he reacted to the word. But the older man didn't move a muscle in response. Instead, he pulled the cork on a new bottle of wine and chomped on a piece of cheese.

"Ah, yes, we have no choice but to do that."

Just where was the dreaded poisoner? Even if David had no sure proof of his guilt, that's how he thought of him. Hoekstra knew where he lived, he knew his habits, he owned his lab for all practical purposes, and yet no word from the man, even though now David was blasted all over the weekly campus newspaper like roadkill. A page-one article reported on the sudden recovery of Frances Hoekstra, department store heiress, important regional philanthropist, and wife of Niels Hoekstra, director of the famed Larson Kinne Institute. Through the power of polarity massage, Alexis Scherbatskoy had somehow "drawn the sick woman back from death," and she had been accompanied by her "close companion, David Oster."

Over the next few days, a number of students from the beach-day geology class had now become Oster groupies due to this very visible article. One of them, a girl with a ponytail, kept shoving little notes under his office door, "Come to a meeting of the Healing Circle—Powered By Light, next Thursday. And visit our website. A Friend." Being a monk for science no longer required a pose but became a necessity, and David avoided his office altogether. To make matters worse, he had become an object of great curiosity to his neighbors as well. From her house two blocks away, Marina watched him with her own set of binoculars, ferret presumably in her arms. Too proud to hound him, Lucy resented that he had been at the hospital with Alexis and not herself, the noted sleuth, but still she often wandered up and down in front of his house, watching him, apparently, but never stopping to say hello. Somewhat ridiculously, Shelby took to giving David a high five whenever he saw him.

This highly localized fame also made another trip to the hospital in search of his notebook impossible. He had called Alexis several times, but she hadn't called him back, and he depressed himself further by picturing Hoekstra's craggy face as he read David's fanciful speculations as to his guilt. Around dinnertime, two days after the article had appeared, the phone rang, but since he could see that it wasn't Alexis, he refused to answer. Viktor motioned him toward it, but he kept waving him off. This went on long enough for the thing to stop ringing. Then it began again.

"Answer it, but disguise your voice," Viktor said, cackling.

He finally picked it up, resigned to whatever madness approached.

"David," a high, thin voice screeched at him, "we are having a demonstration. We need you here." The voice waited. Was this another one of the New Age groupies, maybe having a psychic raising of the dead around Pyke City?

"I'm sorry, I, uh…"

"It's Philo Smallett. Ms. Scherbatskoy has arranged a demo of the horses on the basketball court. It's all hands on deck, Oster, especially you. Three o'clock tomorrow afternoon. I expect your presence."

"Don't worry, I'll be there." He was glad to go, as it would give him a chance to see Alexis and get some sense of the dimensions of his doom if she hadn't gotten the notebook or had forgotten about it or just didn't think it was that important. Did he have faith in her? He wasn't sure.

At the appointed time, his first venture out of the house in days, David considered disguise but finally settled on a cap and a wide green muffler, quite inappropriate for what was the first warm, sunshiny day in months, but a good cover-up. People would think he had a disease and give him a wide berth. Walking up the avenue to the campus, despite his recent despair, he suddenly found the world delicious, poplar trees in bloom, dogwood bending in the clear air. Even the pink rhododendron had survived the most recent rain.

At the deserted gym, David sat in the bleachers and watched the black basketball star and one of his white teammates shooting hoops, thinking how much noise their shoes made. At last Philo appeared and slunk over, obviously feeling as unathletic as David in the face of semipro players.

"Any signs of quadrupeds?" he asked.

"Not yet."

They watched the one-on-one awhile longer, when suddenly, out in the wings, he could see Alexis leading two horses straight toward them. His first overwhelming feeling was joy at seeing her, but he couldn't possibly ignore the deafening noise of the horses' hooves.

Howling in disbelief, the two basketball players ran over to her, shouting, "Get them out of here. You're ruining the floor."

David and Philo leapt to her rescue, and once the name of the august Thornton had been invoked numerous times, they backed off and fled the court. The horses clomped toward them gingerly. Even they knew they were in the wrong place.

"Right away we see a problem." David wanted to take the lead and appear rational.

"Only one?" Philo glared at him.

"We'll have to put something on their hooves to dampen the sound." Alexis sounded very calm considering the circumstances, but she barely glanced at David, who wondered if she was still annoyed at his not going on TV. And had she ever retrieved his notebook, or didn't she take even that—or him—seriously?

"Socks!" Philo screamed.

"Felt of some kind, I think," Alexis said, like an actor in a play trying to be normal while there was a madman onstage.

"Did somebody beat these guys into submission?" David stared at two very docile horses.

"They're old," she offered. "Quite old." Finally she looked at him, smiling slightly.

"Brilliant. They'll be less excitable." Philo ran his hands along his lapels nervously, and David began to fear that he would start hitting himself again.

"The idea I dreamed up was to have most of the act swirl around the horses while they basically just stand there. It could work, sort of." Alexis seemed confident.

"It works for me," Philo said. "Does it work for you, David?"

"I don't know. It's quiet in here now, but the noise of the people and the cheering will change everything."

"Put earplugs in their ears," Philo said.

"They have to be able to hear my voice and commands. Anyway, you can see that they have fairly placid personalities." Alexis was addressing David now, directly.

To him they looked almost dead. "How old are they exactly?"

"Eighteen and twenty, very old for horses. In human terms, they'd be headed for assisted living."

Philo laughed. "You guys are doing pretty good for a couple of faith healers."

"For the last time, I didn't do anything." David's shout reverberated through the gigantic structure, and even the horses seemed to awaken momentarily. "Never mind. I'm going to focus on the problem at hand." Whenever he was around Alexis, he tried to look like a serious adult, but being unable to breathe exactly, he loosed his words like random darts. Her presence always seemed to undermine his best-laid plans.

"They'll be hung with various silks and tassels, so they'll have some style."

"That'll be like putting a wig on a werewolf."

"It'll be strange, but it won't be that bad." Alexis really did smile at him now. "We'll try to keep it short—that's the key—on and off the court."

"Don't we need a status report? Is the team winning at all?"

"They've won three out of their last four games. It's unheard of, a first since 1962. I frankly regard it as the end of the university, but what do I know?" Philo threw out his hands and stalked over to a corner, then began motioning at David to come talk to him.

"I've got a message for you from Thornton," he whispered in the cavernous gym.

"What kind of message?"

"He wants to inform you about Viktor Pelliau. 'An important scientific development,' that's what he said."

"What could this possibly mean?" David wondered if this cryptic communiqué had to do with his research money. Looking over at Alexis anxiously as she moved the horses toward the exit—he absolutely had to talk to her—he said, "Listen, Philo, be careful. I'm beginning to see conspiracies everywhere."

He nodded. "Me too."

Out in the parking lot, Alexis was loading the old geezers into a horse trailer. They both were friendly enough, one of them nuzzling David on the arm.

"What are their names?" he said.

"Jerry and Murray." She didn't look at him.

"Doesn't sound very horsey to me."

"They're named after my father's stockbrokers." And now she turned his way, brushing off her hands on her jeans.

"Ah, why didn't I think of that? Listen, I've been panicked about the book."

But with that, she pulled the little thing out of her pocket and handed it to him.

"Thank God." He wanted to kiss it and then, more importantly, her, but restrained himself.

"It was in the lost and found. The lady there said a nurse had dropped it off, but she didn't know when."

"So that means we have no idea whether Hoekstra read it or not."

"Right. Maybe you'll just have to keep on having faith that he didn't?" She smiled up at him playfully, and he leaned in this time to kiss her, but just as he did so, the very man they both had been avoiding for days crashed his way into the parking lot in his big, mean Mercedes. Hoekstra jammed on the brakes and jumped out, hot-wired with rage.

Before David had time to think up something to say, the old man yelled, "You son of a bitch," and strode across the muddy road straight toward them.

# CHAPTER 18

D AVID HEARD ALEXIS behind him, slamming the
trailer door closed. Hoekstra was gaining fast, but
David stood his ground.

"Get in the truck," he shouted to her. He sounded like an
actor in a cowboy movie. "Get in the truck now!" She did, just
in time to see Hoekstra plant himself in front of the younger
man.

"You bastard." He practically spat at David's forehead.

"OK, Hoekstra, why don't you try to calm down? Go home,
Alexis," David shouted over his shoulder. "I can take care of
this." But he could sense that the truck wasn't moving, and in
a way, he was glad. The man might have a gun.

Hoekstra was sweating, and though he teetered a bit, his
anger seemed to have strengthened him. "You're a traitor, Oster.
I could tell that the first time I met you. You're a traitor to the
male code."

"You read my notebook, didn't you, you spy?"

Hoekstra looked dumbfounded and shook his head. "Your
what? Why should I care about your fucking notebook?"

"Are you sure?"

The man just stared at him, uncomprehending apparently.

"Never mind. I guess not. What is it then?"

"Stay away from my woman."

David shook his head, confused. He hadn't seen Frances Hoekstra since that day in the hospital. Was the old man angry at him for his role in bringing her back to life?

Hoekstra shouted now, "Some things are eternal."

"Like husbands trying to murder their wives?"

Hoekstra backed away from him and leaned on the bumper of his own car. "You're always late to the party, aren't you? I told you it was a mistake. I'm not talking about my wife. I'm talking about Leah." He bellowed the name again, "Leah!"

For one moment only, David admired his capacity to surprise. "You're crazy! I hardly know her. We've only had some... dealings. How about all of your other women, old man of the geyser?"

Alexis yelled from the window of the truck, "What about those letters? How many women did you send them to? It was an industry."

Hoekstra advanced toward him again, flexing surprisingly strong-looking arms, and David felt something hot and mean rise up in his stomach, but he tried to back away. Hoekstra kept coming until he was smashed against the trailer, and as the man lobbed a fist at his jaw, David ducked, then shoved hard against him in the ribs. The older man fell straight backward, crumpling onto the pavement. There was a yelp from Alexis, who got out of the truck now.

"My God, he's not dead, is he?" David said, feeling as if he would faint.

She bent toward him and checked for a pulse at his neck. "He's all right."

They heard a siren. Unaccountably, a police car wound up the road behind Crestole and headed straight for them. Holy crap, were they after him already?

"Quick, what's my story?"

"Self-defense?"

"Yup, that's the ticket." David planted himself beside the trailer as if warding off yet another a blow.

Two policemen strode toward them, stopped, and stared at the man on the ground. David knew he shouldn't speak first, but he did anyway. "Officer, I can explain."

The cop gave him a puzzled look and mumbled something to his partner. Then they both bent down to eyeball Hoekstra. One of them slapped him, first on the right side of his face, then on the left. Sure enough, those heavy-lidded eyes opened, struggling to focus.

"Hey big fella, you're under arrest."

"Again?" he muttered feebly.

The two policemen picked him up and hustled him into the back of their patrol car, while David and Alexis stood there, stunned. Finally she turned to him. "Leah?"

"Leah Burnett. I'm supposed to teach some God-awful, ridiculous class about fish with her. She and Hoekstra are involved—that's only the half of it. Remember, I mentioned her to you before because she got the same letters as yours?"

"Right. I do keep hearing her name, always in connection with you somehow. And he was awfully angry."

"Over-the-top angry. It doesn't make any sense. As for Leah, I've talked to her a few times, but she's just part of my investigations." David could feel himself looking ever more guilty by the second. In the face of his stammering, Alexis seemed not twelve years older but a hundred years his senior, and him the baby of the universe. If reincarnation exists, he obviously had never been a human being before.

Desperate, he looked at her longingly, trying to figure out the proper words about Leah, but before he could frame anything sensible, she rested her chin on her hand and said, "I think you'd better decide exactly what she is to you. Anyway, I've got to get the horses back to the barn." She jumped up into the truck, then leaned out and yelled, "At least you saved me."

That evening, as Viktor sliced up some cucumbers and tomatoes and squeezed a wedge of lemon in their general direction, David recounted to him the day's gruesome events. "As of this moment, we are staring at the butt end of my professional career and my romantic one at the same time."

"Not true, I think you'll see."

"You know, prior to my arrival in Pyke City, I'd never beaten anyone up. Now I've done it twice. I'm a serial puncher."

"How uplifting for you, but don't worry. It's the end of Hoekstra's career, not yours, David. It must be they accuse him, even though she lives."

"I wonder if his wife is helping them make their case against him. Maybe she has some kind of proof that he did it?"

"You never know about husband and wife. A woman in Riga cut off her husband's balls, yet he forgave her. The police charged her anyway, and there they were, huddling in court, him with no balls. It was horrible. Don't worry, you'll figure it all out, dear boy, including your girlfriend. Meanwhile, this makes me director of the institute again, officially. I'm so happy. I'll give out more money to my friends."

"Haven't you already confirmed my money with Thornton?"

"Absolutely."

"Philo Smallett said Thornton wanted to talk to me about you, 'scientifically,' or some such thing. Do you think he's already trying to take it away?"

"It's fine. Everything's done and signed."

He seemed so certain David decided to stop worrying—for a few minutes at least.

However much he tried to pretend that it wasn't happening, the prospect of that horrid undergraduate class now gave a certain structure to David's life. And why shouldn't it since he couldn't get to sea and really had nothing else to do? Viktor had identified a number of professors who might be roped into teaching for him, should that dreadful duty ever materialize, and several days later, he got up early on a gloomy morning to attend a biology class in preparation for begging its teacher to handle at least two lectures for Mysteries of the Sea. Students milled around outside the lecture hall, hundreds of them waiting for Professor Allison Merkel and her lecture on fish, specifically the white sturgeon, a bottom dweller in the Columbia River. As her talk wore on, David learned more about this creature than he ever thought possible. Covered in horny plates, using its mouth like a vacuum, it was singularly unattractive, having evolved over a period of forty million years, and Allison, a hearty scientist in khaki, had a hell of a lot of slides. Before her were three hundred mildly interested Washingtonians. David dozed off for a moment, only to hear that "the young sturgeon is a pesky critter." Several students tittered.

At the end of the lecture, inexplicably, Allison wanted his opinion. He pronounced it brilliant and lined her up for not two but three dissertations on fish for what even she called Wet and Wild. To his consternation, she wouldn't let him go, instead engaging him in an endless discussion regarding possible lectures on salmon, then steelhead trout, along with a brief run at shad.

Later that evening, while wandering through the one and only mall in Pyke City, David ran into Lucy, and he invited her for pizza, thereby inadvertently getting hold of another piece of evidence in the village murder mystery. As they talked over beer and pepperoni, he could tell that she didn't know Hoekstra was back in jail. When he informed her of this, she produced yet another packet of letters.

"You just carry these around with you?"

"Yes, strangely enough, I do." As usual, she was smoking and had curled her legs underneath her in the chair. He reached out for the letters, but she snatched them back. Looking uncomfortable, inhaling deeply on her cigarette, she finally said, "I have a bad habit of falling hopelessly in love with the wrong people."

"Widely shared, I believe."

"I fall in love with rabidly heterosexual people."

David blanked out, at first, to her implied meaning, because he feared things were getting too close to the bone. "Listen, it's none of my business."

She patted his leg. "You're right to look into it. She means a great deal to me." This last "she" bit threw him off. Even though these didn't look like the letters David had seen before, he'd expected the inevitable love moo of the Danish maniac, who apparently took the time to hit on every woman in town. But this was something else altogether, something that would break Viktor's heart.

"No," he said. "Are you joking?"

She nodded, nibbling on a piece of pizza.

"Mrs. Hoekstra?"

"Yes."

David stifled the impulse to laugh. American men automatically think a woman who isn't interested in them is gay, but poor Viktor, it never even entered his mind that his beloved perhaps did not swing his way at all. Instead he blamed himself and plotted and planned how to win her over. At that ghastly party, David had seen certain signs and signals, and of course, she now lived with Marina, but he hadn't really entertained much thought about her life, other than that Viktor longed for her so.

"It's too much. I'm going completely crazy. You and Frances Hoekstra?"

"It wasn't like that."

"Like what? Everybody's related to Hoekstra! Now you're involved with his wife!" He was almost screeching. She started laughing along with him, so he figured he hadn't given mortal offense.

"Actually it was pretty bad, but not the way you think. I don't like to reveal this stuff."

"Oh, reveal it, for Christ's sake. If I stayed here too long, I'd probably be running after Mrs. Thornton."

"Nothing ever happened. It was stupid, really. I mooned around for a while and sent her some letters. Then she wrote back to me. That was what I was looking for, the letters I sent to *her*, and I found them, along with her husband's creepy, waterlogged rantings, so of course that means he knows about us." Lucy stuck the letters back in her jeans pocket. "Just hanging out in my ugly mind, I guess, as usual."

"Doing what?"

"I was very messed up about Frances—and staying right there with it, in my head."

"I do that quite a lot myself. Hoekstra said you took an old letter opener, a pen, and some other papers."

"I did, to throw him off, but I'm sure he knows about it now. The papers I wanted were my letters. Frances told me where they were. Hoekstra discovered them at their house, got pissed, took them away from her, and put them in his desk."

"I wish Viktor were here. He would go nuts with this information."

"We shouldn't tell him! First off, he wants me to be in love with him. And secondly...what would be second?"

"Viktor would try to kill Mrs. Hoekstra himself."

"Marina wouldn't like it either. She'd be jealous."

David had been wrong, oh so wrong, and that knowledge had a bracing effect and reinforced something he had suspected for a long time. Despite his assiduous efforts at finding stuff out, he wandered around in a fog. Now for his roommate he had a newfound sympathy, and deeper than that, pity for his unrequited love. Pity for Lucy, too. She was pursuing Hoekstra's wife right under the old man's nose. No wonder he hated her so much, and by association, her friend Viktor.

David vowed to think more kindly of Viktor, to stop suspecting him of any and all plots and just be grateful for his friendship. He had reasons enough to be grateful for the money Viktor had presumably gotten for him, a gift that Thornton confirmed when he ran into him as he walked to his office the next day.

"You heard about this already, I imagine?" their president muttered. It was raining, but the man had no umbrella and no hat. He slicked back his meager hair with a wet hand, and David could barely see him through the droplets.

"Yes, Viktor told me about it himself."

"He would, since he's living in your house. I've been meaning to speak to you about that, by the way. It's an arrangement that should probably stop—looks damn strange, if you ask me."

"What's wrong with it?" David knew what he meant, had thought himself about the appearance of favoritism, but he enjoyed watching Thornton display his views.

"Now, don't get me wrong. I know you're not a couple of goo goo boys, but other people might think so."

Goo goo boys? There were days David felt that the president had never actually left 1956; nevertheless, he tried to remain solemn. "I thought you meant favoritism, sir. That's my concern," he said as a giant raindrop plopped off his nose. "I want to get him out of my place and into his new house, which isn't finished yet. The police have blocked off the old one for their investigation."

Thornton's voice rose. "Completely unnecessary, totally and completely unnecessary. There is no crime here. The woman is back in her home."

"Her husband's in jail again. The police took him away the other day."

"Shit in a bucket. That wife is crazy. She probably staged the whole thing to get his attention. Believe me, David, I know women. They stage things all the time."

"I'm fairly certain Mrs. Hoekstra did not try to kill herself with a poisoned drink at that party."

Thornton was leading him, against his will, down the street toward the center of town. "Was that the murder weapon? How do you know, young man?" All of a sudden, he was fingering David as the guilty party.

"I've just been throwing around some ideas. There was denatured alcohol in the house, probably left there by the construction people. Looks just like gin. I saw her keel over while drinking a martini."

"There you have it. She staged the whole thing. Who was that woman who drank cleaning fluid last month? Then there

was another one, ran into her own grape picker. No, it couldn't
have been that."

Despite what was now a downpour, David attempted to
speak. "Are all these people who are trying to kill themselves
locals?"

"Goddamn right they are. People kill themselves here all
the time." He seemed proud of it. David wasn't sure where they
were going, but it turned out to be the jail. He quickly fabri-
cated a story about students waiting for him to toss around
ideas on Wet and Wild, but Thornton snorted, "They'll be
thrilled when you don't show up."

The president of Western Washington State University
pounded on the main desk at the jail, then banged on the small
bell. In a threesome they were roaming the cells looking for
Hoekstra, a beefy police officer right behind them.

"We sequestered him for his own safety," the guy announced,
a mysterious remark since no other prisoners were in residence.
At the third cell, they spotted him. He was lying down on
his bunk, reading the *Journal of Bacteriology*, drinking Henry
Weinhard beer, a Gitane burning in an ashtray on the floor.

"What's your bail?" Thornton barked into the cell. Hoekstra moved his magazine slightly, giving them the fisheye. The
cop announced that it was $250,000 now because the charge
had been upgraded to assault in the first degree. "You can pay
that, can't you?"

"Certainly, but I'm enjoying the solitude."

"Don't be absurd. You should be home assisting in your
wife's recuperation."

The accused poisoner looked at Thornton strangely, then
turned his head toward David. "What are you doing here,
Oster? I expected you to be out raising the dead or hitting
people."

"I'm preparing to teach young people how to fish for sturgeon."

"Too bad, that class might impede your scientific progress. Maybe you'd like to go into teaching permanently?" Hoekstra smirked at him.

In due course, they found themselves walking out the front of the police station, Hoekstra still puffing away on his smelly cigarette. David expected the other shoe to drop—the "this guy punched me twice" shoe—but it never did. His sometime boss just kept eyeing him.

Thornton nattered on about his return to work. "Your students are waiting; your colleagues are waiting; hell, even Viktor Pelliau is waiting."

"Waiting for you to die," David wanted to say, but Thornton couldn't be stopped.

"He hasn't done any administrative work at all since you've been gone, just given out money, to his friends, I might add." He looked David's way.

"We'll soon fix that." Hoekstra smiled grimly, but David knew Thornton had already signed off on the funds.

"Excitement is building about this young man's class."

"Wonderful," Hoekstra said. "They'll know how to spot a whale, maybe even tie boat knots."

"Excellent. That's what they need, useful information. No more of this airy-fairy shit." Sure enough, these two old bastards were colluding to ruin him. Why couldn't he find a way to neutralize the both of them?

They walked on in the pouring rain. David noticed that although Hoekstra had on an Irish woolen cap pulled down over his forehead, the students recognized him and turned to stare, even wave.

"It's good to have famous professors, keeps the students on their toes," Thornton whispered in David's ear, almost gurgling.

"He's infamous, not famous."

Thornton gave him a look both horrified and contemptuous. "Fame is the coin of the realm, David. Its source is irrelevant. Milk it, milk it. Besides, she's not actually dead."

These remarks were apparently no less true for being so outrageous, and David noticed that Hoekstra had fallen behind them, surrounded now by a small circle of students eager to have contact with the local celebrity, be he famous or infamous. On the Oster Wet Scale, the rain had peaked, as in fat, round, warm, and pounding steadily. David was soaked through, and water had clotted on his eyelashes.

"Was there anything else you wanted to say to me?" he asked Thornton. "About Viktor, I mean?"

The man wiped his face with his jacket sleeve. "He's important in science. Whatever we may think of his antics— I've been putting up with them for too many years—he's a person to be reckoned with."

"I thought you wanted me to throw him out of my house?"

"I do, I do. Just don't offend him in any way. Higher-ups, you know." At which point he made a kind of baseball referee's gesture, sweeping his hands across each other, as in "safe" at home plate.

# CHAPTER 19

"**I**T'S FUCKING UNBELIEVABLE. Hoekstra's almost a murderer, and look, he's got every idiot on campus clustered about him. Nobody cares about the coma victim." David ranted at Viktor as they sipped coffee at the Bean.

"You don't understand. Women here, they long for romance. They sit in their homes day after day watching people on television getting kissed, but no kisses here, not a one. Their husbands are drunk, or cutting down trees, or chasing young girls. For them, an attempt at murder would at least be some attention, some sign of love. Even the girl students, look at what they've got, guys whose necks and heads are the same size. Believe me, I've met these young men. Complete emptiness. They could test automobiles in their heads."

Several students glared over at them since Viktor's voice had risen particularly high. "Stop it. They can hear you," David whispered. At that moment he could absolutely not relate to the women Viktor described, because the non-desperate Alexis hadn't returned his calls since the parking lot incident. She must be mad at him; that much seemed clear. She wanted explanations, reassurance possibly. David registered all this as unfair, unpleasant, too, because he had indeed harbored distinctly lustful thoughts regarding Leah and felt guilty about them. Worrying over what to do about Alexis had become a pretty constant theme these days, but now he forced his mind to return to the matter at hand. "The point is, we're not getting Hoekstra. He's getting us! It's hopeless. I'll have to quit again."

"Don't be a fool, David. Besides, I am invincible," he announced over a gigantic cup of French roast. "Your money is gotten. Thornton regards you favorably since you went to the jail with him. Don't you want to know how much?"

"I certainly do."

Viktor leaned back in his chair, stared up at the ceiling, and almost whispered to heaven, "Six million dollars!"

"Six million dollars, goddamn. Are you kidding? You got even more? This is fantastic."

Viktor grinned and pulled on his earlobes. "Yes, fantastic and beyond."

With this extraordinary news stored in his addled brain, David decided to forget about quitting and go back to his own work. He did contemplate changing the locks on his office door, but figured that, if Hoekstra tried to get in, he could hide under the desk with his father's .38 in hand. To pass the time, he reread "Hot Bubbles at Juan de Fuca," which had been moldering among his files, and this time with less skepticism. Viktor clearly wanted to use his understanding of ocean wave circulation to find the best possible spot for his experiment, since the less violent the wave movement the better. This was information David would have on board the ship in real time with his current meters and shear probes. Viktor would supply instruments for measuring fusion within the hot chimneys—sometimes called black smokers—but it would be David's job to figure out how to maneuver these into the core.

As he contemplated the fact that indeed, as Viktor said, he hadn't at first understood the proposal, his phone rang. A whispery female voice on the other end said, "David Oster?"

"That's me."

"I've wanted to…I thought I should see you and thank you for being at my bedside."

"Mrs. Hoekstra?" She didn't sound good at all. They set an hour to meet in the late afternoon the next day, again at the coffeehouse, though he volunteered to come to her.

"No, the doctor says I should get out and face the world."

When he arrived for yet another sojourn at the Bean, where he seemed to live lately, the recently cured woman was seated in a dark corner with Alexis Scherbatskoy. Mrs. Hoekstra, Frances, as she insisted they call her, looked pale and shaky. Her honey-colored hair was growing out gray at the roots, she wore no rings, and she was dressed in austere navy-blue clothes, almost like a nun. David had no idea what to say, but Alexis was talking on as if the two women had known each other for years. Alexis barely looked at David, and Frances didn't speak much to him either, but her expressive face responded with deep smiles while she carefully sipped her drink. Everything about her was slowed down, fragile, sometimes tentative, and, as David noted, rather attractive.

Alexis was talking up alternative cures like acupuncture and aromatherapy, but her conversation had the air of nervous chatter, maybe to avoid acknowledging him. Mrs. Hoekstra turned to David, finally, and in a soft voice said, "Niels told me that you had just come to show your support. I'm grateful that you did, because look who you brought with you. Never in a million years would she have come on her own."

Alexis shifted in her chair. "Yes, I'm so glad that I went to the hospital that day. We owe it all to David," she said a bit acidly. They both turned to him, as if expecting something oracular.

He sipped his coffee. "I imagine that your journey, or whatever you want to call it, has changed you."

She nodded.

"Perhaps events and people look different to you now that you've gone..." He flushed with the thought that he was about to go stupid sci-fi on the whole group and start talking about "the white light" and "the edge of consciousness," but the blessed lady came to his rescue.

"It was like sleeping. I don't remember anything about that night, except"—she paused to look around the room as if seeing it for the first time—"the belly dancer." They all laughed, David too loudly.

He wondered if that was really all she remembered. He also wondered if she thought her husband had tried to kill her, and if she knew about his pursuit of other women, about all those goddamned letters.

"Is your husband still being prosecuted?" he blurted out, unable to stop himself. But she took no offense.

"I'm not sure. Apparently I got a bad drink, a martini with denatured alcohol in it. The doctor was amazed that I didn't smell it. Not only was it poison in and of itself, but it reacted with the Valium I was taking for my nerves."

David was ridiculously proud to hear his theory confirmed, and now he had to find out who had mixed that drink. He remembered seeing Frances draw the glass to her lips as Hoekstra reached for her. Had he actually just handed it to her? How would he have known that denatured alcohol was under the sink in the first place? It was possible, of course, that he had put it there.

"Is that really what happened?" Alexis muttered, looking at David intently, knowing the gist of his theory.

"That's what the police toxicologist told me. It does seem like a strange accident."

"Stranger than strange," David wanted to say, but instead inquired, "Was it a gin or vodka martini?"

"It was supposed to be gin."

"Do you know who mixed it?"

"I'm sorry, I've no idea." At this, she seemed to tear up, and Alexis frowned at him to stop. He knew she was right; this woman wasn't prepared for life, let alone any questions about the poison in her glass.

"How did you get here?" he asked, thinking he should at least see her home safely.

"Niels hired a student to drive me around. He should be waiting for me now." Frances didn't say much after this, just glanced around with a strained, tense air, nibbling on the crumbs of her lemon poppy seed muffin.

Outside in the rain, she thanked them again, over and over. A black Lincoln Town Car pulled up, and a jaunty young man jumped out and guided her into the backseat. "Take a load off, Mrs. H," he said.

Startled and unsure, she waved good-bye, and David felt terrible, as if she were going back to a dungeon where her husband probably locked her up with Heinrich the dog so they could fight over his food.

Alexis was clearly feeling the same way. "How totally depressing," she said as she swung her scarf around her neck. "I really think he was the one who tried to knock her off. Nothing else makes sense."

"He keeps saying that it was a 'mistake.'"

"Mistake that she didn't die, probably."

"That's what I thought, but he wouldn't really be announcing that, would he?"

"God knows. He's nuts, and he might just try again."

"I don't think so. He doesn't want to go to jail. Besides, he may be strange, but he's not completely mad." The minute he said this, he realized that he hadn't taken this man's evil seriously enough, hadn't even gauged its dimensions, and so he took Alexis by the hand and tried to pull her back into the Bean.

"No, I have work to do today."

"This will just take a moment. It's important." She didn't want to go with him, but finally gave him a look and agreed. After grabbing the nearest table, he produced his notebook and thumbed through it. "My equations haven't yielded anything terribly interesting yet, but they do present a bill of particulars against Niels Hoekstra. Central to this is Leah." Alexis raised her eyebrows, but then looked over at his silly drawings and laughed, especially at herself on a horse. "Hoekstra asked me to watch Shelby. Shelby is having an affair with Leah. Hoekstra was trying to have sex with Leah in a hot tub, and I saw them."

"Wait, I don't think I knew that."

"I couldn't stand to tell you about it. Anyway, now he's mad at me about her. Before, he kept telling me I shouldn't rat him out to his wife, while she was in a coma! Now he's yelling about 'his woman,' Leah, in front of a crowd of people. If I didn't know better, I'd think he actually wanted his wife to find out about his little hot tub adventure. And you know, Leah was also a target of his letter-writing campaign, along with you and Lucy."

"So this Leah person is central to the mystery?"

"Yes, but not central to me."

At last she smiled at him, relieved apparently. "Shelby is pretty central too."

"I wonder. He seems your garden-variety philanderer, relatively harmless, in a good-humored, amoral way. I kind of like the guy. Except where's his wife?" She shook her head, and he continued. "Shelby could have found out about Hoekstra and Leah, but I still don't see why he would have tried to hurt Mrs. Hoekstra. Perhaps he was after someone else? As a murder weapon, a poisoned drink seems remarkably imprecise."

David described to her the hot tub incident in detail. Did this have a role in what had happened? She thought a moment.

"He's afraid she'll tell Shelby he's impotent, and then he'll be humiliated?"

"I still don't really understand why he keeps yelling at me about her. He must know that she and I are not involved." David really thought he should enunciate this fact as many times as he could.

"He certainly made a scene."

"You know, he's into scenes, big, heavy drama, but I never can figure out about what."

David continued to sketch out the dimensions of the mystery, waxing—or so he hoped—adult and scientific. Most likely Shelby put the denatured alcohol under the sink. Did he next put it in her drink? Why, when he seemed to like her? Did Hoekstra think Shelby was going to try to murder his wife, hence David's assignment to watch him? The problem, as David laid it out before her, was that he couldn't grasp Shelby's connection with Hoekstra, a man who for some reason hated him. Impossible that Hoekstra had been in league with Shelby, but then how did he know where the poison was?

"Thanks to my father, I know exactly what alcohol poisoning will do to you, lab alcohol, wood alcohol, or too much gin, blurred vision, maybe blindness, even coma. It was amazing that she lived."

Alexis looked at him reassuringly. "If the police let Hoekstra out on bail, what can we do about it, short of breaking into the house and rescuing her?"

At that moment, watching her bring her coffee mug to her lips, David was struck with how little he knew of her thoughts, of her heart, with how much he didn't know about love. He couldn't think of a way to address any of this, instead, saying, "We're not doing that. We're not doing any of it. Domestic squabbles are dangerous and none of our business." When you lived in the Oster household, you knew how dangerous domesticity could be. He walked Alexis to her truck, really wanting to drag her back to his place, especially after their new and very welcome rapprochement. Unfortunately, a disturbed Latvian remained in residence.

Not for long, he was to find, because when he got home that night Viktor was feverishly packing. Shelby had told him that his new house was almost finished and that he could occupy it anytime he liked. Even though it contained no furniture, Viktor insisted that he help him load up his belongings in the Buick.

"I must sleep in there tonight, David."

His car, which had always ridden low, had now sunk so far down that its back bumper almost dragged on the ground, so it was a slow trip. Even in the deep, rainy night, the pink edifice was clearly visible as they approached it, and mysteriously, someone else had already turned on lights. The garage door was open.

"A poltergeist?" David said, when Shelby came bounding out of the front door, closely followed by Leah.

"We were just getting things ready for you," he said

"Where's Larry, if I may ask?" Frankly, murder was in the air, and David wasn't about to get shot.

"He's fixing the charges against Hoekstra, working a deal somehow or trying to settle it. They're meeting at his house."

"Poor woman, plotting right under her nose. Someone should rescue her." David still felt guilty about letting her go home alone.

Viktor took his arm. "Not us, dear boy. He would shoot us in the ear. Remember those big guns he had?"

"Want a beer?" Shelby asked David.

"Why the hell not?"

Inside, Viktor's new home was spotless, smelling of wet paint and carpet glue. The walls and ceilings soared white—not the ghastly pink of the outside—and out of the immense glass windows could be seen the town below. Viktor ran from room to room, exclaiming over the beauty of the place.

"We must make a real toast, to the house, recon…recon…"

"You're stuck in a groove," David said.

"Reconstruct?" Shelby said.

Viktor shook his head vigorously. "Like fruit juice."

"Reconstitute," David offered.

"That's the word. Reconstitute the essence of my old home, here, without the killing." He unscrewed the top of a blue-green bottle he had in his pocket and poured them each a glass of his favorite thick, syrupy liqueur, Latvian Black Balsam. "*Prozit, uz veselibu*, to your health. May the new house forgive all the badness and evil at my old house and think only of the joyful times. We are reborn." They drank the strong drink and stared into each other's eyes, the four of them believing for one moment in Viktor's grand vision of a new start.

Unfortunately, at this point, completely confused about Viktor's scientific status as well as his relationship to the institute, David had come to think of him mainly as a giggler, a partier, and a snoop. Still, he would miss his roommate. He was companionable and good with food, and David's house would no doubt feel cold and bereft without his constant chatting and cooking. Viktor had a way of establishing a life wherever he went and didn't need much to do this—olive oil, wine, someone to talk to. At the domed palace, he had lived out of one suitcase, yet the whole place became his, while David existed among his landlord's knickknacks like an interloper and never made a mark on the joint. For him, it might as well have been a motel.

The thought of Frances Hoekstra back in her hellish hacienda kept David awake that night. He knew he had to attend an early class the next day, taught by a guy in marine mammalogy whom Viktor had talked into teaching at least two classes on whales for Mysteries of the Sea. But lying there, looking up at the chipped paint on the ceiling, he couldn't stop himself from trying to imagine the life she had returned to. What would you say to someone who had tried to kill you and failed? Certainly his parents had seemed to want to kill each other; they just didn't have the guts or the wherewithal. It all boggled the mind, but he didn't have to think too long because the phone rang.

"Yes?" he said warily.

"David, I can't sleep." Alexis sounded frightened and strange.

"I can't either."

"We shouldn't have let her go. We sent her home with a man who's under indictment for trying to kill her."

"What could we do? We couldn't stop her. She obviously doesn't believe he did it."

"I'm afraid she won't survive the night."

"You're being ridiculous. People don't just get knocked off in this day and age, just like that, right in their own homes. In addition to which, the guy knows that everyone suspects him."

"David, please trust me on this."

Trust her with the truth, trust her with himself? David wasn't sure he could do this. Nevertheless, the two of them rendezvoused at her house, then drove her truck to Hoekstra's around 3:00 a.m., leaving it hidden down by the road.

"This is unbelievably stupid. I don't even have a weapon," David said, whereupon Alexis pulled a can of pepper spray out of her purse.

"Don't worry, I'll just zap him if he tries anything."

There was something profoundly moving about the Washington backwoods in the early morning, as if the sacred souls of countless Nisqually, Duwamish, and Snoqualmie folk lay slumbering in their graves beneath the Douglas firs. Nevertheless, David and Alexis trespassed among them, crunching their way up the hill, reaching the top only to see Hoekstra's hacienda suffused with light. They stood for a moment behind a clump of bushes as they watched his hulking shape cross in front of a downstairs window.

"I've been here less than a year, and I've become a Peeping Tom," David whispered.

"Do you see his wife anywhere?" Alexis wrung her hands to keep them warm, and finally David grabbed them and put them inside his coat. Just then they heard a rustling behind them. "Quick," Alexis whispered, pulling her hands away and pushed David behind a tree.

They listened while the footsteps along the driveway got louder. A hooded figure in heavy boots appeared, trying its best to tiptoe, but making even more noise than before. Its head turned, and David recognized a pair of owlish glasses.

"Viktor?"

The man's head snapped around, and he darted to the side of the road.

"Viktor," David whispered again, and he now emerged, pulling his hood down. "What the hell are you doing here?"

"The same thing you are, heroic young man. And young woman, pardon me."

"You scared us to death," Alexis said.

"Do we have a plan?" A novel remark coming from Viktor, who seemed to live for the operations of chance.

"We just wanted to see if Mrs. Hoekstra was OK, although how we do that is another question." Now that David spoke normally, his voice sounded unnaturally loud.

"I comprehend you. We search for signs of foul play."

"OK, I have a plan. Let's go home," David suggested. "There's nothing we can do anyway, and I have to attend a fish class at eight a.m."

"No, no, now that we're here, we might as well investigate," Alexis said.

David argued against this as well as he could with a Douglas fir branch practically up his ass, but a few minutes later, they were circling the house, all three of them hanging on to each other's hands. All they could see was Hoekstra pacing and smoking a cigar. There was definitely something odd about it, but then a man recently out of jail yet still under indictment, with the wife he had tried to kill unexpectedly home from the hospital, might well behave oddly. David was just gearing up once again to suggest a retreat when suddenly a howling sound rose up in front of them and kept on rising in a vicious crescendo. Heinrich was on the move. Without looking back, he and Viktor prepared to flee. David tried to grab Alexis's hand, but she yanked it away and turned back toward the dog, while the two men started toward the road.

The howling turned into a high-pitched squeal. David looked around to see Alexis, legs wide apart, fixed like a soldier, planted before the dog with her little can. She sprayed him full in the face. The dog wobbled on its powerful legs, shook its ugly head as if just out of a bath, until it fell over like something stuffed. David raced back to her.

"Thank God for your little canister. It took balls to face him down like that. How long will he be out?"

"Not long, I think. This is what mailmen use, and it doesn't do all that much."

Viktor ran up beside them, completely out of breath. "You see, what did I tell you? Russians all have military training."

By then they heard the unmistakable tones of Hoekstra, yelling after the dog, "Heinrich, get them. Hunt them down, *fass, fass*. Kill!"

"Time to go home," David said, but Alexis was already moving toward the house. "What the hell are you doing?"

"I'm going in to talk to him."

"Don't be insane. The man is clearly dangerous."

She kept walking.

"Wait, you can't go alone. I'll come with you."

"Absolutely not," she called back over her shoulder.

"You're a mother!" David shouted, but she only turned back and gave him a look.

"A mother? Goodness, you work so fast, young man."

"No, she has a son back east."

"Oh dear. Well, nothing we say will matter. She's irrational. Look at Peter the Great." Viktor moved in the other direction down the driveway.

"Stop, we can't go anywhere until she comes back out."

"I am leaving. The dog will wake up and bite my leg, and then…" Viktor thought a moment. "I'm staying. He will bite my leg, and I'll sue Hoekstra for a hundred million dollars. It's the American way."

"Give me the pepper spray. If he wakes up, we'll blast him again." David wasn't totally confident about this, but he said it anyway.

"It's true. You can't leave a woman with a murderer, even if she is Russian."

# CHAPTER 20

"**G**ODDAMN, SHE HAS more courage than we do,"
David said, watching Alexis march toward the house.
"She does not. She has a death wish." Viktor
crouched on the grass and watched the comatose dog like a
hawk, tear gas can poised on his knee.

"Don't give him too much, Viktor. It only takes one shot,"
David said, suddenly worried about the poor canine, but he
became even more unnerved when Alexis disappeared inside
the front door.

"How little you know. These are Nazi dogs. They need the
full blast." Heinrich was still out, and David lay down beside
the dog to watch over him. But he was so exhausted that he
closed his eyes. "You can't sleep now, David. What if he awakens and chews off your head?"

"That would be bad." He closed his eyes again. The sparrows
were already up, which meant morning would follow shortly. It
was peaceful, but it was wet, little fir needles poked his head,
and he had to roll even closer to the dog to get comfortable. He
must have been asleep quite a while when he awoke to Viktor
yanking him by the shoulder.

"He begins to move, David. I think we must flee."

"If we leave two women here in danger, we'll never be able to live with ourselves."

Viktor lifted a booted leg. "If he awakens, I will smash him one."

"Stop it! You're being cruel to this dog." He patted its nodding head. Still nearly asleep, with his body stirring slightly, Heinrich looked almost docile.

At first light, or what passed for light around Pyke City, their surroundings turned more prosaic. They watched the front door, and Alexis finally emerged, but David caught a glimpse of Hoekstra behind her, still in the house, as she marched toward them.

"Mrs. Hoekstra is all right," she announced. "I'm just going to revive Heinrich and let him wander home." She pulled a Baby-Wipes out of her pocket.

"Not while I'm here you're not," Viktor said.

"He'll be fine, so out of it he won't bother anyone." She wiped around his eyes, his ears, all over his snout, and he began to twitch, then make a hoarse breathing sound. Viktor was jogging in place, getting ready to run, and, taking no further chances, pulled a silver flask out of his pocket and downed a swig of Jack Daniel's. He shoved it at David, who took a taste in honor of the cocktail hour in some exotic locale far, far away.

"What happened in there, Alexis? Oh my God, oh shit. What time is it?" He'd forgotten his watch at home and grabbed Viktor's arm to look at his. It was almost eight. "The class, the goddamn whale class. I swore I'd be there." But Alexis wouldn't let David go until an agonizing five minutes passed, as they watched the dog wobble toward the front door.

Finally they ran down the hill, and he and Alexis jumped into her truck, not even waiting to see if Viktor's Buick would start. David's hair stood on top of his head, and all his clothes were rumpled and dirty, but there was no time for him to change, so he told her just to drop him off on campus, where the esteemed Professor Marron, noted explorer and lover of whales, or more precisely, whale music, awaited, probably impatiently. He would have movies, tapes, an audiovisual experience bound to keep the students awake for at least an hour. During the ride, he tried to question Alexis, but she assured him she was fine and would tell him everything later. David lurched out of the truck toward the auditorium, dreading the 150 faces bound to gape at his disheveled condition. After maybe two hours of sleep on the wet ground, he was as woozy as Heinrich.

Marron waited for David onstage, looking natty and great white hunter-y, and had laid his Australian hat on the chair, covering his notes. These whale guys are the movie stars of science, appearing on TV with all the creatures they study and to whom they give cute names, but unpopular with real scientists because they are so rich and happy. He stood when David entered, which was more than he deserved, and gave him a chair near the podium.

"David, so thrilled you could be here. I thought you'd be out looking for leptons." Since this was a class of subatomic particle, he obviously hadn't a clue what David did.

"I'm a little tired today…"

"Rough night, eh?" he said with a bit more of Hemingway than David thought strictly necessary, though a twig hung off his flannel shirt.

"Beyond rough."

"Don't worry, you don't need to do anything here. I'm just going to introduce you and tell them about Wet and Wild before I start my lecture."

"My man." David slapped him on the back.

Marron turned to the waiting faces, them as were awake, and they gazed back at him, some with interest, others with what resembled defiance. "Entertain me, if you dare," that look seemed to say. For David it was like being a lounge act; only he'd slept on the barroom floor all night. In a sincere attempt to make him look good, Marron briefly sketched David's career as a man of the deep oceans, the only one who understood how abyssal waves behaved as they did, but it all sounded unspeakably dull compared to the activities of Dr. Rick Marron, whale watcher, whale saver. Then, to David's consternation, he described Mysteries of the Sea as "the brainchild of this very same man, David Oster."

Proceeding to his own subject, for one solid hour Marron regaled the class with what scientists laughingly call whale "music," high-pitched squeals that appear sequential, blasting out of two huge loudspeakers. In David's weakened condition, having started the day with Jack Daniel's and dog snot, he registered the sounds as fingernails down a blackboard. Typical whale vocalizations run between 150 and 195 decibels, loud and squeaky, but the kids loved it. They had all kinds of fantasies of what the creatures might be saying to each other, or singing, and Marron had plenty of slides and videos showing the animals at play. True to form, he had named his creatures Corky, Blue Jim, Bella, stuff like that, and this Flipperized version of science went over very well, but by the end of the hour, David was ready for the hospital. Alas, Marron insisted they have coffee at the student union and proceeded to engulf him in scientific chatter over hot mugs of organic Sumatra. How David got through it he couldn't fathom, but he definitely wanted this guy to teach classes for him. He kept forcing his tongue to move, making his best effort to appear a sentient human being.

"Wet and Wild, I love it," Marron said, "and you're obviously going to need help."

As soon as he could pry himself away from the man, David raced home to change clothes and take a nap, only to be grabbed by Shelby as he struggled to open the front door. "Did you see the paper today?"

"I can barely see you, Shelby. I certainly haven't read the paper."

"They let him off. Hoekstra. Read it." He handed David the latest *Sentinel*, which had Niels's big smiling face waving at a crowd of well-wishers, or possibly people he had paid to stand outside his house. "Professor Hoekstra was exonerated today in the mysterious illness and near death of his wife Frances," it read. "According to police, Mrs. Hoekstra insisted that she had made the faulty cocktail herself, by mistaking a bottle of denatured alcohol for gin."

"My ass she made it herself. I wonder what he did to get her to say this?" David said. Impossible to think Mrs. Hoekstra had been rummaging around under the sink and just filled her glass with poison. "Who made the drink, Shelby? Did you?" He might as well ask the guy straight out.

"Of course not. Hoekstra must have. They didn't have a bartender or anything, and I saw him hand it to her."

"Did you show him where the denatured alcohol was at Viktor's house?"

"Why the hell would I do that? I probably shoved it under the sink one day when I was in a hurry, and he must have found it. Look, she's a good person. I can see her doing any-thing the old bastard wants."

Shelby seemed to have grown sweet on her himself by virtue of nostalgia and notoriety, and when David told him about their nighttime adventures, he insisted the two of them immediately go out to the horse ranch to get the straight story on Mrs. Hoekstra from Alexis. Exhausted as he was, David knew he ought to check up on her, and when Shelby offered to drive in the elaborate Escalade, he finally agreed.

Alexis seemed remarkably fresh and alive after their hideous night and gave them both coffee in the tack room. "Hello again." She smiled and kissed David on the cheek. They seemed to have segued to a much better place romantically, and he was happy, if so tired he could hardly stand.

He held her a moment and said, "Did you see the paper this morning?"

"Not yet."

He handed it to her, and she read.

"Doesn't surprise me, though. That she would take the blame on herself to protect him," Shelby announced.

"She's changed her story. At the Bean she said she didn't know who made the drink. She certainly didn't make it herself," Alexis said. Now Shelby looked shocked and seemed anxious that she tell him more, especially about what happened during her visit to the Hoekstra home. "We had a talk."

"At that hour of the night? Wasn't he even a little pissed that you were traipsing around in his driveway?" Shelby asked.

A groom was brushing out a horse nearby, so she lowered her voice and spoke almost in a whisper. "He was so glad to see me, it was pathetic. He'd been drinking."

"Now there's a surprise. Where was the little woman?" David said, fighting to stay awake.

"Sleeping, that's what he said anyway, but I could hear her talking on the phone, so at least I knew she was more or less OK."

"And that's all that happened?"

"Well, he also wanted me to run away with him to Argentina, where he knows people."

"Old Nazis, probably," David said.

"He kept saying, 'I'm sorry, I got confused,' over and over again. I assumed he meant the poison drink."

"That's one fucking lot of confusion," Shelby muttered.

"Hoekstra did say everything was cleared up with the police, that he'd seen to that. You've got to understand, guys, he was weeping when he told me this stuff. He had no idea how late it was, no idea that it was weird I was there."

Without thinking about what he was doing, David hugged her to him, and she smiled as if they had known each other a long, long time. Suddenly he felt older—he had more weight in the world.

"I did try to find Frances. I went to the bathroom twice, but that house is huge, and there was a limit to how long I could just wander around, him following me the entire time. He even stood outside the bathroom door, saying over and over, 'I was confused. I'm sorry, I'm sorry.' It was horrible. I felt for him, I really did."

"Did he ever thank you for bringing her back from the grave?" Shelby asked.

"Not in so many words. But he kept grabbing my hands, saying, 'Those hands, those magic hands.' He was totally incoherent, hammered, probably drinking since dinner."

"How did you get out of there?" Shelby said.

"He kept pulling me back, telling me I had to kiss him. I finally broke down and did it."

"Jesus!" David could picture those murderous, rubbery lips.

"Then I promised to come back."

"But you won't!"

"He probably doesn't remember anything that happened, that's how drunk he was." She smiled at David, who still looked horrified. "It was a purely expedient kiss—and very short, believe me."

Shelby didn't say much on the drive to the institute, though David tried to pump him about his interest in Mrs. Hoekstra. Finally, he announced that he was "just bored" and entertaining himself with the mystery.

Later that evening, after a day of unsuccessfully trying to work, David slogged home over the wet leaves. The murky warmth seemed to lift right off the pavement, and there was an edge to the air, electric almost. The month of March, he'd been told, was when the suicide rate began to rise, climbing until the first ray of sun in June. The residents of the state resembled prison inmates, fine as long as they never saw daylight, but insane at the very first glimpse of a break in the clouds.

He had reasons to be depressed that went far beyond the weather. He was guilty of assault and battery on his boss, not once but twice; he was making love to a woman Hoekstra was either pursuing or, at the very least, implicating; and, whether he had read his notebook or not, surely this same man realized that David thought he had tried to knock off his wife. He couldn't do any physics but was instead fully occupied with undergraduates and fish. If he had planned his own personal ruination, he couldn't have done a better job. At least Alexis kind of liked him, possibly, but how long could that last? Once she knew more of his fears, his weaknesses, she might just see him as some ridiculous youth. Contemplating all of this under the dome, sipping a glass of bloodred Cabernet Sauvignon, he stared out the window at the rain, on the Oster Wet Scale, definitely a nine. He picked up his calendar and numbered the days that lay ahead of him until May, a crowd of endless hours that would find him right here in Pyke City. It was beyond pathetic.

With no warning, Viktor loomed outside the glass in his front door, smiling maniacally. "Let me in," he mouthed. He was hyperventilating and, as soon as he pushed his way in, grabbed a glass of wine and gulped it down. "You will not, you simply will…"

"Sit down, Viktor. Calm down. I think we should start our lives over as of today and not get hysterical about everything."

The man still could barely breathe and was motioning for wine. "The dog, the dog!" he shouted. "Instead of going back inside Hoekstra's house, he followed me, jumped up on the seat, and wouldn't leave. How could I touch him? I don't like dogs, but he is drooling all over my beautiful upholstery."

"Oh shit. I haven't slept in two days, and now, damn. I'm not particularly good with animals, Viktor."

"Who could be good with this monster dog?"

"I got news, bub. The dog is not our problem; the owner is."

"I'm trying not to think of that." He now drank straight from the wine bottle. "Oh dear, only a mediocre red."

Viktor dragged David outside to his car, and sure enough, Heinrich lolled on the backseat of the Buick, aggressively slobbering. He had a zonked look on his face and had apparently not yet recovered his killer instincts. David patted him on the head, but the dog stared at him vacantly. He shut the car door and then sprinted back to his front porch, where Viktor now sank down on the steps.

"What are we going to do? I can't take it anymore. I'm exhausted. I've been driving around for hours, waiting for him to eat my head."

"Why didn't you just abandon the car?"

He looked at him, horrified. "The Buick Roadmaster?" It was as if he had asked him to burn the flag.

"OK, think, think. We need to take him back to Hoekstra's and drop him off."

"No, no, absolutely not. That man will shoot us, David."

"The animal shelter. Let's just drop him off."

"What will we say? We tried to kill him!"

"We did not. Don't be ridiculous." He sat down next to Viktor.

He could see lights on at Lucy's house, where she and Marina had now apparently taken up joint residence. "Maybe Marina knows what to do. She's got that ferret, after all."

"I'll kill her if I see her."

Startled at his vehemence, David looked over at him intently. Did Viktor know that Lucy was gay, and that's why she couldn't love him? He certainly hadn't outed her, but perhaps someone else had? Did Viktor talk to anyone other than David? He was awfully isolated, obsessed with women and liquor, science coming in a distant third. He ignored his graduate students and only focused on Hoekstra when forced to.

"What about Shelby? He might know what to do with the animal," David finally suggested.

"He's never home, especially at night."

They both stared at the dog, who seemed to be perking up a bit. He moved his head from side to side and started panting out of the half-open car window.

"Uh oh," Viktor said, jumping up. "I'll kick him if he lunges toward us."

"Wait a minute." David ran inside to get an old baseball bat he kept in his closet for any possible intruders, not that he had any intention of actually hitting the canine, but he could wave it in front of him in alpha dog–type fashion. By the time he got back, Shelby stood right next to the car, with his hand on Viktor's shoulder. They were both staring at Heinrich.

"Thank you, God," Viktor announced. "Shelby's going to think of something."

Alas, Shelby seemed stunned, as stupefied as the two other men. The dog, on the other hand, opened both his eyes at once. He blinked.

"At least he's alive," Shelby offered. "You know, you really could have hurt him with that pepper spray."

"I wish we had," Viktor said gloomily.

The dog rose up. They all stood poised, David with bat, Viktor with fist, and Shelby with nothing. Heinrich had trouble standing on the upholstery and slid down right away onto all fours. Shelby reached out and waved his hand in front of his face, then opened the door a crack.

"No, no, the dog is a killer," Viktor warned, but he looked like no killer David had ever seen. In fact, as they watched, a slight wag happened at the tail end of this killer, then another. Opening the car door a bit more, Shelby patted old Heinrich on the head, and the dog moved its snout up as if to smell them. Viktor and David backed up a foot and watched. The dog had mastered the slippery seat and started to pace back and forth. "Get ready, everybody," Viktor said.

"That's right, lock and load," Shelby laughed, opening the door all the way. "Are you sure you guys have the right dog? Maybe this other one just jumped into your car when you weren't looking or were drunk or something."

Viktor bent forward to assess the dog's identity, pronouncing him the very same Heinrich who had wanted to eat them hours before. As he moved toward the animal, lo and behold, he was licked on the hand, not once but twice, before he could snatch himself away. Indeed, Heinrich, eyes bright and panting happily, riveted his attentions seriously on Viktor.

"He likes you. In fact, I think he's in love," Shelby said in a singsong voice.

Heinrich's tail was moving back and forth like crazy as he pranced on the backseat, trying to lick a Latvian.

# CHAPTER 21

"IT'S A TREMENDOUS thing really, the love of a dog for its master." Shelby seemed bent on torturing Viktor about his new pet, since the creature wouldn't leave his side and kept putting his head up under his hand to be rubbed, while they all still sat on the curb by the car. It would have been touching if it weren't so grotesque.

"You're a sick man, Shelby. I have told you that many times, and now I know it," Viktor said.

"It must have actually followed you into your car out of affection," David suggested.

"Don't you join in with all this 'I love the animals' crap, David. You're my only hope."

"I'm going to bed. I don't care who this animal loves. I can't stand up another moment."

"'Whom,' I think. Anyway, you cannot abandon me with this canine."

"Maybe I should go out and get you some Kibbles and Bits." Shelby punched Viktor in the arm.

The dog posed a definite problem, as it fingered their nighttime activities at the Hoekstra abode. But what the hell were they supposed to do with it, especially at this late hour? After arguing for twenty minutes about their next move, they decided that since Heinrich had obviously been abused by Hoekstra—otherwise why would he now be latching himself on to Viktor, a man terrified of dogs?—they should concoct a story about finding him in the woods and take him to the pound, where if Hoekstra didn't show up, someone nice would adopt him. Heinrich kept schmoozling up to Viktor while he was trying to drive, but he held firm, so it was off to the animal shelter. Their story sounded pretty half-assed, but the night manager believed them, no doubt because the dog was an expensive purebred and well kept, not an animal anyone would just give away.

"Aren't you even a little bit sad?" Shelby patted Viktor on the shoulder as they walked out.

"Stop that, you degenerate," Viktor said.

It was now very late, yet another night of sleep David had missed, and he was beginning to relate to his mother's rare moments of exhausted, frozen rage. "Watch it now, David. She's in the 'decomp zone,'" is how his father used to put it, meaning "decomp" as in "decompensate." She would shrink deeper and deeper into an overly controlled silence, but could erupt at any pinprick of trouble. David himself was definitely in the decomp zone at this very moment, the first sign of which was an unnatural internal quiet, all emotional systems on shutdown.

"I've got to get home right away, or I can't be responsible for my actions." This he said in a hoarse whisper, as if speech might cause him to fall down.

"I'm staying at your house tonight. I'm afraid to dream of Heinrich," Viktor announced, and David was too tired to object.

"You guys are nuts, you know that? I mean, what the fuck were you up to anyway?" In something like a first, Shelby seemed close to real anger as they got out of Viktor's car. "You were totally out of your league, going to the guy's house like that. He just might be a killer. That sounds like something I would do," he grumbled as he crossed the street toward his own house.

"I don't regard this as a compliment." Viktor disappeared into his old room.

By the time David actually got into bed, he was so tired that his legs ached. A wet spot on the ceiling had spread in an awkward pattern, like a cell out of control, and he couldn't stop looking at it. Then the rain started. Again. He recalled that when he was young, he used to sit in his family's enclosed back porch watching a storm, listening to it beat against the screens. What a delicious sense of protection, he inside, the torrent out there unable to get at him, and if his parents were fighting, as on a Saturday night, it was a good place to hide. The deluge seemed closer now, and he wondered how it would sound to the newly opened ears of Frances Hoekstra, alone in the house with a man who had undoubtedly tried to kill her. Suddenly he realized that if she'd lied about making her own drink, she must be protecting him—therefore, she had to know everything.

The very next day, without ceremony, Viktor was stripped of his temporary directorship of the institute. He told David that Thornton hadn't even looked up when he announced, "You're out, boy." As David approached his lab, everybody was whispering about Hoekstra's return, which had thrown the place into panic. How does one act around a man in that extraordinary circumstance? Nobody knew, but the newly reinstated director solved the problem by announcing a happy hour on the central bulletin board for that very day.

As for David Oster, he had the giddy sense of having lost everything. When someone had mismanaged his situation as badly as he had, who cared what his boss thought? He was lucky not to be in jail himself. The only reason for cheer, he was also in possession of a letter from Thornton confirming all the money and ship time due him and was clutching it in a file folder. If anyone tried to take it away from him, he was prepared for extreme measures. Predictably, Hoekstra summoned him almost immediately. On the way down the hall, his thoughts raced. What did the old man know about his activities, and when did he know it? He was rehearsing a look of total ignorance when Hoekstra appeared in the hallway, grabbed him by the shoulder, and steered him toward his office. All David could do was fling himself deep into the green velvet chair, affecting nonchalance.

"David," Hoekstra said in that awful baritone, "I feel that our relationship may need a bit of repair. I don't wish you to take personally what I am now about to say."

Bloody pictures filled David's head, much of it clearly actionable. He pulled himself up a bit, trying to get his bearings, and cleared his throat in preparation for God knows what.

"Remember what I told you at the beginning of the year?"

David coughed again, wondering what he could possibly mean. He had told him so many insane things that he was lost in the ozone of confusion. "About Viktor?"

"Of course not. I saw immediately that you'd come under his sway, the way everyone around here does. Once you're his creature, there's no hope."

"Ah," David said noncommittally.

He stood glowering in self-righteous fervor, quite a feat considering he had been released from jail only days before. "No clue?" He waggled that unnaturally long index finger of his. David shook his head stupidly. "I asked you to keep an eye on Shelby Burns," he said and leaned forward over the desk.

This was a surprise. The only person on his list of suspects who kept dropping down to the harmless level remained the object of Hoekstra's obsession. Perhaps the man really hadn't tried to kill his wife; he had been trying to kill Shelby, and something went awry, hence the repeated avowal of a "mistake." He must have been in love with Leah and wanted his rival dead.

"Yes, yes, of course you did, and I have been, I can assure you that."

"You have become his friend." This last word he made sound criminal.

"I wouldn't go that far." The minute he said this, David felt so craven for denying one of two people here who actually seemed to like him that he stood up. "Of course he's my friend. I'm not clear why you're inquiring into the matter."

Hoekstra turned away, his hulking back toward him as he stared out the window. "You are in receipt of a financial commitment from the university, are you not?"

David's file folder remained very close to his foot. "Yes. Thornton has signed off on it."

"I know, I know. Due to my own schedule, there's been a slight delay about going to sea, so you'll be free to prepare for your teaching duties. Later you can make all those little discoveries. Of course, it's even more essential now that I go with you." The ghoul was smiling as he turned back his direction.

"My duties?"

"After you teach Mysteries of the Sea."

Perhaps Hoekstra would be in the penitentiary by then? Or maybe David would be? Suddenly he saw his future as an eternity of dashed hopes perpetrated by semiprofessional criminals like this one.

"Is that legal?"

Hoekstra fixed him with an inhuman stare. It was like a horror movie, the vampire trying to drill holes through his chest with his eyes. "Any problem with that, Oster?"

"Yes, actually…"

"When I said watch Shelby Burns, I meant watch him like a hawk. Don't let him out of your sight. Wear those binoculars around your neck."

His face was turning red, and David sincerely hoped he would fall down and die. What did he care about the old man's vendetta against Shelby, who now, he remembered, actually possessed the binoculars himself? He decided to go on the offensive.

"I don't want to inquire into your personal life, Hoekstra, but wouldn't you say that the horses are out of the barn, so to speak?"

He fiddled now with an unlit cigarette and fixed upon him the full force of his awfulness. "What the fuck do you mean by that?"

"Aren't your problems somewhat bigger than Shelby Burns?"

"I don't think you really know my problems, Oster, and even if you did, I'd never take advice from some fruitcake from Southern California. I won't stand for your kind of moral degeneracy."

David went straight for his desk and slapped his hands down on it loudly. "You son of a bitch, how dare you talk morality to me?" He didn't know what he planned to do, but Hoekstra jumped back as if David were about to throw yet another punch.

When the phone rang, he grabbed it, shouted, "Yes," listened a moment, then flung his arm out, indicating the door. He waved so vigorously, the veins stood out in his neck, and David could hear him shouting into the receiver as he walked down the hall, "You have to do something! You must do something!"

David buried himself in his lab for hours. His head pounded with anxiety and self-loathing. This had been a pivotal moment in his career, because, after frittering away a fair amount of time at his postdoc, he had landed this potentially wonderful position, a chance to make a name for himself. He wasn't getting any younger, and youth, for a physicist, was about as important as it was for a starlet. Despite the demented Hoekstra, the Kinne Institute was well-known, and if the director of it failed to vouch for him, he wouldn't be able to get another job or funding anywhere else. These were not solid thoughts, but a feeling that expanded in his body like a balloon about to pop somewhere beneath his eyeballs.

In pain, he grabbed a tattered old folder that he always kept on his desk labeled "Big Trip." It contained historical information about all the intrepid researchers who'd gone down in the ocean in submersibles, and he had been keeping it for fifteen years, something to inspire him when he felt miserable about his work. He had begun it after a field trip to New York City with his high school class. This trip included the Coney Island Aquarium, where they got to see William Beebe and Otis Barton's 1930s bathysphere, a ball-like craft that measured four feet nine inches and weighed five thousand pounds. Packed into the tiny vessel, tethered to the ship with a thirty-five-hundred pound cable, the two scientists descended 1,426 feet under the ocean off Nonsuch Island in Bermuda and watched as the fish swam by. "The only other place comparable to these marvelous nether regions must surely be naked space itself," Beebe wrote and marveled at the awesome life he could see a half mile down, comparable to the magnificence of the planets and the stars.

In 1960, Jacques Piccard and Don Walsh took their own bathyscaphe to a depth of 35,820 feet at the Marianas Trench off Guam, and no one had since broken their record. It had long been David's dream to ride the *Eddy*, a modern submersible named after marine biologist Edward F. Ricketts, straight down to the Endeavour Segment of Juan de Fuca, and the amount of money he'd been given would actually make this possible. Not that such an adventure would advance his knowledge of physics one bit, but it would let him become an eyewitness to the extraordinary forces he could now only envision through abstract measurements visible on his charts.

These musings made him feel infinitely worse, and so when Viktor arrived at his office and announced that they must, absolutely must, attend the happy hour, David said, "I'm not going. I want to stay here with my dreams, as hopeless as they are."

Viktor stared at him a moment, then picked up his old file and leafed through some of the pictures, shaking his head. "You have to go."

"Please, you don't seem to understand my situation. I should be filling out job applications. Not that I'll get any of them. You're looking at a wasted life."

"Nobody cares what you actually do up here, David." Viktor was determined, and David decided that, after all, he might as well go and get drunk.

Happy hours were held in the institute common room, an uncomfortably minimalist setting furnished in fifties furniture that was either retro or just old, depending on your point of view. David had never liked it, especially not its uncomfortable square-backed leather chairs and its short little bulbous lamps that cast no light at all. Even the Lucite pendulum clock failed to cheer. The emotional landscape was even more oppressive, with people looking over their shoulders, not knowing what to do with a formerly suspected felon who also had just been reinstalled as their boss. A number of senior scientists were present, but it was mostly graduate students and assistants glancing at each other furtively and whispering. Was there any protocol for this situation? Hoekstra circulated and spoke to people he routinely ignored, intent on normalcy, but there was a serious problem with the punch, since everyone was afraid to drink it. Only after Hoekstra hoisted a tankard of the stuff himself did the assembled group pitch forward to imbibe. He had laced the brew with vodka, so things achieved a giddy hideousness, and Viktor kept raising his eyebrows at David as usual.

"Are you trying to tell me something?" David whispered to him above the din.

"Of course not, old man, just delighting in the tableau. I brought my Busy Bee honey bear in case the punch proved unsatisfactory." He pulled the distinctive plastic dispenser out of his jacket and squirted a shot into his mouth. David noticed that Hoekstra kept glancing over at the two of them, and when he told Viktor about their recent meeting, his former roommate's real reason for wanting to come to happy hour became clear. Obsessed, he kept repeating, "The dog, David, the dog, hasn't he asked after it?"

"He didn't say one word about the dog. Maybe it was her dog?"

"No, no, don't you remember the way he talked to it, like an SS officer on a railroad car? No woman would have that creature as a pet."

"You miss the dog. I can see it in your eyes. You miss the goddamned dog."

"I do not. And keep your voice down. There are spies everywhere."

"You fucking love that dog, Viktor. Where is it now?"

"He's still at the pound."

"Aha, you went to see him."

"I was just doing what any human individual would do, David, as opposed to yourself, who would let him rot down there."

"No, no, I assumed the owner would look for him there first and retrieve him."

"Tell Hoekstra. You must tell him, or they'll give him the gas."

"Jesus." It was too much. Elbowing his way among hysterical happy hour guests, David scribbled on a lab sheet "Your dog is at the animal shelter," folded it up, and handed it to his nerve-racked Latvian friend. "You find a way to get it to him," he told Viktor and exited the party.

Walking away from the institute, David contemplated his next move. He didn't have to think too long since he spotted the dreaded Thornton hotfooting it toward him, yelling, "Oster, Oster, the basketball team is on a streak. They could actually make it to the Final Four."

David had forgotten about the whole grotesque business, what with his extensive detective work.

"Do you have any idea what this means? For the first time in over forty years of basketball, we're about to win something. It was under my watch. I am proud to say that, sir, under my watch."

"Congratulations."

"So get to it. The preparations must begin!" He flung his arms up in a sort of cheerleader's salute and walked off.

David was trying to digest what this meant for his shaky career, when he thought he saw a ray of sunshine. It jetted down from the big gray cloud that hovered over Pyke City and began to spread, suffusing the sky with light and warmth. It seemed to promise all, to give back life. Yes, he could endure, possibly prevail, despite whatever fresh torments Hoekstra concocted for him, whatever asinine assignments Thornton demanded of him.

In the first real daylight he'd seen in what seemed like forever, he determined to grill Shelby, to force out of him whatever he was hiding, and, in addition, to get back those infamous binoculars. Hoekstra wanted vengeance, and you could bet that it wasn't about Shelby's extensive use of state cars, which continued despite the Escalade. For unclear reasons, that magnificent vehicle remained more often than not hidden in its owner's garage. In service of this, David walked over to his front porch, where the man stood nonchalantly by one of the pillars as a pretty dark-haired woman and a small boy played ball in the yard. My God, there was his wife, and a very comely one too, soft and curvy, dressed in the desperate peasant mode so favored in the Pacific Northwest. She lived! He stuck out his hand for an introduction and learned that it was indeed Ellie Burns and little Chuckers. When she smiled at him, he felt the weight of all his guilty knowledge of her husband's life.

"How about a walk around the block?" Shelby said to David.

"I want to come, I want to come," screamed Chuckers.

"Come on, kid." Shelby turned to David. "This man is a scientist. He won't say anything you can't hear."

The neighborhood was just beginning to show signs of springtime life. Chuckers muttered and sang, skipping all the while in front of them.

"Shelby, this guy Hoekstra has a serious problem with you. He's asked me to watch you now several times. Are you sure he doesn't know what you and the missus were doing that day?"

Chuckers was almost to the corner and no doubt couldn't hear them, but Shelby still spoke very softly. "Of course he knew about us. You couldn't fart in that house without his knowing. He's like a fucking vampire. He is a vampire."

"So the innocent little boff was...?"

"No boff is innocent, David. Don't you know that?"

Chuckers turned back and ran toward them, then gave out with a bright smile. "Hi again," he said to David.

"Hi," he said back. Shelby smiled at him fondly, the first time David had seen him give evidence of any paternal feelings. The little boy raced off toward a dachshund just coming around the corner. "How does this relate to the divine Leah, if I may ask?"

"It doesn't relate; it coexists."

"And Mrs. Hoekstra?"

"I'm in love."

"You're in love?" Now this was the last thing he'd expected, Shelby Burns in love. It was hard enough to get him to commit to a beer, let alone a person. "Congratulations."

Shelby gave him a pained, quizzical look.

"With whom?" The question hung alone in the empty air.

"I'll let you figure that out yourself," he said as they cycled back toward his house, son in tow.

David was so stunned he forgot to ask for the binoculars.

# CHAPTER 22

I T WOULD BE some days before David learned the identity of Shelby's beloved. All the man would divulge was that the affair with Mrs. Hoekstra had lasted longer than he originally said. Still, he seemed remarkably free of guilt about his multiple involvements.

He explained soberly, "I need the illicit. Don't you understand? Without it, I can't think of a reason for living."

As David sipped coffee in his lab, he contemplated Shelby's remark and the fact that he absolutely did not want to end up where Shelby was right now. Because of his feelings for Alexis, he intended to show seriousness and maturity in his actions toward her. How to behave from this point weighed upon him, and he drank in this determination along with the hot brew for a time, until he heard the unmistakable tones of Philo Smallett outside his door.

"Oster, Oster, let me in. It's no use trying to hide." The man he greeted seemed even more frenetic than usual. He threw down a bunch of newspapers on David's desk. "Read. Weep," he announced, then slapped his forehead with his hand.

Sure enough, the *Sentinel* was filled with scores, with names of stars, with the basketball team's emergence from the deep misery of years of sporting loss. While he read, Philo compulsively fingered some papers in a manila folder, thumbing through great yellow sheaves, which randomly fell on the floor around him.

"The die is cast. Our fate is sealed." That was his drift. He seemed to have gotten most of his phrases out of Emily Brontë, and he kept invoking the gods of bad weather to intervene.

"They play indoors, Philo."

"But nobody will come to see them. They'll stay home."

"No one cares about the weather here. It can be pouring, and people will be out in their sundresses. It's a continuing fight against reality, and you know it."

"Not if there's something really big. It's that time of year, you know, when the rain mixes with the storms coming out of northern Russia."

"Damn, we aren't that far from Russia, are we?"

"Through northern Alaska. It can be quite dramatic. I would think you, as a scientist, would know all about this. We need to pray." He was mumbling, still sorting through the interminable papers.

"It's ridiculous to look for divine intervention in this business. We'll just have to leave the state. It's what I've been waiting for, actually."

"Sorry, bub, no can do." He waved a note in front of him. "We are Thornton's personal guests at the next game, expected to meet the great Larson Kinne himself. Everybody will know it was us. We'll be introduced to all the rhubarb farmers that way."

David stared at the scope of his ruin, humiliated in front of colleagues, rich patrons, his new lover, even animals. The author of the performance, that's how he would be known.

Coinciding with the end of his career in physics, it was a fitting conclusion, but almost immediately he upbraided himself for his internal whining. "No mewling or puking" as Old Dave would say. After all, there were plenty of other things he could do. He could buy a piece of land around here, where it was cheap. Maybe start a junkyard. Perhaps a dead car farm or a discarded appliance dump?

Needless to say, he didn't mention these notions to Philo, who was still staring at him, and instead asked, "Have you ever done this before?"

Philo looked at David oddly, then jolted himself out of his haze. "Of course not. What do you take me for?"

"Not the horses, I mean meeting all the rhubarb farmers."

"No, it's considered a great honor, shaking hands with the big donors. There weren't any to meet recently, because the teams never won." He cackled hysterically now. "Maybe they won't win, or they'll all be killed in a bus accident—"

"How can they be killed? The next game takes place here."

"The black player could leave town, or we could bribe him."

"Philo, we've come down a long road together. We're almost at the end." David put his arm around the man's shoulders and wheeled him toward the window, where Oster Wet Scale rain came down at the rate of about 7.82. "That road is wet, it's bleak, but we're going to survive." He sounded like a preacher.

Philo looked up at him with cow eyes, and David could tell that for one second he believed, but that second passed, and the veil lifted, almost violently. "Don't kid yourself. We're fucked. I know whereof I speak." With that, he grabbed up his falling paper collection and backed out the door.

At last he called Alexis. Forewarned about the team's possible victory, she asked him to come over as soon as he had some free time. Formerly he would have catapulted himself to her house in an instant, but with his new resolve in place, he suggested an afternoon visit hours hence. When he finally spotted her in the late February twilight, he could only think how incredibly lovely she was, as fresh and startling as the day they had first met. Watching her in her silence and self-containment as she brushed the tails of the horses, he worried that she was positively beyond him. She had that reserve, that poise he had noticed in other "animal people," dog trainers and the like. How could she ever fall in love with him?

She smiled when she saw him and gave him a hug in what he interpreted as a hopeful sign. David's opening speech suggested the apocalypse or worse, but she refused to take any of it seriously.

"I've done things here you wouldn't believe."

His mind segued to a sexual theme, despite every good intention.

"They always seem to work out, just not the way you thought."

Drinking her hearty coffee, he was content to watch her wander around her kitchen, putting cups away, pouring a bit of cream, anything, really, to see those hands at work. She had a soothing quality, or perhaps he just imagined she did. If there was anything his recent romantic adventures had taught him, it was that he knew nothing; he thought he knew what he was doing, but he didn't. He didn't know what other people were doing either. In fact, the black hole of ignorance surrounding his life had, up until now, been profound and permanent. He wanted to convey all this to her, but she stopped him with a curious look that made him fear she might be reading his mind.

"I never thought I would be hanging out with Washington rhubarb farmers," David finally said.

"Hops, peas, and loads of apples, that's what they farm. I would describe them as practical, focused."

"Great. I just don't want them to focus on me."

They made arrangements to get together an hour before the so-called show to make sure everything was ready if and when it became necessary, but then he didn't want to leave. He wanted to tell her he loved her, if only he could find any sort of language that would be real. Explanations were the very life-blood of courtship, it seemed to him, although his father was of the "tell them nothing" school of thought. "The less women know, the happier they'll be. They live in a dream world, David, just swimming around in the emotional ether."

Alexis didn't look dream worldly, but he wasn't sure if it was too soon for such a conversation. "I'd like to talk to you," was as deep as he could get. They kissed, and before anything else was said, he found himself making love to her on the floor.

Afterward she said nothing about his wish to "talk," so he figured he'd met the one and only woman who didn't hunger after discussions.

"See you before the big event," was all he could muster, and she kissed him with that soft burning mouth of hers.

He emerged from her house into a real storm. Driving down the stone road, he saw black clouds in front of him that looped around each other in circles over the horizon. Steely rain pummeled the back of his jacket, and sharp needles rico-cheted off the hood of his car, truly an over-the-top Russian-Alaskan downpour, no doubt about it. Could this stop the team? A thousand-pound steelhead trout couldn't stop them now.

Despite his elaborate new residence, Viktor had taken to reoc-cupying David's house whenever he felt like it, and David never found any reason to object. On this particular evening, drinking red wine and staring morosely up at the dome, Viktor for once appeared drunk. His eyes wandered, and he returned to the same subject over and over again, Lucy.

"She doesn't love me, old man. Now I see that. She walked past me today on the road, and I might as well have been a spike."

"Speck? Is that what you mean?"

"Speck. Less than a speck."

"You personally cannot change the sexual inclinations of another person, Viktor," but as David said this, he wondered how explicit he was going to have to get with him.

"Of course I can, like Lohengrin. Force of personality is what mystical sex is about. She has to feel the force of my sex."

"Mystical sex, hmm, possibly I haven't had that." The pounding was terrifically loud on the roof, and he began to worry about the condition of the dome.

"You have, David. I know you have."

"Viktor, she lives with a woman. And I'm pretty sure that's not the first—"

"Stop. I can't bear to think about it. It's making me sick." Viktor motioned toward Marina's house, and suddenly he brightened. "But it's good that no man is my rival. Excellent, in fact. I should be happy. I can beat out any woman, especially that coma woman, even if she is still alive. How's the poisoning detective work?"

So he did know about Lucy and Frances! Was this why he hadn't wanted to visit the woman in the hospital, because she was his rival?

"I'm still trying to figure out who made her drink. It must have been Hoekstra, but how did he know there was denatured alcohol under the sink? Wouldn't people have seen him rummaging around under there during the party?"

"So many people, David, all swaying with the belly person."

"Fuck, is this weather normal?" It was beginning to sound scary.

"It's not too bad. Could be worse."

"As in Noah and the flood?"

"Don't know him." He started cackling and fell forward onto the floor. Rather than try to lift his logy body, David straightened him out and put a blanket over him. Viktor curled his hands under his chin and smiled up at him like a fallen Buddha. "I am resting, dear boy." Then he passed out.

Shelby's lights were on, so David figured he, too, was formulating a defensive strategy against the rain, and undoubtedly this would include a quantity of buckets, some of which David might be able to borrow. Despite the hour, he ran across the street and knocked on his door. It opened to a domestic scene, with Ellie sipping something out of a mug, while Chuckers's little head rested on her lap. Shelby was hard at work on a chair leg, which he was sanding.

"Hey, Professor. Come have some hot chocolate." Shelby's hands were covered in dust, and he wiped them on a towel, then went into the kitchen to get David a cup.

Ellie waved at David and smiled, putting her finger to her lips to warn him to be quiet. He sat on the couch and sipped the cocoa, marveling at the peacefulness of this scene. Even knowing the base behavior that lay hidden under the rug, it still seemed appealing, still like the kind of life he would never have, doomed always to be outside someone else's family, looking in. How on earth did Shelby carry off his indiscretions with, it seemed, nary a ripple in the marital calm? To his credit, he apparently didn't want to be found out. His love life appeared to be without aggression, whereas some guys David knew tortured their wives with obvious late-night activities.

Shelby took him up into what he called his reading room, part of an attic blocked off by two-by-fours, with a desk, a chair, and a couple of wooden shelves. The book collection tended toward *How to Build Your Own Home*, which he had recently used, and *Paint: Varieties and Suppliers*. He reached into the desk drawer and brought out a bottle of clear liquid, then picked out two liqueur glasses. He poured them both thick streams of grappa.

"Buckets, Shelby, I sense that I'm going to need buckets!"

"There are plenty out in the garage. Don't worry."

The rain thundered down upon the roof. It was horrible, as if the heavens had a migraine.

"Do you have a plan, I mean a personal one of some kind? Your wife seems like a lovely woman."

Shelby stared at him, apparently assessing the risk of telling the truth, then reached behind the desk and handed David the binoculars. "I thought you might need these back," he said.

Feeling tremendously guilty at the thought of conspiring against the man or even of suspecting him, David didn't know what to say and looked down in silence.

"In fact, I don't have a plan. I've sort of been floating along, living on crumbs."

"You seem remarkably unconcerned about other people's husbands." David offered this as the second glass of grappa went down.

"If they were real husbands, I wouldn't be in the picture. I was doing a public service."

"Noble of you."

Shelby poured them each a third glass, although the rumbling in his stomach should have told David not to drink it. "What I really have here is a problem of choice. I have to choose, and I know it's going to be soon. I don't want to choose. I want everything the way it is now."

Aha, the fourth woman, besides Ellie, Leah, and Frances. Perhaps now David would learn her name. But he was conscious that the grappa had hold of his brain and was trying to break it apart because he heard yet another terrific noise. Was it knocking, banging?

"Am I drunk, or are there sounds other than weather approaching?"

Shelby looked around like a watchdog, sniffing the air. "Goddammit, you're right, Professor." He leapt out of his chair and stood listening at the top of the stairs. A definite banging.

Downstairs, Chuckers was nowhere to be seen, and neither, for the moment, was Ellie. Someone pounded loudly on the door.

"Who the hell is it?" David asked.

Shelby pulled a rain jacket from out of the front closet and opened the door a crack, finally going outside. There, on the front stoop, David could see Leah, her hair streaming down her shoulders, down clothing that was plastered to her body. Crying Shelby's name over and over again, crossing her arms up under her magnificent breasts, which rose out of the darkness like wet fruit, she glanced at David with a stricken look. Shelby grabbed her arm and steered her onto the lawn.

"Go ahead. I'll take care of things here," David said, carried away by the insanity of the moment.

They moved off down the front path, holding each other close. The minute David closed the door, he knew he was in trouble. Where was Shelby's wife, and what disgusting lie would he have to tell to clean the business up? In service of this potential sham, he stood there holding the heavy binoculars, listening for Ellie's footsteps above the din of the storm. Finally he went into the kitchen, just in time to hear her coming down the stairs.

"David, are you still here?" She had on a thick velvet robe, and her hair was piled on top of her head, like a madonna.

"Yes, yes, Shelby asked me to wait for him…" He was about to go on, but she cut him off.

"Ah," she said calmly. "He's out?"

"Yes, just for a moment." They stood there listening to the blasts of rain that pummeled the house. No one sane would go out in this weather, no one at all, not even Shelby.

"Would you like something to drink?"

"I just had some grappa, and I think I'm a little drunk already. I'd better stop." There was a momentary bleep in time during which they stood silent, and then she came over and spoke to him quietly. "It's all right. You can go home. If I need you, I'll call."

"Shelby said I could borrow some buckets, and I'll do that if you don't mind, but you can call me if you need me. I'll see you with these." He waved the binocs at her, and as he burbled on, she showed him the door to the garage.

Outside, buckets in hand, David saw that the rain had gone solid it was so thick. He turned back to look up at her window, where she moved in the strange light, before stumbling toward his own house.

# CHAPTER 23

B Y THE TIME David made it to his own house, his jacket was soaked, heavy like a tarp, almost as heavy as the buckets he was carrying. In his earlier hurry, he had forgotten keys, wallet, and cell phone, so now he was reduced to pounding on the front door, which Viktor must have locked while in a drunken stupor. David circled around the yard, slogging through mud to peer into windows, and finally he spied him in the kitchen, sitting shit-faced beside a glass bowl. While David pounded on the back door, the older man merely stared upward, then moved the bowl over slightly to catch errant drops, wiping his face all the while. By this time "torrential" was an understatement for the velocity of those drops. It was a howling, screeching gale, the kind he had seen only in tropical hurricanes.

David banged with two fists and screamed his name. Viktor looked around, waggling his neck curiously, as if shaking water out of his ears.

"Open the door, you fucking criminal!"

After a shuffle of movement, the door swung open with a blast of rain, and he almost fell into the drunken man's arms.

"David, David, what on earth are you doing out in weather like this?"

He was gasping for breath, and a lake of water was falling off his clothes. "Oh, just wandering around enjoying the countryside."

"Well, this is hardly the time to do it."

"You drunken bum. I could have died out there." David registered Viktor's costume, a slicker and Bermuda shorts.

"But I thought you were in here."

"When last you were conscious, I was."

"Ah yes, I did imbibe, did I not?" Viktor cackled, then grabbed his arm. "We have a serious emergency, my boy. Thank God you brought buckets."

"Nothing weather related could upset me after the night I've had. Shelby appears closer than ever to a romantic meltdown."

Viktor waved him off. "Shelby always has a crisis. My home building was a rest from the sexual soup in which he swims."

Viktor took him by the hand and led him into the living room. Two buckets dotted the floor, and rain fell steadily into each one, but it also poured onto the yellow carpet and the yellow silk chairs.

"Oh my God." David looked up; it seemed to be raining pretty hard at various points inside the whole house, hardest even through the dome. "Other than the buckets, what can we do?"

"Pray, drink, dance around in the rain, and then we can drink some more."

"You were drunk when I left, Viktor."

"Silly boy, I was not. You see how brilliantly I adorned myself in foul weather gear." He pulled his slicker up some, wiping water off his face. Just as he did so, the rain stopped. It stopped instantly and completely. A shocking, drippy silence followed the pounding.

"This is the way it always is," Viktor whispered.

David whispered back, "Does rain like this happen often?"

"It happens, it happens…I can't remember…maybe two years ago."

They stood staring around at the sodden interior. Chairs and carpet were soaked through, the buckets were full to over-flowing, and water still dripped from the ceiling. The weather had actually moved inside the house; it was the end of shelter as they knew it.

"What the hell. It needed a good cleaning." David wanted to focus on whatever bright side was plausible and determined to sober his roommate up with some strong coffee.

Resigned to it all, the two men sat on the front porch swilling the dark brew and waiting for the dawn. Looking back, David thought a kind of madness had set in. They no longer had any refuge and had no choice but to fall asleep in their wet clothes, wrapped in blankets on their damp beds.

The next morning the house looked even worse than it had the night before. "We will open doors, and the sun will cure all." Viktor went from window to window, flinging each one open. The sun indeed was out, and it illuminated the bleeding yellow of the place. It did little to cheer David up. Seeing Leah last night had reminded him that he'd promised to attend her class that very morning—the last place he wanted to be.

"Because of you, Viktor, I have to go to a class with young people and with Leah, whom I ran into last night with Shelby in a very uncomfortable situation. I don't have time to stand here and clean up."

"Don't worry. I'll fix everything. I am so grateful for having lived in your house; I'll fix it up perfect."

Soon they would have worms, was David's only thought as he walked toward the campus, but then an even more horrible possibility struck him. Would Leah actually show after the crisis of the night before? If she didn't, he might be compelled to cover for her. Would he, God forbid, actually have to talk to the young people of the state of Washington? David panicked as he watched the students pile into the giant lecture hall, so many of them, enough to muster several platoons. The clock kept ticking, the kids kept filing in, plentiful, no doubt, because Leah's beauty had increased enrollment, especially among the athletes. In fact, it appeared whole teams had signed up for this class, and they sat in well-muscled clumps leafing through real pages of real books.

David had just begun devising plan B, which consisted of his lecturing on the significance of rogue waves in the imagination of Herman Melville, or some such rot, when none other than the dreaded President Royce Thornton walked through the door. He stood uncertainly at the top row of seats, looking around, and it occurred to David that he must greet their president. Up the steps he went, hoping against hope that Melville was a subject dear to Thornton's heart.

"David, just wanted to hear Professor Burnett, a genius, I've heard, just brilliant."

"Wonderful, I didn't know you were interested in literature."

Thornton jerked a bit and then glared at him. He seemed to be having trouble breathing.

"Is anything wrong?"

He started coughing and wiping his nose with his ever-present handkerchief. "Isn't this the lady scientist, the one

doing"—now he pulled a syllabus out of his jacket pocket—
Lake Trout: Habits and Availability?" All became clear. Thornton had the latest list of topics for next year's Wet and Wild
and had gotten the classes mixed up. He wanted to know about
fishing, and Shakespeare's *The Tempest* was the furthest thing
from his mind.

David took his arm. "Professor Burnett is in the English
Department."

Once again he registered alarm. "I must have my days
confused, but no matter. I love a book. Many's the time I've
said to Lettice, 'I love a book,' and you can quote me on that."
He grinned toothily. David ushered him down the steps, and
Thornton took a seat beside him in the front row. "Tremendous
number of bodies in this room, Oster, just tremendous. Do
they do a head count?"

"You mean call the roll?"

"Of course."

"No, no, I think they prove their attendance by writing the
papers and passing the exams."

He looked at him as if he had announced the discovery of
fire. "Excellent. Good plan."

The students, David noticed, tended to get rowdy when
not actually occupied in a task or focused on a point of
attention at the front of the class. He began to hyperventi-
late. Rogue waves were no substitute for Leah's boobs, and
he knew that he could have three hundred enraged children
of Washington at his throat while the president of the school
looked on. As soon as the hands of the clock hit five past the
hour, Thornton turned toward him, lifting his wrist, help-
fully pointing at his own watch. David nodded and tried to
breathe, but the tide of talk was rising, and who knew when a
fistfight might break out?

Suddenly the rustling moved its trajectory, and heads turned. There Leah was, striding down the steps as if last night had never happened. In white blouse, black jacket and skirt, she looked truly stunning, and even the most doltish of the athletes roused themselves to observe. She now did something that heightened the tension. She took off her jacket, revealing those perfectly formed breasts, round in their white cocoon. David glanced at Thornton to see his reaction. He squinted over his nose through his half glasses, looking perplexed. Right then David suspected that he had no idea who this woman was, though she had been on the staff for at least four years. The man who could forget Leah Burnett was no man at all.

David eyeballed the auditorium, where the students now gave her their full attention, no rustling, no coughing, just a quiet sexual hum. Then she began to speak. In conversation, her voice sounded rough, not gravelly, but a little husky. Now it rang out vivid and strong in the great hall as she talked of writers of the sea for the last two thousand years, Viking to Anglo-Saxon to Celt to Virginia Woolf and inevitably, even including Joseph Conrad. In a nod to the village drama, or maybe just to David, she actually read a passage from *Victory*, one of Hoekstra's favorite sources for his letters. She was the bearer of the beauty of the ages, and kids he assumed to be meatheads had gone quiet and thoughtful. Even the gum chewers rested their jaws and listened to her, entrapped in her poetic visions. With such beautiful art before him, David almost wanted to cry. Where was he? Where was his own work?

The hour swept on, propelled by the majesty of the authors she invoked. Thornton stared at her and actually seemed to listen, but unfortunately, it was over too soon. She wrapped things up with a poem by Wallace Stevens, "The Idea of Order at Key West," which began, "She sang beyond the genius of the sea," and the mighty words sounded through the room as she summoned up the mysterious heart of nature itself. No one knew she was finished until she pulled her shoulders back, picked up her jacket, and once again covered those precious breasts. A sigh went up, then thunderous applause. Even the specter of salmon fishing off the Columbia River would never get them so worked up.

As they continued to clap and cheer, Thornton leaned over and whispered, "Brilliant, brilliant, Oster. Where did you find her?"

"She works here, sir."

"Of course, you're right," he said, without conviction. "I've seen her before. But I thought she was a secretary or something low, you know, lower down..."

"On the food chain?"

"Exactly. I can't keep track of all our personnel. I can't police everybody." The unnaturally chatty Thornton had him cornered, but David turned away and clambered over several rows of seats to grab Leah and thank her.

"That was wonderful. Guaranteed to outdo even 'Tide Pools and You.'"

She laughed.

"Please say you'll teach a class for me, or two, or three, no matter how much your husband hates me."

She smiled again and buckled up a swanky black briefcase. "Of course, for you, David, anything." She looked not one wit less attractive for her late-night visit to Shelby.

"Your career has also taken an upward turn, as our president now seems to know who you are."

"He didn't know me?"

"That stream is not swiftly running, if you read me."

"I do." She ran her hand through her hair and looked after the retreating students, still silent about the ravages of the previous evening.

David touched her on the arm. "Are you all right?"

"I'm not sure," she said, then walked up the long steps away from him.

Thornton had been watching this colloquy from nearby, and before David could follow her out, he stopped him. "This has been a fantastic hour, Oster. The sheer knowledge of books gained here, incredible. She did forget one person, though, Robert Service, poet and great man. 'Oh how I love the laughing sea, Sun lances splintering; Or with a virile harmony in salty caves to sing.' 'Sea Sorcery,' do you know it?" The only thing worse than talking to Thornton was hearing him recite poetry. "Above all, Oster, and this you can never forget, bodies, bodies everywhere. That's the key to this kind of thing. Your class could have twice as many."

As they emerged into the sunlight, Thornton steered him along the sidewalk. "Excuse me, sir, I'll be back with you in a moment." David raced over to where Leah was talking with a few students and hustled her off under a tree. "Are you really all right? Tell me how I can help you."

She looked searchingly into his face. "It's over, David. I love him, but he doesn't love me. I was hoping to get away from Larry and make a life with Shelby…"

At this, he started. Tough concept, this "life with Shelby" thing.

"He doesn't love me at all. I need to turn around and face who I am and deal with it."

David bent down and kissed her on the cheek, though he sensed Thornton looming somewhere near them. "I'm such a failure at love myself, I don't know how to talk about it even, but you'll be much happier when you do that, I know." For a moment he sounded like a grown man, but just then he heard a characteristic snort raffling toward them and had to suppress a laugh.

"By way of reward, I have decided that you have reconnoitered this hill yourself, you have planted your flag, and far be it for me to tear that flag down. You found this woman, Oster"—Thornton was vaguely embracing her now himself—"for Mysteries of the Sea, which will be your class exclusively. You shall be Wet and Wild—yes, I know the nickname—for the duration."

A power spike surged up David's spine, jolting him with "no, no, no," but he couldn't choke out a word. The rest of his natural life—let's see, conservatively another forty-five years—would he be up in front of three hundred innocent youths, teaching them how to fish? Would he begin tying flies and putting on waders? An image of himself as some very fat guy on a television comedy flashed before his eyes. It was not him. That was critical. This could not be him.

# CHAPTER 24

THE WALK BACK home to his ruined rental could not have been long enough that sunshiny afternoon in March. There was nothing in his professional future that he could look forward to with anything but dread. Hearing all that poetry had fired up his personal desire to go to sea, but also the grim knowledge that he wasn't doing anything about it, that he couldn't. Soon his work would consist of cheering on bikini-clad bimbos as they demonstrated water volleyball to three hundred undergraduates.

When he finally trudged into the house, Viktor lay in wait and raced toward him, but not before he could see the state of what surrounded them. Sun had compounded last night's problem; stains had dried irregularly on the yellow silk chairs, the still-sodden carpet was slowly baking, and the whole house had a biologically active smell. The house hadn't dried; it had composted.

"It is drying, David, it is. I can feel it, slowly though, slowly."

David grimaced at him and went upstairs, drained and depressed. Sleep presented the only solution, then maybe the car's exhaust pipe down his throat, but as he lay down on the bed, he couldn't stop obsessing over the villains in his benighted landscape, his boss, the university president, maybe even his roommate. The $6 million commitment could be a total fake. The only person who presented an image of warmth and solidity in his life was Alexis, and he made himself think of her as much as he could. Trying to rest his mind, each time he closed his eyes, he pictured working at Juan de Fuca, managing his equipment, making his calculations. Down there, in that torrid, turbid world of extremes, how could he discern the workings of a fifth force so slight that it showed itself in traces, in small tugs at the universe? The other four forces are loud and noisy; they hit you in the head, or they blow you up. But the fifth force is like the potential energy of a hummingbird's wings, only known in its sly beatings. David was self-aware enough to realize that his desire to pin down this hitherto unknown force was, in part, a wish to rule all the elements impinging upon him, even while sensing that they were uncontrollable. Still, he felt certain that if he completed measurements around Juan de Fuca, he would come close to measuring its existence firsthand. But first he had to get there.

He must have drifted off, dreaming of green women under the sea, when suddenly Viktor's gleaming face appeared above him. "David, David, wake up."

"This had better be important because I could shoot someone today. Do you understand?"

"I do, of course I do, but it's Shelby."

"I'm sick of Shelby."

"I know, but he says it's urgent, that he and 'a friend' want to see you right now. There is no other time possible."

"No, I refuse to participate in that lunatic's life. Do you hear me? I refuse to participate in his life!" He yelled this last bit toward the window, in the general direction of Shelby's house, but Viktor put his hands over his ears.

"Be quiet, dear boy. He's not even there. He just came by and said you must meet 'them' right away at the coffeehouse."

"I'm trying to sleep." David rolled away from him.

In what seemed like moments, Viktor was back, this time looking really worried, peering down at him like a medical doctor. Viktor rarely worried. He affected the attitude that life was too absurd to fret over, but this time he seemed truly agitated.

"He wants you now, David. I do believe that it really is serious."

"Why hasn't somebody shot Shelby? That's what I'd like to know."

"Oh, he's good with a gun himself."

David got up in a rage, waving the man out. No one's company seemed attractive, but he might as well just go because Viktor was now in hounding mode, which meant he would give up only when tanks appeared.

Even the sunny afternoon, something he had awaited since September, failed to cheer him as he walked the glistening streets. Everything and everyone were too smiley. They should be depressed, like himself. As he walked toward the Bean, he guessed that Shelby must have changed his mind, and he felt resigned to his spiriting away the second most beautiful woman in town. Perhaps Shelby had determined on some end to the ridiculous couplings and recouplings going on, and now obviously David would have to encourage him, be "supportive," in that particular way that he loathed.

Inside the Bean, where he recognized Shelby's wide back, the man turned and waved, then motioned David to a table in the corner, behind the sacks of coffee. He decided to delay by getting a stiff swig of espresso, so he waited while they fussed and fumbled with the grinder, but once he held the steaming cup in his hand, the moment could be postponed no longer. As he maneuvered between the bags, trying not to scald youthful Washingtonians, he barely looked up. When he did, he almost dropped his cup. It was not the winsome, poetic Leah; it was not the wifely little woman; it was Frances, none other than Frances Hoekstra herself, looking positively radiant. She smiled; she cuddled Shelby's arm; she laughed like a girl. David backed away, stopped, then started forward again. Could this be the fourth woman, actually the third and fourth?

Shelby pulled out a chair, and he had to sit down. "I hope you'll be cool about this, but I thought we should explain before we leave town."

"Leave town?" David coughed into his brew. "What are you talking about?"

Shelby took Frances's hand in his own now, and the happy couple sat beaming at him. Somehow people in love, even if they are a midget and a giant, emit a fatal dewiness. It would be rotten to ruin it, so he just sat there, prepared for the worst.

"I told you I had to make a choice, and I did."

Frances leaned forward, fixing David intently. "You played a special role in our lives, don't you see? We thought you should know first."

"Know what? I mean, are you guys kidding?" He realized right away that calling Frances "guy" was stretching it. "Mom" would have been more like it. Now she looked crestfallen. She had, after all, recently come back from the dead. Who would have imagined that on her return, she would encounter Shelby and mistake him for someone she could trust?

Shelby straightened himself up in his chair, and David noticed that he was actually wearing a blue shirt and a spiffy sports jacket. "I didn't confide in you because of our mutual acquaintances, but shit, man, I knew you would understand."

"What I understand is that you're stealing the wife of a man who may have tried to kill her once, in public, in full view of fifty people." He spoke loudly, and Frances clasped her lover's arm and put her finger to her lips.

"He'll be glad, then, that we're leaving," Shelby said, not illogically.

"I don't think so."

"No, no, David, it must have been an accident," Frances said. He couldn't decide whether she was willfully naïve or just dim-witted. "He did make the drink himself. I saw him, but I'm sure he picked up the wrong bottle or made some mistake."

"The only mistake, lady, is you sitting here," he wanted to say. Then another line came to him; "Flee, flee this one too. He'll probably try something himself in a year or two, and he will definitely plan it better." But nothing came out of his mouth.

"We love each other, and we're going to make a life together, not here," Shelby said.

"You're damn right not here. He's loading his shotgun this very minute. This must be the reason he wanted me to watch you, Shelby. He must have known all about your affair."

"Don't you think we know that? We're leaving on Thursday. You're the only person we've told because we trust you, David," said the lying philanderer, looking him right in the eye.

Frances rose. "I'll be back in a minute." She sidled through the coffee bags.

David leaned over to Shelby. "What the fuck are you doing?"

"I'm leaving town and going straight."

"Sure you are, Shelby, sure. What about your wife and little Chuckers?"

"They don't want me around. In fact, she got into business school at the University of Washington. Listen, she's been ignoring me for years, and Chuckers, he's eight now. He's an independent little guy, and he'll do fine. He'll visit me plenty."

"But why Frances?" He knew the very asking of the question in a certain tone of voice could end their friendship, but it seemed about to end anyway. Shelby frowned a moment and sipped his coffee. "Look, I know you. You are not, so to speak, a one-woman man."

"You know me here, David. I feel like a piece of shit compared to all these educated guys. What do I do? Fix houses, fix cars, all of it good work, but just crap to the brainy jerks wandering around town. They're everywhere."

"Still, Shelby, I'm not prejudiced or anything, but she has to be…years older than you." He didn't want to number those years, but they brought her damn close to Medicare.

Shelby just smiled now as if his companion were hopelessly infantile, then leaned forward and whispered, "*She owns department stores.*"

David had known that already, of course, but was so accustomed to Shelby being motivated by sex, not money, that the remark surprised him. Before he could respond, Frances reappeared, carrying a brownie and another cup of coffee.

Then suddenly their scary little domestic drama was interrupted as the world of basketball, specifically March Madness, erupted right in the coffeehouse. It started as a vibration, then a hum of conversation, then a chant. Six or seven students rose as one and started screaming at the television screen perched atop the counter, "Steelheads, Steelheads," on and on. Several other people stood, jabbing their fists in the air, kissing each other, and jumping up and down.

"It's karma," Shelby said, grinning. "The universe thinks we're cool."

"It's basketball, and there's nothing cool about it. My fate is sealed. They seem to be on their way to the Final Four," David said. Frances gave him a puzzled look as she munched her brownie. The crowd exploded again. It appeared the team had won. "I can't explain my role in this, really. All I can say is if you're determined to do so, you've picked the very best time to run away together, right before the big game on Friday."

"Shit, man, I never miss a game," Shelby said. "We can't leave. This is their first winning season in modern history."

"Don't endanger yourself for a sporting event, Shelby. In fact, I myself plan to skip town. Could I go with you?" David's speech got Frances to laugh, but Shelby seemed serious about staying.

"We can keep our secret a few more days," he said to his ladylove. As he got up to leave, though, it occurred to David that they were hardly furthering their deception by sipping coffee together in public.

Out on the street, David watched them depart together, and watching Frances from the rear was a very big deal. Maybe Shelby really did mean to change his life, since he was obviously not destined for gainful employment, so why not please a rich and very sweet woman? She was attractive, she was charming, and she might leave him all her worldly goods, or he might take them away in a van. David laughed out loud at the thought of Shelby as a department store mogul, but he was pleased that at least now he could eliminate him as a suspect.

These strange thoughts confounded David as he strolled up toward his office. He knew he should immediately seek out Philo Smallett, but that wasn't necessary, as the man already occupied a chair in his lab. "Have you heard?"

"Yes, unfortunately."

"I was counting on them to lose. No one can be trusted these days, least of all students. Snot-nosed little shitheads. The black kid must have inspired them."

"It's their job to win, Philo. I mean, it's not un-American."

"Oh, shut up. I'm totally beyond an appeal to patriotic sentiments. What I want to know is, shall we go with the woman's plan? It's two nights away, you know."

"Don't you mean, do we have tickets and to where?"

"They'll just find us and drag us back."

"Look, Alexis knows what she's doing." David hoped to God she knew, because he certainly didn't.

Just when it seemed the big game couldn't become any more apocalyptic, Viktor greeted him at home by announcing that he planned to turn the game into a reconciliation party with Lucy, so he had invited Marina to come with them, although he feared she would bring the ferret.

"Viktor, this really isn't a fiesta, OK? It's a certified disaster, the end, kaput, *finito* of yours truly."

"You're so negative, David. The bright side is just around the corner."

"Right, the corner of another state. What the hell? Do whatever you want. Only I'm going to be behind the scenes when the throwing of large vegetables begins." Also, possibly, the throwing of the ferret. Did Lucy know that her beloved was leaving town with Shelby? Probably not, but there was no way David was getting into the middle of that particular quarrel.

Viktor eyeballed David seriously. "You see, I thought Shelby would provide us with drama, but it is you, dear boy, the least likely, if I may say so."

"Why least likely? I've had plenty of drama in my life, too much, as a matter of fact."

"Don't go on so. I believe you, but as usual, you completely misunderstand me."

"That's right. I don't understand you, and I don't understand anything or anyone else either."

"Oh my God, don't take your neuroses so seriously. It doesn't become you!" For the first and only time, Viktor seemed genuinely angry with him, so enraged that he didn't speak to David at all for the next two days.

During this interval, David had talked to Alexis several times to arrange the upcoming festivities. She had been rehearsing the horses with the cheerleaders, arranging costumes, even one for herself. He tried to help as best he could, but she seemed so competent, so unafraid of what he saw as a potentially horrendous event, that he didn't want to infect her with his fears. It had become an overriding concern not to appear too "young" in front of her, unserious, self-obsessed, naively focused only on the problems of his own work. Alas, this concern had effectively shut him up. He was tongue-tied and kept his communications with her brief, but he hoped heartfelt. For her part, she had taken to teasing him about the physics of horses and girls falling onto the basketball floor. Had he calculated this properly? Would the fifth force impinge on gravity, allowing their pompoms, inexplicably, to hover a tenth of an inch above the floor? Impossible calculations, as was everything else in his world.

As David and Viktor made their way on that dreaded Friday evening to Crestole Pavilion, which was already full up with Steelhead fans, the two men still weren't talking to each other much. Viktor went up into the stands, while David rummaged around behind the scenes, hearing with a gathering sense of doom the roars, the chants, the unbridled violence that was embodied in any crowd of sports fans when their team was on a winning streak. He searched for Alexis, getting lost amidst television cables, coolers of Gatorade, and absurdly tall men, until finally he found her behind the building itself, calming Jerry and Murray while combing their tails. They looked grand, incredibly so, but she had brought along two other horses as well.

"Who the hell are these guys?"

"They'll be fine. They're ancient. I thought two looked skimpy."

"'Skimpy' is the least of our problems."

Blue-and-green satin skirts hung down to hide their mangy haunches, and the brushing had resulted in a pleasantly furry hide on all of them. Their eyes were open, almost bright, so perhaps the drugs hadn't kicked in yet.

"Are they going to be stoned?" David certainly hoped so.

Alexis shook her head. "I hope they don't need it. They've been calm all week, and I've been feeding them extra barley with some herbs to mellow them out."

He grabbed her arm. "Alexis, these are horses, not hippies! Out there is chaos."

"I know."

"No, you don't know." His voice was rising.

"Just relax. I've been lulling them to sleep each night with a CD of screaming Marines. I got it from the recruiting center." She handed him a disk labeled *Semper Fi, Sounds of the Corps in Action*.

"Oh God." He was hyperventilating as the sounds of the crowd grew even louder. Not knowing what else to do, he sat down on a cardboard box, expecting the worst. Viktor had performed the ultimate sacrifice and loaned him his flask, from which he now took a swig. It was that Latvian stuff, Black Balsam, and he held the thing out to Alexis, who shook her head no.

"I should be sober during this, David."

"I should be drunk." He proceeded immediately to imbibe a significant portion of the flask's contents in gulps taken in thirty-second intervals, while the noise rose like a wave from a place that seemed four hundred miles away. Murray, Jerry, and their two companions remained calm even though David kept lurching over to them and patting their manes. Perhaps God would intervene, and the team would lose. But the Steelheads were on a streak. If you haven't won anything for over forty years, the Lord perceives you as an empty bowl, so the yogis say, and there was no doubt this was one deep-down, bottomless-pit empty bowl.

Philo Smallett was nowhere to be seen, but David spotted Thornton approaching; even through his liquored-up haze, he recognized that manic grin. "We're winning, Oster. Money and bodies, money and bodies. It couldn't be better. Are you ready?"

Alexis gave him a thumbs-up, or was it the finger? In any case, he snorted as he turned back to David.

"Play your cards right, and this could be an annual thing."

David tried to say, "I'm so glad," but it came out something like "I have sore gums."

Thornton slapped him on the back. "Go to a dentist. You've got the money now." Off he lurched, waving back jauntily. "Come up and meet Larson Kinne later."

Only then did David remember he was supposed to socialize with a man who was that absolute real thing, a genius. What would Kinne think of him after this whole catastrophe?

With each loud buzzer came another series of shouts and a horrendous chant that went, "Steelheads, Steelheads, crush them dead." After what seemed like forever, a hush fell. It was half time.

Still backstage, David was beginning to feel more confident, sort of, and sat down on a camp chair as the girls trooped out in front of him, wearing their blue-and-green short skirts, singing along to the strains of "Washington, My Home." Over the PA system, the announcer counseled the crowd to stay in their seats after the game, because a "stupendous extravaganza" would follow if the Steelheads won. David's head hurt, and he leaned back in his chair against the wall, contemplating the scene before him, willing the horses to remain calm. He must have dozed off because when he woke up, the game was thundering forward in a clear crescendo. That could mean only one thing.

"Out of the desert, into the oasis, we will win. 'We,' I said 'we,' didn't I?" David murmured, and Alexis came over to kiss him on the forehead. "Yikes, I'm one of them now." He started sweating.

"Just sit here, David, and I'll take care of everything. Better yet, go out into the stands with Viktor."

David hated to leave her alone there, but she decisively shoved him toward the waiting crowd. Reluctantly he strode out toward the basketball court, staring all the while at five thousand hungry Western Washington State University mouths, pouring diet soda, contraband beer, and popcorn down their gullets. He looked up at the scoreboard: 118 to 110. They were going to win. Thornton, Mrs. Thornton, the hateful Hoekstra sans Frances, Philo Smallett, and a very tall man, Larson Kinne or possibly a rhubarb farmer, occupied a central box, but there was no way David would put his head into that particular noose. Tempted to flee the whole place altogether, he suddenly spotted Viktor's waving hand and his ridiculous smile flashing out at him, and, after injuring several people in his climb, he plunked himself down beside him. The fact that he was able to aim his ass so perfectly suggested to him he should be slightly buzzed all the time.

Marina and Lucy looked pretty tight, as in tightly together and also tipsy. Contrary to Viktor's explicit orders, the ferret was present in a red knitted jacket of some kind, and it snuggled in a carry bag beside them.

"Are you coming to the performance?" Lucy said.

"I'm here already." David edged away from the ferret.

"No, no, the cello piece I've been composing for the dance performance, the one Marina and I have been working on since we met."

"Oh, that," he muttered, although this was the first he had heard that it was actually finished. She'd been talking about "making dances" for months, so much so that he'd lost all faith in this, as in so many things.

Viktor was in his usual state, halfway between hysteria and coma. "The game is almost over. Here come your horses," he whispered in his ear, and at that moment, the announcer took advantage of a time out to boom his name through the loudspeaker as planner, organizer, major domo of everything they were about to see, should the Steelheads dribble to victory.

This disembodied voice screamed, "Dr. David Oster, stand up and take a bow."

David planted his rear end into that seat as firmly as he could, but Viktor and Marina vaulted him upright, then thrust his right arm forward in what appeared to be a Nazi salute.

"Stop it, you idiots," he shouted at them, waving, nevertheless, ceremonially, like the Queen of England, a little too long. They yanked him down by his jacket after the cheering subsided.

"Enjoying your moment of glory?" Lucy wheezed into his ear. She clearly had imbibed way too much of the Latvian sauce.

"I do not acknowledge your right to interrogation." She looked at David strangely, and, at that moment, he lost his balance and toppled over onto the floor.

# CHAPTER 25

THUNDEROUS APPLAUSE GREETED David's return to consciousness, but not for him. The victorious Steelheads leapt around the court, hugging and kissing one another. They had won; unaccountably and unbelievably, they faced the prospect of competing in the NCAA Final Four. Launching themselves into hyperdrive, screaming hysterically, students and rhubarb farmers alike raced down onto the basketball floor, jumping at the players despite the security guards' efforts to push them backward.

Into this melee blared the announcer's voice, "Please, ladies and gentlemen, vacate the court. Our victory celebration is about to begin."

Before anyone knew what was happening, the same twenty girls last seen at half time marched single file through the deafening crowd, swinging their pompoms and batons and shaking their well-toned bodies. David sobered up in an instant, waiting for Murray, Jerry, and their two older pals in skirts. As people scurried off the floor and back into their seats, the four senior animals appeared, led by Alexis.

"They look beautiful," Viktor screamed into his ear, while loud music filled the hall.

Frank Sinatra sang: "The record shows, I took the blows," and the crowd joined in, screaming even louder, "I did it my way!" Murray and Jerry remained calm, while Alexis, in a shapely ringmaster costume, marched them forward, and the two other horses followed behind. People were standing up, shouting, singing, sliding ever nearer the court, but above the din, David could still hear the banging of the horses' hooves.

The girls, the players, and the horses lined themselves up facing the crowd, so orderly they might have been in the cavalry. The cheering subsided a moment, and then over the sound system, a rap group screamed its frenetic version of "America the Beautiful" as if sung by a bunch of parrots on crack. David expected the worst, but the horses endured the grotesque noise, only turning their heads toward the girls, who threw their batons up expertly. In perfect unison, all four horses turned and faced the crowd on the other side, while yet another roar went up. All in all, it was going well as the cheerleaders swirled around the placid animals.

David began to breathe again, especially as he knew the number ended shortly, and even he started to clap and join in the fun. All of a sudden, a siren blasted out from the upper reaches of the stands, a loud siren very like that of the police, and everyone looked around in confusion. Though it was only some frat boys with a Radio Shack gizmo, the crowd reacted like Pavlov's dog, clutching each other and heading toward the aisles. The horses reared their heads, and at just that moment, one lone baton swirled up toward the infinity of the ceiling. David watched it crest, and, as if in slow motion, it fell right on Murray's —or was it Jerry's head? The horse jerked his neck and snorted, then whinnied. The siren still blared, now joined by kids chanting through a bullhorn, and at this very moment, the ferret jumped out of Lucy's arms, disappearing beneath the bleachers.

Viktor screamed at them all, "Get out! We must reach safety."

"There's nothing wrong. Just sit tight." David's advice proved useless, surrounded as they were by the madness of hot bodies in a crowd, and every single other person in the hall straining to flee, but he stuck to his seat, watching those god-damned animals. One of the older horses shied at the noise, and then the one on the other side swiveled around as if on a music box. Out of his left eye, David spotted the ferret. It scooted onto the basketball court directly under Murray, who reared back, and even though Alexis still moved among them calmly, he bucked and then sidled away from her as the cheer-leaders screamed. Everyone, including quadrupeds, thought it was a fat rat. One of the horses bolted straight for an exit, with people racing right behind him, and the noise on the basketball floor was horrendous. Earlier the slightest clip-clop had been loud, but now it was as if a thousand pounds of bricks banged from side to side in a clothes dryer.

David tried to climb over the seats, but his knees buck-led, and when he got up, the unthinkable happened. Murray relieved himself on the basketball floor. There, in a welter of steaming horseshit and pompoms, horses, players, ferret, cheer-leaders, and Alexis all converged, slipping and sliding. David raced down the steps and lurched onto the court. Everybody else scrambled off in several different directions. Suddenly Alexis fell into the goo, and at the same moment, one horse backed into her. It looked to be about to fall on top of her, and did fall, but not before David yanked her arm and pulled her up and away from the creature. The two other horses pawed anxiously at the wooden floor, finding it maddeningly unlike dirt. David managed to grab them both by their bridles, while Alexis coaxed the fallen horse to its feet and pulled him determinedly toward the exit.

Just as they got to the door, the horse David was holding with his left hand strained forward against the bit, snapped his head from side to side, and lunged straight through the crowd toward the parking lot. People around him were still panicked, and one man grabbed his arm.

"What the hell happened?" he yelled.

Another guy screamed, "That way, that way!"

David could see nothing except the retreating rear end of his horse while he clung for dear life to the bridle of the one by his side.

Alexis left him there and raced outside, her animal in tow. Within moments she returned and took charge of David's remaining horse. "I got the other one in the truck," she said.

"I couldn't hold mine. I'm sorry." His renegade quadruped had just kept going, now a speck on the horizon. "Should we go after him—them, I mean? The first one took off right away."

"No, no, I'll call a ranger, and he'll pick both of them up."

Now he got a good look at her, she was covered in dung and torn bits of pompom. She didn't smell too great, but neither did he. She winced at his condition, then glanced down at her own. He didn't know how long they stood there, but most of the crowd hotfooted it away. David had a wonderfully empty feeling, as if he'd lost every single thing and was therefore light as air and pure as the day he was born.

They were headed back to her truck when who should come bearing straight down upon them but President Thornton himself, followed closely by the tall, thin man he had seen sitting beside him in the stands. Thornton led with his neck and clasped a Steelhead cap in his hand. Hoarsely he shouted, "Oster, Oster."

David said to Alexis, "Thank God almighty, I'm about to get fired." She clung to him as the two men loped into their faces.

"Oster." Thornton seemed to be having difficulty breathing and just kept repeating his name. Finally he straightened up and placed his Steelhead cap on his head. "Oster, you're a hero, a goddamned hero, saving this little lady like that." He reached over and patted Alexis, despite the filth all over her. "Can't tell you how impressed I am? And I speak for Lettice when I say you are the man of the hour. I want you to shake the hand of Larson Kinne, your personal benefactor."

"No, no, I didn't do anything, sir." David tried to back away, embarrassed at his condition.

Nevertheless, Thornton grabbed his dung-covered hand and stuck it into the hand of Larson Kinne, the osmium king. He really had changed world history with his amazing engineering feats, but right at that moment, he looked just like Abraham Lincoln and smiled at him with the benevolent eyes of an intensely amused man, despite the fact that he held a very dirty hand in his own.

"I expect great things from you, Oster. I've been following your work."

"You have?" David was immediately conscious that he looked like a filthy, drunken bum and smelled much worse.

"Certainly, and I admire your perseverance since discoveries like yours will take decades. Young scientists like you are usually so anxious for instant gratification."

David sure was, but obviously didn't say so, basking dumbly in the warmth and confidence of the great man.

"You're a hero, even my Lettice said so," Thornton chimed in again. "Get back to those horses, little lady," he said to Alexis, snorting, pounding her on the shoulder, but before David could introduce her to Larson Kinne, confide in him about his work on the fifth force, or even apologize for smelling so bad, he and Thornton went off into the crowd.

"Do salads talk to that man?" Alexis asked incredulously.

"Lettice is the name of his wife."

Making for the horse trailer, they ran into Viktor, Lucy, and Marina, all purposefully headed their way. Marina was on the attack. "Cruelty to animals, that's what I call it! What would you call it, Lucy?"

"More fun than a barrel of monkeys," she said acidly.

"Ha," Viktor laughed, then frowned.

"That mangy rodent of yours was entirely at fault. I hope he's now being eaten by a dog." David glared at them.

"The horses are fine, by the way, despite your red-coated pet, who should never have been here," Alexis said angrily.

Marina turned to Lucy. "Our poor little Viktor, out there somewhere all alone, prey to eagles, even coyotes."

"It's animal abuse," Lucy cried out at Alexis. David could see that she and Marina were loaded. They must have emptied Viktor's cooler.

"Ooh, catfight!" Viktor grinned idiotically.

"It's people abuse, don't you see, that's doing us in," David suggested. To Alexis he muttered, "Let's get out of here."

"Now you'll have to get a new pet." Viktor smiled wickedly.

"Shut up, old man," this from Lucy, who was clutching on to Marina to prevent her from throwing a punch. They were all bombed.

Out of his left eye, David saw Shelby and a familiar dark-haired woman guiding Chuckers through the crowd. He had indeed postponed his elopement—to see the game with his wife! David looked around anxiously to see if he could spot Hoekstra, but he must have already fled. In any case, his own duty was clear. Get Alexis safely into the truck, out of the clutches of the crowd and other irate Washingtonians who might question their animal rights position. As he closed the truck door, she leaned out to him and kissed him firmly on the mouth.

"You do just keep saving me. It's wonderful."

"It is wonderful, isn't it?" David said, still dazed from the evening's events but proud of himself nevertheless.

Pulling the trailer slowly out of the parking lot, Alexis waved to him and blew him another kiss. Viktor had observed this scene and shook his head violently. "I knew you'd get her, old boy. It was only a matter of time."

It was over. That was the very best thing he could say about the day. The horses survived, and rangers rounded up the last two only an hour after the event. Hops farmers and students alike had witnessed David's disgrace, but fortunately they had no vote on the Nobel committee, and his insane hopes seemed blessed now by the formidable Larson Kinne himself. The team's triumph was greatly glorified in the next day's paper, but nobody read about it, since the celebration lasted two solid days with no letup. Public drunkenness became the rule, and the town was littered with confetti, balloons, empty beer cans, and other celebratory objects. An enormous papier-mâché replica of the Steelhead cap had been placed on top of the courthouse. Surprisingly, the excretory hullabaloo on the basketball court dropped into oblivion, although the *Sentinel* mentioned several injured cheerleaders, "equestrian confusion," and a small furry creature in a red snood. In this upbeat atmosphere, people didn't even mention the business to David, supposed author of the event, except to congratulate him. As the public hysteria gradually subsided, classes also wound down, and David deeply hoped that personal dramas were also on hold.

Not so. In the early morning hours three days after the big game, a moving truck appeared in front of the Burns residence. David peered out his front window in time to see Shelby's wife and Chuckers directing the men. Her husband was nowhere to be seen. David sauntered out, trying not to look too curious, but she came over quickly and gave him a big hug.

"I'm sure you know that we're off now."

"Off? I knew something…"

"You don't have to play dumb with me, David. Shelby left a letter for you." She handed him a white envelope.

"You mean he's gone already?"

"They had to get out of here in secret. Her husband's a maniac."

"You know about all this?"

"Of course. What do you take me for? We were just friends, David. The romance went out a long time ago."

"Well, yes, he did speak to me about his plans."

"He must have liked you. He didn't like many people here. Look, if there's anyone he should have run off with, it's her. She's older, she's smarter, and she's richer than anyone he's ever known. With that kind of backing, there's no limit to what he can do."

David nodded, though he was really thinking of certain illicit activities he might tackle. "You're right, I guess. I admire you for being so…"

He was about to say, "supportive," when she interrupted with, "so realistic." Then she hugged him, just as Chuckers ran up and squeezed himself in as well. What a sweet domestic picture, sadly, of people who barely knew each other.

Such were his thoughts later on as he wandered up to his office, preparing to check out potential lecturers on sturgeon fishing and how to spot a smelt. He had Shelby's letter in his pocket, saving it for a quieter, happier moment. As the current king of Wet and Wild, he was so depressed he thought then and there of abandoning his research, despite the good words of his benefactor. Who really cared? Maybe people wouldn't want to know that another force existed in the universe. Even though it would affect fundamental physics, it would have no practical application whatsoever. Like Kepler or Galileo, David might be vilified, hounded out of the profession. Ludwig Boltzmann, prominent in his little, hitherto unfinished notebook, had established the mathematical basis of thermodynamics, but ended up killing himself right before experiments would prove his equations right. Suicide or derision, the unhappy lot of the visionary. Then, suddenly, he laughed out loud at his own pretensions.

"Yeah, right, buddy, you certainly have proved yourself to be another Kepler." A couple of students gaped at him.

To his surprise, as he reached the front entrance to the institute, Larson Kinne's luminous, craggy face rose up again in front of him. He appeared to be in a hurry, but he stopped short and stuck out his hand. "Keep going, Oster. You're my man. I believe you have a line on the fifth force and will get critical evidence in your next experiment."

Which experiment was he talking about? How did he know he was even pursuing the fifth force? He had mentioned it only once in an earlier paper and in a very guarded way, calling it merely "an unknown force." Before he could say anything more, Kinne sprinted away to the parking lot. David stood on the curb watching him, stunned. At least this time his hands had been clean.

As he turned back toward the building, he saw Alexis coming toward him. "Larson Kinne again?" she said.

"A great man."

"*You* are great." She looked particularly radiant.

"What are you talking about?"

"The basketball horses."

"Oh, be quiet. From you I expect at least a tiny drop of rational thought."

"No, no, you were masterful. I had to come tell you that," she said, slipping her arm through his. He looked at her and realized that he couldn't think of anything charming or seductive to say. She had that effect on him; around her, the normal ploys evaporated.

As they strolled toward the Bean, now completely abandoned by the locals in favor of taverns and pizza parlors, he recovered from his awkward daze enough to tell her the latest news in the Hoekstra saga. "The aged Dane is now on his own. The errant Shelby hath spirited Frances away to a happier land."

"Shelby and Frances? You're kidding," she said, and if eyes could bug out of that beautiful face, hers did. "I wonder where they went?"

"Maybe the Yukon, some romantic spot like that."

"Romantic?" She seemed offended by the whole business. "They told you about this in advance?" When they had gotten their coffee and sat down, David told her the whole story. She kept shaking her head. "Shelby, Shelby going straight, I can't believe it."

"He's not necessarily going straight. He's going in another direction. But I wonder about poor Leah, stuck with old Larry." The minute he said this, he started nervously. Despite the fact that he thought he had cleared up the question of his relationship to this woman, he didn't even like saying her name, mainly because of Hoekstra's constant enraged invocation of it.

Happily, Alexis reacted more to the news of the recent elopement. "I think Frances tried to explain all this to me, but I was willfully misunderstanding her. She felt an obligation, she said, because of my spiritual role in her life. I was so afraid that I would have to confess about her husband's letters that my mind froze up. They always say Russians like to confess, but I don't."

"Lucy will be upset about Frances too."

Alexis shook her head and sighed. "I thought I was the only one to see what was going on there. Poor Viktor, he never had a chance."

"Shelby left a letter for me, and I want—" But before he could read it to her, from across the room, the man she had just mentioned lunged toward them.

"Hoekstra is looking for you," Viktor announced.

"For me?" David gulped his coffee.

"Of course for you," he said, glaring at them.

Before they had time to leave, who should appear in the doorway but the abandoned man himself? He loomed, a sinister figure by any measure, his heavy shoulders sunken even further, his wild, angry energy tamed momentarily by the doorjamb.

"Let us flee," Viktor hissed.

"We can't keep running." David stiffened himself for whatever kind of fight was to come. Alexis had a stricken look on her face, as if she would be called upon for some ultimate sacrifice.

Before any plan at all came to mind, the wounded giant screamed across the empty café, "Oster, she's gone!"

# CHAPTER 26

T HEY WATCHED AS Hoekstra rushed toward them, arms outstretched.

"Coffee, sir?" rang out a cheery voice from behind the counter.

Ignoring the inquiry, he powered his way through the sacks of beans, loomed above their table, wobbled, then sat down with a thud.

Alexis fixed him with a close look. "We know about Frances."

"How could you know?" He pulled out a Gitane, shoved it into his mouth, and looked around madly at the lounging students.

"Hoekstra," Viktor said, most authoritatively, "it has always been that everybody knows everything that happens here. It has ever been thus."

This confused pronouncement, delivered in a silky voice, shut everybody up, and they gulped their coffee like dying men, not having any social cues at all for this extraordinary occasion. A woman just out of a coma leaves her murderous husband for a rogue and a lecher twenty-five years her junior. What was there to say?

Hoekstra was the most befuddled of them all, but he finally did go up and get a mug of coffee as David and Alexis tried to figure out a way to disappear from the room. He sat down again and said nothing, just kept spooning sugar into his drink, though occasionally he would look over at Alexis like a spaniel.

"Perhaps it will all end up for the best," David said, rubbing his hands together.

"For you maybe." This sounded ominous, but Viktor kept winking at David so idiotically that he couldn't respond. Instead, under the table, David smashed Viktor's foot with his own.

"Yow!" Viktor screamed, and this set Hoekstra off.

"What's wrong with you, you Latvian mental case? I should have fired you years ago. They all told me you would get the Nobel Prize for your crazy bubbles, but have you? Have you?"

"Stop it, Niels," Alexis said.

Viktor shoved himself away from the table. "I will get an award of some very big kind, Hoekstra, and I expect you to weep and moan and bite your teeth and die." He screamed this last word practically back to Latvia, standing and vaulting himself toward the men's room.

Alexis and David exchanged horrified looks, but clearly Hoekstra was hardened to insults. "He's a hopeless fool. Nothing he says can touch me. If he ever got the prize, he'd try to shoot the king of Sweden."

Viktor popped his head back out of the men's room, screeching, "And where's your fucking dog?" then marched out of the place altogether. David perked right up at this, and Alexis started to laugh but checked herself.

"What did that maniac say?"

You would have to have been three hundred feet underground to miss Viktor's words, but like a boob, David repeated, "Where's your dog?"

Hoekstra cocked his head to one side. "I don't know. He left one night, and the ungrateful little hound hasn't returned." But surely he did know. Hadn't Viktor given him David's note?

Alexis now sweetly smiled at him. "Have you looked for Heinrich at all?"

"I haven't had the time. Besides, Frances was the only one who cared about him, and she was hardly ever home. She started living at a hotel. Did you know that? She preferred the Bel Air Hotel to me!"

"It was your wife who loved the dog?" Alexis said softly.

"Certainly."

David inhaled deeply. "Why all those love letters, Niels? What was the point?"

Hoekstra fixed him with bleak eyes. "Do I have to tell you? It's humiliating." He glanced around the Bean as if looking for someone. "I loved my wife, madly."

"But you kept trying to seduce other women."

"Did I?" He stared at him and drew little invisible circles on a napkin with his finger. "What if I left the letters out?"

"So you were doing what? Torturing her with them?" And then it hit him. "You were trying to make Frances jealous?"

"I was trying to get beautiful women to come after me, yes, so my wife would want me more."

"And when you wrote that their affections were becoming violent?" Alexis looked angry.

"I wanted to deflect suspicion from myself, for her illness, without harming anyone, really." He tried to smile.

"Why were you always so angry with me about Leah?" David hated to mention her name, but he had to.

"I wanted you to keep away from her. Surely someone like her could make my wife very, very jealous, and I suspected Leah had a thing for you. She thought you were attractive."

Alexis eyed David intently, and he tried to frown in a way that expressed total disapproval.

"Leah was the linchpin in my plan to get Frances back, and the only one to respond at all to my letters."

"Then why did you keep pressuring me not to tell your wife about you and Leah?"

"You'd been warned against it so many times, I just assumed, knowing how you must feel about me, that at some point you or your girlfriend would. Frances would get even more jealous."

Slowly Alexis turned back to Hoekstra and said, "So you did love Frances, in the end."

"Totally," he growled.

"And that's why you wanted me to watch Shelby, because you were jealous of him?"

"Yes. That evil bastard, going after a married woman!"

David stared around at the few innocents in the coffeehouse, talking, laughing, cheerily bringing cups to their lips, confident in the safety of what they imbibed. He thought back to that terrible night, the music rising, Hoekstra's wife gulping at her drink, and in a kind of screen memory, he could see her husband moving toward her, trying to stay her hand. What could that mean?

"You kept saying you made a 'mistake.' What kind of mistake, I wonder?"

"Perhaps if you start using your mind, David. Think about body mass."

David pondered this a moment, amazed at his peculiar thoughts, but felt emboldened enough to explore them out loud. "Who was the drink for?"

The old man raised his eyebrows and smirked.

"No, I don't believe it. Was it for you? A drink of denatured alcohol? You were going to drink it yourself? You could have died." Even for a young man brought up around grotesqueries, this was a radical idea.

"Not really. I'm a big man, bigger than Frances, and could monitor how much I took in. But we got into an argument, and the music was so loud, then I yelled at her to stop, but before I could do anything, Frances grabbed the drink out of my hand."

"How did you know there was denatured alcohol under the sink?"

"I saw it there earlier in the evening while looking for the garbage. The idea just came to me, and with so many people milling around, they had no idea what I was doing."

Alexis was watching David, with admiration he hoped, and so he pressed on, in spite of the many off-the-wall ideas running around in his head. "You were going to drink the cocktail to make yourself deathly ill in front of her?"

Hoekstra swiveled his formidable being in David's direction. "I wanted her to love me again."

"But when she was in the hospital, you hardly seemed to care."

"I was horrified, in shock, but relieved, at least, that she wasn't with Shelby."

David could feel Alexis beside him, boiling with rage. "You staged the whole thing. You miserable motherfucker, you deserve everything you're getting." She stood up, slammed her chair down hard, then strode out.

David rose too. "Why don't you go home and drink something else lethal?"

Outside of the Bean, in the crisp, clear afternoon, Alexis waited for him and took him in her arms. "It's sickening," she said, and he held on to her.

"Let's see Shelby's letter." David took it out of his pocket.

It was written on notebook paper with the little serrated edges torn off, and the handwriting was large and dramatic. He read it aloud. "'Dear David, Much as I have enjoyed our friendship, it must now end for a time. Frances and I are going underground, so nobody should know, but I will tell you it's Greek, and it's an island, and it'll be fun. When Hoekstra gets over the shock, which Frances says should be in about a month, we'll be back. I won't say where, I won't say when, just we'll be back. Don't worry, old buddy, I'll be in touch, and don't bang anybody I wouldn't. Your friend, Shelby Burns.'"

"This letter will someday find its place in the optimist's hall of fame," David said to Alexis as she looked at him in wonder.

"No kidding. It's horrible, all of it. Do you think he really loves her—Shelby, I mean?"

"Does he? Could he? Does he even know what love means?" David realized with a jolt that he himself was in love and would have to find a way, very shortly, to say so.

"I've got to go, a riding lesson."

"No, don't go," he said, trying to hold on to her somehow.

"I'll see you later."

"Come with me to Lucy's dance performance this evening, will you? Viktor drags me to them all the time, and I don't think I can handle all this alone."

"Yes," she said, and they kissed.


As he wandered back home, David mused on the heroine of this damp drama, Frances Hoekstra. To think that a woman old enough to be his mother, a woman large of ass and fortune, had been the romantic idol at the center of these bizarre plots. It was too much. It had a Wagnerian quality, complete with a Washingtonian Brunhilde. He had been so wrong, so totally wrong, it was refreshing, as sheer arrogance had done him in.

David thought that by letting people hang around with him, men and women alike, he could laugh at their mad doings, just observe them without feeling anything, but instead, they'd become his friends. For good or ill, he cared for them, worried about them. God help him, he was a resident!

David pulled out his little notebook and thumbed through the equations. So quaint they seemed to him now, especially in their foundation in logic, in quantifiability. Still, he had had all the right elements, just could never formulate their correct relation. It was Leah who worried him the most. That face, with the rain streaming down over her black hair, the face of anguish and hopeless desire. What pain Shelby had brought to her. Once inside his front door, he sank down on one of the stained-looking yellow chairs, exhausted but at least happy that he would shortly see Alexis again.

Unfortunately, the phone rang, and it was Viktor, almost incoherent, who announced that he had to come to his new house right away, that very minute. The man's panic actually sounded real. When David swung into his driveway ten minutes later, the pink palace looked even more dejected in the sun. Viktor's home still hadn't been completely finished, and now that the contractor was in Greece, David doubted it ever would be. The front door looked open, and David pushed on it.

"Viktor, Viktor."

No response except, finally, a strange, low growl. He turned, and none other than Heinrich, looking hale and hearty, bounded across the hardwood floor, ready to eat him.

David jumped into the hall closet and slammed it shut, but the overheated canine stood outside, panting and whimpering. He heard Viktor command, "Stay, boy, *stavi, stavi*," and in a louder voice, "Don't worry, I'm teaching him to speak Latvian, but until then, he's controlling his own self." He opened the door, the beast now tethered to his side. Heinrich's tongue was hanging out, and the fearsome creature gazed up at Viktor with a fixed stare.

David stepped gingerly out of the closet. "What the hell are you doing now? If it's a new plot, you can count me out!"

"I couldn't help myself. The dog, all alone like that, who knows when they will shoot him, and he's one of God's creatures, after all."

"Are you telling me you're keeping this animal?"

"Of course I am. It's my American duty."

"What about Hoekstra?"

"He doesn't care for him. He left him in that cage for forever. After I gave him the note, David, he still didn't do anything; you know that yourself." At this point Heinrich was nuzzling up alongside Viktor's leg, and even David had to admit it looked like love. The two walked lockstep toward the back patio, where Viktor had wine and slices of Brie laid out on a small wooden table, beside which were two camp chairs, the first signs of real furniture. Naturally Heinrich hied himself over to the food, but Viktor yelled, "*Sedi, sedi,*" loudly. "'Sit' in Latvian, you see how well I teach him?" He went on and on about the fate of the dog until he stopped short. "Ah, but David, I have to tell you something."

"You're running off with Leah."

"No, no, much better than that. But I don't want you to be upset."

"Come on, upset me."

"I'm on the short list for the Nobel Prize."

"What?" He gaped at the man. "You're making this up."

"No, my friend Lunde Erdeberger called me. He would never lie. The Swedish never lie. The Danish, yes, God knows I've seen it myself. Hamlet was right."

"Stop, stop. I don't believe you. No one would just tell you this."

"Why not? It's important to be prepared. You don't want to get a call from Sweden and hang up on them. Besides, all I know how to say in Swedish is 'No more herring.'" Heinrich panted at his side. "I'm so happy, really. It makes up for goodbye to Lucy. She is lost to me; there cannot be a doubt. Did you underestimate me, dear boy?"

It's true, David had underestimated him. He had even suspected him of complicity with Hoekstra, but now he realized that this must be the momentous news Thornton had been trying to convey to him. For years Viktor claimed to have detected free neutrons in the water around his imploding bubbles, an important step on the journey to controlled fusion. Unlimited cheap energy for the world—a magnificent discovery. Because he never saw Viktor do any work, and he mostly just ran after women and dogs, David had lost all sense of him as a real scientist.

"You're trying to get me going about the prize, aren't you? I'd suspect you of anything at this point. The dog is probably the beginning of another murder investigation."

"Oh, David, you never understand, and I still have such high hopes for you."

"This I do understand," and he explained all that he had just learned about the Hoekstra love triangle.

His Latvian friend didn't seem surprised, merely quizzical, but at least proud of him for dragging the truth out of Hoekstra. "Just when I lose hope, you arise!" he said and threw up his hands. "Come, we'll be late for the dance performance."

"Damn, you're right. I'm supposed to meet Alexis there."

Despite his wish to hear more about the Swedes, off they went on foot to the Arts Council Hall, dragging Heinrich behind them.

"You should leave him home," David suggested, but Viktor insisted that he would be too lonely.

When they arrived, the concert had already started. David and Viktor spotted Alexis, so visible with that hair, and climbed over a number of people to get to her, scaring them all with the dog. She kissed David on the cheek as they sat down. Center stage, Lucy crossed over to a fake wall, lugging her cello, then hoisted herself up onto the top of it, legs clasped around her instrument. Electronic music blasted from speakers on all four sides of the room, dissonant stuff remarkably like squirrels sharpening their teeth on emery boards. Suddenly two figures in black leotards appeared on either side of the stage. The first one, clearly Marina, then the other, whom David didn't know, leapt barefoot into a pile of peat moss in alarming postures that went with the music, to which Lucy now added mournful soundings from the Vuillaume. Jagged leaping, legs thrown sideways, heavings of the torso—the two women performed these moves staring down the audience and next turned around and did it all again backward. David wondered who would crack first, himself or the potential Nobel laureate, or possibly Heinrich, who had lifted up his head and was sniffing around, because each time the women moved, a spray of moss flew up and emitted its distinct perfume.

At some climactic point in the music, the women rushed toward each other, arms outstretched, then swung themselves around in what was morphing into brown goo. Atonal bleeps ratcheted up higher and higher.

David leaned across Alexis to whisper to a pained-looking Viktor, "This is affecting my synapses."

"I got my experiment idea from this piece," Viktor said a bit louder. "Look at Lucy playing. Harmonics on stringed instruments are standing waves that depend on the length of the string. I created acoustic standing waves in the laboratory, but where in nature could I find them? In the black smokers, the chimneys near Juan de Fuca, I say. Inside, there's very hot and very cold water, so you have high-frequency water waves causing the bubbles to implode. And of course seawater is loaded with deuterium, a necessary component to the reaction. Do you see?"

"Shh." Alexis seemed intent on Lucy, who was moving her bow nimbly amidst the cavorting dancers.

It was difficult to get the full flavor of Viktor's theory, lost as David was in the cacophony, but it sounded audacious enough to be right. No reply to him was possible, however, because Marina and the other woman were firmly intertwined, rolling from side to side like Siamese twins in a windstorm, while Lucy sawed away sympathetically.

Finally Viktor leaned over and said very loudly, "This reminds me of Soviet art!" He stood up, yanking Heinrich, and so man and dog once again clambered over students and matrons alike. David and Alexis just sat there, praying for it to be over. She grimaced at him several times, but they endured until the very end.

Outside near the parking lot, blessed silence, but David's ears were still ringing. Viktor had waited for them and kept shaking his head from side to side, while Heinrich started howling, which was not good, as the newly single Hoekstra had availed himself of what little culture existed in Pyke City to attend this very concert. David knew this because shortly thereafter he was standing right next to them. Heinrich certainly wasn't glad to see him. He quavered behind Viktor, tongue out, tail hanging between his legs.

"I'm going to kill you for this," Hoekstra yelled at Viktor, trying to grab the dog's leash. "That dog cost me five thousand dollars. I was going to sell it."

"You said your wife was the only one who loved it," David said, rather grandly, conscious that he was trying to show off again for his beloved.

"Shut up, you California panhandler." Hoekstra now circled the two men as if about to throw a punch. Viktor kept backing away, the leash curling around his legs, while Heinrich whimpered. Hoekstra glowered at Viktor, and David feared that yet one more time he was going to have to deck him. Though he seemed to be in knots, suddenly Viktor thrust out one leg, then another, and finally kicked upward, connecting with Hoekstra's knee. The Nordic pestilence fell down onto a bush.

"Hee-hee," Viktor giggled and jumped up and down. "I am on the short list for the Nobel Prize. Never cross my path again." Then he placed his booted foot on the man's stomach and pushed down hard. Evidently the dog was undisturbed by the fall of his former master, clinging ever closer to Viktor.

"Stop it. You don't want to kill him." David stood in front of Alexis to protect her from the mayhem.

"I do. Maybe Heinrich will eat him. *Uzbruc, uzbruc*! Look how he hates him. Eat, eat, feel free. I must take up violence, David. It clears the head."

"What are you doing?" Alexis yelled at him.

"Yes, stop it, Viktor." David bent down over Hoekstra, who appeared just to have had the wind knocked out of him, but could also have been more gravely injured. He motioned to Alexis. "You'd better call an ambulance."

Now, as luck would have it, the concertgoers chose this moment to exit the hall. They had to step over the fallen man and around Viktor, while Heinrich began to howl. Suddenly President Thornton appeared, along with his wife, who wore a small doily around her neck. They stared at the four of them, and Lettice reached down to pat the dog.

"Is he dead?" Thornton said, with no emotion in his voice.

Hoekstra's head now rested on David's knees, as he had squatted down beside him. "He's alive, but something is definitely wrong." At that moment, he had a vision of holding his father in just the same way. In real life, he had never had the chance. He got a phone call about his death and later a small scribbled note that Old Dave had written at the very last, saved by a nurse. It read, "Onward, Motherfucker."

"He was just overcome by the performance." Viktor grinned.

"I know how he feels." Thornton grimaced.

"Oh, darling, it was wonderful, you know it was, the Earth Mother and the Moon Goddess." Lettice seemed thrilled.

"What's wrong with these people?" Alexis bent down and whispered into David's ear, but he couldn't figure out how to reply since the pathology spread itself so wide and deep.

Viktor giggled, and everybody looked at him. "Sorry. I think you all should know. I am on the short list for the Nobel Prize."

"I know you are, you lunatic." Thornton snorted at him, then announced to the group, "Some dope smoker called me last month from Woods Hole to give me the news."

David felt Hoekstra's pulse and realized the man was gasping for air. As if in a dream, he now did something that never in his young life would he have pictured. He actually rendered mouth-to-mouth resuscitation. Was it to impress Alexis, or to impress himself with his wonderful altruism in the face of the older man's evil, or was he merely reacting instinctively to another suffering human being? Whatever the reason, he,

David Oster, had physical contact with those fat white lips, and as he breathed life into him, Hoekstra opened his eyes, blinking several times. He fixed his savior with a pained look, then clung on to him and said in a hoarse voice, "David, David?"

"Yes?"

Hoekstra wheezed at him hard, and David could hear a siren in the distance. His eyes bugged out as Rasputin's must have when he refused to expire; his forehead was clammy, his face sallow.

"She was in love," he croaked out. David could hear Heinrich panting a few feet behind him. The old man stared up at him, and a tear, a real tear formed at the side of one eye. "Frances was in love with Shelby." At that moment, David felt sorry for the old bastard, all his bad acts done in the service of love for his wife.

"So how did the pornography figure in?" he couldn't help but ask.

"I just wanted to turn her on."

"Isn't that sweet," Lettice sighed as the ambulance snaked its way toward them.

David was still cushioning Hoekstra's head with his hand when he looked up to find the paramedics standing beside them. Hoekstra shooed them away and brushed his long hair back over his forehead, struggling to speak. He did speak, looking at David.

"You saved my life. I tried to kill myself again by letting him stomp on me. You brought me back from the grave."

David pulled back. "No, I didn't. You just woke up." He could feel Alexis's warmth behind him.

Thornton leaned forward and whispered into David's ear, "What did I tell you? People try to kill themselves here all the time."

Hoekstra licked his lips and attempted to hug him. It was horrible. "Say the word, David. Anything you want, I'll make sure you get it."

Viktor broke into powerful giggles, and David swore he heard a note of triumph. Suddenly it hit him. Viktor had won, won it all, not only the possibility of a Nobel, but the total capitulation of his archrival. Viktor and Hoekstra had been jousting like medieval knights, over women, over dogs, and most importantly over him, who now might occupy the benighted state of Washington forever. As he stared at them, they both gazed back with cow eyes, adoringly because, alas, the fair blushing prize was none other than himself, and Viktor had definitively won. He'd gotten him to agree to do his experiment, gotten the millions to do it, and reduced his rival to begging on the street.

Astonished at his own thoughts, David had only a moment to gloat because right beside the two paramedics, he spotted another uniformed entity. Incredible legs stood before him, atop which rested the navy blue skirt, vest, and jacket of Alaska Airlines, then the razor-cut short blonde hair. Cosmo!

She grinned at the assembled personages, this apparition from the air, and rushed David with a hug. He struggled to break away as she cooed, "I've been looking for you everywhere. My goodness, what a town."

David backed away, into Alexis, as a matter of fact. Terror closed his throat, stopped his mouth. What the hell was Cosmo doing here, and more awfully, more hideously, why now? He gurgled something, but suddenly, breaking into his panic, David heard a familiar voice powering its way toward them. It was Larry Burnett shouting, screaming his name. Jesus, the only person who had no reason to hate him, and now here he was. Above Thornton's stooped shoulder, David saw the golf club—he thought it was a nine iron—upraised and threatening.

"My wife left me, you scumbag!" He seemed ready to swing the club right at him. "You put Leah up to it. I know you did."

David clamped his jaw shut in horror. His mind had simply stopped, and when he turned toward Alexis, she glared at him with a look that contained every self-loathing thing he'd said to himself over the last two years. Paralyzed, he watched as Thornton reached up for the club the madman held as he lunged toward Viktor.

"I'll kill you, you miserable Latvian. I'll burn your ugly-ass house down, you evil troll." Thornton now had taken hold of the shaft, so Larry was swinging both the club and the university president's arm around at the same time. He pulled it out of Thornton's reach and connected straight to Hoekstra's shoulder, screaming, "You old fraud. You were in on it too. I found those letters. I'm gonna sue you all. You'll be tied up in court for fucking ever. Your lives are over, over!"

Surprisingly, the injured Hoekstra gathered himself up and pushed the man backward, shouting, "Of course Leah left you, you sniveling little sleaze. You never touched her, a gorgeous woman, gorgeous!"

At that moment, Viktor snapped the leash off Heinrich, who lunged toward the irate golfer, fangs bared. The last David saw of Larry, his ass was two inches from Heinrich's formidable jaws.

"Gee," Cosmo laughed. "I think I might have come at a bad time."

David still hadn't said a word to her and now found he absolutely had to. "Cosmo, I, uh, it's been so long." He wanted it to sound like three hundred years.

"Not that long. I was in Seattle and thought I'd just pop down, but it took me forever on that terrible freeway. I missed you." She giggled again and sort of bounced on her high heels.

David felt dead air space behind him where Alexis had been moments before. Had she fled? He turned to look for her, but just as he did so, Thornton laid his hand on his shoulder.

"I back up Hoekstra's offer one thousand percent. You can have everything you want, Oster, provided Wet and Wild stays just the way it is for the rest of your natural-born life."

Viktor started jumping up and down with triumphant glee, and David began to choke and cough, but really he wanted to cry. No matter that he could do the perfect experiment on the fifth force, now with a possible Nobel laureate—which would cost seven, maybe eight million dollars, max—no matter the technicians, radioactive tracers, submersibles, and Viktor's hot bubble theory, which would take another couple of mill. It would all mean staying in this damp, crazy place forever—probably, it now seemed, without his beloved. Still, for one mad moment, he was tempted.

"Anything?" David said, and it started to rain.

# CHAPTER 27

ALEXIS WAS INDEED gone, as David found out the moment he surveyed the parking lot. He wanted to pack Cosmo off right that second, but of course he couldn't and ended up escorting her to the Old Sawmill, where he downed two martinis with lightning speed. He didn't have to say much at first because Cosmo just kept marveling at the aforementioned scene and how odd it was that "smart types, men of science," appeared to be behaving so stupidly, attacking each other, clearly engaged in some kind of violence.

Despite his worries over Alexis, his urgent need to go find her and explain everything, David began, especially after the third martini, to find Cosmo's jauntiness refreshing, her tart observations of their loony little world quite telling. She was right. He must have lost his mind up here. He didn't say much as she regaled him of her world travels on her off days, the beaches of Phuket, a yoga retreat in Pune, India, and those two only within the last several months. Her life was a riot of cultures and adventure. As David stared up at the deer antlers on the wall, he found his current isolation in the Pacific Northwest comical or pathetic, which one he wasn't sure. Had he been wrong to blow her off so quickly, he wondered? She was a sexy little thing, and she had produced innumerable laughs.

"So, are you feeling any better? You seemed really anxious to get out of LA." She smiled at him seductively.

"About some things, yes, about others, no." He could feel himself lurching back into the sort of mystery-speak he had cultivated with his old lovers. Everything was a half-truth or a confabulation, lies sprinkled in among facts like salt, just enough to add a little zing. How he had cultivated that ambiguity, always leaving them wanting more.

Cosmo mentioned the Bel Air Hotel. "The only decent place to stay out here in Bumblefuck."

That name caught David up, its implied contempt, its ugliness. "It's not so bad. In fact, Mount Rainier is beautiful. I can see it from my bedroom window," he said, looking for some way to stake out an authentic stance with her. As he felt himself go hot inside, he fell into a rush of words and explanations. "I can't see you anymore, Cosmo. I can't go back to the hotel. I shouldn't even be having dinner. I can't do any of it."

"What are you talking about? After I came all the way to see you?" Despite their long hiatus and every other sign of an end to their always casual relationship, the rejection made her angry.

"In L.A. I was improvising because I couldn't figure out how to tell you the truth. I was seeing a lot of other women at the same time I dated you. It was just, I don't know, fun, childish, great, not my life, an interlude, if you want to call it that. I'm in love."

"Who with?"

"The woman who was standing behind me this evening, with the white hair."

"That old woman?"

"She's not old at all. The hair just makes her seem so."

Cosmo stared at him and then said, "Let's go." He paid the check, and they walked outside, where a damp, misty warmth prevailed. "You know, I kind of figured that's how it was."

For his part, David felt relieved and calm. Whether he had lost Alexis or not, at least he had dealt with one woman honestly. This boded well. Maybe the periodic stabs at truth telling with his new love had finally penetrated his frozen heart and precipitated a thaw. When he and Cosmo parted, it was as friendly old compatriots from some sort of war.

By the time David got home, he felt an odd mix of wasted and relaxed. He had to fight his urge to call Alexis, but it was too late at night, and he wasn't clear what he should say. This was a woman with a child! What must she think of him? He wasn't really sure he had ever straightened out the murkiness around Leah, and hearing her name shouted at him for the umpteenth time must have raised old doubts. Now he had to explain about two women, one of them standing right in front of them acting like a giggly schoolgirl. Worse yet, amidst the wonders of his personal life, he had been engaged in a pissing contest with a bunch of crazed colleagues. Lying in bed, listening to the blessed silence of no rain, he reasoned that, at least in terms of the fisticuffs, much could be laid at the feet of months and months of scientific frustration brought about by his boss, no less so by his sometime roommate. After all, weren't they all too old for this? They were, but he wasn't, was he? Not a good argument because she probably saw him as a child already and always would. The very worst of it was that he had disappointed her. He had felt that in her look and flight. She must be laughing or—horrors—crying about him right now. He hated to think of her in pain. What an infant he must seem to her, an unfaithful fool who played my-dick-is-bigger-than-yours games outside a dance concert.

Days later, David was still wretched and still hadn't called Alexis. She certainly hadn't called him. What could he say? It might take hours to explain, and none of it would be to his benefit. He knew he hadn't figured it all out himself, so burbling on about it, even in low lighting and with liquor by his side, seemed like a horrific idea.

His only good news—they were going to sea in two weeks' time, though the identities of the "they" kept changing because Viktor, unaccountably, ridiculously, did not want to go. First off, he claimed he was afraid to travel upon the ocean at all—"I might fall off the boat." Next, he tried to convince David that he could carry out the experiment without him, using his notes alone. This was folly, of course, and he couldn't really persist in this vein, so ultimately he fell back on the dog. He couldn't leave Heinrich behind because he was a traumatized canine, and who would ever have the guts to dog sit for him?

David knew that the real source of Viktor's reluctance was the fact that right up until the very last moment, Hoekstra made obvious, elaborate preparations to accompany them. Returning again and again to the thought of being stuck in a confined space with the "Dreadful One," as he kept calling him, Viktor announced, "He wants me dead, David, I know it. He will hit me in the head with a winch."

"No, no. He's forgiven you, I think, and I'm his hero in a weird sort of way. I'll work on getting special permission for the dog to come along."

Despite Viktor's worries, David assumed he would eventually just acquiesce to the presence of their disgraced leader. But no. Viktor threw himself into action, actually phoning up the Latvian ambassador in Washington, who, of course, was thrilled to hear from one of the most famous sons of the home-land. Through his intervention, Hoekstra was called to the embassy right away to consult on a project for the Riga harbor, and so peremptory and lucrative an offer could not be ignored, especially now that he was no longer in department store funds. About his triumph, Viktor was intensely proud and told every person he could buttonhole at the institute the details of his plotting.

On May 5, Viktor, David, and Heinrich set out to embark on the *Elysium*, a 150-foot research ship, from the Friday Harbor Marine Station at San Juan Island. It was a sunlit morning when graduate assistants, scientists, and crew members, fifty people altogether, hovered at the dock and helped load the tons of equipment necessary for the voyage. Viktor stood aloof, nodding occasionally to David, who was supervising the cargo, when suddenly an agonized expression came over his face, and he gesticulated wildly as Hoekstra pulled up in his Mercedes and alighted with a spring in his step. Viktor clambered on board to avoid the older man, but David had to craft a wel-come of sorts.

"Fantastic, you're here. Did you finish your Riga project?"

"I did, raced through it. How could I miss this voyage, especially going down in the submersible?" This six-ton object, the *Eddy*, was being loaded as he spoke, an amazing vehicle capable of spending ten hours on the deep ocean floor and sustaining human life up to seventy-two hours. It looked like a peanut-shaped baby submarine with stern propellers. David had the distinct feeling that it was the mission of Hoekstra's life to go down in this craft, but he assumed that there would be several trips, and he and Viktor could avoid accompanying him. Slowly the *Eddy* was lowered onto its hangar on deck, and

David watched it shimmy and sway. Viktor had disappeared. David wondered if he had jumped ship, entirely possible under the circumstances. Then he saw Heinrich run toward him, and he knew Viktor couldn't possibly have abandoned this, his newest best friend.

After steaming through the placid waters around Juan de Fuca Island, the ship plowed its way toward the strait, where predictably, they encountered twenty-foot swells. As they turned north toward Vancouver Island, headed for the Endeavour Segment of the ridge, things really got rocky, and several of the research crew retired to their bunks, Viktor included. For the first several days, Heinrich, too, was seasick and wobbled uneasily through the corridors. He would plunge a front paw forward just as the ship rolled and then sort of fly or skip above the moving floor, landing off-center. After this difficult period, however, he became surprisingly agile and made friends among all the crew, even as Hoekstra pretended to ignore his existence.

When Viktor finally did emerge from his cabin, he collared David in his onboard lab and started complaining. "How could you have done this, drag me out here?"

"You wanted me to do your experiment. It was your idea."

"Yes, but I could have just e-mailed you and told you what to do, because you like to rock back and forth on this awful ocean. That's obvious." The sea's endless motion seemed to offend Viktor personally, and as the time approached for them to help Hoekstra lower his enormous yet delicate instruments over the side of the ship, with the mighty diesels attempting to hover over a single spot, he became almost frantic and decamped once again to his bunk. Still, after another two days of complaint, he threw himself into the voyage and worked through eight-hour shifts with the heavy equipment, albeit scowling whenever he spotted David. Hoekstra wouldn't speak to him, so at least he was happy about that.

The old man's own research involved running hundreds of feet of rubber tubing down into several of the sulfide chimneys in order to suck out the hyperthermophiles living therein at temperatures of up to seven hundred degrees Fahrenheit. Hoekstra was enchanted, laboring with almost no rest. David found himself helping with the heavy work, hoisting the huge hoses into buckets where they poured forth their multitudinous biological wonders. He couldn't help thinking about all those letters. Yes, it was dangerous, and wet and dirty, and, dare he admit it, perhaps even heroic.

"I gave myself up to the vigorous enjoyment of my first scientific command," he recalled and had to sigh.

David mapped deep-sea wave action via current meters that he could monitor from his onboard computer. Using an injection sled, he dropped sulfur hexafluoride (SF6) in a constant band around the most active vents, and, as a result, for months thereafter had a remarkably clear picture of vertical wave action against the ridge. With David's help, Viktor managed to place his neutron detectors into the biggest black smoker—forty-five feet high, in fact—and after eight days of solid, backbreaking effort aboard a rolling ship, David and Viktor seemed joined at the hip. They no longer saw much of Hoekstra, who spent all day and most of the night in his lab, and for this they were grateful.

Their biggest trial, however, was yet to come. It soon became clear that, because of fuel considerations, there would be one single voyage of the *Eddy*, and that their boss would be its pilot. Since it could hold only three people, David and Viktor would be stuck in cramped quarters, under the crushing weight of the ocean, with a definitely crazy and very likely dangerous man.

"He already tried to kill himself once, sort of," David whispered to Viktor, who was quaffing beer and regaling the crew with stories of his homeland.

"No, no, are you sure? He was just trying to impress his wife."

Several able-bodied seamen guffawed. They didn't care for the old man, either. While his imperial diction and his habits of command had at first been a joke, they had now become a matter for serious dislike.

"Can't anybody else pilot the thing?" David asked, sipping his Diet Coke. With the start of this voyage, he had cut back significantly on his drinking and intended to continue the practice.

One of the crew spoke up. "The captain has to pilot the *Elysium*, and the first mate has to deal with lowering the *Eddy* onto the seabed, a complicated deal, that one. It takes serious training to command the sub, and Hoekstra is the only other person on board with the know-how."

Viktor and David looked at each other in horror, the former pouring himself yet another beer. "He might not want to kill himself anymore, but he probably wants to kill us."

This seemed like a hilarious suggestion to the assembled sailors, who habitually responded to the scientists as if they were not only inept but also certifiably nuts. One patted David on the back and suggested he "fake sick" to get out of it. Another offered up a reason for hope: "He says he thinks he'll discover something major. Murder might not be on his to-do list, at least not right now."

As they made their way toward their cabins, Viktor announced quietly, "We are doomed. This is just what he's been waiting for," then hovered by his bunk, more upset than David had ever seen him.

"We can't panic. It's his life dream. We don't really need to go down there, but he certainly does, and he can't go alone. He needs us to point out certain geological and physical features."

"You're right. You are right." Viktor held his head and rubbed it right at the crown. "I must accept my fate, whatever that may be."

Despite his reassurances to Viktor, David wasn't too sure about any of this himself, and had almost as much anxiety as if they were taking off into outer space.

Nevertheless, the next morning the three men climbed into the submersible and huddled together as it rocked and swayed its way to the sea floor. Viktor did not speak during the descent, and neither did David, each apparently thinking final thoughts; in any space and time this was a dangerous activity, no matter who was at the helm. Yet Hoekstra radiated complete confidence, turning the toggle switches for the sub's robotic arms with the skill of a virtuoso. He smiled, laughed, and nodded at them whenever he performed another feat. But his unnatural friendliness only spooked them more. At 650 feet, sunlight completely disappeared; at thirty-two hundred feet, they felt a powerful thud as Hoekstra released half of the ballast steel. Each man had his face plastered to a window. At first it looked pitch-black, but as their eyes adjusted, they could see the fiery glow that arose around the volcanic fires. Transparent shrimp floated before them, five-foot-long red-and-white worms waved in vast fields atop a forest of chimneys, and clumps of bacteria the size of snowflakes swirled gently as if in a watery, colorful winter.

"This is how life must have existed thousands of years ago," David said softly.

"Yes, the primordial world," Hoekstra muttered.

Viktor sighed loudly. Giant bleached-out crabs floated past the windows, and then strange white fish, apparently adapted to this cold, lightless environment. All the while Hoekstra captured everything he could in the vessel's mechanical arms, greedy to take home a sample of every mysterious species.

"The life density here is incredible," David said, "far exceeding anything known on the surface of the earth."

"These little critters demonstrate chemosynthesis, not photosynthesis, as their source of life, so elemental they don't need the sun. What do you think, Pelliau?" Hoekstra asked.

"Very lovely," Viktor sputtered.

The *Eddy* twisted its way carefully around the vents—it looked as if they were at an underwater Yellowstone—and happily, David spotted several of his current meters tethered to their immensely strong moorings. With their paddle-wheel rotors allowing them to move freely around the rods they were attached to, they showed no signs of disturbance or disintegration. A fifth force. Could he hear it; could he see it? Never. But his little wheels might be feeling its resistance right now. They might be in it and of it. They turned with the turning of the world here below.

After eight and a half hours—two and a half hours of travel time down, and six hours of bottom time—they had inspected every instrument David had dropped, filled their basket with sulfide structures, ocean-floor rocks, life-forms, and samples of water. During this whole voyage, their silence was only sporadically broken. Viktor was too terrified to speak. He didn't want to be on the ocean at all, and he positively didn't want to be under it. David actually began to find Hoekstra's calm professionalism reassuring, and he felt many of his fears vanish, crushed by the silence of fathoms of water. They were at the very heart of the world, cracked open before them like God's forge.

Slowly, slowly they began their ascent. Up through the wavering fires of the black smokers, thence through the white fields of bacterial snow. Now fish glided past their windows, and David followed closely their unblinking eyes. Look into the eyes of any animal, no matter how wild, how alien, and you will see God, such was his amazed thought. He wanted to cry. Upward the little craft rose as the sun began to jut across the blackness, up, up into the light, into a rolling, rocking ocean surface that blazed with warmth. Like a man reborn, David breathed that light into his soul.

Landing their craft on the deck of the swaying ship proved fully as dangerous as anything else they had done, but at last the *Eddy* came safely to rest. When he finally crawled out of the hatch, David felt as if he had just returned from Mars and was exactly that proud of himself for going. He waved to assembled students and crew as if at a photo op.

Not to be outdone, Viktor flung himself facedown onto the deck, kissing it and shouting, "We live!"

# CHAPTER 28

AS SOON AS he could, David flopped onto his bunk and slept for almost twelve hours, awakened only by pounding on his door. Naturally he expected Viktor, who always liked to rouse him with a crisis. But it was Hoekstra, motioning excitedly for David to accompany him.

As they strode along the corridor, rocking from side to side, the old man seemed beside himself with joy. "It's the smallest fish I've ever seen, the smallest in the world, I believe, seven point nine millimeters. I think it's from the hake family. It lives on acid!" Once in the lab, David peered down into the microscope at the tiny thing with a transparent body. He could see its miniscule skeleton. "It has a complete vertebrae in a body that small, but very few other attributes of adulthood."

"Amazing."

"This will make my career. Forget all those fuckers who said I was only an administrator. What should I name it? The hake is called *Merluccius merluccius*. Hmm. This one's a male, with this strange grasping fin. His little brain has no bony protection whatsoever." He strode back and forth across the lab. "Imagine, it's the baby of the universe. Probably his species was here before recorded time began."

David reacted with a start as he realized that was how he thought of himself in relationship to Alexis. How odd that he should now be in the presence of the real thing. He looked up at Hoekstra, who was squinting down at him, anxious to get back to the microscope himself.

"A significant find, very important. I congratulate you," he said to his boss. At long last, this proved itself the ritual acknowledgment the old man had wanted, and before he could get away, Hoekstra embraced him. It was a moment the two recognized as closure, of sorts, to their long history of mad interaction, and as he held the older man, David found himself growing teary. If only this had been his father.

David again made for his bunk and lay staring up at the swinging cabin light. Einstein famously said a space traveler would get younger if he vaulted himself into the stars on a spaceship, because time itself had slowed down. David, like-wise, seemed to have somehow gotten younger by going in the opposite direction, toward the bottom of the world. He was a reverse astronaut. Perhaps instead of fighting against Alexis's view of him as a child, he should move right into the center of this fear, both his and hers. Obviously he couldn't continue the jerky, childish stuff that had been his refuge of late, but he could acknowledge the great gap between them, surrender to it inside and not stage-manage his behavior so much, thereby making himself look even more childish. He had to start by being present.

With this fruitful thought in mind, he went to the computer room and sent her an e-mail.

Dear Alexis, Hello from the ocean, both above and below. I don't know how to say this carefully or subtly, so here it is. Cosmo sailed back at me from the past like a torpedo. I broke it off in Los Angeles, but so ambiguously that she felt she could return with no notice. And of course I was never anything but a friend to Leah. I need to see you and talk to you. Love, David.

Looking out a porthole at the vast ocean surrounding their ship, he pondered the consolations of physics, specifically of his old friend, the second law of thermodynamics. Entropy had ultimately suggested the solution to his problem, as his hero Feynman had predicted. Not the inevitable running down of things, but its opposite—order. That was what he craved, and that was what he determined to find in his life and work.

While the *Elysium* glided over placid waters back toward Friday Harbor, David stood on deck, wondering what awaited him. He wasn't sure what his instruments had shown, but he did know that the eight million the institute had popped for this little voyage would not soon be matched again, so it had all better pay off. He wasn't going to get another chance with his beloved, either, if he screwed up from this point on.

"I'm going to go find Alexis," he announced to Viktor as they disembarked.

"Now?"

"Yes, now. She thinks we're all insane."

"Poor creature. And she's known us for such a short time." Viktor seemed so preternaturally happy that he had finally done his experiment and braved the seafloor that nothing anyone said to him could jar his psyche.

Inside his house, where everything still looked a little seedy and smelled damp, David contemplated his next move. Should he just drop in on her? That seemed like a terrible plan. Now that his vivid, outrageous neighbor Shelby had decamped, he no longer had any sort of distaff example of how to get from point A to point B with women. Coffee, dinner, it all seemed so prosaic. The sun was shining, it was a cloudless day, and momentarily inspired, he called Hoekstra on his cell phone to confirm that he was in his lab and had a long talk with him.

Then he called Alexis. When she answered, he detected a marked coolness in her voice. "Welcome home." That was it, said without much passion.

"We had a fantastic, incredible voyage. I'd like to show you something from it."

"I've got a lot of riding lessons this week."

"This is important. Meet me at the institute, please, tomorrow around noon."

"I can't do that. In a day or two. I'll call." She hung up.

Given his LA love life, and even before that with his mother, David thought he knew how to behave around difficult women, but he had never been treated quite this way. With Alexis he felt he was going to have to be patient, a truly novel stance, but the only one he could think to adopt now. At last she called, they did make a plan, and in the bright sun two days later, David watched as his beloved strode into the institute lobby, looking ever so much like the horsewoman she was, not smiling, not cowed by the august scientists wandering about the place.

"Thank goodness you came," he said nervously.

"Of course I came, though I'm afraid to think what's next around here, fights, drink, CPR, golf clubs, old girlfriends!"

"No, no, something much more significant."

At last she smiled slightly and this time finally looked him in the eye.

"Follow me," he said.

When she saw Hoekstra's name outside the door, she pulled back. "What now?"

"You don't trust me."

"I don't trust anyone these days."

"Please," he said and knocked on the door. This was Hoekstra's lab, not the office that had been the scene of so many unfortunate episodes in their mutual past. David had never been inside it, but predictably it was enormous, twice the size of his own. Hoekstra's assistants had been told that this huge scientific discovery, a secret of massive proportions, was something they could make known only to this one woman, of all the women on Earth. The old man apparently couldn't resist being present as well and appeared with a cup of coffee in hand, heartily greeting the both of them. David wasn't surprised, but a horrified Alexis seemed to want to back her way toward the door.

"No, no, it's all right." David took her by the arm, and Hoekstra motioned for them both to sit down at a bench where an enormous microscope stood. She pulled up a stool as Hoekstra adjusted the apparatus, directing her to look down.

"It's the *Merluccius francescus*, named after my absent wife." Acting the gentleman scientist, Hoekstra seemed at once sad and pleased.

Alexis bent down and peered at the poor little see-through thing with its bizarre grasping fins and tiny vertebrae.

"It's the smallest fish on record. Hoekstra found it at Juan de Fuca," David said. "I can only hope my own work there will prove half as important." Alexis stared at him as he nodded collegially at his boss. This was a far cry from the fistfights she was used to witnessing. "I wanted to share this with you."

"It's beautiful." She sighed and smiled warmly at him.

"Thank you, Hoekstra," David said and drew Alexis toward the door.

In the lobby, he fully expected her to run away from him again and was desperately trying to think of something he could say to keep her there. But he was so befuddled that he blurted out, "It's the baby of the universe."

"It is?"

"Yes, for now anyway. Some of us, scientists mostly, comprehend what that means, scientists and Zen Buddhists. Since I've been to the bottom of the sea and back, I think I know what it means in relationship to me. If I'm lucky, I'll learn how to walk and talk, in time. I thought you would understand."

"Ahh, I think I do." She clasped his arm, and in front of a dozen weedy physicists, a few graduate students, and the bust of Larson Kinne, she kissed him.

# DEEPER WATER

T HUS, INDEED, THEY returned to Pyke City as better
men.

While they were away, one of their number, Shelby
Burns, had certainly improved his position socially and finan-
cially; whether it included a moral shift as well remained to be
seen. David found in his mailbox several glowing postcards
from Greece with admonitions to "stay cool" and "don't blow
it," whatever that meant, but eventually Shelby called him from
Seattle and told him that he would be living there permanently
with Frances, whom he planned to marry. Two months later
the rather tanned-looking twosome—with Shelby in a well-
cut dark suit—graced the cover of *Seattle Today* magazine. The
headline read, "Seattle's Global Couple," though the meaning
of that particular phrase seemed open to debate, given Shelby's
previous reach. The article inside contained pictures of a magnificent mansion under construction on Orcas Island, their
"future hideaway," the piece asserted. Yes, "hideaway" would
be the operative word.

Very shortly after the voyage of the *Elysium*, Niels Hoekstra became, briefly, a darling of the press. Baby *Merluccius*

*francescus* enchanted the American public, and its discoverer proved a garrulous guest on late-night television. Of course, for all his trouble, he only had a fish, not the real Frances; nevertheless, the old heathen exuded a bittersweet glow.

Another player in the Pyke City drama, Larry Burnett, ultimately left town. After his divorce from Leah, he departed for Idaho to run a gun camp for troubled teenagers. Naturally, his ex-wife got nothing of their mutual assets except the house, but this left her the next-door neighbor of one Viktor Pelliau. Life adjacent to the second most beautiful woman in town must have proved more and more delightful, because David rarely saw the guy.

Nine months after they returned from their voyage, Viktor published his now-famous research report, "Hot Bubbles at Juan de Fuca." With those remarkable instruments of his, he had finally succeeded in measuring nature's very own fusion reactor at the bottom of the sea. Viktor didn't get the Nobel Prize, but he was short-listed again that year.

David's own paper, "Gravity's Little Helper," published in *Physics Today*, asserted the probable existence of a fifth force, since the $SF_6$ tracers proved definitively that deep water rose only near the largest underwater ridges. This was not only an oceanographic advance, but also an indication that there might indeed be a substance-dependent, intermediate-range force equal to 1 percent that of gravity. His results caused a furor and created a cottage industry of new "fifth forcers" trying to replicate his findings. A crew member on the *Elysium* had snapped a picture of David triumphantly waving as he debarked from the *Eddy*, and that same photo appeared on the cover of *Time* magazine, causing the SETI project to contact him about possible applications in outer space.

In the aftermath of these wonderfully strange and invigorating events, it struck David forcefully: we are always in deep water. We guess, we estimate, we assume, but we are controlled by huge forces in this universe, like the waves in the sea, and that elusive fifth force is ever ready to throw off all our calculations. As we yearn for better days, we have no choice but to wait for a better wave.

He and Alexis were out walking in the woods near her farm, where he has lived since shortly after he returned from his voyage, when they spotted a ferret. Was it *the* ferret? They'll have to watch for traces of the red snood.

## THE END

# ACKNOWLEDGMENTS

S O MANY PEOPLE helped me with this book. Thank you all, but if your name is not listed here, please know that I am still beholden to you.

Steadfast critics and/or cheerleaders: Joyce Engelson, Judith Ehrlich, Jeanne Martinet, Ted Bell, Gia (Nurse Pebbles) Gittleson, Sally Shore, Jean Casella, Phil Dusenberry, Kathryn Bundy, Regina Leeds, Patricia Zehentmayr, and Wendi Woods Chandler.

I am so grateful to my major science advisor, Dr. Zaven Arzoumanian, astrophysicist at NASA, senior research scientist on NICER, the Neutron Star Interior Composition Explorer. He and I had much fun imagining the future of so-called cold fusion and making up theories that were plausible, if not possible. Dr. David Boyd at the California Institute of Technology helped as well, with jokes on the second law of thermodynamics and other diversions from his important work in nanotechnology.

My devoted readers and counselors I must also thank: Dr. Dorothy Duff Brown, Diana Ketcham, Nancy Drosd, Leslie Techolz, Pamela Rose, Jorge Rosales, Jeff Levi, Katt Lowe, and Mark Baldwin.

Marina Lavelle, web designer extraordinaire, did the cover art, and I admire her no end. Thank you to Jesse Holcomb, Savannah Holcomb, and Alex Silvester, our esteemed art support team.

The person I am most indebted to is my beloved daughter, Vanessa Taylor.

For
McMillan Robinson

# ABOUT THE AUTHOR

A. R. Taylor is an award-winning playwright, essayist, and fiction writer. Her work has appeared in the *Los Angeles Times*, the *Southwest Review*, *Pedantic Monthly*, *The Cynic* online magazine, the *Berkeley Insider*, *Red Rock Review*, and *Rosebud*, among others. The New Short Fiction Series featured her short stories, and her work has been performed at Tongue & Groove, the Annenberg Center, and the Federal Bar. Taylor herself played the Gotham Comedy Club.

Her awards include the DeGolyer Prize in American Studies, a nomination for the Henry A. Murray Award at Harvard, and the Writers Foundation of America Gold Statuette for Comedy. She has received recognition from the NBC Program for New Writers, the Dana Fiction Awards, and the Actors Theatre of Louisville. In addition, she was head writer on two Emmy Award-winning series for public television.

lonecamel.com

CPSIA information can be obtained at www.ICGtesting.com
Printed in the USA
LVOW13s0859300314

379521LV00001B/91/P